D1422991

THE
UNICORN
WAR

Tor books by John Lee

THE
UNICORN
WAR

JOHN LEE

A Tom Doherty Associates Book ▪ New York

This is a work of fiction. All the characters and events portrayed in this novel are either fictitious or are used fictitiously.

THE UNICORN WAR

This book is printed on acid-free paper.

Edited by David G. Hartwell
Maps by Nancy Westheimer
Design by Lynn Newmark

A Tor Book
Published by Tom Doherty Associates, Inc.
175 Fifth Avenue
New York, N.Y. 10010

Tor® is a registered trademark of Tom Doherty Associates, Inc.

Library of Congress Cataloging-in-Publication Data

Lee, John.
    The unicorn war / John Lee.
        p.   cm.
    "A Tom Doherty Associates book."
    ISBN 0-312-85913-9
    I. Title.
    PS3562.E3538U55   1995
    813'.54—dc20   95-15463
                                                            CIP

First edition: July 1995

Printed in the United States of America

0 9 8 7 6 5 4 3 2 1

For Arthur, the progenitor; for
Susan and Carole, midwives; for
Michael, who combines a talent
for proofreading and the
uncommon sense never to
comment.

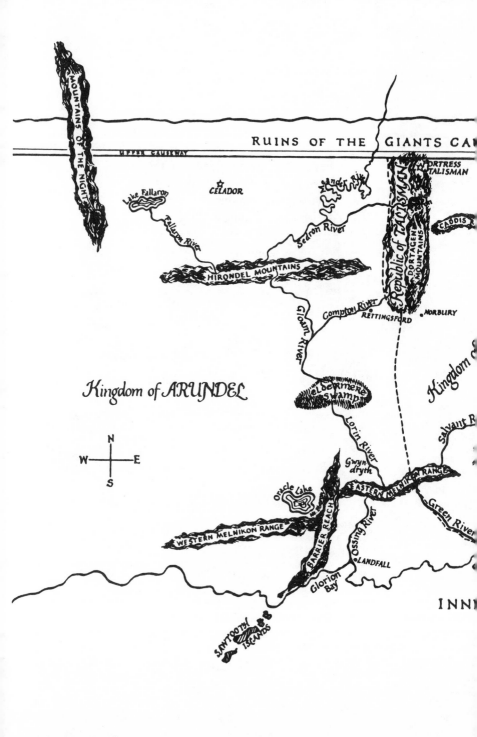

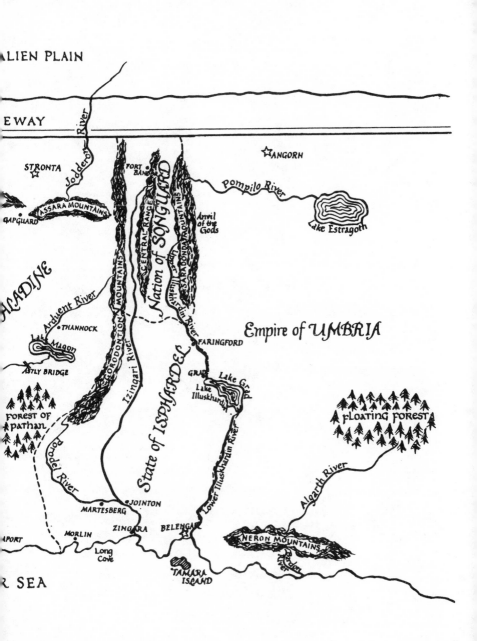

PROPOSAL for the DISPOSITION of CONQUERED OUTLAND TERRITORY

Kingdom of ARUNDEL

The
ARUNDEL

UPPER CAUSEWAY

Republic of
TALISMAN

TALISMAN

Kingdom
of
PALADINE

Alien
PALADINE

State
of
ISPHARDEL

SONGUARD

SONGUARD

ISPHARDEL

Empire
of
UMBRIA

Plain
UMBRIA

THE
UNICORN
WAR

I

⚜ ⚜ ⚜

The traveling party wound its dusty way along the Southern Route. There was a carriage for the Mage of Paladine, though it was unoccupied. There was a contingent of guards, armored, armed and beplumed, and an overloaded baggage wagon. Behind the wagon rode an assortment of servants including the cook and his helper. The mood was relaxed, the weather had, as always, been predictable, the provisions, courtesy of the Holding of Gwyndryth, more than adequate, and there was a Mage along to cope with any unforeseen trouble. Sleeping on the ground at night was not the most comfortable of propositions, but, all things considered, it wasn't a bad life.

Jarrod Courtak, the Mage of the empty coach, rode well ahead of the small column. He enjoyed the illusion of solitude that being a half mile in front of his entourage afforded. At this moment, the sun had scarcely cleared the horizon and was streaming horizontally through the woods surrounding the rutted road that led toward Stronta. The air still had a chill on it at this hour and all the scents of the countryside were individually clear. It was a time that breathed renewal, and the solitude provided refreshment from the family squabbles he had escaped. The smooth canter beneath the overreaching boughs banished thoughts of the disagreements at Gwyndryth.

There was a rider up ahead, trying to master a plunging mount, and Jarrod automatically drew rein. As he stared ahead, there was movement in the brush beside the path beyond the capering horse. Unease prickled up the nape of Jarrod's neck. Acting upon impulse, he turned his horse's head and, as he spurred back down the road, he heard the ululations of the men who had been hidden in the bushes. Brigands, he thought, old soldiers disenfranchised by the war's end.

"Ambush. Ambush ahead!" he cried as he approached the train. He pulled his mount back to a standstill. The leader of his guard trotted up to him.

"How many men, Excellence?"

"I don't know," Jarrod said, shaking his head. "There was one man on a horse on the roadway and a lot more in the bushes on the side."

"You saw them?"

"Well, not exactly. But they were there. I felt them. I can't be sure, it was too fast, but I think about fifty."

"You think, Excellence?"

"It could be more, it could be less. I didn't stop to count," Jarrod said testily.

"Very well, sir, I'll deploy the men." He paused. "Will you return to the carriage?"

The question was put casually, but Jarrod knew that there was a wealth of unspoken criticism behind the question. If he was a Mage, why hadn't he dealt with the situation? If he was a Mage, why was he not ordering people around before he went out and burned their adversaries into embers?

"No, I think not," he said quietly. "And the answer to your questions are, I didn't destroy them because I don't know who they are. They may be former colleagues of yours reduced to brigandage, who will be frightened away by a show of force.

Two: you are the man in charge of the security of this column and I did not want to usurp your authority unless you proved yourself incompetent. And three: magic is not a toy to be used at the snap of the fingers. You may rest assured that if those people up ahead don't melt away when it becomes apparent that this party of travelers is adequately protected, I will see to it that you and your men are shielded."

Jarrod looked at the Captain, whose jaw had dropped, and sighed. "No," he said, "I didn't read your mind. I used common sense, although that seems to be a bit of a misnomer. Now, if I were you, I'd get your men together, present a broad front, and make a great deal of noise. I'd have some men in the rear, too, just in case they're sneakier than we expect them to be."

"As you command, Excellence," the Captain said, awe still evident in his voice.

They advanced with a semicircle of armed men in front. The woods around them were silent, the birds having fled with the ruckus the humans had made. There was no sign of an enemy up ahead. Their own advance was far from silent, what with the creaking of the wagon's wheels, the jingling of harness and the snorting of horses. Jarrod rode just behind the guards, senses probing ahead. Despite the manifold noises of their passage, the sudden whine of a machine cut across them like an affront. Jarrod knew that the noise was aimed at him. Magicians could not tolerate machines and the high-pitched screech, while an annoyance and distraction to the rest of his tiny column, was meant to disable him.

This was no haphazard venture by sturdy beggars, he realized as men materialized across the path in front of them. This was an attack made with him in mind. As he quieted his horse he addressed the possibilities. His mind had been inured to machines by the Guardian some fifteen years ago, but nobody on Strand knew that. If the troops could not deal with this situation and he had to intervene, all the attackers would have to be killed, without exception. His immunity was obviously a secret worth keeping. He put his hands over his ears, as if to block out the sound and, to make it look better should one of them escape, rocked from side to side in the saddle, as if tormented. The Captain's shrill order to charge was slightly muffled when it came.

As the troopers spurred forward, swords aloft, Jarrod continued his charade while keeping a sharp eye on the proceedings. He threw up a light force field between the converging groups. It was not strong enough to stop the spears that were being thrown by the bandits, well-armed bandits, he thought, but it was sufficient to deflect them and slow them somewhat. Then the two lines met and there was nothing he could do to protect his men. Not that they needed help. They were well mounted and well armed and their adversaries were on foot.

He tried to peer past the melee and the dust, but he couldn't see the horseman who had alerted him to the trap, nor could he locate the machine. The strident whine continued unabated. It was aggravating, but in no way debilitating. Still acting the part, he turned his horse in a tight circle, scanning the woods to either side as he did so. Nothing. The baggage wagon, the presumed object of this attack, was drawn up in the middle of the road, protected by a small contingent of his escort.

He turned back to see how the fight was progressing and, as he did so, caught a hint of movement. There was no time to cast a spell, scarcely time to unsheathe his sword before the rider came crashing out of the undergrowth. Jarrod's horse reared and he was able to block the other man's blade before it had gained the full momentum of the downswing. The shock of it tingled down his arm nevertheless. He grabbed the reins with his free hand and pulled his mount around to face his enemy. There was a flurry of cuts and parries, of tight-turning horses and reflex actions. Fear-driven excitement bloomed in Jarrod's veins and lent urgency to his blows. Even so, he was being pushed back toward the baggage cart. Then his opponent jerked up and forward simultaneously before slumping over his horse's neck. A crossbow quarrel protruded from his back and blood began to stain his jerkin. Jarrod, obscurely disappointed, leaned over, grabbed the dangling reins and led the other horse back to the wagon.

"My thanks to the bowman," he said as he dismounted. "Let him present himself after this is over and I'll see to it that he is rewarded."

A ragged cheer announced the rout of the brigands, and, with their flight, the noise of the machine stopped abruptly, leaving an eerie afterringing in the ears. By the time the guard had regrouped, the lone horseman had been stripped and his clothing searched. There was nothing to identify him and no way of determining his nationality. The same proved true of the men that the soldiers had killed. There were two badly wounded prisoners, but they died almost immediately. It was puzzling, but Jarrod had some bleak suspicions. He had come close to death and, had he not ridden out ahead that morning, the results of the encounter might have been very different, escort or no escort.

The last time I was ambushed, he thought as they continued their journey, I was searching for unicorns. It had been Umbrians then. His mind drifted back to the days when he had shared his life with the unicorns. He had felt then that the key to Strand's salvation lay with them and, in a way, he had been right. His thoughts skittered away from Beldun's death. Without them Strand might still be fighting the Outlanders; without them he would never have encountered the Guardian and then he would have succumbed to that whining machine. He owed the unicorns so much and he missed them. Nastrus had been the last to leave, but somehow Jarrod thought that they would come again. That was what he wanted to believe.

"We are delighted to see that you have returned to us unblemished, my Lord Mage," Naxania said. "Reports that we have re-

ceived say that you were waylaid on your return from Gwyndryth."

"Indeed I was, Your Majesty," Jarrod replied, "and within
the borders of Your Majesty's realm. The troops that Your Majesty assigned to me provided the means for my escape and I
commend them to you highly."

He straightened out of another bow and regarded his sovereign dispassionately. Naxania of Paladine was still a very handsome woman. Her long, black hair was straight and glossy. Her
throne was set up so that the light coming through the windows was behind her, and if there were any lines in her face,
they were invisible. Since she was sitting, it was impossible to
get an accurate impression of her figure, but her face showed no
signs of a gain in weight. The lips were thin and had been red-
dened. The brows were too regular not to have been plucked.
She must, Jarrod thought, be in her mid-forties, but she looked
no more than thirty.

"Mere highwaymen, ill-advised enough to attack a well-
protected convoy?"

"I think not, Your Majesty. They had a machine with them
that did nothing but make noise and they used it while we were
advancing on them."

"And that says something to you?" The Queen was openly
skeptical.

"I do not think that it was a chance encounter," Jarrod said.
"The only reason for that machine would be to disable a Mage,
or at least a Magician. That, to me, smacks of the Empire."

Naxania looked at the man standing in front of the throne.
He has become a force to reckon with, she thought. She had
opposed his elevation to the rank of Mage of Paladine and she
had lost. She had not opposed him, contrary to popular opinion, because she had desired the Mageship for herself, though,
as a member of the High Council of Magic, she had the right.
No, she had opposed it because this selfsame Jarrod Courtak
was, by quirk of inheritance, Duke of Abercorn. The Duchy

held extensive lands from the crown and the Duke was one of her chief vassals. It was hard enough to hold the aristocracy loyal when she herself was Talented. Now the Mage of Paladine was also a major landlord. There were rumblings among the laity that the Discipline had too much influence in the realm. It wasn't true. Neither she nor Courtak had abused their positions, but the perceptions were there.

"We would doubt that," she said pleasantly. "It is common knowledge that Magicians and machines cannot coexist. The fact that this machine only produced noise, was, in truth, a simple artifact, might well mean that a local gang, learning that there was a Mage in what would otherwise be a profitable convoy, contrived a means to neutralize him. Of course, if there were any captives taken, we could have them questioned."

"That is the other strange thing, Majesty," Jarrod said. "Two captives were taken. Both swallowed some potion before they could be questioned. They died very quickly. That in itself is unusual."

"Very true, my Lord Mage, very true. But scarcely grounds for pointing fingers at Umbria. No, we must congratulate ourselves on your escape from brigands and leave it at that." She cocked her head slightly and produced a wintry smile that denoted that the audience was over.

"I trust that Your Majesty will have no objection if I make some discreet inquiries."

"So long as they are truly discreet," Naxania allowed. "The Emperor has no great love for your family and we do not want relations between our countries strained."

"As Your Majesty commands," Jarrod said, and bowed one final time.

He sat in his own rooms in the Outpost with decidedly mixed feelings. It was good to be home and, when all was said and done, this was his home. He extended a booted foot for the Duty Boy to tug on. His family, still a rather alien word to him despite five years of marriage and two children, his family lived at Gwyndryth, but, while he was comfortable there and loved them dearly, Gwyndryth would never be truly home to him. He had grown up in this place. The children he had played with were fellow Magicians now. They, too, were a part of his family, the only family he had had when he was growing up.

He gave the boy his other foot. Was he being unreasonable about the attack on his party? Was the Queen right? Had the machine been mere local ingenuity? No. Robbers did not take poison. Once the attackers had realized that they could not break through the line of soldiers, they had fled into the woods, taking the machine with them. Surely that was significant. But why would the Emperor want him dead? If Varodias wanted to avenge the insult given him by Joscelyn, why wait this long? Joscelyn was his stepson, but still it made no sense.

He stood up and began to take off his court clothes. The Duty Boy handed him his plain blue Magician's robe and began to put the grander, lay garments away in the press. He remembered the lad from a previous turn at serving, but he seemed to have grown at least a foot.

"Nip down and ask the cellarer for a flagon of ale," Jarrod said to him. "Talking to Queens is thirsty work."

He doubted that Naxania believed that the attack was the work of simple brigands, though there were certainly enough of them about. She had been thinking in diplomatic terms. Her thrust about his family had made that clear. It had been five years since his stepson had vanished on the back of a strange unicorn, but the incident had not been forgotten. Marianna was still not received at Celador. The boy had not been seen or heard from since and though his mother never mentioned him, she had taken it hard. Jarrod shook his head. It was pointless to speculate. He would ask Marianna to have her factor in Belengar keep his ears open. Rumors had a habit of surfacing in the Isphardi capital.

The Duty Boy appeared at the door with a tray bearing two flagons of ale. He smiled nervously at the Mage.

"His Eminence, Agar Thorden, is coming to see you," he said, Adam's apple bobbing prominently, "so I thought a second ale would be proper."

"Quite right," Jarrod said reassuringly. "Your judgment is impeccable. Is he at hand?"

Eminence was a title reserved for Mages, but Agar Thorden had run the Outpost and administered the Discipline in Paladine for so long that the appellation seemed natural.

"On the landing, sir."

"Show him in. Show him in."

Jarrod advanced across the room to embrace the older man. Thorden limped these days, especially when the weather was damp, and his neatly trimmed thatch of hair was white. His gown was the standard Magician's blue, save that it had a white key design around the hem and the ends of the wide sleeves. The conceit was all his own and his only concession to vanity.

"Come and sit by the fire," Jarrod said. "It's a bit feeble at the moment"—he shot a meaningful glance at the Duty Boy— "but I've only just got back from the palace. It'll be blazing in a minute."

The boy handed the men their ale and then raced to apply the bellows as the two settled into chairs close to the fire.

"So, how have things been while I was away?" Jarrod inquired.

"The royal treasury is late with the Tithe, as usual. We're a fortnight behind with the bookkeeping, thanks to Tokamo's continued absence. The Weatherward in the mountains to the east of Gapguard was bitten by a hognose snake and his replacement has little or no practical experience. I am told that the Village Magician assigned to the Astly Bridge area has scandalized the folks thereabouts by taking up with a fifteen-year-old girl; there's a petition addressed to you demanding his removal. In short, business as usual." Thorden looked up from under shaggy eyebrows and then took a long, slow, pull at his ale.

"Well," Jarrod said with a broad smile, "I can quite understand why you came to see me the moment I was back."

"Oh, not quite the moment," Thorden said, unbeguiled. "You saw fit to see the Queen first."

Jarrod spread his hands placatingly. "Only because my party was attacked by a band of men who used a machine—whether to spook the horses or neutralize me, I cannot say for sure. Since the attempt took place within the borders of her realm, I felt that Her Majesty should be informed."

"A machine? What kind of machine?" Thorden asked sharply.

He may be old, but he isn't slow, Jarrod thought. "All it did was make noise."

"And who knew that you were returning to Stronta?"

"It was no secret at Gwyndryth," Jarrod replied. "We stopped at a couple of post inns on the way." He raised both hands in a kind of shrug.

"I see. I don't like the sound of it, but then neither do you, I'll wager."

"If you hear anything, I'd be obliged if you passed it along." He paused. "But you didn't come here to talk about my troubles, or the lateness of the Tithe." Jarrod let the sentence hang.

"No, I did not," Thorden said bluntly. "There's been trouble in Songuard."

"What kind of trouble?"

"Three young Weatherwards, newly sent there to fulfill our part of the Concordat, have disappeared. Two of them were raised here. Gerdain Bervis, dark-haired lad with a slight squint, is one."

"I seem to remember a Duty Boy like that."

"That was nine years ago. He's twenty now. The other is

Nadal Aristach's son," Thorden added, naming a fellow Magician.

"Jubal?"

"That's the one."

"He was very gifted," Jarrod said. "How did he end up as a Weatherward?"

"The Collegium has been putting a lot of emphasis on Weatherwarding and he felt the pull of far places. Much as you did."

"And there are no indications as to what might have happened?"

"None that I know of," Thorden replied with a sigh. "They were in remote areas, naturally. The first hint that something was wrong was when the work crews building the new Isphardi roads through the valleys began to complain about the weather. A party was sent to investigate and all three stations were found abandoned. The local clans had just returned from wintering on the lower slopes and claim to know nothing."

"There are Umbrian press-gangs in the mountains," Jarrod said, remembering his own encounter with them. He sipped his ale. "How long have you known about this?" he asked, looking up.

"A day or two above a sennight," Thorden replied. "The message came through the Isphardi Ambassador. He was professionally sympathetic, but he made it quite clear that his government wants new Weatherwards in place, though what he thinks we can do about it from Stronta is beyond me."

"We have to find out what happened to the first three before we send anybody else," Jarrod said. "By the way, where was the third one from?"

"Somewhere in Arundel."

"So the Archmage will know about this."

"I assume so, though I haven't heard from him."

"The trouble is, Songuard is so bloody far away. If only Nastrus . . ."

"Oh no you don't," Thorden cut in. "You're the Mage now and you're needed here. Your days of gallivanting around on a unicorn are over."

"I still think we should try to find out what happened. We owe it to the lads and their parents. Can you get me a map with the stations marked on it? Perhaps that will stimulate some ideas." He took another drink and then said, "I'm probably seeing conspiracies where none exist, but doesn't it strike you as odd that there should suddenly be two attacks on the Discipline?"

"Why would anyone want to attack us?"

"I don't know. I just have the feeling that something's afoot."

"I'll see what I can do about a map," Thorden said, finishing off his ale. "When I'm caught up on the paperwork, perhaps we can go over the accounts together."

"By all means," Jarrod replied with as much enthusiasm as he could muster.

The following morning, having Made the Day and breakfasted in the Hall, Jarrod approached the stables intent on taking a ride beyond the Causeway. As he walked through the archway into the stable area, he felt a prickling sensation between the shoulder blades, as if he was being watched by someone. He swung around, but there was no one behind him. The sensation persisted and suspicion dawned.

'Nastrus?' he thought out.

'And about time too.'

At that moment, Lazla, the head groom, came trotting out of a loose-box at the far end of the courtyard, his face lit by a huge grin.

"Oh, Eminence, Eminence."

"I know, Lazla, I know. I hear him."

He strode across the cobbles and into the loose-box.

'Where have you been, you rascal?' He flung his arms around the unicorn's neck and hugged him.

'Oh, here and there. Up and down the Lines of Force; exploring.'

'Well, it's good to see you again.' Jarrod stood back and took a long, fond look at his friend, noting the shaggy coat and the grey around the muzzle.

Nastrus turned his head and returned the gaze. *'You're not looking any younger yourself, you know,'* he remarked.

'We can't do anything about the aging,' Jarrod replied evenly, *'but I can see to it that you get groomed.'*

'I'll have you know that I've just come from a world that's considerably colder than this one. This is my winter coat and I'll start shedding by tomorrow.'

Having once traveled beyond the confines of Strand, Jarrod took the assertion of other worlds in stride. *'And you finally missed us and decided to visit,'* he thought back.

'You humans never change,' the unicorn returned with mock resignation. *'You think that the universe revolves around you. As a matter of fact, I came to see how my offspring are adapting to life at that castle we built.'*

'Take me with you,' Jarrod said impulsively.

'Yours is still there, is he?'

'I don't know,' Jarrod admitted. *'We haven't seen him since Ragnor's funeral. That son of yours, what was his name?'*

'Astarus,' Nastrus supplied.

'May have taken him to the Island at the Center for all I know.'

'He hadn't been there when I last was there, and that wasn't too long ago.' He read the fear that the boy was dead in his friend's mind and refrained from further comment.

'It'll be like old times,' Jarrod said, rallying. *'Unfortunately, I can't stay away long. Old Thorden will have my hide if I do.'*

'When do you want to go?'

'I've got to make sure that there's nothing important on the cal-
endar, and besides, we can't have you turning up there looking like
an over-the-hill shire horse.'

Nastrus snorted his disapproval of the image and Jarrod
patted him affectionately. He left the stable smiling and feeling
better than he had since the attack.

II

❧ ❧ ❧

They must die! Have the Imperial Guards seize them
and bring them in chains to Angorn. We shall make a
public example of them. Their arms and legs will be hacked off
in the public square, then they will be dragged through the
streets on hurdles and, when they are brought back, they will
be eviscerated and then hanged in full public view."

The Emperor Varodias' voice rose steadily throughout the
peroration and reached an almost-soprano climax of determined glee. He sat on the throne in the Audience Chamber, his
high-heeled shoes drumming on the footstool, gloved hands
beating on the arms of the carved chair with its high, overarcing
back. From anyone else it would be the ranting of a madman,
but this man was sole ruler of the Empire of Umbria, and his
word, if translated into action, was law. He calmed himself and
sat back into the throne. He was immaculately dressed, as always, in the pearl grey that he had favored for the past two
years. The puffed-out velvet sleeves were slashed to display
plum-colored silk. The pantaloons, less puffed, were similarly
striated. He wore a short cape, pinned at the shoulders by mas-

sive, uncut, but polished, rubies. A standing collar framed his waved and thinning white hair. The face was lined, but the sharp, little eyes missed nothing. The chin, with its pointed beard, only quavered when he wanted it to.

Malum of Quern stood quietly before the throne, head bowed, waiting for the ritual tempest to blow over. That he was privileged was manifest in the fact that, apart from the Emperor, he was the only person visible in the vast room whose walls were decorated to resemble a forest. Even the floor had fallen leaves painted on them. Visible was the operative word, for he was fully aware that a scribe sat, shielded by the throne, transcribing every word that was spoken. When he judged that it was safe, and that the silence had stretched to that exact point where an answer was required, he raised his head.

"Your Imperial Majesty is infinitely wise. Treason cannot be tolerated and the offenders must be made an example of." He broke off and waited. It was a game that he had learned to play. They both used the Formal Mode of speech to their own advantage.

The Emperor was not mad, unless it was a madness sent by the Divine Mother to further his fortunes. It was a guise that he liked to exploit, as was his age, which he used to ruthless advantage when it suited him. The Empire was in turmoil, had been for almost a decade. There had been peasant rebellions, workers' uprisings and challenges against the throne by a handful of disaffected or overly ambitious Elector-Scientists. The Emperor had, with, he had to admit, his own modest guidance, managed to outwit them all. Now there was another wave of unrest and the Emperor saw, or pretended to see, Malum was not quite sure which, a massive conspiracy ahatching.

"There is a 'but' waiting on the back of your tongue, sirrah," the Emperor said, slitting his eyes and staring down at his Secretary. The gloved right hand moved up, index finger wagging. "We know you well, my lord. You cannot dissemble with us.

Do you take the side of these recalcitrant and opprobrious vassals?"

"The Mother forfend, Your Gracious Majesty," Malum said, managing to meld injury and sincerity. "It simply occurred to me that if you took up the chiefest conspirator and hung him in a cage from the battlements until he starved to death, that would serve to affright his cohorts. Meanwhile, you could send the Imperial forces into the other disaffected Electorates to quell the local unrest and then occupy certain strategic castles as just payment for saving the Electors from the insurrection of their own people. The garrisons would, of course, have to stay there to guarantee that insurrection does not recur and I would think that the Electors would be grateful enough to pay for their upkeep."

Malum inclined his head again and waited. He heard a low, rumbling wheeze and knew that he was home free. The wheeze built into a chuckle, was interrupted by a fit of coughing, and became a clear laugh at last. The voice, when it came, was clear, lucid and cold.

"Admirable. Rebellion will be contained and the exchequer will benefit. A capital idea. We should reward you for this." There was a pause while the white fabric fingers played on the arms of the throne. The Emperor sat forward and smiled. "The Elector of Darrendorf is getting old, revenues are down. Mayhap it is time for him to retire to his estates." This time it was the Emperor who left things dangling.

Malum had lowered his head again and was glad that he had. What he was being offered was the third most powerful position in the Empire. The Keeper of the Exchequer was second only to the Lord Chancellor in the Imperial order of government and the opportunity for enrichment was infinitely greater. It was extremely tempting, but it would mean coming out of the shadows and, when all was said and done, he did, in fact, exercise more influence. But that, he realized, didn't matter. The Emperor was testing him. His stomach began to churn. If he accepted the honor, the Emperor might decide that his aim was self-aggrandizement and not the Emperor's service. If he declined, the Emperor might be insulted, and that could result in exile, or the loss of one's head. He took a deep breath and, when his head came up, he was smiling. It wasn't a good smile, but it was the best he could muster under the circumstances.

"If Your Imperial Majesty will permit an observation," he said, the ghastly smile firmly in place. "Mederich of Darrendorf is not responsible for the falloff in revenue. That, in my humble opinion, is the result of the combined and evil machinations of the Isphardis and the Magical Kingdoms. Now, it is true that the Elector is not as young as he used to be, but he is somewhat younger than Your Majesty, and Your Majesty demonstrates every day that experience has only served to sharpen Your Imperial Majesty's judgment."

The fingers of the royal right hand had begun to dance again and Malum, knowing the sign, hurried on. "I am overcome with joy that Your Imperial Majesty would single me out for doing nothing more than my duty to His Imperial Majesty and to the Empire, but I desire no rank above the one I hold, so long as I have the confidence of Your Majesty. Without that, I am nothing. No position, no title, can replace the inestimable feeling of being, in some small way, Your Imperial Majesty's councillor."

That much, though expressed in terms for which he despised himself, but were also necessary for survival, was true. He looked at his master's face, reading it like the expert he had become. The lines around the mouth had softened—a good sign. The eyes were still slitted—he had not passed whatever test it was that his master had set. Money? No. This ruler hated to disburse from the Treasury unless it was absolutely essential. He had already played on that to his advantage. No, what Varodias distrusted was the man who seemed to want nothing. He

had held the throne for over forty years and had been surrounded by ambition. That he understood. The sacred nature
of an oath of fealty, the putting of the Empire's good over personal considerations, were all ideals he espoused, expected
from others, but did not believe in. Malum knew his value to
the Emperor, knew that the Emperor knew it too and also knew
that it made no difference to a man who had been an absolute
ruler for such a long time and whose whim was law.

"Since Your Majesty has been graciously pleased to acknowledge my humble efforts," Malum said, "I should be infinitely grateful if the estates adjacent to Quern could be made to
acknowledge my fealty and, perhaps, a portion of the Imperial
taxes might accrue to Quern, together with the right of fines
and fees usually reserved to manorial courts?"

Varodias' smile was thin and knowing and, for a moment,
Malum wondered if he had made a fatal mistake. The gloved
hands lifted from the arms of the throne and the fingertips
tapped together. The smile persisted. The voice, when it
emerged, was soft and rife with sarcasm. "So you would remain
anonymous, but be rich," the Emperor said. The left hand went
up to stroke the short, pointed beard. The changeable, hazel
eyes bored down. "Very well, Master Secretary, we shall order it
so. In fact, we shall give you judicial and seigneurial rights over
the whole Shire."

"Your Majesty is entirely too generous," Malum said, bowing low. Indeed. His income had just been quadrupled.

"Yes we are," the figure on the throne said coldly. "You are
going to have to earn this. We want the Electorate of Oxenburg
neutralized." A hand waved. "We know that they pretend to be
loyal, but they have no hostages at Court. We do not trust
them. We want the Margrave under our eye. Next, weather
control is being established in Songuard; your reports say so.
We want it eliminated and we want it done in such a fashion
that it will not be traced back to Angorn."

Varodias leaned forward over crossed arms. "Do we make

ourselves entirely clear, Lord Malum, newly appointed Seneschal of the County of Cleremont?"

Malum bowed low to cover his consternation. He had already taken steps to disrupt the ordering of Songuard's weather in order to curtail the Isphardi's road-building efforts, but he had done it on his own initiative and the Emperor did not always appreciate initiative. Had he found out? Was this a subtle warning?

"Entirely clear, Your Imperial Majesty," he said, keeping his voice steady.

His mind was already maneuvering as he backed from the presence. He had three Weatherwards in custody and the seasonal rains should be falling over Songuard. Word of that would get back to the Emperor soon enough. He hoped that he wouldn't be forced to kill them. Most Umbrians discounted Magic as mere superstition, but Malum had spent time in the Magical Kingdoms and knew that the Discipline, if roused, would be a formidable foe.

The Oxenburg problem was something else again, but he had an idea that might provide the answer to another problem at the same time. Though he had kept his eyes down, as etiquette demanded, through most of the interview, he had scanned the Emperor's face for signs of illness. Varodias had to be well over sixty, a good ten years beyond the norm. It was time to cultivate the Prince, but it would have to be done subtly; any hint of a transfer of allegiance could have grave consequences. Varodias feigned illness from time to time to flush out possible cabals, so one had to tread with the care of a cat. Nevertheless, a group was beginning to form around the Crown Prince, and it would be to Malum's advantage if the Prince were to leave Angorn for a while.

Estivus, Margrave of Oxenburg, dismounted wearily, kicked a body out of the way, and wiped his blade clean on the grass.

The sky was a limpid blue and a soft breeze wafted puffy white clouds across it. A perfect day for a fight, good visibility, cool enough for full armor, but he felt none of the residual elation that battle engenders. Slaughtering peasants was not his idea of honorable combat. He looked down the gentle slope and saw the ill-dressed corpses, the scythes and homemade pikes. Pitiful, he thought. Above his head, the kites were already wheeling, drawn by the scent of blood and their instinct for death. He shuddered briefly and sheathed his sword. The larger scavengers, human as well as avian, would soon be on the scene.

"Good fight, what? That should teach the treasonous bastards a lesson." The cheery voice came from behind him and Estivus turned.

"Indeed, Your Royal Highness," he said to the red-faced man on the magnificent grey destrier. "Another resounding triumph for your Imperial father." He did not bother to keep the irony out of his voice, knowing that it wouldn't register on the Emperor's only surviving son. The sole thing, besides eating, that Prince Coram excelled in was hunting.

"No pickings for the men from this lot," the Prince observed, "and certainly there was no one worth ransoming." He spoke in Umbrian, which was normal enough between soldiers, but unusual coming from a Prince of the Blood. Common, the lingua franca of Strand, was what they spoke at Court.

"You have the right of it there, Your Highness," Estivus said as he climbed back into the saddle and turned the horse's head. "No more than a half-starved rabble."

"They would have plundered the Imperial granaries if we hadn't stopped them," the Prince said placidly.

And who could have blamed them? Estivus thought. Four years of bad harvests had taken their toll and now the Imperial Cavalry was being used to kill men bent on trying to find grain, any grain, to feed their families. This present task did not sit well with him, though he knew that his oath of fealty demanded it. He nudged his horse into a trot toward the crown of the hill where his men had regrouped. Prince Coram trotted after him.

Coram's presence in the Margrave's troop was supposedly a signal honor and a sign of Imperial trust. Varodias, having cloistered the Prince for the greater part of his life and executed or otherwise disposed of his brothers, had suddenly decided that his only heir needed some practical experience and had entrusted him to the Oxenburgs. The Prince's entourage was an unwelcome expense, but the Prince himself was an easy and undemanding guest. When Estivus had suggested that he might join the unit for a while and live the life of an ordinary cavalry officer, the Prince had agreed and had brought only two servants with him. The problem was that His Royal Highness regarded warfare as another form of hunting. He made no distinction between men and game.

"Nothing more to be done here, Highness," the Margrave said. "The Shire will be quiet for a while, though the tax gatherers will have a hard time of it."

"Shouldn't we bury them?" Coram asked, nodding down the incline toward the litter of bodies.

The question surprised Estivus. It suggested a sensitivity that the Prince had not thus far manifested.

"The thought does you honor, sir," he said gravely, "but it is best to allow the families to claim their own. Proof of death is necessary for inheritance and the local lord needs to know how many men he has left to work his fields."

"Ah yes. I hadn't thought of that. They're going to be short-handed come harvest."

"The Mother grant a sufficient harvest for it to be a problem," Estivus said gently.

They rode in silence to Hallentor, the family hunting lodge that was doubling as a cavalry post. The presence of the Prince beside him sent Estivus' thoughts ranging over the recent events in the Empire. It was not something that he ordinarily did. He concerned himself with his family and his men and left greater affairs to others. He had, he knew, the reputation of being a good commander and a loyal vassal—also of not being overly ambitious or overly bright. It was an image that he had been at pains to foster. Ambition in the son of an Elector was a dangerous thing in Umbria. Being clever was almost as bad.

Things had not been going well in the Empire, everyone knew that. Banditry and food riots were endemic and, while Simlan the Hermit seemed to have disappeared, there was still unrest in the manufacturing towns. Varodias seemed to be getting more willful as he got older. Just a couple of years ago he had had the Electors of Ondor and Flaxenholme arrested for treason and dragged off to Angorn to await trial. They were still there.

Most of the senior officers that he knew disliked the fact that the army was being used to cow the people. Fighting the Outlanders had been a clear, clean, necessity. Taking the field against bands of old soldiers reduced to highway robbery by a lack of land and employment, or the ragtag starvelings that they had put to the sword today, left an unpleasant taste. He had been a soldier since he was seventeen, had never wanted to be anything else, but he had been thinking of late of resigning his commission, using his eventual governance of the Electorate as a reason. Indeed, there was some truth to it. He knew little enough about managing the family's considerable holdings.

They clopped their way into the bailey of the lodge and threw their reins to the sudden cluster of adolescent grooms, all of whom were vying for a permanent position in a knightly household. Estivus dismounted heavily and found a dark-haired youth at his elbow. The boy hesitated to speak and Estivus, sticky and, even in his own nostrils, odorous, was more interested in a bath, but, remembering his own days as a squire, looked down and raised his eyebrows in question.

"The Lord Malum of Quern is within and desires an appointment, an it please Your Lordship," the lad said in Common, using the Formal Mode.

This one comes from Angorn, the Margrave thought. "Has your master lodging?" he replied in kind.

"Rooms in the tower have been put at his disposal and, were he here, I know that he would tender his thanks."

A smooth-tongued stripling, Estivus thought, and presumptuous with it. "Give his lordship joy of this unexpected pleasure, and do you tell him that I shall join him when the stink of fighting has been washed from my body." The boy bowed and walked proudly away.

Malum of Quern here, Estivus mused as he clumped across the courtyard, his sabatons ringing on the cobbles. "The Emperor's crow" as he was called behind his back. Rumors about Varodias' Secretary had penetrated even this far into the countryside. There had never been such a position at Court before and, from the title, it should have been held by a senior scribe, but Estivus knew that Quern was a fairly young man. It was also said that, though rarely seen, he wielded considerable influence. The Margrave had not been quartered in the capital for some years and had no firsthand knowledge of the man, but, if Quern was an envoy from the Emperor, and why else would he be here, he would have to be treated with the respect due. The Margrave was in no mood for Court niceties, but he knew his duty. There would have to be a feast, though there was precious little game left in the larder.

Newly washed and barbered and wearing his second-best clothes, Estivus of Oxenburg presented himself at the door of what used to be his mother's quarters. The same young man showed him in and the Emperor's Secretary rose to greet him, advancing with palms extended.

"I am honored to make your acquaintance, Margrave," Malum said as their hands touched briefly. The accompanying smile was easy and open. "I must apologize for appearing so unexpectedly. The messenger I sent ahead seems to have been waylaid. Your people, however, could not have been more courteous or accommodating."

"I regret that I could not have been here to welcome you in person," Estivus replied politely, "but there was a local matter to attend to."

"So I understand and I hear that you dealt with it in your usual masterly fashion." He gestured toward a group of chairs. "His Imperial Highness speaks glowingly of your conduct."

Estivus smiled stiffly. He distrusted flattery. "You have spoken with the Prince?" he asked as he took his seat.

"Not in person, no," Malum admitted. "I have, of course, sent my compliments, but his Imperial Highness is doubtless wearied by his exertions. No, I was referring, rather, to the letters that His Majesty has received from his son. The Emperor is most grateful to the Elector for his hospitality and to you for showing Prince Coram some of the realities of his future realm."

"His Imperial Majesty does us too much honor," Estivus replied warily. "It is a privilege to have the Prince among us."

He looked carefully at the man opposite. Quern was a short, thin, pale man with black hair and eyes that were either black or dark brown, depending on the light. The face would have been on the pretty side of handsome, but for the sharpness of the features. He wore a black jacket and long, black trousers, black stockings and black shoes. The only relief came from his silver buckles and a small, old-fashioned, white ruff. His nickname, Estivus thought, was well earned. He wished the man would get down to business. He obviously hadn't come all this way to administer a pat on the back on his master's behalf.

"Would that it could be for longer," Quern said as if anticipating him, "but there are problems developing on the international front and His Imperial Majesty feels that it might be to His Highness's benefit to be at Angorn during the early stages." The smile this time carried a hint of knowingness and complicity, but if he expected the Margrave to express an interest, he was disappointed. "A furtherance of his education," he added unnecessarily.

"We shall, of course, be sad to see the Prince go," Estivus replied gravely. "My daughters have formed a great liking for him and he is popular with the men, but His Imperial Majesty's command is ever our law."

"Just so," Quern agreed. "I am glad to hear you say so. It makes the next part of my message so much simpler."

The friendly smile came again and Estivus braced himself.

"His Imperial Majesty requests," Quern continued with a slight emphasis on the "requests," "that you accompany Prince Coram to Angorn."

Estivus bowed his head as his mind raced. It was the Emperor's habit to require major vassals to keep a family member at Court. It was one of the reasons that the two Electors accused of treason had presented themselves at Angorn without a fight. Did this mean that his father was under suspicion? Surely not. The Oxenburgs had never meddled in Imperial politics, but, with Varodias, one never knew what to expect. He lifted his head and looked squarely at Quern.

"Is it His Imperial Majesty's intention that I escort the Prince to Angorn and return to my command, or that I should stay a while at Angorn?" He tried to make the question sound as offhand as possible.

"The Emperor would deem it a favor if you would consent to take a position at Court," Quern said smoothly. "The Prince has few friends there." The smile flashed out again. "Hunting cronies, yes, true friends and counselors, no." The dark eyes were shrewd. "You need have no fear, my lord." The voice was soft, reassuring. "The Emperor has nothing but the highest regard for the House of Oxenburg. It is the Prince's good opinion of you that has prompted this. Indeed, you will find that His Imperial Majesty can be generous."

The confounded man is reading my mind, Estivus thought. Irritation was mixed with a certain amount of admiration for the way in which Quern was handling him. The Secretary's tone made it seem as if Estivus had a choice, whereas they both knew that he had none. Well, perhaps one.

"Am I required to give up my command?" he inquired, pleased that the words had come out as neutrally as he had intended.

"Alas, yes," Quern said and Estivus' heart seemed suddenly free of the constriction that had been gradually tightening around it. To refuse preferment at Court in favor of continued service in the field could not be construed as disloyalty.

The Secretary raised a hand to forestall comment, got up and went over to a saddlebag propped against the wall. He unbuckled the flap and drew out a rolled parchment adorned with a ribbon buried in wax. He advanced on the Margrave, scroll held out, with a look of pleasure on his face.

"It is my privilege to present you with the letter patent of your appointment to the rank of Brigade General." He paused for effect. "Not, as you will see, of the Imperial cavalry, but of the Imperial Army proper." He handed it over and stood back, beaming.

Estivus drew in a deep breath. He had just been jumped up three ranks, unheard of in peacetime. He did a quick calculation. There were only four other Brigade Generals and he was their junior by a good fifteen years. That wouldn't sit well with them. On the other hand, it would mean a doubling of his pay and that, in turn, would mean a new roof for the dower house.

Malum watched the Margrave's face and saw the emotions that played across it as well as the slight flush that rose from his throat. He had judged the man aright. He was susceptible, so long as it squared with his sense of honor. Furthermore, the man was no dissembler. Everything that he had read about the Margrave, an embodiment of the old-fashioned "virtue" of the Umbrian aristocracy, was proving to be correct. He would make a most suitable companion for the Prince and, if played correctly, could provide an excellent entrée to the upper echelons of the Army, where Malum's intelligence was particularly weak.

"Of course," he said, "you will have to have some kind of official position at Court." He sounded apologetic. "You know how status-conscious those people are. I thought perhaps Chief Gentleman-of-the-Bedchamber to the Prince might suit. He has a Chamberlain to run his household and the formal duties are minimal. The position carries an annual stipend of ten thousand imperials."

Estivus pursed his lips but stopped short of whistling. That, on top of his military salary, would make him a rich man in a couple of years.

The bear will growl, Malum predicted to himself. Too much unearned good fortune is unacceptable to him. It must, therefore be suspect and, if suspect, challenged.

"And what, precisely, am I supposed to do to earn this generous stipend?" the Margrave asked on cue.

"Attend His Royal Highness, hunt with him, remain on sufficiently good terms with him so that your advice carries weight. Make sure he does not get into trouble when he is drunk or is too badly fleeced in the whorehouse." There was no charm or bonhomie in the voice now and the eyes were level and penetrating. "The Emperor's heir is an innocent," he said flatly. "You have come to know him somewhat. He is bluff, good-natured, bloodthirsty, inexperienced in statecraft and not particularly eager to learn. In short, he is an easy mark for the greedy, the unscrupulous and the ambitious." He stopped and gave Estivus a melancholy little smile.

"Prince Coram," Malum said so softly that the Margrave leaned forward to hear, "is, like it or not, the only peaceful future for the Empire. His father, alas, has devoted little time to his training." He shrugged. "If the truth were known, he has paid scant attention to the Prince all through his life. Coram is devoted to his mother, but the Empress Zhane is dropsical. If she is bled properly, she may last another couple of years.

When she dies, the Prince will be adrift, looking for an anchor. It is my," Malum checked himself and then continued as if no break had occurred, "it is the Emperor's hope that you might help to fill that void." He let the words hang, but the Margrave made no reply.

"I will not cozen you, my lord," he resumed after a while. "This is no cozy Court position. This is no glorified and over-paid nursemaiding. I pray daily to the Mother that our sovereign lives to a ripe and acute old age, but the Mother has Her own inscrutable ways and the realm needs someone solid and reliable at the Prince's side."

Malum had waxed vehement. He had allowed the fiction that he spoke entirely for the Emperor to lapse. It was a calculated gamble. He permitted himself to look slightly ashamed of his fervor and ducked his head.

"Forgive me," he said. "My former master, the Elector of Estragoth, always looked to the longer good of Umbria and he instilled the same cares in me. I seem to have absorbed his concerns for the long range, but I have yet to master his dispassion." He raised his hands and his mouth tightened. "I am devoted to His Majesty," he said simply. "Without him, I am nothing, and yet I worry." The look on the Margrave's face told Malum that he had chosen exactly the right tack.

"I shall need some time to break in my successor here and to make my farewells to my family," Estivus said.

"You could bring your family with you," Malum suggested, and then saw the look on the Margrave's countenance. "But then again," he added, "perhaps not. The womenfolk like to take their time about such things. They like to try to anticipate the fashions." He smiled easily. "I recommend that you include details of what the ladies of the Court are wearing in your letters home."

"Does the Prince have no say in the matter?" Estivus inquired.

"I have not, as you know, had an opportunity to broach the

subject. I have an Imperial order for his return to Angorn and in that he has no say. I have no doubt that he would welcome your company."

"How long before we leave?"

"A sennight, I think. There is an Imperial forest a league off, if my maps are right. We have an heir to the throne on hand who has the right to hunt in it. It would be a shame to pass up such an opportunity."

"We'll find you a good mount, my lord," Estivus said, and prepared to take his leave. At least, he thought, that will solve the larder problem and enable the post to provide a fitting farewell feast for the Prince. Breaking the good news to his wife was going to be a lot harder.

III

✣ ✣ ✣

M alum sat, shoes off, doublet unlaced, in the one comfortable chair in the two-room suite he had just been allocated and contemplated his situation with some satisfaction. The Emperor had seemed pleased when he had shown up with the Crown Prince and the Margrave of Oxenburg in tow. Though the offer of new quarters had come from the Chamberlain, there was no doubt that the impetus came from Varodias. Though far from grand, they were infinitely better than the pawky room in which he had lived since entering the Elector of Estragoth's service. Furthermore, their modesty was unlikely to elicit envy or invite unwanted attention from the other young courtiers. If the knucklebones fell right, he should be able to retire a wealthy man.

While his power and standing in his own county had improved immeasurably, his estate was small and marginally profitable. There would, he was sure, be larger holdings in his future and, presumably, an heir to leave them to. He was well content to wait. Marriage into an Electoral House was his aim and for that his influence with the Crown Prince would be key.

Besides, this was no time to be looking for a bride at Court. The Empress's ladies in waiting were all elderly, the Prince was unmarried and, hence, there were no young women in his household. Given the current political climate, Electors were unwilling to send their unmarried daughters to Angorn. Why put more hostages within the Emperor's grasp than one had to? There were wives at Court, of course, some of whom had a roving eye. Not for Malum, however. He was neither important enough nor handsome enough to be a feather in the cap and this, too, suited him. A man with few friends cannot afford to make enemies.

Not that he lacked for protestations of friendship. He smiled wryly to himself as he sipped his watered wine. He was summoned too often to the Emperor's presence for that. Those who sought offices or Imperial favors invited him to hunt and took pains to establish fellowship. Some offered gifts. He accepted some of the invitations, his love of hunting was undiminished, but he refused all gifts. Once in a while he would bring a petition to Varodias' attention, or, when asked, venture an opinion on an appointment. He took care to promote only those things that were in the Emperor's, or the Empire's, best interest. He was sedulously building a reputation for incorruptibility and disinterestedness.

The Margrave of Oxenburg, though Estivus was not aware of it, had been Malum's choice for the Prince's mentor. It fitted in with the Emperor's desire for a body from that family at Angorn and the man had a reputation for unswerving loyalty to the Crown and a lack of interest in politics. Now, having met him and traveled in his company, he felt drawn to the man in ways that he did not care to analyze. One thing was obvious. The Margrave would be a good influence on the Crown Prince and already commanded Coram's admiration.

Matters were progressing satisfactorily on other fronts as well. The news from Songuard was good. Severe storms had disrupted the Isphardis' road-building efforts. The kidnapping of the Weatherwards was paying off more rapidly than he had expected and he had told the Emperor what had occurred. He had omitted to mention the date. Such an operation could not be mounted again without making the Empire's role obvious, but this early discouragement might produce disproportionate results. A victory, however clandestine, was badly needed just now, if only to sweeten the Emperor's mood.

Weather seemed to be the key to that, too. Four years of disastrous harvests had produced shortages and civil unrest, especially in the towns. That had affected manufacturing and that, in turn, limited the ability to import grain. Salvation might well lie, eventually, with the Alien Plain. Water was the big question. Veterans from the war against the Outlanders were settling along the borders of a lake, most of which was, in fact, inside territory allotted to Isphardel. By the time the Isphardis reached it, however, they would be confronted by a fait accompli. In any case, it would be years before the Alien Plain was producing enough to feed the rest of the Empire.

There was a knock at the door and Malum looked up, annoyed. Attendance on the Emperor was a nerve-racking business and it took its toll on a man's spirit. Once he had allowed himself to relax, he resented intrusions.

"Come," he said grudgingly.

The blond head of Brandwin of Gottschalk, the sixteen-year-old son of a southern neighbor, poked hesitantly round the door. He had good reason for his caution. If the Lord Malum deemed the intrusion unnecessary, Brandwin would have to strip and submit to a switching. He was newly arrived, sent by his father hard on the announcement of the Seneschalship. Everything was strange, but he was learning fast. His predecessor as His Lordship's page had been dismissed and sent home to his parents in disgrace. He did not intend to make the same mistake.

"Beg pardon, m'lord," he said in his heavy Southern burr. He sidled into the room and made an awkward bow. He swallowed, trying to remember the exact words. "The Emperor desires that you attend upon him at your earliest convenience." He looked up and smiled in relief, pleased at his performance.

"And where shall I attend upon His Majesty?" Malum asked, half-hoping that the boy would get the answer wrong.

"There is a Gentleman-of-the-Bedchamber waiting for Your Lordship in the corridor," the lad said promptly.

"Oh very well," Malum said, putting down his goblet and pushing himself to his feet. "Come over here and lace up my doublet. I don't know how long this will take, but my bed better be made up when I return and I shall require a hot posset before I retire."

The boy did as he was bidden and then brushed the clothes before securing the half cape to the shoulders of the doublet. It might be a long wait with nothing to eat, but at least he hadn't been cuffed. Whether he was caressed or beaten later would depend on the Emperor's mood. He was resigned to either. He had, he reminded himself, a place at Court in the service of an important man who talked with the Emperor.

The Emperor Varodias sat upon his bed, dressed in a silk sleeping robe with a velvet cap covering his thinning hair. His brocaded slippers swung a good foot off the floor. Malum advanced across the herb-strewn space, his footfalls releasing drily aromatic scents. He made his obeisance and waited.

"We have been thinking," the Emperor said in his high, melodious voice, "that we should use these Magicians from Songuard that you have told us you have captured, a feat we appreciate, to do something about the drought that is afflicting our provinces. The Songeans have too much rain and we have too little—save"—a hand waved negligently in Malum's direction—"for the coastal region."

"Your Imperial Majesty's perspicacity is an example to us all, as ever," Malum replied smoothly, while his stomach began to tighten. "In this particular instance, however, there are some practical problems. To begin with, very few people know that these individuals are in Umbria. They may suspect it, but they cannot prove it. The weather patterns, however, have changed abruptly . . ." He let the sentence die away. "Secondly," he resumed, "it would be extremely dangerous to allow these men the freedom to practice Magic. They are presently bound hand and foot and gagged. If they are loosed, there is no knowing what kind of unnatural disaster they might call down upon our heads." His tone was studiously respectful and his use of the Formal Mode impeccable.

"Still, it seems to us a shame to waste the potential, and the need is great," Varodias countered peevishly. "Cannot they be convinced?"

Malum paused before replying, weighing how best to put his point of view across. Why, he wondered briefly, did he always feel that he had to justify himself, prove himself anew, each time he faced the Emperor. He was a grown man, a man of demonstrated abilities. Varodias was his Emperor, due his loyalty, respect and his best efforts, true. He was also his father, though the man did not know it, and the Mother only knew what that demanded of a bastard, but Malum of Quern had forged his own destiny independent of that knowledge and had earned the right to be truthful when it was in the Empire's best interest. He was conscious, nevertheless, of the sweat trickling down his sides. He took a breath.

"If Your Imperial Majesty will permit a personal observation," he ventured.

"You may speak."

"I spent five years in Stronta during the negotiations on the Outland Treaty and I had a chance to see Magic and Magicians at firsthand. I must tell you, Majesty, that the Discipline will be a fearsome adversary if roused." His hands came up and waved in front of his chest as if deflecting comment. "I am aware that the Mother Church discounts Magic entirely and most of your subjects regard it as charlatanism, but I must tell you, from my own observation, that it is powerful. I have seen it in operation and it destroys anything in its path. It is not a force to be dismissed."

Varodias looked down from the canopied bed, eyes lidded, silent long enough to make Malum fearful. "You saw it," he said at length, "when they wanted you to see it." He smiled. It was not a reassuring smile. "They did it so that you, young and impressionable"—he managed to get a measure of contempt into the phrase—"would be convinced." The Emperor sat back in his throne. "We should have done exactly the same," he said, "but both of us know that, confronted with our machines, and our superior knowledge, this so-called magic will crumble." He paused slightly. "We were talking of the Magicians from Songuard. If reason does not answer, try torture. They and their unnatural tinkering with the forces of nature are responsible for this drought. They should be made to reverse it." The fingers of the right hand flicked in dismissal.

Malum bowed deeply. "As Your Majesty commands," he said, and backed from the presence.

Once outside, he swore under his breath. The Emperor's mind was beginning to deteriorate. To reveal, in any way, that the Magicians were in Umbria could have dire consequences. It had been a mistake to bring them to Angorn. He would have to move them out of the capital and away from Varodias. He could say that they had to be in the mountains to influence the weather. Indeed, that might well be true. Perhaps they could be induced to make it rain around Angorn. Then he could have them taken to some other area to make it rain there. He was thinking quickly as he made his way back through the passageways to his rooms. Yes, perhaps he could pull this off after all. By the time he reached the door he was looking forward to his posset and to having the new page sleep at the foot of the bed.

He awoke shortly after dawn. Brandwin was already fussing over the fire, readying water for chai and for his master's bath. The boy was performing better, Malum thought, no doubt about it. He would, perhaps, reward him with a new suit of clothes. The youngster was beginning to look frayed and shabby and that reflected badly on himself. Malum's own clothes, black velvet jacket and trousers, white shirt with a short, pleated ruff and cuffs, lay on the lid of the press.

He had worn the same basic outfit since he had first arrived at Angorn. He had had little money in those days and black lasted longer and required less cleaning than the grander fashions of his contemporaries. He had been made sport of for it and had continued to wear black as a gesture of defiance. Now it had become his signature. He was well aware of his nickname around the palace. The laugh that accompanied it these days was, more often than not, nervous. He was content that it should be so. He stretched, threw back the coverlet and repaired to the garderobe. One of the virtues of these rooms, and one of the reasons that he had chosen them over more spacious quarters, was that they had their own privy. It was a luxury denied to all but a few.

On his return he looked at the boy as he labored, the pale skin red from the heat and the exertion, the blond hair darkening with sweat, the movements adolescent awkward as he tried to lug the hot kettle over to the tub. Something stirred in Malum, something prompted by the desperate effort to please that the boy seemed to exude.

"If you lean forward slightly," he said, "and hold the handle toward the base, like this, it'll go much easier." The flashing smile of gratitude he received warmed him and made him turn away with an awkwardness of his own. He felt a muffled conflict of emotions, an instinct to instruct, closely allied to domination, and perversely, considering their respective ranks, an instinct to protect. He dismissed the feelings as irrelevant; he had more important things to attend to.

He breakfasted sparingly and then descended to the dungeons. The turnkey accompanied him through dank, stone corridors to the area where a steam generator hissed and clanked.

The air was full of the smell of burning coal. They stopped at a door and he stood aside while the turnkey unlocked it. He had chosen this location for the captive Magicians himself. It might not satisfy the Emperor's notions of torture, but Malum knew what effect the proximity of machinery would have on the prisoners.

"Ungag them," he ordered, and waited while they worked their mouths to get rid of the feeling of constriction. "Give you goodday, gentlemen. I have spoken with the Emperor as I said I would." He watched them.

The three were young and all had the indecent extravagance of height that marked Magicians, but that was where the likeness ended. The one called Aristach was the tallest and usually the most self-assured, but incarceration next to the boiler room had given him eyes that blinked constantly and a mouth that twitched in counterpoint. Bervis had black hair and eyes that never looked straight ahead. The third, Gordiam, was shorter than the others, though not by much. When he had been taken prisoner he had been plump. Now he looked haggard.

"As you know," he continued, "I have opposed this imprisonment since I first became aware of it. I pleaded for your return to Songuard, but His Imperial Majesty remains convinced that you are responsible for the drought."

"We've been through all this before," Aristach interrupted, the voice scratchy from lack of moisture. "The drought began well before we got to Songuard and kidnapping us hasn't changed a thing."

"So you say," Malum replied patiently, "but the Emperor chooses to doubt your veracity." He gestured in a plea for understanding. "What else could you say under the circumstances?" He raised a hand to forestall objections. "I took a risk last night in bringing the matter up again." He sighed and shook his head. "Dealing with an absolute monarch is no easy task, I assure you.

"Knowing that your protestations of innocence carried no

weight with him, I pointed out to His Majesty what the possible repercussions might be, both from the Discipline and from your respective rulers, if your presence in Umbria became known. I reminded him that we have always had cordial relations with the Magical Kingdoms, that we relied upon them to restrain the territorial ambitions of the Isphardis." He smiled. "The Emperor agreed with me and ordered your execution forthwith." He paused to let that sink in. "I ventured to suggest," he continued, "that if you could create some rain locally, or if you could use your arts to divert some of the unwanted rain falling on Songuard . . . He agreed, somewhat reluctantly, but he agreed."

He watched the hope creep back into their eyes. "There are a couple of conditions, however. In return for your freedom, the Emperor requires that you bring us a consistent, soaking rain, so that we can count on a wheat crop this year and that you swear a holy oath that no mention be made, ever, of this, ah, temporary relocation."

"And in return for this small favor, we regain the freedom that is rightfully ours?" Jubal Aristarch's voice was full of skepticism.

Malum smiled again, an easy, friendly smile. This one dies first, he thought. "Well, to begin with," he said, "you get out of here and away from the machinery. You will be saving several thousand people from possible starvation, restoring the livelihood of others, preserving international good relations, in short, doing the kind of thing that dedicated young men such as yourselves would want to do."

"That's all very well," Jubal said wearily, "but we can't just make it rain whenever we feel like it. It doesn't work that way. We explained that to you. We have to be as close to the natural weather patterns as possible and changing them is a slow and difficult process."

"We could take you back to the mountains, our side of the mountains of course," Malum said. "I would need your oath that you would not try to escape or make mischief." He looked from one to the other. "Consider the alternatives. We have received no inquiries about your absence and if we do, we shall send out search parties." The smile was wolfish. "We shall be so disappointed when they come back empty-handed." He paused and looked them over again. "Let me give you until tomorrow to think about it. Oh, and I'll leave you ungagged."

He signaled to the turnkey and left well satisfied.

"Well, what do we do?" Jubal asked as the sound of retreating footsteps was absorbed by the noise of the pumps.

"I don't trust that smooth-tongued little viper," Gerdain Bervis said.

"What harm would it do to agree?" Gordiam said in a voice that wavered. "We have to get out of here. Those bloody machines are giving me a permanent headache."

"If we do what he wants, we'll be killed," Jubal said flatly.

"If we don't agree, we'll be killed even faster," Albio Gordiam argued. "Besides, why wouldn't they let us go after we've solved their problem? It wouldn't do any harm to shift some of the rain eastward. Isphardel and Songuard get too much rain at this time of year anyway. All we were doing was moving it north at a faster rate and dumping it over the Alien Plain. If he had us killed, it would cause an international incident."

"Don't be so naive," Jubal said, shaking his head. "How long have we been away from our stations? A month? Longer? The weather patterns over Songuard must have changed; someone will have been sent to find out what's going on. Alive, we are a liability. Dead, the Emperor can always deny all knowledge. The Discipline will suspect, probably suspects already, but you don't create international incidents over suspicions."

"I suppose you're right," Gordiam admitted, "but if they take us back to the mountains, there's a chance that we could escape. If they leave us here, they won't have to kill me. Those motherless machines will do it."

"You have a point there, Albio," Bervis said. "If they let us make Magic, they won't be able to have machines around. If we make Magic, we ought to be able to get away."

"Even if we don't, I have no intention of dying cheaply. I'll take as many of the bastards with me as I can." Aristach sounded venomous.

"Listen," Bervis said. "For the rainfall to do any lasting good, it'll have to keep up over a fairly long period. The best way, even from their point of view, would be to let us go back to our stations and do the work from there. Just add that component to what we would normally do."

"I suppose it's worth a try," Jubal Aristarch concluded. "Is it agreed then? We go along with this scheme for the meanwhile and see what develops?"

The other two nodded.

IV

❧ ❧ ❧

*W*hy *all this sneaking around?*' Nastrus asked as he made his way through sleeping courtyards with Jarrod on his back. '*I thought you were an important person. Have you been disgraced since I've been gone?*'

'No, I have not been disgraced. *I'm still an important person, and that's the problem. I've got a great deal to do during the day and people get nervous when I disappear.*'

'*Too important for your own good, eh?*' Nastrus teased.

'*I expect to be back by morning, but if I'm not, I'm not,*' Jarrod replied, refusing to rise to the bait. '*We'll deal with things as they come up.*'

They walked quietly through the outer gate, left open and unguarded in these days of peace. Fear of Magic, or at least what a Magician could do to you if you were caught, was enough protection against thieves. Jarrod was uncomfortably warm under his double layer of clothing and his wool cape, but it had been a long time since he had journeyed through Interim and whatever immunity against the cold of the Lines of Force he had accrued was probably gone. His saddlebags were full of food and he carried a waterskin and another skin for wine.

They trotted across the kina-cropped turf and turned to the north, facing the dim outline of the Place of Power, of which Jarrod was the Keeper. Beyond, lost in the darkness of the night, lay the Upper Causeway.

'*Are you ready?*' Nastrus asked.

Jarrod leaned forward and grabbed two handfuls of mane before laying his body down on the long neck. '*Ready,*' he said.

Between one breath and another, Nastrus went into Interim. An impenetrable grey surrounded them. Bone-biting cold slid past wool and silk and gnawed at the vitals. Before the pain grew too great, oblivion intervened.

When Jarrod came to, he was aware of intense hunger on two levels. His stomach was growling and Nastrus' need filled his head. He felt weak and realized that, with the unicorn's head down cropping grass, he was in danger of falling off. He pushed himself upright, taking deep breaths to dispel the dizziness. He worked his fingers, still clenched convulsively in the coarse hair of the mane, until he could disengage them. He slid off Nastrus' back and scrabbled at the buckle that held the saddlebag closed. The need to eat was a compulsion that had to be satisfied.

Finally sated, he washed the meal down with water and looked around. There, on the mountainside, silvered by the nightmoon's light, was the castle he had built. He had expected the unicorn to come out of Interim on the plateau that fronted the building and did not look forward to the scramble uphill. Still, if they were to get back by morning, there was nothing else for it. He reached out for Nastrus' mind, but the unicorn was still too intent on grazing to pay him heed. He was considering starting off by himself when a shadow detached itself from the foot of the slope and came toward them.

"Joscelyn?" he said hopefully. The word came out raspingly.

"Welcome, my Lord Mage." The boy spoke in Common and used the Formal Mode.

"I'm glad to see you. Are you well?" Jarrod used the conversational intonations.

"I am well an' I thank you, Eminence."

"Oh come on, Joscelyn. There's no need for such formality," Jarrod said, irritated by the boy's attitude. This wasn't going the way he had expected. "I haven't come to reprimand you, or drag you home. I wasn't even sure you would be here, though I hoped you would be. Nastrus wanted to visit his offspring and I jumped at the opportunity."

The young man stayed where he was, about fifteen paces away. He was taller than Jarrod remembered, but he was wearing what looked like a red cloak with the cowl up and his face was in shadow. "Am I permitted a hug?"

Jarrod moved forward and opened his arms. Joscelyn hesitated and then advanced. He was stiff and uneasy in the embrace. He was also, Jarrod thought as his arms circled the boy, desperately thin. He held him briefly and then pushed him gently back and gazed into the face. The face was gaunt and drawn, what he could see of it. Most of it was covered with hair.

"Your mother misses you, and so do I," he said.

Joscelyn bowed his head. There was an awkward silence and then, "Have my . . . have there been repercussions?"

"Nothing serious. Neither Arabella nor Naxania has forgotten the incident, though, and I wouldn't visit Angorn if I were you." He tried to make it sound humorous, but knew he had failed. "I think I'd like to go up to the castle," he said. "Nastrus ought to have had enough to eat by now."

Joscelyn nodded, turned and began to walk away without a further word.

'He is not very welcoming,' Nastrus commented.

'I expect he's out of practice,' Jarrod replied as he swung himself up onto the unicorn's back. 'I'm probably the first person he's

seen in a long time.' He was disappointed nevertheless and knew
that Nastrus was aware of it.

To their surprise, Joscelyn was on the plateau ahead of
them. He waited beside the steps that led up to the massive
door to the Hall. Jarrod paused to look at the full sweep of the
castle. It seemed exactly as he had left it, though daylight would
probably give the lie to that.

"Come inside where it's warm," Joscelyn said as his stepfather approached. "There isn't much, but I made all the furniture myself." Jarrod noted the pride in the statement. "Of
course it isn't what you're used to," he added, an edge in his
voice on the comment.

The younger man led the way to the undercroft door with
Jarrod following him. The undercroft had been designed for
storage, but it made sense to use it for living quarters. It would
be easier to heat and the boy certainly wasn't going to be enter-
taining. Once inside, Jarrod wasn't sure that living quarters was
the right phrase. There was a pallet in front of the fireplace.
There were odd-shaped chairs dotted around and a large,
sturdy-looking table off to one side. Joscelyn saw the look on
the other's face and produced a creaking laugh.

"Unfortunately, I have more ideas than talent. You never
taught us carpentry at the Outpost. In fact there are a lot of
things you didn't bother to teach us."

Jarrod put his saddlebags down against the wall. This was
turning into a confrontation he did not want. "You didn't exactly give the system a chance," he said moderately.

"The system is the problem," Joscelyn said heatedly. "It stifles people."

"You've done much better than I could have," he said, diplomatically changing the subject. "You know, I never expected
to see this place again. It's rather nice to see it occupied."

Joscelyn sighed, drawn into the shared experience. "Occupied is right. It certainly isn't lived in." The tone was bitter and

Jarrod raised his eyebrows. "It was supposed to be such a noble and romantic undertaking, but I've turned into a farmer and fisherman instead." He looked at Jarrod for a long moment and his shoulders sagged. "You wouldn't happen to have any spare food in that saddlebag by any chance? It's been such a long time since I've had proper food."

"Yes of course." Jarrod picked the saddlebags up, carried them to the table and began emptying them. "You might build the fire up while I do this," he said. "I'm still feeling the effects of Interim."

Joscelyn smiled. "You've no idea how glad I am that you thought to put in a fire down here."

"Where did you find the wood?"

"On the other side of the mountains. I, ah, I went back to Arundel through Interim and stole an ax and a saw." He looked up see how his stepfather was taking the news. "I'm not too proud of that," he said defensively, "but without tools I couldn't have survived. Even so, it was a job and a half getting the wood back here. The unicorns weren't exactly happy to be used as beasts of burden, but they finally did it."

He was talking quickly, hungrily, and Jarrod realized how lonely he must be. "Speaking of unicorns," he said so as not to have a silence, "I rather expected to see Astarus."

"Oh, he left a couple of years ago," Joscelyn said as he came to the table, bringing a chair with him. He turned back and got another. "He wanted to see other worlds."

"Takes after his father," Jarrod said conversationally, not wanting to add to the tension. "Are there others that come and visit you?"

"Oh yes. All the time. I can't communicate as well with most of them, though." He sounded wistful. "A lot of the ones that helped build this place come back and in the last year or so their foals have come to see what their parents did. It's all in the Memory."

"A remarkable thing, that Memory," Jarrod said, watching the boy tear into the food like a starving animal.

"Mmph." Joscelyn looked up, his mouth full. "You and Mother are in there," he said when he had swallowed. "It's odd, though, because the unicorns don't understand half the things you did or why you did them. Of course, you were the first humans they'd ever encountered." He returned avidly to the food.

We'll have to find a way to get him back to civilization, Jarrod thought. This can't go on. But how? Even as he put the question, a possible answer came to him. Two birds with a single stone and success would ensure a return at least to Oxeter. That would make Marianna happy. Three birds in fact. He smiled in satisfaction.

Joscelyn of Gwyndryth came to his senses in the middle of an immense bowl of vine-covered cliffs. The portion that was in sunlight was a waterfall of multicolored flowers. The rest of the circle was a dull green and, down at the bottom, was a lake whose surface echoed the black of the rock beneath it more than the blue of the sky above. He was in the Anvil of the Gods, where he intended to be. He was cold and he was furiously hungry. Malloran, the unicorn that he had picked for this journey, or who had consented to accompany him, depending on the point of view, cropped contentedly.

He slid off the unicorn's back and felt his legs fold down as if from long disuse. He had lied to Jarrod about his familiarity with Interim, not wanting to lose this chance to be out in the world again. He walked around until his legs felt steady, oblivious to the beauty around him, and then he attacked the food that he had brought in the saddlebag. Only when those necessities were over did he take stock of his surroundings. It hit him then that he was in the place where his mother had first come upon the unicorns. He turned slowly, taking in the sheer, vine-covered walls and the obsidian lake at the center. This, he thought, was the beginning of it all and, in a gesture that he didn't quite understand, he lifted his arms up to the sky and wheeled around, embracing it all.

In the light that remained, he explored as much as he could, trying to find the terrain described by his mother in countless nursery tales, but nothing seemed to match. When dusk came, he scrambled to gather dry wood and forage for food that would not upset the unicorn. The fire was comforting, but the meal left a lot to be desired. As he prepared for sleep, he went back over the recent past. The advent of his stepfather had changed everything. He still wasn't sure that he liked the man, but he had to admit that, without him, this present adventure would never have happened. On reflection, his previous rebellion, and he'd held to it and hadn't given in, had achieved very little, nothing if he was honest. If he pulled this assignment off, he could, he might . . . He drifted off before his dreams could be articulated.

He awoke feeling more certain. He couldn't explain it, but he just knew that if he kept the map he had been given in his head, Malloran would be able to find his way. Malloran, when consulted, was less sure. The map, as far as the unicorn was concerned, was woefully inadequate. None of the weather stations shown on the map Joscelyn had been given seemed to be in Malloran's family Memory. Joscelyn refused to be daunted. He would do it, he told himself. He was his own man again. This time he knew; this time he was in charge. He looked around at the shrouded valley waiting for the sun and felt a challenge. He mounted Malloran prepared to meet that challenge, whatever it was. The unicorn reserved judgment.

He was nervous nevertheless, when the moment arrived. He had selected the closest site for their destination and he had the map of the area between it and the Anvil of the Gods clear in his mind. He sat, sweating, astride the unicorn, his mouth dry, and concentrated. Even though he was expecting it, the transition into Interim caught him by surprise. He fought to keep the picture clear, but the featureless cold leached it away. With a feeling of helplessness, he surrendered to the inevitable.

The weather station was situated in a fold in the mountainside that afforded some protection from the winds. The simple one-room hut was dwarfed by a massive fireblanket tree, its lowest limbs a foot or two above the roof. At the edge of the flat space a spring-fed pool tumbled away down the steep slope. There had been an attempt to start a vegetable garden, but none of the plants had survived. Though the view was spectacular, the place had a sad, abandoned look.

Joscelyn walked slowly over to the cabin and tried the door. It had been nailed shut, presumably by the search party. There was a window on the south side, but it was shuttered and a tug showed that it was latched on the inside. He grabbed the bottom of the right-hand shutter and yanked sharply. The latch gave and both shutters swung open. As he had suspected, there was no glass. He hefted himself halfway over the sill and looked around. A pile of grasses in the corner, a rough table, a pile of kindling on one side of the fireplace and three or four logs on the other. No cooking pot. They stole his cooking pot, he thought.

'How long has the one you seek been gone?' The thought surprised him and he realized that the unicorn must have come up behind him.

He did not have the total communication with Malloran that he had had with Astarus. With Astarus it had been instantaneous and complete. The unicorn knew what he thought and what he felt and Joscelyn, in turn, had known everything that Astarus was feeling. He had never in his life known that kind of closeness and when his friend had decided, on the spur of the moment, to go off exploring on his own, it had left a void and a scar. He had chosen Malloran for this expedition because he was a little older than the others and, he hoped, more reliable. With this unicorn, it took a deliberate effort to communicate.

'*I'm not sure,*' he thought back carefully. '*About a month I think.*'

'*There are a number of scents,*' Malloran replied, '*but they are too faint to disentangle.*'

'*You can tell the difference between one group of humans and another?*' Joscelyn asked.

'*Of course. They eat different things and they smell different.*'

Joscelyn boosted himself back off the window. '*Perhaps the scent will be clearer at the other stations, or perhaps you can find a common thread.*'

'*Is there nothing that your senses tell you?*' the unicorn asked.

Joscelyn closed his eyes and let his senses reach out. There was something, faint but familiar. It teased his memory and then he had it. He opened his eyes. '*Magic has been performed here.*' He smiled ruefully. '*That's rather obvious, isn't it? We come to a place where a Weatherward has been changing the flow and direction of the winds and, surprise, surprise, I can detect the lingering presence of Magic.*' He stroked his newly trimmed beard as an idea occurred to him. '*Put your head through the window,*' he said. '*See if you can pick out one human scent that is stronger than the others.*'

The unicorn complied. '*One is clear.*'

'*And the same one is outside?*'

'*Undoubtedly, but I cannot single it out.*'

'*Pity. I thought we might be able to track it and that might give us some indication of where the Weatherward has gone, or at least in which direction.*'

'*My sire says that Magicians are more powerful than other humans. Why did these ones not protect themselves?*' Malloran asked.

'*A sudden, unexpected, blow to the back of the head is a marvelous equalizer,*' Joscelyn replied grimly. '*Well, there's nothing more to be learned here. Let's try the next one. It's about a hundred miles south and at about the same elevation.*'

'*My bloodline has a history of taking unnecessary risks,*' the unicorn replied, the thought tinged with humor.

Joscelyn awoke in the middle of an oval of grass surrounded by the silver trunks and fluttering leaves of cinder trees. He pushed himself upright and surveyed the area. No hut; no sign of human habitation. Uneasiness began to percolate through him and he reached out for the unicorn's mind. Malloran was too preoccupied with eating to heed the call. Had he failed to keep an accurate picture of the map in his mind? Was the map itself wrong? What in the name of the gods were they going to do if they were lost? The questions blotted out the hunger pangs and propelled him off the unicorn's back.

His legs felt steadier this time and he made his way to the edge of the clearing. Off to the right there was a break in the trees that might be a path and he set off to explore it. The trail led uphill, curving around boulders and ancient, broad-trunked trees whose names he did not know. He stopped to catch his breath and the need for food welled up again. He closed his mind against it and pushed on. After what seemed like a very long, steep time, the path broadened and ended abruptly in another clearing. The sight of a cabin hard up against a sheer cliff calmed his racing heart, and the stream, tumbling down from somewhere above and burbling off into the woods, brought home his thirst. He ran over, flung himself down and buried his face in it.

When he was done, he rolled onto his back, face, beard and the ends of his hair soaking wet, and let the sun warm him. After a while, he propped himself up on his elbows and looked at the weather station. It was larger, sturdier and better built than the last one. This young Magician was either better with his hands or had had help. He got slowly to his feet and went to investigate, driven by duty, curiosity and the thought that there might be some sort of food inside.

This door had a proper handle and it was not locked. Joscelyn opened it wide and went into the gloom. He unbarred the windows and pushed the shutters outward letting in shafts of sun in which the motes of dust kicked up by his feet danced. A table with a bench, a wooden frame to hold the bedding, a well-made chair by the fireplace, a chest against the far wall, a shelf in the jog formed by the fire. His eyes took quick inventory of the room. No trivet in the ashes and no cooking utensils, though they might be in the chest. He crossed over and raised the lid. It was empty. He turned back toward the fireplace and saw that there was something on the shelf. He investigated. Two shriveled onions and some spongy tubers. Without bothering to clean them, he started to chew.

Joscelyn did not feel like taking another trip through Interim that day. The near miss of the last one had shaken his confidence. Malloran was just as content to stay as to move on, so they spent the night at the second station. In the morning, Joscelyn Made the Day by the stream and dedicated the ceremony to the three missing Weatherwards. That done, he ate sparingly from the saddlebag before poring over the map. The last weather station was near a pass that led to the Umbrian side of the mountains. Jarrod had warned him about the press-gangs. While what he could judge of the probable terrain made a mishap unlikely, it would not do for him to be found in a weakened condition. There was no way, however, for him to guess what kind of schedules the press-gangs kept, or even if they used this particular pass. They would just have to hope that the gods were with them.

The third station proved to be no more revealing than the other two, but Malloran said that the human scent was freshest here and that all three of the Weatherwards had been present at the same time.

'Is there any indication of where they went?' Joscelyn asked.

'Down toward the pass, but I do not think they went alone. If they did, another party followed within days.'

'Can you tell how long ago?' Joscelyn's pulse quickened. This was the first real sign that the three might still be alive.

'I am not good at judging time by your standards,' Malloran admitted, 'and it has rained several times since they left. The scent

*is not recent; stronger than in those other places, but ill defined nev-
ertheless. It yields little.'*

What now? Joscelyn wondered. He had no proof that the
Weatherwards had been kidnapped and taken to Umbria, but it
certainly looked that way. His uncle, as he still thought of him,
had expressly forbidden him to enter Umbria, but if he reported back with suspicions based on a unicorn's sense of
smell, the powers that be would never let him go home. Jarrod
would order him back to the castle and that was no longer good
enough. He had rusticated long enough. He was tired of being
hungry. He loved the unicorns, but he needed some human
contact. He needed to learn more about Magic and how to use
it.

He sat on the short grass and watched dark clouds gather
over the valley. Behind him, over the Umbrian Plain, the sky
was clear. Malloran and he had been lucky with the weather for
the past few days, but soon it would rain. All the more reason to
be on the far side of the mountains. He couldn't go back now.
He needed more information. He would be careful, avoid the
Umbrians as he had avoided the Songeans, but he ought at least
to see the lay of the land. If he could get a line on the whereabouts of the Weatherwards . . . a dark thought floated across
his mind, mirroring the weather, or if he found they were dead,
he would have something worthwhile to report. Then perhaps
they would let him get on with his life, make up for lost time.

He got up and stretched. There was no way Jarrod Courtak
could stop him. He might be anywhere in the mountains as far
as Stronta was concerned. No, there was no choice really. He
scratched his beard and started to think about finding something for supper. If things went on like this for much longer, he
would have to set snares. Malloran would be offended by his
eating meat, but he would need to maintain his strength if he
were to do any good.

V

✣ ✣ ✣

J arrod Courtak put down his quill and flexed his fingers before sprinkling sand across the parchment. He had brought his telling of the history of Strand forward to the fairly recent past. Recent when compared to the work he had done earlier in the Archmagial Archives beneath Magicians' Court. He had found the research intensely satisfying, almost addictive. There was so much material to review, so many connections to be made, lacunae to be filled, that the temptation was to avoid actual writing. It was all valuable, all worthwhile. He was restoring a common past to his civilization. No, not restoring, he reminded himself. Giving it something it had never had. The decision to record no history while the Outland Wars were in progress was a strange one. Perhaps, in the beginning, the Allies had thought that the battle would be brief, but it had dragged on for centuries until all that remained of the early days were legends and old songs.

Now he was setting down his recollections of the end of those wars, an end in which he and Marianna and the unicorns had played a part, and he was confronted by a dilemma. If he told the truth about what he knew firsthand, he was likely to destroy belief in the rest of his History. How could he explain the Island at the Center to a people who believed that the stars revolved around Strand? Who would give credence to a being like the Guardian, a creature of infinite age who had no need of a body? His musing was interrupted by a knock on the door. "Come," he said. The Duty Boy peered around the frame. This one was completely unfamiliar. They must have changed the roster again, he thought.

"A message from the Duchess of Abercorn," the boy said tentatively.

It was a title that he still wasn't used to, though his wife had embraced it with gusto. "A bunglebird," he said, rising from his desk.

"No, Excellence. A message from the palace."

"She's here?"

"I, I think so, Lord." The boy had edged into the room, but looked as if he was prepared to flee at any moment.

Poor little wight, Jarrod thought, but then most of them started out like this. He took a breath and smiled reassuringly. "Suppose you tell me what she says."

The boy bobbed his head and swallowed. "She sends her greetings to her noble husband and she and the children want to see you." A smile of relief started and then froze. "No," he said. "She and the children crave your presence as soon as it is convenient." He nodded to himself and looked up triumphantly.

Jarrod smiled again. "Thank you, my boy. You may leave." Had he ever been that intimidated? he wondered as he watched the youngster scurry from the room. Probably. Greylock had certainly daunted him while he was growing up. Was still capable of doing so on occasion, if the truth were known, though he no longer let it show.

He thought about the implications of the message. For Marianna to turn up at Stronta unannounced was highly unusual.

For her to travel with the children was unheard of. He glanced at the water clock. Seventeen hours. He turned back to the desk and rang the hand bell. The Duty Boy reappeared almost immediately. He hadn't retreated that far.

"Send a message to the Chamberlain," he instructed, "and tell him that the Mage of Paladine will be dining at the palace tonight and that he would appreciate it if his wife could be seated next to him. Tell the stables that I shall require a carriage with the full complement of outriders and footmen. After that, I shall need a bath and you are to lay out my second-best formal robe, the pale blue silk one with the sapphires." He paused. "Do you have all that committed to memory?"

"Yes, Excellence."

"Good. Put the tub in front of the fire before you go and tell the kitchen about the bathwater before you go looking for the messenger. Clear?"

"Yes, Excellence."

"Oh, and send up the barber."

"Yes, Excellence," the boy iterated before he turned and fled.

Two and a half hours later a shaved, sleek and perfumed Jarrod was being admitted to his own suite of rooms at the palace by a young attendant that he did not recognize. Marianna was waiting for him in the anteroom, looking, to his eye, as lovely as ever. Their embrace, though warm, was made formal by the farthingale that she was wearing.

"It's so good to see you," he said with the enthusiasm that he felt, "and I hear you brought the children. Can I see them?"

"Of course you can see them," Marianna replied, linking an arm through his and leading him into the withdrawing room. "The baby is asleep, but there will be real trouble if you don't say good night to Daria. She has sworn that she won't go to bed until you do."

The sound of their voices triggered the explosion of a shiningly scrub-faced small girl from the sleeping chamber, pursued, arthritically, by the venerable Mrs. Merieth.

"Daddy! Daddy!" the young bundle yelled as it launched itself into the air in order to attain huggable height. Jarrod gathered her in, oblivious to the damage it might be doing to his robe.

"Hello, precious," he said tenderly into her hair.

She pushed herself back so that she could look into his face. The green eyes were bright. "We've been on a 'venture, Daddy."

"Indeed you have, my poppet," Jarrod said as Mrs. Merieth bore down to detach the child. "It's all right, Merry," he added.

"Indeed 'tis not," Mrs. Merieth said emphatically. "'Tis way past her bedtime and the main room is no place for a bairn in her nightclothes. Now, kiss your father good night and off to bed with you." She reached up, being none too tall, and plucked the reluctant Daria from her father's arms. "It's good to see Your Lordship again," she said, attempting a curtsy, before she bustled the child out.

"I'll wager Daria is much like you were at her age," Jarrod remarked, smoothing out the wrinkles in the gown.

"So Merry keeps reminding me," Marianna replied with a touch of acid. She clapped her hands and the attendant appeared.

"Wine," she ordered. "And don't dawdle. We have to be downstairs in twenty minutes."

"I don't recall that young man," Jarrod said as the servant withdrew.

"No. I took him on when I visited your estates," Marianna said casually.

"My estates? You visited Oxeter?"

"Well, I thought that an unannounced visit by the Duchess would be instructive."

"I see." His tone made it clear that he was displeased.

"Your friend Tokamo was an excellent choice for Seneschal," she continued, trying to blunt his displeasure. "He is scrupulous, he is hardworking and, as far as I could judge, and I am a very good judge of such things, he is absolutely honest."

"I am glad that you approve of my appointments." Jarrod's voice was cold.

"A very wise choice," Marianna agreed. "He has brought a sense of order to the estates. I went over the books with him. Productivity and harvests are up considerably since he took over and I totally approve of his centralized accounting system."

She was rattling and Jarrod knew it. The servant entered again, bearing the wine and two glasses. Jarrod used the time to try to sort out his wife's odd behavior. She had the right, of course, to visit his lands in Paladine, but to do so without telling him was highly unusual. Had the circumstances been reversed, he could have expected a tongue-lashing. He lifted his glass in a silent toast to her.

"I had no idea that your holdings were so large," she continued with a false brightness. "They make Gwyndryth seem quite small. Mind you, there are improvements to be made. It needs modernizing and it needs creative stewardship."

"And you intend to do that from Gwyndryth," Jarrod concluded.

Marianna took a nervous sip at her wine. "Well, no. As a matter of fact I thought I would do it from Oxeter," she said, and looked at him quickly.

"Something's happened," he said. "I would have sworn that nothing in this world could make you give up Gwyndryth."

She sighed and her hands moved in inconsequential little gestures. Her mouth twisted slightly to the side. "So would I," she said, "and then along came my father."

"Ah, I felt that things weren't going too well."

She tossed back the rest of her wine. "He's impossible. He butts in everywhere, he disapproves of everything I do. He hates the idea of his family being 'soiled by commerce,' he countermands my orders and we fight constantly. Frankly, I can't take it anymore. We had the most tremendous row and I just packed up the children and left." She looked at him, defiance in her eyes. "I'm not going back, you know," she said. "I can stay here if you insist, but I would much rather be at Oxeter." She came across the room and laid a hand on his arm, looking up into his face.

"The potential is so great," she said, something close to wonder in her voice. "I have the structure to export the produce in place already. I could make you incredibly wealthy."

He was somewhat unnerved by her intensity. "My dear," he said, "we are both extremely wealthy as it is. I am still paid pensions by every country for my work against the Outlanders. We both came back from the Island at the Center with a fortune in jewels. The Duchy is prosperous. What is this rage to make money that possesses you?"

She withdrew and poured herself another glass. When she turned back to him her face was composed. "I am sorry, husband," she said, voice carefully neutral, "I must seem somewhat wild and overly ambitious to you. The truth is that I have just been dispossessed of lands over which I ruled. I built the fortunes of Gwyndryth to heights they had never known. Never in our history have our folk and our tenants been so prosperous. Never has the influence of Gwyndryth extended so far. And all without recourse to arms. But this was unacceptable. And why? Because it was achieved by a woman, that's why. My father could not stomach it and, upon a whim, or in anger, he took the lands away. It was his Holding to do with as he pleased. The profits and the well-being of the tenants be damned." She paused and began to pace.

Jarrod looked over to the water clock. Ten more minutes before they had to go down to dinner and he still hadn't seen his son. Probably wouldn't now. He had known her a long time and he knew how she was feeling, knew how much Gwyndryth meant to her. He could also understand Darius' point of view.

His father-in-law had retired, bruised by Queen Naxania's rejection of him, to his own estates. Having lived for years under the rule of a willful woman, he found his home occupied by another.

"What you don't understand," Marianna said, turning to face him, "is that, for a woman, power comes in two forms. It either derives from her father or her husband, or she earns it for herself by being rich. That way she is in charge of her own life." She paused. "I love my father, though he can be a motherless bastard at times, and I am proud to be his daughter. I love you and I am proud to be your wife, but I want to be something for myself, independent of both of you. I have a talent for commerce. I was brought up to be a boy and I am very good at the management of estates. Doing those things makes me feel in control. I matter. They wouldn't be done as well without me." The fierceness had returned. "Can you understand what I'm talking about?"

He put his wineglass down on a table and went over to her. He took her hand in both of his and looked down at her. Her bosom was heaving and her eyes were still flashing. She reminded him of the girl who had gone hunting unicorns. He smiled, knowing that it would annoy her and not caring. "Do you know that I love you very much?" he said. "I've known you since you were Joscelyn's age, were disguised as a boy and made me call you Martin. You've always been headstrong, you've always felt that you had to prove yourself, even when you didn't. It's one of the reasons that we work so well together. You always push yourself forward, I always manage to back into the limelight. It's lucky that I'm Talented and you're not, or the relationship wouldn't work at all. Of course I understand. I've always understood. If you want to set up house at Oxeter and run the estates, be my guest. You and the children will be a lot closer than you were at Gwyndryth."

He put his hands on her shoulder and rocked her back slightly. "You have to promise me one thing. You'll be deferential, well, deferential isn't the right word, respectful, to Tokamo. He's my oldest friend and he's doing us a favor. When you can manage the estates by yourself, he can return to the Outpost, but, until then, if you have a disagreement, even if you think he's wrong, you give way. Agreed?"

"Agreed," she said. She looked up and smiled. "Have I told you of late that I am glad I married you?"

He leaned down and kissed her. "No, and if we don't hurry we shall be late for the obligatory drink with the Queen."

After an entirely insincere half hour with the Queen, they were ushered to their seats. Marianna was seated two away from Naxania on the left, Jarrod next to her. Between Marianna and the Queen sat Osmir Dan, a young nobleman who was currently Naxania's favorite. Technically speaking, Jarrod, as senior vassel present, should have sat next to the Queen and, in other circumstances, the lapse would have irked Marianna. The young nobleman's smiles and obvious appreciation of this newcomer to Court seemed to mollify her. Jarrod smiled to himself. His wife, in her dark green gown, dark red hair brushing her bare shoulders, was sight enough to turn any young man's head, but, if this particular young man wished to keep his head upon his shoulders, he would do well to look away.

The soup was served, a time when one conversed with the diner to the right. Paradoxically, though this was the most public of functions, once the servers had withdrawn, there was more privacy than they could normally expect.

"I've seen Joscelyn," Jarrod said quietly.

Marianna's spoon checked fractionally and then continued on its path. "How is he?" she inquired as if they were talking of a mutual friend.

"Thin," he replied, "but otherwise healthy. He has grown and he has a beard."

She took two more spoonfuls of soup before asking, "And where is he now?"

Jarrod admired her evenness of tone. "I sent him on a mission." He smiled and raised his left hand as if making a point.

She returned the smile and he could see how strained it was. "You sent him on a mission?" The eyes were round, but the look was hard.

Jarrod threw back his head and laughed. It wasn't a very convincing laugh, but it was done for the benefit of the eyes glued to the High Table. "If he pulls this off, dearest," he said, his face still a rictus of mirth, "he may be able to return home with honor. He asked me to send you his love. He says he misses you."

She inclined her head coquettishly and laid a hand on his arm. "You putrid piece of animal feces," she said sweetly. "How could you do this without telling me?"

"There was no time, love of my life," he replied, "and the important thing is for him to be able to come home. Come to think of it, Oxeter would be a good place."

"Where have you sent him, you conniving bastard?" she cut in, voice pure honey.

Jarrod leaned back in his chair as if beguiled by his partner. "To Songuard, dear wife."

Her eyes narrowed. "If any harm comes to him," she began, and then, sensing the approach of the page to clear the dishes, "so he said to me, 'it's only my leg that's wooden, m'lady.' " They both laughed and Jarrod turned to the Chamberlain's wife who sat to his left with a sense of relief. The respite was, he knew, only temporary. He would have to answer Marianna's questions when they were back in his suite.

VI

The Oligarch Olivderval sat at the desk in her counting-house. The ribbed, stone vaulting came to a point in the dimness over her head. It was quiet down here after the clerks had gone home and, being belowground, it was cool. Both were important to her. The former because she had to compose a report on the morning's Council meeting for Mage Courtak, her chief ally among the ranks of the Discipline, though by no means the only one, she thought with a smile. The cool was soothing to her now that the humidity had set in. She shifted in the heavily cushioned chair. Her bulk made it harder to breathe these days and conditions had worsened since the weather had reverted to its old ways. That, she was convinced, could be laid to the Umbrian's door, along with the continued expansion into Isphardi territory. She took up a quill, examined the nib to see that it was sharp enough and dipped it into the inkwell.

The administrators met this morning, she began. No greeting, no naming of the person to whom the missive would be addressed. Her couriers were reliable, but there was no sense in taking risks. If the report fell into the wrong hands it would look, at first glance, like a business document. *The matter at hand was the land in the North that you had inquired about. It grieves me to inform you that a certain foreign gentleman has taken it upon himself to encroach upon the estates in question and has even established farms and demesnes in the area in violation of legal property rights. Because of the remoteness of the location, nothing, at present, can be done to remedy the situation.*

The Cloudsteed Wing, hired at considerable expense from Talisman, had reported continuing Umbrian expansion along a large lake on the Alien Plain, a lake that was clearly within the territory allotted to Isphardel by treaty. The cloudsteedsmen had also reported Imperial rotifers in the area and, since the Emperor Varodias had sole contol of the Rotifer Corps, this was colonization by Imperial design. Isphardel had no troops to respond with and the agreement with Talisman precluded hostile acts by the Cloudsteed Wing.

There was considerable discussion among the administrators as to how best these flagrantly illegal moves might be countered. Some of my partners recommend the imposition of trading sanctions, but there were differences of opinion on the matter.

Now there's an understatement, she thought as she laid down the pen and went over the scene in her mind. Festin Manyas had proposed a grain embargo. Easy for him, he didn't have warehouses bulging with wheat and rice. Both she and Rully of the Narbonesa had gambled heavily on the continuing bad harvests in the Empire and were about to make a very nice profit on their investment. Her fellow Oligarchs who were not in the grain trade were not above trying to kill someone else's deal out of envy, malice or just general competitiveness. This, of course, had been hidden behind pious invocations of the national good above personal profit. Asphar of the House Urcel had been the most egregious; no surprise there. He had been an adversary, sly and smooth-tongued, since childhood. She took up the pen again.

In the event, it was decided to make no overt move for the time being, though the idea of forming a citizens' watch was floated. On this, there was general agreement.

Instituting a citizens' militia had been her idea. It would mean that the troops they had been training in secret could come out into the open and be merged with the new recruits brought in by the popular outcry against the Empire once Varodias' seizure of portions of the New Territories was made public. If these troops could be trained and equipped by means of a public subscription engendered by that same popular outrage, it would save the Oligarchs the not-inconsiderable sums that they had been paying out secretly to bring an army into being. There was no need for Jarrod to know that, of course. It was sufficient for the Discipline to know that Isphardel was moving toward protecting itself. The neatness of the maneuver gave her a great deal of personal satisfaction.

In conclusion, she wrote, *one of your relative's factors has been making inquiries about certain unfair practices. While I have no proof, my best guess is that the same man who is responsible for the illegal occupation of estates is also behind this other move.*

I trust that this letter finds you and your family well. Our company continues to do as well as can be expected, though we are all discommoded by the continuingly unsettled weather. The cause remains a mystery to us—the habitual sacrifices at a variety of temples have produced no results. The weather remains, as in ages past, something beyond our comprehension and control.

She signed the name they had agreed upon at the bottom of the page with a flourish and sprinkled the whole with sand. The message did not begin to describe the tension that the Oligarchs felt or the divisions within the Council, but it would have to do. Courtak had shown himself to be shrewd enough when negotiating the Concordat. He would just have to read between the lines.

Olivderval did not know it when she wrote, but the Weatherwards that she had referred to so obliquely were journeying back toward the border. A caravan of four steam chariots and three steam wagons was chugging down the evenly graded, packed-gravel road that joined Angorn to the mining town of Harrenberg at the base of the Saradonda Mountains. Malum of Quern rode with his page in the lead chariot, the Magicians, with two guards apiece, were divided among the other three. The wagons contained provisions and tents, should they be caught between refueling stations, and the entourage. Once away from Court, Malum allowed himself the indulgence of such a display.

As the Emperor's surrogate, he was expected to maintain a certain amount of state. In this case that meant a cook and his assistant, three servingmen, a barber and, at his insistence, a Wisewoman. It was, he felt, a modest retinue. Two of the servingmen doubled as interrogators and the Wisewoman was needed to keep the prisoners alive should the interrogators err on the side of zeal. The contingent was completed by twenty mounted Imperial Guards to protect them from bandits and to impress upon those they encountered that Malum was an official envoy.

This journey presented some risks for him, though they were not to be found upon the road. For a man whose power rested on his influence, absence from Angorn was always risky. There were others only too eager to gain the Emperor's ear. Moreover, the outcome of this particular venture was hard to predict. If the Magicians—his nose wrinkled with distaste at the thought of them—produced the fortnight of gently soaking rains that were needed, he would have saved the Empire from potential disaster. If things went awry, the Emperor might well have his head. Either way, the Magicians would have to die. The thought made him smile. It would be a pleasure to teach these stiff-necked, overgrown children a lesson.

On the sixth day after their departure from Angorn, the cortege rolled into Harrenberg. Housewives appeared in doorways, eyeing the sooty smoke with disfavor. Small children cavorted and screamed and chased after the vehicles. Steam chariots were a rare sight on the outskirts of the Empire. The road followed the bank of the river, passing coal barges bound for the East. It crossed via a handsome stone bridge and continued toward the Elector of Estland's palace, which sat solitary and serene atop a hill that had once been a slag heap. Now, carefully landscaped gardens sloped down to the riverbank. The road wound through a double file of fir trees and ended at the coaching area.

The Elector was not in residence, was seldom in residence, was only there if he absolutely had to be and, in any case, would have made a point of not being there on this particular occasion. He had been informed that the Emperor required the use of the place, but, since the Emperor himself would not be there, he had decided that discretion would be the better part of obedience. The resident staff, without that option, greeted the Emperor's representative with an obsequiousness that Malum found satisfying. He, in turn, was gracious.

He woke the next morning in the Elector's great bed. Brandwin was sleeping at the foot as usual, but, stretching his legs as far as they would go, Malum could not touch him. This, he thought, was truly luxurious. One day . . . The boy sat up, fright and sleep in his eyes. It was light and his master was awake before him.

"Chai, then a bath and have the barber come up," Malum said pleasantly. Brandwin relaxed. The man was in a good mood. He said a short prayer of thanks to the Great Mother as he scrambled off the bed.

"When I'm done," Malum said as he sat up, "you'll take a bath too—and add your clothes to mine and see to it that the staff here washes them. One can pick up lice on a journey."

"Yes, Master. Right away." Brandwin wondered what he would do for clothes in the meantime, but that wasn't a question to ask the master. He ducked his head and scurried out of the room.

Freshly washed, shaved and fed, Malum descended to the cellars, where the Magicians were being held. He was accompanied by two guards bearing lanterns. Outside a stout wooden door a man stood winding the handle of a compact machine. A low howl filled the corridor. Malum gestured and the noise died. He hefted the key ring, chose one and unlocked the door. Signaling to one of the men with a lamp to follow him, he stalked into the room.

Jubal Aristach was perched on a wine barrel. His dark blond hair and beard were tangled, the hazel eyes, preternaturally large in the gaunt face, glittered in the lamplight before he turned his head away. His wrists and ankles were fettered and a chain ran between the two sets of bonds.

"Get a bucket of water and a dipper," Malum ordered, and the guard, setting the lantern on the floor, complied.

Malum maneuvered another cask into the center of the room. He drew a kerchief from his sleeve and flicked it across the top before spreading it out fastidiously. The guard returned with the bucket.

"Ungag him and give him some water." The guard did as he was bid and Malum watched as the Magician gulped greedily. After three dippers, he waved the man away. Aristach's head came up and he turned to face Malum, drops of water spangling his beard and moustache.

"This simply will not do," he said.

"I regret the inconvenience and the lack of a personal privy," Malum replied urbanely, "but, under the circumstances . . ." He spread his hands and smiled.

"Oh," Jubal returned, "I'm not referring to the accommodations, mephetic though I consider them. I was commenting on your policy of starvation. The theory, I presume, is that if we are in a weakened condition, we will be less likely to escape. However, you also expect us to perform Magic for you." He motioned to the soldier and drank again.

"Now you, my lord, if memory serves, have spent time at

Stronta and, being both observant and intelligent, must know that the performance of Magic takes a toll on the practitioner. If we are not strong to begin with, we will not be able to cast spells. Weatherwarding is a slow, continuous performance. If you hope to use us, you will have to feed us." He leaned back and produced a wan smile.

Malum admired the man's spirit and detested him the more for it. "Any other demands?" he asked scoffingly.

"Other than a guarantee of freedom after we have done as you ask?" Jubal replied, equally sardonically. "Well, as a matter of fact there are. If you expect us to pull this off, we are going to have to work together. We are talking about a major diversion of prevailing weather patterns. We'll need time together to come up with the proper combination of spells and who does what and when. We shall need the herbs and simples necessary for the potions we shall have to consume to protect our bodies while the Magic courses through us. We shall need freedom of movement and speech to effect the spells and we need to be high enough up in the mountains to be able to reach out and influence the weather coming in from the south."

"Is that all?" Malum made no effort to hide the sarcasm.

"Not quite. That bloody machine will have to be turned off at least two days before we begin to prepare. We'll need the time to recover from its effects and all our wits about us when we try to harness and divert the winds."

"And what assurances do I have of success if I accede to your requests?"

"None really," Jubal said with a shrug. "I wish I could say otherwise, but I can't. We've none of us been in touch with the weather for a long time now. I assume that it has been uncontrolled since our, ah, abrupt departure. The patterns have probably changed and, though it chagrins me to admit it, there are some storm systems that we simply can't control.

"What I can tell you is that, if the conditions aren't met, we have absolutely no chance of bringing regulated rain over the

Empire." He cocked his head and drew his lips in. "It would do you more harm than good," he said, "if we brought an unbridled storm system over the Umbrian Plain. With the land so dry, the flooding would be catastrophic." A tight smile came and went. "If that happened, you'd kill us and the Emperor would probably have you executed. I don't think either of us wants that." He paused. "D'you think I could have a bit more water? I haven't done this much talking in sennights."

Malum got up, filled the dipper and tipped it slowly into Aristach's mouth.

"Thank you. Now, where was I? Oh yes. Control. We shall have to start off with showers to soften up the ground. That will take a sennight of pumping cloud formations eastward at intervals. Once that is done, a second sennight can be devoted to continuously soaking rains."

"And that will be enough?" Malum interjected. This whole thing was becoming far too complex.

"It will have to be, for the moment at least, since you won't let us return to our stations and do it from there." The Magician gave Malum an appraising look. "You can't tamper with the prevailing winds for too long, you know. Any alterations that you make up here have repercussions down the line."

"For instance?"

"Oh, if you want a for instance," Jubal said with sweetly malicious reasonableness, "the vortex that we shall have to create will draw the coastal winds to the west. That means that the rains that would normally fall on the south of the Empire will be diverted.

"Now," he continued before Malum could ask another question," if I remember my courses in Geography from the Collegium aright, the primary cash crop in southern Umbria is sugar cane and sugar cane requires a lot of water at this time of year." He raised his manacled hands apologetically. "If we are successful, those who depend on sugar cane for their livelihood are going to have a very bad year. That's the way it is with Nature. What you gain in one area, you lose in another."

Malum smiled sourly. What he was being told by this motherless mongrel was that, if his plans worked out, his personal revenues from Quern would be severely reduced. The trouble was that the fellow made a lot of sense. Perhaps if he agreed to his conditions, the eventual degradation and death of all three would be the more pleasing.

"You make some good points," he admitted blandly. "I shall give them some thought. In the meantime, the machine stays on." He retrieved his kerchief and left the room, trailed by the guard with the lantern.

Jubal Aristach sagged back as the door closed and the key grated in the lock. He winced as the whine started up again. He had played a dangerous game and he really shouldn't have brought up the bit about the sugar cane. He smiled in the dark. He ran the conversation through again in his head. Yes, he had made all the points that he had meant to make. At the very least he had gained them some time and, with a little luck, they would end up in decent enough condition to make an escape. In the meantime, the Discipline might take action. Surely they would take some action.

VII

🔱 🔱 🔱

Joscelyn and Malloran rode through the pass and into Umbria. Behind them thunder growled and storm clouds raced northward. By contrast, the sun shone on Umbria. They had been back to the castle so that the human could regain some strength and smoke some lake fish for the further journey. He had restocked his saddlebag and returned to the col. Malloran came to a halt and they looked out over the vast plain. From this height the only outstanding feature was the river running east into the haze of the distance. The path zigzagged down until it lost itself below the tree line. It was not unlike standing on the battlements and looking out over the Alien Plain, save that there he was de facto lord of all he surveyed and here he was an intruder.

They headed down, crossing small streams made boisterous by the melting snow from the peaks. Somewhere below there were mines, that much Joscelyn knew from his mother. If the Magicians had been captured by slave raiders, they could well have been put to work in the mines. He would have to study the terrain, find possible places where they might be held and then watch patiently until he spotted them. The problem was that neither he nor Malloran was exactly inconspicuous.

As they negotiated a hairpin turn, the shadow of a raptor swept across the path in front of them. Malloran, startled, pulled up abruptly. Joscelyn shaded his eyes and looked upward. A large kester hawk was outlined against the sky, hanging in the air on spread pinions. Now there, Joscelyn thought, is the perfect spy. If he could see through the raptor's eyes . . . He shook his head. There was no way that he could capture the distant bird and bend it to his will. Besides, while he had done the obligatory anatomy lessons, he had never had any actual experience of shape-changing. That was one of the disadvantages of leaving the Collegium early.

'If you look to your left—slowly—you will see the answer to your dilemma,' Malloran said in his mind.

Joscelyn turned his head obediently, thinking that familiarity was improving their ability to communicate. What he saw was a mountain ram with a shaggy coat and fiercely curling horns. He was rubbing himself against the corner of a rock, leaving clumps of wool behind.

'I can't turn myself into one of those,' he said regretfully. *'I don't have the necessary skills.'*

'You do not have to turn yourself into a sheep. You only have to see through his eyes.'

'True, but I don't think that I could impose my will on such a large creature.'

'You will not have to,' Malloran said. He sounded complacent. *'He knows what you require and he is prepared to cooperate so long as he is not required to go near other humans. It is not a question of your subordinating his will, but of you being entirely directed by his.'*

'Are you sure about this?' Joscelyn asked, unconvinced.

'Of course. I have communicated with the sheep.'

'I didn't know that you could do that.'

'The occasion has not arisen while we have been together. Besides, there is much that you do not know.'

Joscelyn smiled at the unicorn's tone. It was the first time that he had smiled in a long time. He dismounted and unslung the saddlebag. He took it over to a flat rock and sat down while Malloran moved off to graze. He glanced over at the ram. It was standing about forty yards away gazing, apparently unconcernedly, out over the plain. He searched his memory for the steps he would need to take to project himself into the animal's mind. It was worth a try at least.

He ought to prepare a potion to ready his body, but looking around he could see nowhere for the herbs to grow. He would have to put himself into a really deep trance. This was a remote area and he was unlikely to be disturbed, but it would be better if he was out of sight. He got up and moved to a spot behind an outcropping of rock. He was a lot closer to the ram, but it didn't move. He settled himself and began to repeat the litany of concentration, stilling his mind and emptying it. His breathing slowed and his eyelids drifted down. He reached the quiet center of himself and formed a picture of the ram as he had last seen it. He visualized his spirit hovering above the head and then slipping down between the circling horns and into the skull. Once there he stayed very still, not wanting to startle the beast.

He became aware, little by little, of the ram's heartbeat and allowed himself to examine this strange body. Strong, thick neck, massive shoulders, deep chest with capacious lungs, supple back and strongly corded hindquarters, ready to explode into motion at any moment, all these bespoke an animal in its prime. He did not seek out the emotions but let them percolate into his consciousness. Pride and certainty were uppermost. If Joscelyn thought that his host was in his prime, the ram was certain of it, gloried in it. This mountainside was his and woe betide any other male who dared to trespass on his domain. He would be driven back, horns broken and flanks bleeding.

Was there anything, Joscelyn wondered, of which this creature was afraid? As if in answer there came the image of a man. Men were to be avoided. It was supplemented by the picture of a wild warcat. The feeling about this one was somewhat different. Joscelyn knew, without knowing how he knew, that if they were confronted with a warcat, they would give as good as they got. There was an aura of distrust. Warcats were sneaky and given to ambushes. Communication, of a kind, had been established.

The ram started to move off and Joscelyn suddenly saw the world through its eyes. The viewpoint was disorienting. This close to the ground, things seemed to come at them faster and the animal's rocking gait moved the landscape up and down in a dizzying fashion. The details were extraordinarily sharp, but the colors seemed to have been bleached. There was a distinctly grey tinge to the grass and the rocks were darker than he remembered. They stood out distinctly from their surroundings. As he was thinking this, the ram trotted up onto a slab and, without the slightest warning or hesitation, launched out into space.

Joscelyn's heart, had he possessed one in this form, would have been in his mouth. The next second they landed on another rock some twelve feet down the slope and then were airborne again. The ram skipped down the mountainside from outcropping to outcropping until it reached the trees. It wasn't even breathing hard. Now that he was used to the exhilaration, Joscelyn was sorry when they slowed down to make their way through the sparse undergrowth. The ram stopped from time to time to pull up new shoots or tear off leaves, but it made steady progress across the slope, moving farther north all the time.

After a while the trees died out and they trotted across a tussocked incline. They pulled up at the rim of a cliff. The ram swung its head to the left and Joscelyn saw houses and the beginnings of a broad wooden chute that went straight down the mountainside. He became aware of a mixture of strong scents, none of them to the ram's liking. Horses, coal dust, dung, grease, smoke and cooking odors mingled and, permeating them all, the distinctive, acrid smell of man.

The mountain sheep retreated from the edge and continued along the cliff top. It seemed to take a long while before the stench of the mining community dwindled away. They stopped twice to graze and once, halfway across a stream they were fording, to drink. Other than that, they maintained an even pace for what seemed like a league and a half before the ram slowed down again. The cliff edge was still to their right, though it had been broken in several places along the way. In some spots water had cut ravines into the scarp and in others the land had subsided to form shallow valleys.

Joscelyn had been expecting them to stop. The smell of another encampment had been in the air for some time. This operation was larger than the first. There were two chutes here and water was piped into them from a source he could not see. Carts were pulling up on either side and discharging their loads. The overall pace was faster. There were many more cabins and stables and the sounds of a smithy cut into the noise of the slurry. Set apart from the rest was a two-story house. There was a well-traveled road that took a gentle curve downward. If the Magicians were being held in the mountains, he thought, this might well be the place.

There might be other mines, other settlements farther north, but Joscelyn was aware that the ram was nearing the borders of its territory. He would not go beyond them. As if in response to the thought, the ram began to angle uphill and Joscelyn knew that it was going to check the edges of its domain before returning. When they approached a point roughly in line with the northern boundary of the mining village, he caught the faint smell of another sheep. They turned and headed straight up for the snow line.

They moved higher, stopping every now and then to leave a scent marking on a rock, a scrubby tree, a clump of alpine sage. Once they got close to the snows, they turned south and worked their way across the broken terrain. Crags rose to their right with deep, dark clefts riven by time and the weather, a receding series of ledges climbing on up to the sawtooth peaks. Below them, the wind-twisted shapes of stunted trees dotted the scarp.

The ram stopped suddenly, lifted its head and inhaled deeply. It turned slowly and faced the way it had come. The head moved from side to side, seeking. A deep rumble of anger came from somewhere in the chest cavity. Joscelyn concentrated. Another ram had invaded the territory. Younger, a known quantity. There had been a battle the previous year and the challenger had been driven off. The nostrils flared with displeasure and Joscelyn's host gave a great snort before moving stiff-leggedly forward. This time the impudent challenger would be taught a decisive lesson. Fighting anger was building, the blood coursing into the muscles, the breath deep and controlled.

The massive head of the rival ram appeared around an outcropping and then it was standing sixty feet away, eyeing the incumbent. It was large, every bit as large as Joscelyn's host. Its coat was smoother, most of the winter shag gone, and Joscelyn could see the play of muscles across the shoulders. The curving horns glinted in the sunlight. It snorted and pawed the ground with its right forehoof. Joscelyn's ram did the same. He could sense that the animal was quivering, not in fear, but with pent-up hostility.

Without the young man's being aware that a decision had been made, they were moving, accelerating toward the foe. The other ram was charging, too. They covered the uneven turf in great bounds and then sprang at each other. Joscelyn saw the lowered head, the great, curling horns approach with dream-like slowness, growing as they neared, blotting out everything else. The two heads crashed together and Joscelyn felt the shock of the encounter clear through the ram's body. They fell back briefly and then launched themselves again. This time the two pairs of horns locked and they swayed together, wrenching their heads viciously from side to side, each trying to overbalance the other. The strain on the neck was enormous, but there was no diminution in the fury his host felt, no loss of confidence. Both animals pushed and twisted this way and that, seeking advantage, feet adjusting nimbly to the changes, but to no avail. The horns slipped apart and they both retreated, chests heaving, breath coming short.

They circled each other warily, looking for an opening, trying to keep to the higher ground. Now and again one would feint, the other retreat only to counterfeint. The intruder was bigger and stronger than he had been last year. He had to be driven off now, crushed and humiliated, before the ewes came. Hatred blazed up at the thought of losing females and the ram charged. The move was ill considered because he charged uphill. His opponent shifted stance and butted him on the shoulder. It wasn't painful, but it slewed him round. He was upslope, but off-balance. The next charge pushed him back into the mouth of a ravine. As they retreated, Joscelyn became uneasy. To his way of thinking, this was not a good idea. The ram felt the same way and made a short charge to regain the open ground. There wasn't the room to get up sufficient speed and he was easily blocked. Joscelyn wanted to look back and see what they were being pushed into, but he had no control over physical functions and the ram, sensibly enough, was more concerned with its opponent. It had regained its wind and was looking for a moment of inattention to launch an onslaught that would regain maneuvering room. The young ram, however, was not about to surrender its advantage. Joscelyn's host still felt confident, but it was watchful and wary now, the overweening anger subdued.

It was ready for the next charge when it came and met it head-on. Once again horned heads crashed together and Joscelyn's senses went momentarily numb. When he focused again, he saw that they had been driven back. Not much, but enough so that the steep walls of the ravine were visible on either side. Now the ram risked a look over its shoulder. No ledges within jumping range and not more than twenty yards to the back of the cut. There was some room for lateral movement in their present position, but the ravine funneled down to a mere dozen feet across. The back looked as if it had been sheared off square. As if it had been quarried, Joscelyn thought.

He wasn't aware of the transition, but they were racing forward. There was a ringing crack as the heads met, but the challenger was not dislodged. Joscelyn's ram gave ground and the foe advanced and planted itself foursquare in the mouth of the ravine. It stood there, head lowered, pawing the ground gently, confidently. Joscelyn sensed a change in attitude in the older animal. The terms of the contest had changed. This was no longer a matter of territorial rights. It had become life and death.

His ram backed up quickly and then threw itself at the enemy. The other managed only a short spring, but the massive shoulders seemed to absorb the impact. They wrestled head-to-head, each trying to push the other back, trying to twist the opponent off-balance and expose the stomach to the slashing forehooves. They staggered to and fro, neither one gaining more than a momentary advantage. The effort, however, was taking its toll. The older animal was tiring and its instinct told it that the eventual outcome would be defeat.

At this point, in other circumstances, survival would become paramount. It would have broken off the contest and fled, like the younger ram the year before. Fled to rebuild its strength and plot its revenge. Here and now, penned between the rock walls, flight was not an option. Joscelyn's champion broke off, spun around, retreated to the back of the cut and whirled back to face its nemesis. It stood there, trembling with fatigue. The other ram paced forward slowly. Its strut showed that it knew that it had won, that its opponent was worn down and demoralized. All that was left was the killing charge.

No, no, no, Joscelyn thought. I'm not going to die like this, trapped in the body of a sheep. He saw the rival, poised, through the dull eyes of his host. Think, he told himself. How do I take control? How do I get us out of this. His mind raced furiously, trying to recall the lectures that he had found so boring in another world, a lifetime ago. He reached out through the blankness that was settling over the ram. He concentrated, mustering his will, and tried to make one of the front legs lift. The hoof rose suddenly and then dropped. The ram quivered in surprise. Joscelyn calmed himself and reached out along the neural passageways.

The ram stayed quiet, not a hint of opposition, but no cooperation either. So little time. If only he had paid more attention when he was being schooled. He experimented. The muscles of the rear legs coiled and the ram sank down as if about to spring. The movement was not lost on the opponent. Its eyes narrowed and it backed off a couple of paces, waiting to see what the older animal would do.

Joscelyn used the time gained to swivel the head from side to side so that he could gauge the space that he had to work in. The ram, luckily, seemed to remain catatonic. As he surveyed the surroundings, the plan began to coalesce in his mind. From what he had gathered while watching his host from within, this was not a natural venue for such a combat. It explained, in part, what was paralyzing his host. His solution wasn't a natural one for this species, which was precisely the point. If he relied on the ram's instincts, all would be lost. He spread his awareness throughout the unresisting animal, taking control of the body, preparing it for action. An interior part of him exulted in the power.

He concentrated on the leg muscles and advanced the mountain sheep a couple of feet before resuming the half crouch that preceded the leap. The ram was recovering from its shock, though it still made no move to regain control. It will have to be now or never, Joscelyn decided. He lowered the head as if preparing to charge. The opponent took the bait and launched abruptly into a preemptive charge of its own. At that instant, Joscelyn threw all of his energy and every scrap of compulsion he possessed into the series of muscle movements he required of his ram. The tightly thewed haunches uncoiled, but, at the same time, prepared to launch sideways instead of straight ahead. His host sprang into the air, but not in a forward direction. It threw itself to the side and took a glancing blow on the left flank.

The other ram had no reason to expect such a move. It was contrary to custom and instinct. It was fully committed to what it believed was the final encounter. It had no time to slow, change direction or rein itself in. It had intended a killing stroke and was moving as fast and as hard as it could. Its leap took it past its older foe and the horns smashed, full force, into the rock wall. It collapsed in a heap, horns shattered. The body tremored and lay still.

Joscelyn's ram had caromed off the side of the ravine and had its own troubles regaining its feet, but regain them it did. Joscelyn relinquished all control and crouched within, awaiting the ram's reaction to his usurpation. It staggered a few paces forward, gathered itself and turned to look at its rival. It was clearly puzzled. It ought, by rights, to be dead, and it wasn't. It came all the way round and, favoring its bruised leg, nuzzled the inert body of its foe. It still lived, but a glance at the ragged stumps of horn projecting from its forehead made it quite obvious that it would never fight again.

It wasted no time in speculation. It had survived, no matter how. It had time to grow strong again and ewes to collect and dominate. That was what mattered. It turned back toward the entrance to the ravine and limped wearily to the opening. Joscelyn felt the aches and the numbed throbbing of the flank. He experienced the depletion of spirit now that the stimulus of fear and battle were gone. He felt his hold on consciousness slipping. He wanted to stay awake to make sure that they got back to his own body, but this time he had no choice.

VIII

🙣 🙣 🙣

The Mage of Paladine, your Eminence," the Duty Boy announced at the top of his lungs.

Jarrod frowned at him for the volume and the Boy, catching his drift, said, in a normal voice, "He doesn't hear that well, so I have to make it loud." Jarrod nodded and proceeded into the chamber.

Greylock rose and smiled, extending his palms for the ritual touch. To Jarrod's eye, he seemed to have shrunk. "This is a pleasant surprise. Why didn't you tell me that you were coming?"

"I took advantage of a visit from Nastrus, sir, and I promised Agar Thorden not to be away for more than two days." He spoke more loudly than he had meant to.

"Oho, so he's treating you the way he treated me, is he?" Greylock said, with a degree of satisfaction. "Invaluable man, Agar. Keep on his good side."

"I do my best," Jarrod said.

"So, what brings you to Celador?" Greylock inquired, gesturing to a chair close to his desk.

Jarrod nodded, hitched his robe and sat down. This close, the effects of aging were more noticeable. The hair was still grey, but it was sparser. Greylock's eyes looked watery and the pouches under them were new. He had taken a long time to recover from his imprisonment in the Place of Power, but he had seemed so much stronger at the time the Giants Causeway was cleared. This was the man, Jarrod reflected, that had been the major figure in his life, a man who could reduce him to abashed silence with a look. As Archmage, he was still one of the most powerful men in the world, but it was sad to see him so diminished.

"I came to talk to you about the disappearance of the Weatherwards in Songuard," he said.

"Ah yes, bad business. The Isphardi Ambassador has made quite a fuss. Replacements are being prepared, but it takes so long to get there."

Jarrod hesitated for a beat. "With respect, sir, the real question is, what happened to the three Magicians we had in place?"

"My sentiments entirely," Greylock said with an approving smile. The eyes no longer seemed watery. "Your concern is admirable, but I fail to see why it necessitates a trip to Celador."

Now there's the man I knew, Jarrod thought with a smile. He has no intention of replacing the Weatherwards until he knows that they'll be safe. "Two of them come from Paladine," he replied, "and this is a serious matter for the Discipline. We have a Concordat with the Isphardis and if the Umbrians are involved, which seems likely, there are international repercussions."

"Indeed?" The bushy eyebrows rose.

Oh no you don't, Jarrod thought. You can't intimidate me that way anymore. "What do we do if they've been kidnapped by the Umbrians?" he asked bluntly.

Greylock sat back in his chair and rubbed his hands together. A pointy-eared cat appeared out of nowhere and leapt up onto his lap. The Archmage ignored it. "Nothing for the moment. There's no proof that they've been kidnapped. The stations have been searched. There was no sign of a struggle at any of them. We have asked the Umbrians if they have seen any signs of the missing men. They say they have not. Besides," he added, scratching the cat's head absentmindedly, "I don't think they want to provoke us just now."

The old boy's looking smug, Jarrod thought. "Any particular reason for that?"

"It seems that the Umbrians are busy settling in the Alien Plain with no great regard for borders."

"And we are not going to do anything about that either?"

"Absolutely not." The tone was sharp. "The Discipline waged war on behalf of all the people of Strand, but it has no business taking sides in disputes between countries."

"But we could make some investigations in the matter of the Weatherwards—very discreet ones?" Jarrod ventured.

"What can we usefully do?" The hands came up in inquiry. "By the time someone got there . . ."

"That's why I came to see you, sir. I'm afraid I've taken matters into my own hands, in the interest of time. I already have someone in the Saradondas."

"Ah, your Songean friend, what was his name?"

"Sandroz? No. I haven't heard from him in years. He may well be dead. No, I sent my stepson." Jarrod sat back and waited.

Greylock steepled his fingers slowly, then he looked up. "Joscelyn?" he said in a neutral voice. "Has he come back?"

"Not exactly. I found him and I told him that if he carried out this mission, discovered the whereabouts of the Weatherwards—no more than that—and came back to report, I would put in a good word for him."

Greylock pursed his lips. "Not the person I would choose to go anywhere near Umbria," he said shortly.

"I agree, sir, but he had one overwhelming advantage. He had a unicorn."

"Ah, I see." Greylock sniffed. "Don't expect my blessing. If he gets caught, he was acting entirely on his own. If Varodias wants to hang him, I shall raise no objection."

"I understand. I just wanted you to be aware of what I had done." It wasn't exactly the reaction he had hoped to get from the old man, but he knew better than to press.

Greylock was silent, stroking his thin beard. "If they are being held by clansmen, I'm prepared to use force, if necessary, to get them back."

"And if they're being held by the Umbrians, being forced to work in the mines for example?"

"If we have convincing proof, we shall make the strongest of diplomatic complaints and demand their return. I could probably get both Naxania and Arabella to join us. The young men are, after all, Arunic and Paladinian subjects."

"And if Varodias refuses?"

Greylock shrugged. "I can't see either of the royal ladies going to war with the Empire over three Weatherwards, can you?"

Malum of Quern sat in the solar of the house that belonged to the Governor of Mines in the mountain village of Darran, maintained for the official's occasional tours of inspection. The morning sunshine flooding through the windows that faced out over the distant plain did nothing to sweeten his mood. A fortnight had passed and nothing had been accomplished. The Magicians, may the Mother lay a curse of impotence upon them, had eaten enough to feed an infantry platoon. Had, if they were to be believed, been reacquainting themselves with the air currents high above the peaks—just that, nothing more. Now they wanted to be allowed to wander around looking for plants they claimed they needed before they could perform. He didn't know enough about the techniques of Magic, was a good enough Maternite to have an abhorrence of things Magical, to know if they were telling the truth.

It was a dangerous undertaking either way. Chained and staked to the ground, there was a reasonable assurance that they would not escape. There had been no attempt so far at any rate. Wandering around, even if attached to a guard, was another matter altogether. He had a portable, mechanical noise-maker, twin to the one abandoned in the Paladinian woods by his erstwhile agent, but he was by no means certain that it would work. It had failed to disable Courtak, though he had only the agent's word for that. The man might have misused it, or even failed to use it at all. Indeed, the rogue had confessed as much. Mind you, by the time he did, he would have confessed to seducing his grandmother.

No matter, the pace would have to be forced. The Emperor was not a patient man and Malum had been away from court for far too long as it was. He got up and walked over to a side table and rang a small, brass hand bell. Brandwin appeared promptly.

"Go fetch the Magician called Aristach," he ordered. "Have him brought here under guard."

When the boy had scurried out, Malum moved his chair so that he sat with his back to the window. He seated himself, knowing that his face would be in shadow, and waited. Five minutes passed and then he heard the clank of chains and the clump of boots on the stairs. There was a knock on the door and then the Magician came through, followed by two guards.

"You sent for me, my lord," Jubal Aristach said, with an indication of a bow as he approached.

Insolent cur, Malum thought, but his face showed nothing and his voice, when he replied, was pleasant.

"Indeed I did. My master grows weary of your delays and he is not a forbearing man. It would be to the advantage of us all if your, how shall I put it? your mission? was undertaken in the exceedingly near future." He permitted himself a smile, though he doubted that the Magician could see it.

"It takes as long to build a man up as to tear him down, my

lord," Aristach replied. "Besides, as I have explained before, magic is a delicate art. You cannot whip a performance out of a Magician as you might a trained bear . . ."

"Do not trifle with me, young man." There was steel in Malum's voice. "I have been very patient with you, but the sands of my patience have well nigh filled the bottom of the hourglass. You and your colleagues have a sennight to show me some substantial progress." He let his right hand drift out into the sunlight. "If not, alas, I shall have to abandon this experiment." He smiled again. "I shall, of course, tell his Imperial Majesty that you and your friends were killed while trying to escape."

Aristach took a deep breath that sounded suspiciously like the sigh of one trying to teach a dull child its letters. "I have explained to Your Lordship that we need certain ingredients for potions to protect ourselves from the effects of the Magic we must make. You have been unable to supply them and you have refused to let us seek them out. Without the potions we will be consumed on the first attempt. His Imperial Majesty wishes us to bring rain to Umbria. We have told you that we will cooperate. You may tell him what you want about the manner of our deaths, but I do not think that he will be pleased."

Malum's mouth tightened briefly, but his tone was reasonable. "I think, master Magician, that I am a better judge of that than you. Nevertheless, I am prepared to let you search for these 'simples' as you call them. I shall, however, insist that you do it one at a time and you will be accompanied by my men. They will be carrying a machine capable of disabling you should you try anything foolish." He paused and looked at the man opposite. "It is somewhat stronger than the one downstairs. I should tell you," he added, "that we have tried the device out on another member of the Discipline with gratifying results. Pick one of your number to go foraging tomorrow and give him the proper warning. Oh, and should anything untoward occur, it will not go well with the other two." He looked across at the guards. "Take him away," he said.

Joscelyn moved easily, bouncily, as if the ram were still in him, he in the ram, even though it had been a couple of days since he had been divorced from the sheep. At least he thought it was two days; there was an area of opaqueness. He was nearing the second mining area that he had seen through the ram's eyes. It was close, he could smell it, though not as keenly as he had before. He approached the rim of the cliff and lay down. He studied the village below. He peered, wishing for the ram's keen eyes. There, by the big house, were two mechanized chariots, the kind that the Umbrian contingent had arrived in for the old Archmage's funeral. There were also soldiers. His heart quickened. Something was afoot.

He lay there for a long while watching, but he saw no sign of the Weatherwards. Let them be there, he said to himself. He eased back from the cliff and stood, dusting himself off. He began to pace, talking to himself and gesticulating. Some of the words, as is common with those who are alone most of the time, were audible. Some were not. If his colleagues were down there, he would have to find some way to free them. As he paced the conviction strengthened. This was not something he could leave to the powers that be, people who were prepared to let him languish in exile. No, no. This was something he had to do. He returned to the cliff edge and watched until the light faded.

He was back at his post the next morning. He watched the settlement come to life, smoke curling up from chimneys, men and women making their way to the privies, pit ponies being watered and fed. Then the men gathered at the mouths of the tunnels and disappeared into the mountain. There was activity around the big house, but no sign of a Magician until close to midday. A Magician, there could be no doubt of that, was led out. He appeared to be tethered to a soldier and Joscelyn felt anger stirring. The pair headed toward the cliff, and he scrambled up and ran to the grove of trees that bordered the little plateau. He crouched down and waited. He could hear sounds of ascent and then the Magician appeared, hauling himself up onto the level ground. He was followed by the soldier to whom he was attached by a leather line. Shortly afterward two more soldiers appeared, one of whom was carrying a box.

This, Joscelyn realized, was a chance to make contact, but he would have to move quickly. He willed himself to relax and then went within. It was a long time since he had invoked a spell of invisibility, but it was a simple one. He envisioned himself as others might see him and carefully and methodically made adjustments to the way his skin and his clothing reflected the light. He started at the crown of his head and worked down to the soles of his boots; back, front and sides, with an extra effort for the leather and the buckle of his belt. He checked himself twice before he was satisfied. Only then did he turn his attention outward.

He had expected the party to have moved away, given the long leash and the mysterious box, but the Magician was stooped over in the middle of the grass as if hunting for something. Of course, he thought, he would have known that another Magician was here as soon as I began the spell. He slipped cautiously through the fringe of bushes, trying not to make any noise. The soldiers were concentrating on the Weatherward, but there was no sense taking needless risks. He walked across the short, springy turf and glanced back to check that he wasn't leaving footprints.

The Weatherward straightened up as he approached and began to move forward slowly, head down, peering at the ground. Joscelyn fell into step beside him and said in the lowest voice he could manage, "Keep walking. I'm here to help."

"Thank the gods," Aristach replied softly. "We were beginning to think that the Discipline had abandoned us."

"The Mage of Paladine sent me. Where are the other two?"

"Back at the house down in the village. I'm supposed to be gathering simples for the potions that we'll need. We've stalled as long as we can. If we don't produce rain over Umbria at the end of this sennight, they'll kill us."

They had reached the edge of the grass. Ahead lay the rocky incline with scrubby bushes and an occasional wind-warped tree. Aristach stopped and turned.

"Give me some extra line," he called back to the trailing guards. "I'm going up there for some megswort and theriac. No sense us all crawling around."

"You keep in sight," the soldier said, paying out more line. "First sign of trouble, we turn on the machine."

"I'll be good," Aristach returned. He hitched in some of the line and started up the slope.

"What does the machine do?" Joscelyn asked.

"Don't know, don't want to find out. Nothing pleasant, you can be sure of that."

"How are we going to get you out of here?"

"I was rather hoping that you were going to tell me that. How many of you are there?"

"Just me and a unicorn, but I may be able to get some help."

"You have six days." Aristach bent down and pried a plant loose. He dropped it into the bag at his waist. "You know," he said as he straightened up, "it might be beneficial if we knew what you intend. That way we could help when the time came."

"I'm not sure yet. I shall have to go back and consult with the Mage of Paladine; in fact I should have reported to him before now, but I wanted to find you if I could."

"We're a lot stronger than we were, but I wouldn't recommend trying to storm the house. It's well guarded and they keep us down in the cellar with a machine going that makes spell casting impossible. They are only letting us out one by one to gather simples. If I suddenly disappeared, they'd kill Bervis and Gordiam. I'd say that your best chance would be when we are performing the weather Magic they want us to do. We'll all be up here in the open, we'll be as strong as we're going to be and we will have prepared ourselves the night before and drunk the protective potions."

"That makes sense," Joscelyn agreed, "though I don't like the thought of leaving you here."

Aristach laughed softly. "It will be a lot easier to bear knowing that rescue is at hand. Now you better be off and let me find the plants we need. This isn't exactly a botanical wonderland."

"Six days from now, then," Joscelyn said. "I'll be back. You be ready."

"Oh we shall. Have no fear."

How do we get them away? Joscelyn wondered as he made his way back down the slope to where Malloran waited. He had come this far by himself and he wasn't about to rely on a bunch of timid old men. If he brought the Weatherwards home safely, they would have to let him go home, but if he went back and reported, someone else was bound to take the credit. And then an idea began to form and his pace quickened.

'*Malloran, I need your help,*' he blurted out when he was in range of the unicorn. '*We'll need the assistance of the unicorns at the castle. D'you think . . .*'

'*Slow down, my friend,*' Malloran cut in. '*Your emotions cloud the pictures in your mind.*'

'*Well, I . . .*'

'*No. Do not try to explain. When you make words, things seem to become less clear. I want to try something. We have not done this before, you and I, but, if I read the Memory aright, it once, long ago, was common practice between human and unicorn. First you must relax and be calm, then you must not oppose me.*'

'*Talk about not making things clear . . .*' Joscelyn began.

'*Please,*' Malloran interrupted, '*do as I ask.*'

Joscelyn shrugged, clasped his hands loosely in front of him and closed his eyes. Almost immediately he felt a swelling sensation, a pressure that intensified. It was as if there was a foreign object in his skull, an object that was getting larger. I wonder if this was how the ram felt? he thought. The presence in his head ceased to grow. It wasn't painful, but it was uncomfortable, like having eaten too much at a feast. Then it was gone.

'Very interesting.' Malloran was clearly pleased with himself. 'It will be easier the next time. I saw that you have very harsh feelings toward these Umbrians. I do not entirely comprehend why. I can understand one herd defending its pasture against another herd, but not this distrust and dislike simply because they are not of your herd. No matter. I agree that we should go back. You need to rest and gain strength. I shall find three of my kin to help with the rescue, but I must caution you that there is great danger in Interim for humans, especially the first time.'

'I know,' Joscelyn agreed, 'but it's a chance we'll have to take. If we are captured, they will surely kill us.'

'If one of us should die,' the unicorn remarked, 'it will be in a noble cause and so recorded in the Memory.'

Six days later Joscelyn was seated, cross-legged, on the castle battlements facing in the direction whence the sun would come. He had spent the previous hours in a pentacle performing the rite of purification. The three potions he had consumed filled him with feelings of confidence. Being in his own place, sleeping beside a fire, eating fish he had caught and vegetables he had grown had had a powerful restorative effect. He felt more than equal to the task ahead.

He prepared to Make the Day, even though it was hours too early. He had noticed in his trips backward and forward that the day was more advanced in Umbria and he wanted to arrive there as close to dawn as he could. Despite the inappropriateness of the hour, he felt, as he had often felt before in this particular spot, that he was the last Magician in the world. Without his effort, the sun would not rise, birds would remain silent, waiting for those first intimations of light. Would the daymoon sail up over the horizon anyway? he wondered. Would it wait for the sun to precede it? And what about the nightmoon? Were the three linked by some invisible filament? He smiled at himself and his speculation. Being alone did that to a person. He began the litany of concentration.

An hour and a half later, four unicorns appeared on the slope just to the south of the wood in which Joscelyn and Malloran had hidden. The stars were beginning to pale as the lone human slipped down and tested his legs. He could feel the hunger radiating from the unicorns, but the potions seemed to buffer him against it. When they had satisfied themselves, he led them in among the trees. Everything seemed normal. The habitual wind created the usual subdued roar in the canopy. There were no signs of leaves being torn off, the humus underfoot was dry. There had been no storm hereabouts recently. He was in time then.

Joscelyn settled the unicorns in the center of the little wood and took himself to its northern outskirts. The level patch of grass was empty save for the three new iron chains attached to spikes in the ground. So, the Weatherwards were going to be allowed to work only when attached, and to iron, most intractable of metals. Not entirely unexpected, but a setback nevertheless. Still, with four Magicians, not an insoluble problem. Perhaps if he went out and loosened the stakes . . . His train of thought was interrupted by the sounds of men on the move. Too early for the mining town. He ducked down behind the screen of bushes that marked this side of the wood.

Nothing happened. He waited, crouched down, and nothing happened for ten endless minutes. Then things started to happen very quickly. Helmets appeared at the top of the crack and the soldiers they belonged to heaved themselves up onto the grass. They made their way to the far side of the plateau and were followed by more of their kind. A second party appeared, carrying a large box with a handle protruding from its side. It was carried to the far side, set down carefully and the handle jutting from its side rotated several times. Clockwork of some kind, Joscelyn thought. Next, a large wooden armchair was manhandled up and squared off on a flat rock well behind the machine. Cushions were placed on it.

A small man, all dressed in black, was boosted onto the plateau and escorted, with considerable deference, to the chair. Joscelyn couldn't see his features clearly through the screen of leaves and twigs, but he seemed to be the only civilian present and he was obviously important. The soldiers ranged themselves behind and to either side of him. There were, Joscelyn estimated, at least fifty of them and twenty or more carried crossbows. Last of all came the Weatherwards, hands bound behind them. He was pleased to see that they wore cloaks. They would need them.

He watched as his colleagues were led to the stakes and the chains attached to their ankles. The sight caused a ripple in his calm, but it was gone in an instant. Their hands were loosed and he saw them doff their cloaks. They gathered briefly to discuss something that he could not hear, and separated, turning to face each other. Stupid, he said to himself as he felt the prickling along his skin that denoted the commencement of Magic. I should have done something to let them know that I was here, that help was at hand. Too late now. They were deep in concentration; the lines of their bodies showed it. The intensification of the tingling he felt attested to the fact that they were beginning to make serious Magic. The hair on the back of his neck itched.

For a while nothing seemed to happen, at least outwardly. Joscelyn could hear an interweaving chant rising in intensity, but the Weatherwards themselves stood slackly, hands to their sides. The only overt sign that they were doing anything was the fact that their heads were tilted back and they seemed to be staring at the skies. Joscelyn began to itch all over his body. It was all that he could do to resist the urge to scratch. Something powerful was undoubtedly going on. He glanced over at the Umbrians. None of them seemed to be affected, though their gazes were riveted on the three Magicians and there were indications of nervousness, bows on the half-ready, tenseness of stance.

The susurration in the canopy became louder, began to sound like the surf off the Barrier Reach of his boyhood. The wind was picking up. He glanced over his shoulder and, in confirmation, saw branches swaying. He looked back at the Weatherwards, saw their mouths moving, knew the chants were continuing, but could no longer hear them. He transferred his attention to the Umbrians. They, too, had noticed the change. They stood closer to each other now as their short cloaks began to flap in the wind. Umbrians, Joscelyn had been told, did not believe in Magic. Well, there were fifty odd across the grass who were certainly becoming believers. The two who were crouched over the box were looking fixedly at the man in black, waiting for a signal. He smiled harshly to himself. They and their like deserved the fear. The man in the chair, however, appeared unaffected. He sat at ease, legs crossed, watching impassively.

There were cloudsteed tails streaming over the mountaintops now, heading on a slant for the Upper Causeway. The wind seemed to be dropping though the tension caused by the spell casting was still building in him. Then he understood. The wind was coming from a more westerly direction and the Saradondas were acting as a shield. He could hear the chanting clearly now. The three Weatherwards were facing east, backs to the mountain, and seemed to be directing their energies out across the Umbrian plain, their arms held out before them. He concentrated and tried to follow the flow. Somewhere, out in the middle of the Empire, heat was building. He marveled at the distances and the forces involved.

He wished he knew more about Weatherwarding. He, and most of his peers, had always assumed that it was a rather inferior branch of Magic, for those with lesser Talents, but they were obviously mistaken. This took great strength and an enormous amount of control. He looked up at the sky. The clouds were thickening and moving toward the sun. Within the space of half an hour, these three had shifted the wind into an entirely different quadrant and, if what Aristach had said was true, this was only the beginning. He looked at them with new respect and then looked back up at the sky. The clouds were moving faster and becoming darker. As he watched, a thin grey veil dropped down over the mountaintops, obscuring them.

Within minutes, rain began to patter down and a cheer went up from the Umbrians. The Magicians lowered their arms and donned their cloaks. A number of the soldiers began to wind back their bows, but stopped when the chanting resumed. The rain got heavier. Another ten minutes of this and their bows will be useless, Joscelyn thought. He noticed that the man in black had turned in his chair and was staring eastward. He followed the man's gaze. The infant sun, not far above the horizon, had created a gigantic rainbow. When the man faced front again, hair plastered against his scalp, his face wore a look of grim satisfaction.

Thunder rolled overhead and the wind picked up again, gusting. The clouds hung lower. Time to get ready, Joscelyn thought, and began to wriggle backward until he was certain that he could not be seen. He stood and made his way to the little clearing where he had left the unicorns. He conferred briefly with Malloran and then led them to the edge of the wood. The figures of the Weatherwards were indistinct and the Umbrians on the far side no more than a blur. The rain had soaked through the canopy and was falling around them, but Joscelyn, fueled by the potions and keyed up by the coming encounter, scarcely felt it. The thunder came again, louder. The sky turned white for a moment, dazzling the eye.

Joscelyn began the spell of invisibility. It went quickly and easily this time. When he was satisfied, he pushed his way through the bushes and made his way across the sopping grass toward the group of Weatherwards. They turned to face him, sensing the presence of a Magic not of their making.

"Keep on doing what you're doing," Joscelyn said. "There are unicorns waiting in the wood. I'll call them out when you're free. Get on them and grab the mane. Make sure you have a good grip. We'll be escaping into Interim and people always black out when that happens. If you fall off it will be the end of you."

He bent down by the closest Weatherward and struggled with the metal manacle round the ankle. It was locked tight and there was no way to undo it without using another spell. It was a simple enough one to be sure, familiar to the lowliest village wizard, but, with the distractions of the situation, the growling thunder, the flickering lightning, the watchful soldiers, Joscelyn wasn't certain that he could pull it off without losing his invisibility, and that might give the game away.

"You're going to have to help me," he said. "I need you to do the unlocking spell."

He had his hands on the shackle and felt the tingle that ran through the iron. The metal would have parted had he not held it together.

"That's done it. Just move your cloak a bit so that the chain is hidden from the Umbrians. When you're all free, I'll give the word and you head for the unicorns."

He moved swiftly to the next and repeated the process. When the last clamp was open, he stood up and thought out to Malloran. As the unicorns emerged from the wood he yelled, "Now!"

What alerted the Umbrians Joscelyn never knew, but, no sooner was the word out of his mouth, than the air was split by the high wailing of the machine. The Weatherwards froze and the cloak of invisibility fell from him. He tried to run, but his feet seemed pinned in place. The unicorns, disoriented but not immobilized, reared and bugled.

IX

✤ ✤ ✤

Jarrod wiped his mouth, pushed his chair back from the table and watched his wife finish her chai. They were having a very early breakfast in his quarters at the palace. The children weren't up and the lone servant had been dismissed.

"You cannot stay any longer," he said, reviving a discussion from the night before. "The royal progress will reach Oxeter in a fortnight and you will have to be there to greet the Queen. You know that."

"I am not leaving until I know what has happened to my son," Marianna iterated stubbornly.

"Naxania knows that you are in Paladine," he said wearily. "If you are not there, it will be taken as a deliberate slight."

"Then you'll just have to go to Songuard and find out what happened to him."

"You know I can't do that."

"Then I'll go. You aren't the only one that can ride a unicorn, you know."

"But . . ." Jarrod began.

"Where is Nastrus anyway?" Marianna asked.

"He's in the stable downstairs. I intend to ride him back to the Outpost. He needs the exercise. Young Lazla spoils him rotten."

"So, if I took him for a little ride, no one would be the wiser." She smiled sweetly.

"Oh no you don't," Jarrod said. "He's been entrusted with an important task and the last thing he would want is for his mother to be checking up on him." He raised a hand to ward off an interruption. "Listen to me now. You haven't seen him in a long time and he isn't a little boy anymore. He's as tall as I am and has a full beard, albeit a very scruffy one. He's full of rebellion and self-doubt. He knows that he did something stupid when he defied Varodias, but he believed in what he was doing at the time and he won't admit, at least to us, perhaps least of all to us, that he made a mistake. I've given him an honorable way out.

"Now, I don't altogether trust him not to do something foolish again, but I had to take the chance. He thinks he's grown up, that the past few years have annealed him, made him an adult, but there's still a lot of childish rage in there."

"But why, Jarrod? I don't understand why. He's had a loving home; he wasn't mistreated at the Outpost—unless you've lied to me. Why this anger?"

Jarrod sighed. "I'm not exactly an expert on young men, except that I've been one. They're all rebellious at his age."

Marianna gave a short bark of laughter. "You? Rebellious? You forget, my love, that I knew you when you were Joscelyn's age. You were biddable to the point of puppyhood."

He ignored the thrust. "That was only because I didn't know how to deal with women." He allowed himself a smile. "Especially not young women like you. But the anger and uncertainty were there. I was lucky enough to have an adventure to expend those feelings on. And speaking of women, I think that part of Joscelyn's problem stems from your remarriage."

"Oh, come now . . . ." she started to object.

"No, no. Hear me out," he interrupted. "Boys can't tolerate the idea of their mother's having sex. Joscelyn and I got on extremely well until he found out that we were going to be married. From that moment on, he's been hostile. Immediately after the wedding, he ran away."

"Suppose you're right," she said reluctantly, setting down the chai mug she had been grasping tightly, "what are we going to do?"

"There's nothing that we can do, my dear. We can hope that he fulfills his mission well, that we can get him back into the Collegium and that he can finish his growing up in a normal manner."

"Nothing more?"

"Nothing."

"That's so like you, Jarrod," she said, folding her napkin and ringing the hand bell for the servant to clear. "You just sit back and wait for everything to turn out for the best."

He laughed, stood up, walked around the table and kissed her on the top of the head. "Well, it worked where you were concerned, didn't it?"

She picked the napkin up and flung it at him, but her eyes had lost their anger. "You are one of the world's most impossible men," she said, rising. She reached up and kissed him on the cheek. "You are also no fun to fight with."

"Stay a couple of days," he replied, "just in case he shows up. Then you go to Oxeter. A royal visit is not the kind of thing that you can leave to Tokamo. Agreed?"

"Very well," she said, her voice mock grumpy. "The Duchess will do her duty."

He smiled at her, kissed her hard, and took his leave.

Jarrod came out into the predawn dark and fetched Nastrus from the stables. They rode through the deserted streets and squares. They paused while the guards opened the gate for them.

'*You are troubled,*' Nastrus commented as they headed north.

'*I hate it when Marianna and I disagree,*' Jarrod thought back.

'*A good gallop will make you feel better,*' Nastrus said, moving into his smooth canter.

'*I think that ought to wait until it gets light.*'

Nastrus pulled up sharply.

'*I didn't mean you to . . .*' Jarrod started. '*What's wrong? Are you hurt?*' he asked anxiously.

The unicorn stood with its head up and its ears pointing forward. '*Some of my colts are in trouble; somewhere down the Lines. We must go. Hold on.*'

Before Jarrod could ask another question, the frigid, grey void of Interim closed over him.

They emerged on a small, gently sloping, grassy area high on some mountain. That much was obvious to Jarrod's muzzy mind as he tried to shake off the effects of Interim. A heavy rain was falling, masking much, but certain things were quite plain. To his right, hard by a ragged copse, were several unicorns in a state of distress. Closer to him were a group of men whose height declared them to be Magicians. To his left, at the edge of the greensward, was a group of soldiers whose lack of height marked them as Umbrians. The mechanical keening that was competing with the thunder was reminiscent of the noise he had heard in southern Paladine.

He shifted in the saddle for a quick look at the landscape behind him. A steepening scarp, large outcropping of rocks and lowering clouds. There was no time for subtlety, or even for preparation. Fortunately there was plenty of energy running loose, some generated by the storm, some Magician made. He swiveled in the saddle again and concentrated on a group of boulders. The ground beneath them would have been softened by the downpour. He reached for the energy stored in the clouds and directed it down onto the mountainside. A play of lightning flashed, grounding itself at the base of the rocks. The boulders, dislodged, began to roll, gathering speed, leapfrog-ging one another.

They headed toward the Umbrian soldiers, who broke and ran. The screech of the machine cut off abruptly. The group of Magicians was still frozen in place. The boulders swept a couple of Umbrians away and plunged out of sight.

"To horse! To horse!" he screamed, aware of Nastrus' half-amused disapproval of the term in his mind.

He watched them scramble across the soggy turf and strug-gle up onto the backs of the unicorns. He could hear Joscelyn's voice urging them on and then, one by one, they winked out of existence. He gave one last look round and saw a small, dark figure shaking a fist at him. He thought he heard cursing, but with the thunder and the hiss of the falling rain he couldn't be sure. Brave man, he thought, before urging Nastrus to follow his offspring. A moment later the lone Umbrian was the only one left on the scarred patch of green. The downpour slanted down around him. It would continue to rain for hours.

Malum followed the Chamberlain down the corridor that led to the Emperor's private quarters. He had expected the sum-mons for the past twenty-six hours, ever since he had returned to Angorn. He had had little or no sleep and his nerves were ragged. Even the beating he had administered to Brandwin had failed to calm him. Now that the moment was drawing nigh, his stomach was in knots. He had run relays of horses into the ground on his way back to the capital so that he could be the first to describe the happenings, but one never knew with Va-rodias.

His mouth was dry as they approached the double doors with their impassive guards. He swallowed and tried to get moisture to his tongue. He must not seem nervous. That could be, quite literally, fatal. The doors opened smoothly and he found himself in the spacious and unfurnished anteroom.

The Chamberlain bowed and withdrew wordlessly, leaving

Malum alone. He stood, hands clasped behind his back, resisting the urge to pace. For the hundredth time he rehearsed his speech of explanation. The inner door finally opened and a Gentleman-of-the-Bedchamber beckoned to him. He was led through the main chamber with its ornate bed, where the traditional levees were held, and ushered into what appeared to be the Emperor's private cabinet. It was a room he had never seen before.

"The Lord Seneschal of the County of Cleremont," the courtier intoned, taking Malum by surprise. The advancement must have been published in the *Palace Gazette* while I was gone, he thought.

Varodias sat in an austerely carved armchair beside the fireplace in which, despite the season, a small fire burned. The room was unexpectedly plain. No pictures, just a faded tapestry on one wall. The beams on the ceiling were painted, but the colors were dull with age. The furniture was sparse. There was an antique table-desk in front of the mullioned window, with a padded chair and footstool and a few side chairs up against the walls. The floor was lightly covered with herbs and rushes. He walked quickly across them and made his reverence.

The Emperor was dressed in grey with dark red sleeves and ruff. He wore grey gloves and his hose and soft leather shoes matched the red of the sleeves. The pointed white beard seemed almost sculpted, the thinning hair carefully brushed back. There was color beneath the high cheekbones, but there was no indication of humor, either good or bad, on the face.

"Welcome back, my lord," Varodias said. There was no welcoming smile to accompany the words. "We hear that there has been rain over the central and western portions of the realm. May we assume that you are, in part, responsible?"

Malum cleared his throat. "Your Majesty is entirely too gracious. The initial experiment was successful and that is what brought on the rain. There have, however, been certain unforeseen complications." He hoped that the cadences of the Formal Mode were disguising his continuing nervousness.

"What kind of complications?" The voice rose slightly at the end of the question.

This was the time for the speech. "A most heinous and criminal act, Majesty." Malum allowed a tinge of indignation. "The young Magicians were performing their spells, the winds had changed directions and the rain was falling, spreading out over the Empire as planned, when a band of other Magicians suddenly appeared on the mountain. They were all riding unicorns."

"Unicorns?" The exclamation was fierce. "Are we to be plagued again by these beasts?"

"It was certainly the case on this occasion, my Liege. There were at least twenty of them. They brought lightning down from the sky and they caused a landslide. A number of my men were killed and considerable damage was inflicted on the mining community of Darran, which lay below." He paused.

Varodias' gloved fingertips were tapping together, the color in the face had heightened and the mouth was grim. The voice when it came was level, cold but level. "And were our weather Magicians killed in this assault?"

"No, great lord. They disappeared along with the invaders." He swallowed. This wasn't going the way he had planned. He had not expected to be questioned until he had finished his explication.

"Disappeared?" The color in the Emperor's face deepened.

"Aye, Sire. One minute they were there and the next they had vanished. We were taken completely by surprise."

"We thought that you were going to take precautions, had machines that could disable Magicians." The Emperor was leaning forward, feet tucked back, fingers of the right hand drumming on the arm of the chair. A vein to the side of his forehead was standing out and pulsing.

"I did, it was used, but a boulder crushed it, killing both the operators. In the resulting confusion, the Magicians escaped."

"This is monstrous! How did they know where you were?" The eyes narrowed. "Did you allow those young men to communicate with anyone?"

"Absolutely not, Your Majesty. Of that I am certain. They were under guard from the moment they left Angorn to the instant they disappeared. They were kept bound and even while they were performing their Magic, they were shackled." He had begun to sweat.

"Then how did the others know where they were?" The voice rose to a scream.

"I have thought of nothing else since it happened," Malum said truthfully. "I can come up with only two possible explanations." He risked a look at the Imperial countenance and was not reassured. "One is," he hurried on, "that the invaders were in Songuard searching for their friends, observed the changes in the weather and traced those changes to their source. The other is that they used some kind of scrying mirror to find their companions."

"It makes little difference. The facts are that our realm has been invaded, the one seeming chance that we had to restore the fertility of our crops has been denied us and the miscreants have gotten clean away." A clenched fist slammed down with scarcely a sound.

Malum regarded his master with increasing alarm. The man was sitting rigidly, but the body was trembling. No, he thought, not trembling; tiny, little jerking motions. The eyes were wide open and unblinking. He waited for the Emperor to say something more, but no words came. "Majesty?" he said tentatively, but Varodias made no reply. He was about to turn and call for a Gentleman-of-the-Bedchamber, when the figure in the chair seemed to come back to life. The eyelids blinked rapidly, the breathing quickened and the mouth began to work.

"Let there be a bounty declared on unicorns," Varodias said. The words were slightly slurred.

"As Your Imperial Majesty commands," Malum replied, somewhat reassured but still wary.

"A murrain on those Magicians!" The voice was gathering strength. "May the Mother blight them and their offspring. How dare they violate our borders." The eye that fixed Malum was quite steady. It was as if nothing had occurred. "We shall give a thousand imperials for every unicorn brought us."

A thousand imperials was a very great deal of money, Malum thought. "I shall see to it, Lord," was what he said. He decided to proceed with the second part of his speech. "There is a possible advantage to the realm in all this."

The Emperor was suddenly still again. "Say you so?"

"It is clear Sire," Malum continued, encouraged, "that the Isphardis conspired with the Discipline to create this famine that our people have been suffering. They invited the Discipline into Isphardel to regulate the weather. It was done under a secret Concordat. What else may have been agreed to in that Concordat? Why was it secret if it contained no malice toward the Empire?"

"Go on." Varodias was alert. Everything was back to normal.

"Our, ah, young guests were on the verge of success when this unprovoked attack occurred and one of our most important mining centers was damaged. It would seem to me that the incursion was a clear attempt to harm the Empire."

The Imperial right hand lifted, fingers fanning out. "And you are suggesting?"

This was the crux and Malum's mouth was dry again. "It would seem to me, Your Imperial Majesty, that you would be well within your rights to declare war." He stopped and took a deep breath.

The Emperor sat back and began to stroke his beard. There

was a long, drawn-out silence. When the eyes turned back to Malum they were hooded. "We are beset on all sides," he said bitterly. "We have enemies within and without, all bent on our overthrow. They think us old, and enfeebled, but they misjudge us." He produced a wolfish smile. The old man's caught fire, Malum thought with relief, and waited for him to continue. The Emperor, however, seemed lost in thought.

"There would be certain advantages to declaring war," the Secretary ventured. "Neither the Discipline nor Isphardel command armies and Your Imperial Majesty could annex the Isphardi portion of the Alien Plain in reparation for the damages caused by this incursion. We would lose trade with them, of course, but there are always some who will put profit above country."

"Aye, they are a nation of money-grubbing heathens," Varodias said, nodding.

"Paladine and Arundel will still have need of our manufactured goods and there is nothing to stop us developing a land route across the Plain. Indeed, without a middleman, profits would be greater. Rainfall is plentiful in the new Isphardi territory and that could, in time, supply our grain and kina."

The Emperor's face had brightened. "War is good for the economy and there are certain other advantages. Electoral retainers become Imperial soldiers and owe their allegiance directly to us. Additional taxes can be raised."

"The people have already suffered a great deal in recent years," Malum cautioned.

The Emperor's hand waved dismissively. "To suffer for no reason provokes hostility. Suffering caused by an enemy incurs loyalty."

"Your Imperial Majesty is most wise. Of course," he added, "there is the fact that the rulers of both Paladine and Arundel are members of the High Council of Magic . . ."

"They are rulers first and Magicians second. Besides, they are both women and women have no stomach for war. If we do nothing directly against the Discipline, they will have no reason for intervention."

"It would be as well to have more intelligence of the Magical Kingdoms, Your Majesty."

"And we suppose that means more money for your operations," Varodias said sourly.

Malum shrugged. "Reliable men need reliable reimbursement."

"Very well, but see that you account for every groat of it. In the meantime, I shall have to summon the Imperial Council and the Mother Supreme will have to be sent for. She hates the Discipline; they all do. We shall have support from the pulpit, and about time, too." He paused, searching his mind for something, then his face cleared. "Is that seditious hermit still alive?" he inquired.

"He is, Sire."

"If we let him loose, will he cooperate, preach a crusade against the Isphardis?"

"I expect so." Malum permitted himself a brief smile. "For a hermit, he does not take well to solitary confinement."

"See to it then. We shall call you again when we need you."

The audience was over and Malum backed from the presence filled with mixed emotions. It seemed clear to him that the Emperor had had some kind of a seizure. It was a frightening thought. His career depended upon Varodias and continued Imperial favor. If the Emperor was incapacitated, he had no other protectors. Coram would be Regent, presumably, and might look favorably upon him, but it was too soon to tell. More than that, it could be disastrous for the Empire at this critical juncture. As he walked back down the corridors toward his quarters, it occurred to him that there was yet another layer to his concern. This man was his father, whether he knew it or not, and the thought of his death was deeply disturbing. He was committed to his course, however. Over and above his self-protective instinct, was the belief that what he was proposing was in the best interests of the country, buttressed by a feeling of loyalty to Varodias. He smiled ruefully to himself. Phalastra, the former Elector of Estragoth, mentor of his youth, had done his work well.

"He's done what?" Jarrod exclaimed.

"He's declared war on the Discipline," Greylock repeated.

Both men were in Greylock's chamber in the Archmage's Tower. The windows were open to admit the breeze and the sunlight, which shone with equal vigor on the spires and turrets beyond.

"How can he possibly do that when he had three of us kidnapped and tortured?"

"That is a question that I asked the Umbrian Ambassador. He said that, quite the contrary, a band of Magicians invaded Umbria, killed a number of soldiers and civilians and demolished a major mining installation. 'A case of naked aggression and an attempt to cripple the Umbrian economy' were his words. Oh, and by the way, since you all arrived on unicorns, the Emperor has placed a bounty on unicorns. One thousand imperial crowns for every horn I think it is."

"But this is insanity. Did you tell him that we could produce the Weatherwards and have them tell their story publicly?"

"Of course I did. He smiled and said that he did not doubt that there were any number of Magicians who were prepared to lie at my behest. If there was any truth to my assertion, why had I not complained officially before? Once our true intentions toward the Empire had been revealed and the Discipline had been held accountable, such belated denials would scarcely be believed by the populace."

"The bloody man has a point there," Jarrod admitted. He forebore to mention that he had opposed Greylock's decision to keep the matter quiet.

"I have already issued a proclamation. We can only hope

that our reputation for honesty and fair dealing will carry the day." Greylock didn't sound optimistic.

"And what if it doesn't? And even if it does, what difference will that make to the Umbrians?"

"Useless speculation," the Archmage said sharply. "These are matters for the High Council to discuss. Handrom will be here from Talisman tomorrow and Naxania will arrive the following day. She's been on a progress, so I'm not sure how much she knows."

Adversity sharpens him, Jarrod thought. "I saw her at Oxeter and I told her about the rescue," he said.

"How did she react?"

"She seemed pleased enough, though I wouldn't care to speculate on how she'll take this latest development."

"And where is that stepson of yours now?" Greylock asked.

"Dean Beriman has taken him back into the Collegium. Keeps to himself, mostly, from what I hear. It's to be expected."

"Given the circumstances, I'm not sure that he should be at Celador. It might be wise to send him to his mother at Gwyndryth."

"His mother's at Oxeter, but I agree with you about his not staying here. He's a very strong Talent, but he has a streak of wildness still. On the other hand, he has a great rapport with unicorns. It's not the same as Marianna's and mine—not that ours is exactly alike. With your permission, sir, I think he should go back to the castle and the unicorns, but it must not seem as if he is being exiled again. He did the Discipline a considerable service and showed a great deal of courage."

"What do you suggest?"

"I think you should summon him and commend him personally," Jarrod said. "And then I think you should ask him to take on a special task. If the current situation does degenerate into open warfare, we may need help from the unicorns. Joscelyn is already known to them, can communicate with them and would be the best person to act as the Discipline's official liaison."

A thin smile crept onto Greylock's face as he listened and he stroked his beard. "You've grown practical," he said. "It's not a bad plan. Someone from the Collegium should accompany him so that he can keep up with his studies. I'm sure that Beriman can come up with someone suitable. They should be properly supplied, too. That will entail unicorns, so I'll leave that up to you. Yes," he nodded, "that might well be the best thing to do."

Jarrod's smile was broad and fond. "You always were shrewd, sir," he said.

X

🙰 🙰 🙰

Celador had been the center of the Discipline for time beyond memory. Magic, it was said, had built the delicate spires and turreted walls. The faded inscriptions over the gates were universally believed to be runes of protection. The High Council of Magic commonly met there. On this occasion the members were gathered in the Great Hall. Jarrod remembered it as the place where his life had changed forever. It was this same Hall that had been the site of the historic Conclave when Archmage Ragnor, assisted by a much younger Greylock, had unveiled the future. That had led to the quest for the unicorns and that, in turn, had led to his sitting at the soskia-wood table on the dais.

He glanced around. At the far end was the minstrels' gallery, where, as a student, he had sat taking notes. There had been rows of benches then, filled with the great ones of Strand. The room was empty now, save for those around the table, and it looked even larger than it had then. The fan tracery still spread lacily upward, but the ceiling above the three vast chandeliers was blacker. The colors that the sun threw down onto the floor from the stained glass windows were as vivid as those of memory, but the colors in the battle flags around the walls had faded.

Of the five Adepts that had sat on the dais so many years ago, Greylock, Arabella of Arundel and Naxania of Paladine remained. The two women had been young princesses then. Now each was queen in her own right. The others at the table were Sumner, a Magister then, Mage of Arundel now, Sommas Handrom, once Dean of the Collegium and currently Chief Warlock of Talisman. To Jarrod's left sat Handrom's replacement as Dean, Effcam Beriman, a man in his mid-forties with an unremarkable face surmounted by pale, straight hair. The blue eyes were slightly protruberant and he gave off a general aura of vagueness. Jarrod knew better. The man had been Head Spellmaster when Jarrod had been at the Collegium. Beyond him sat two Magisters he did not know and, at the foot of the table, two scribes rounded out the group.

Greylock took off his spectacles and rubbed the bridge of his nose. He coughed to attract attention and the quiet conversations died. "This session of the High Council of Magic is called to order. Let the record show that all are present and that two members of the Collegium staff are here at our invitation." He coughed again, this time in earnest.

"As you all know," he continued, "the Empire has declared war on us and upon Isphardel. We are accused of invading the Empire with twenty or more Magicians, mounted on unicorns, of killing a number of Umbrians and deliberately destroying one of their mining installations. The Isphardis are accused of abetting us. I ask the Mage of Paladine to explain what really occurred."

Jarrod rose slowly to his feet and began to tell the story. He moved his attention from one listener to another as he continued the tale, trying to gauge their reaction. "And so," he concluded, "we managed to make our escape. There was no planned incursion. The only Magicians involved were the three kidnapped Weatherwards, who, I may add, had been subjected to torture by the Umbrians, Joscelyn and myself. The rockslide may have inflicted some damage to a mining installation, but I could see no signs of one. If there is a grievance in this matter, it is ours." He sat down and the silence continued.

"How many more times is the Discipline to be jeopardized by this stepson of yours, Abercorn?" The voice that broke the silence was Sumner's and he used Jarrod's lay title. Jarrod bristled inwardly, but kept his features still.

"We are not here," Greylock said quickly, "to discuss Joscelyn of Gwyndryth. There are matters of far greater import."

"Well, let me say for the record that I think that the Mage of Paladine has acted most improperly. He did not consult this Council before proceeding and it is his actions that have led directly to our present predicament."

"Your comment is noted," Greylock said. He acknowledged a look from Arabella. "Majesty."

She smiled around the table. "I have spoken with one of the young Weatherwards and there can be no doubt that Varodias was trying to change the weather over the Empire to alleviate a drought that he blames on us. He is a volatile man and his disappointment was probably exacerbated by the reports of unicorns." The corners of her mouth twitched up. "He has no great love of unicorns. I take this declaration of war to be a venting of spleen. One, moreover, that serves to divert the thoughts of his people from the problems at home." Arabella sat back.

She's put on weight, Jarrod thought, but she's still a good-looking woman.

"I concur," Naxania said, looking very regal in a red dress with a darker red surcoat. "Our Cousin of Umbria knows full well that there is nothing he can do to hurt us."

"And what of our allies the Isphardis?" Sumner asked.

"They have a long, common border and there is a dispute over the northern territories," Handrom added, pointing out the obvious.

"The Concordat does not call for our intervention under such circumstances, but the Treaty of Partition calls for the Magical Kingdoms to go to Isphadel's aid if it is attacked."

"And you were the one who negotiated that treaty in our behalf, were you not, my Lord of Paladine?" the Mage of Arundel asked.

"Your Eminence is well aware of that," Jarrod replied coldly.

Sumner pushed back his chair and surged to his feet. His chins quivered. Jarrod eyed him with dislike. He had grown fat in Celador and his eyes seemed to have shrunk. "Fellow Council members. It is obvious that both the security and the good name of the Discipline have been called into question by a series of actions perpetrated by the Mage of Paladine. It seems clear to me that, without him, we would not be in this situation. I suggest that he be removed from this Council and that the Emperor be apprised of that fact."

"You are out of order, Sumner," Greylock said, frowning and waving the man to his seat. The Mage of Arundel subsided slowly, scowling.

"Perhaps I should remind the Council," Jarrod cut in, "that it was this body that designated me to represent it on the Commission for the Outland, approved the Treaty of Partition, debated the Concordat and approved it too."

"Just so, just so," Greylock exclaimed fussily. "Let us move on."

"I suggest," Naxania said, "that we issue a strongly worded denial of having participated in any raid or having any hand in the weather over the Empire. They haven't mentioned the Weatherwards; why should we? Without them, we have no motive."

Heads nodded in agreement, but Handrom asked, "What about the Isphardis?"

"Perhaps the Mage of Paladine should visit the Oligarchs and confer with them." The recommendation came from Queen

Arabella and Jarrod shot her a grateful glance. "He has had more contact with them than the rest of us. They trust him and he has the added advantage of being able to travel by unicorn. I do not think that we can afford to waste time."

"We have two motions to put to the vote," Greylock said crisply.

Naxania's suggestion was passed unanimously after a discussion as to the precise wording. Jarrod's trip was approved, but the Mage of Arundel abstained ostentatiously. The meeting broke up without the usual informal conversations, though the two queens left together. Jarrod accompanied the Archmage back to his tower and said as they crossed Great Court, "Sumner was in rare form."

"The man is so transparent in his ambition. However, I think his outburst probably did you more good than harm. When will you leave for Belengar?"

"I'll send off a bunglebird to Olivderval this afternoon, give it three days to get there, give them time to discuss—about a sennight."

"Enough time to get the text of what you will say approved by the Council," Greylock returned with a wintry grin.

The High Council of Magic was not alone in pondering the ramifications of Varodias' actions. Five hundred leagues to the east of Celador, Estivus, Margrave of Oxenburg, paced the ramparts of Fort Bandor. The ancient bastion had been built by an early Emperor and had the dubious distinction of being the only major installation on Strand to have been occupied by the Others. The damage inflicted during the occupation and the subsequent recapture was no longer evident, though the keep had never been rebuilt. Bandor had, in the years of peace, expanded southward beyond the walls, but the view to the north remained as it always had.

To the left and right were the peaks, snowcapped still, of the two great ranges, succeeded by the corrugated plunge of hills that ended a league short of the Upper Causeway. Beyond, the Alien Plain stretched until it merged with the sky. Under different circumstances, Estivus would have been happy to be here, far from the civilian bustle and intrigue of the Imperial Court. He hadn't been abroad often, only once before, really, to Celador for Ragnor's funeral and that hadn't turned out very well. He sighed and turned on his heel.

Things weren't going right, to his way of thinking. There was too much duplicity. Take this assignment. He was here, ostensibly, as Prince Coram's aide, on a state visit. A state visit with eight hundred fighting men. The Prince had been admirably diplomatic. He had met with the Songean clan elders, gone hunting with them and, as far as one could judge, had impressed them with his bluff manner and down-to-earth speech. The appearances were precisely as they should be. Yet, out on that distant plain, an army gathered and Estivus had sole command of it. Or, rather, the Prince had nominal control and the Margrave was the military commander.

Corner tower, step and turn. How had he arrived here? Because he was the Prince's companion. Because you are a cavalry officer of proven worth, he told himself. He blew breath out in annoyance at himself. He was the Emperor's sworn man and the Emperor had given him this commission. It was not for him to question. He paused and looked out over the battlement. Whether it was, or wasn't, questioning was what he was doing. He always had. Probably not a good trait in a senior officer, but it was too late now. His mind went over the situation yet again and it still didn't make too much sense.

Both the Emperor and the Church were saying that the Discipline and the Isphardis had conspired to ruin the harvests and had destroyed a mining center. It seemed extremely unlikely, but the country was fired up, no doubt about that. The statue of the Archmage and his helper, erected after the defeat of the Outlanders, had been pulled down by an angry mob.

They believed that bloodthirsty Paladinians would be swarming over the border. The military High Command, of course, knew better than that, but, just as a precaution, a force was sent to occupy Fort Bandor while a proper army, complete with rotifers, which seemed to be on the scene already, cannons and battlewagons that had been captured from the Others and converted, mustered on the Alien Plain. It all seemed a little excessive.

The Isphardis were no threat. They had no army. They had no fighting tradition. The Magical Kingdoms were another matter. They had fought formidably in the Outland Wars, but that was a long time ago. They had rusted since then and the Umbrian forces, the core of them anyway, had stayed keen. Nevertheless, it would be a mistake to underestimate them. He pushed off the merlon and resumed his walk. He had had a meeting with Quern before his departure from Celador. The man had talked about water rights on the Alien Plain and a grain embargo by the Isphardis. Didn't mean much militarily, but he had learned in his months at the capital that my Lord of Quern was not a man to be taken lightly. He sighed aloud.

Three hundred leagues to Estivus' south, the Oligarch Olivderval was thinking much the same thing. She stood in front of a long mirror of real glass, worth six months' labor in the fields if you could find one, and regarded her image with distaste. She was fat, but she was used to that. She'd been fat for a very long time and it had never held her back. Her bed was occupied when she had a mind to share it, and her coffers were full. What displeased her were the crepe marks around her neck. She was preparing for a meeting with Jarrod Courtak, but her thoughts were on Malum of Quern. She knew he was the enemy, the mind against which she fenced at long range. She had no proof, he had been too clever for that, but she knew. And knowing, she had allowed herself to fantasize a little. The image in the mirror did not measure up and she threw an almost transparent scarf around her shoulders, knowing that she could adjust it later.

Stupid, she said to herself as she turned away from the mirror. You have a presentation to make, so concentrate. She took a deep breath and went over the last meeting in her mind. She began to walk back and forth across her bedchamber. Her lips did not move, but her hands carried out a silent conversation in front of her. The two waiting women who effaced themselves by the door knew better than to distract their mistress when she was in one of these moods. They just waited, which, after all, was what they were, in part, paid for.

When Olivderval greeted Jarrod, there were no signs of unease. "My Lord Mage, I bid you welcome to my humble dwelling," she said, just before sweeping across the floor and holding out her arms to be embraced.

Jarrod bent low, he being overly tall and she being on the short side. "My dear Oligarch," he said formally as he straightened up, "I rejoice to see you in such good health."

"Your Eminence is entirely too gracious," she replied in the Formal Mode and loud enough for the servants to hear. She took his arm and steered him toward a bank of cushions. With her welcoming smile firmly in place, she said quietly through her teeth, "I'm going to dismiss these long-eared attendants of mine and then you and I can talk like reasonable human beings."

Jarrod bent his head and smiled. "Most High Plenipotentiary," he said, inventing a title for her enjoyment, but keeping scrupulously to the cadences of the Formal Mode, "I bring you greetings from the Archmage."

Olivderval indicated a section of cushions with her fan and sank onto the ones she had selected for herself. They were piled somewhat higher than those of her guest. A serving girl came with silver beakers of iced fruit juice and disappeared. Olivderval dismissed the other attendants with a couple of waves of the fan.

When they were gone, she pushed herself round and looked at Jarrod. "You don't have to tell me everything that's happened since last we met, I'm easily bored, but how have things been with you personally?"

Jarrod grinned at her, seduced by her personality yet again. "Married, children, international incidents. The usual; and you?"

"Oh, business, the Council, the Empire, war. Much of a muchness." She smiled broadly and her nose wrinkled. The smile disappeared. "You want a report, don't you?"

He shrugged. "I came more to discuss what happens next, but I probably should know what has happened here first."

Olivderval pushed herself back against the cushions, took a sip of her fruit juice, cocked her head and looked at Jarrod askance. "You put it very gently, friend Jarrod," she said. "But the truth of the matter is, as we both know, that you are here representing the Magical Kingdoms. The Empire has declared war on us, occupied our territory before the declaration of war, and we are powerless. Without the help of the Kingdoms, we shall be swept away." She paused, ducked her head and drew in a large breath that enhanced her considerable bust.

Jarrod looked at her and laughed. "You never stop, do you?" he said.

"Well," she said good-humoredly, "it used to work. But," she added, "the problem's real enough."

"Suppose you tell me."

"I assume you know that we have hired a Cloudsteed Wing." Jarrod nodded. "They report that the Umbrian army has moved into our new lands in force and are marching toward Fort Bandor where, quite coincidentally, of course, the Emperor's heir apparent and a general called Oxenburg are making a state visit. I don't know very much about either of them." She looked at him as if trying to foretell his reactions. "Umbrians have been in our territory for some time," she added, "but this is of another measure of magnitude. Naked aggression with a probable threat to Songuard. There is nothing we can do. We have no army, and even if we did, we couldn't supply them so far from home. The Magical Kingdoms and the Discipline must intervene."

"We have sent the sternest possible messages to His Imperial Majesty," Jarrod said blandly.

"So have we, much good may it do us," she replied.

"Surely there must be something that Isphardel can do," Jarrod prodded, "even though it would hurt business in certain quarters."

"We've done that too. We slapped on a grain embargo." She sighed. "It's going to cost me a fortune. I've got warehouses full of the stuff." She shot him a sly glance. "Shan't be able to buy wheat from your wife this year, I'm afraid."

He smiled to acknowledge the thrust. He waited.

"Don't think it was easy," Olivderval said, allowing irritation to show. "Some of my colleagues on the Council felt, with some justification, I may add, that a grain embargo would bolster Varodias' assertion that Isphardel and the Discipline were trying to starve the Umbrian people." She switched abruptly out of the Common Mode into Formal. "What make you of that, Eminence?"

"Not too much, Oligarch." Jarrod started out in the Formal Mode and modified downward. "I would guess that you were outvoted."

"Guess again, Magician. It was my idea." She drained her cup and wedged it between cushions. She looked over at him again, speculatively. "What says the Discipline to that?"

Jarrod rearranged his length among the cushions. "Not very much, alas," he said, deploying his left hand in an open gesture that conveyed regret and a question in the same movement.

Olivderval popped open the fan and swept it slowly back

and forth. "In addition," she conceded, "we have been training a local militia . . ."

"I am very well aware of that. With the best will in the world, you won't have a fighting force for at least the next two years." Jarrod raised his eyebrows much as a knucklebones player when the pieces are in the air.

"Are you taking to the lists, Eminence? I thought we were on the same team." Olivderval looked downcast.

"And we are, my good friend, we are," Jarrod said with equal sincerity. "But put yourself in my position. I come seeking reassurances of positive action on the part of the Oligarchy, and I find half-truths and semirevelations."

Olivderval snorted and rang the silver bell hidden in the folds of the cushions. "You've changed, Eminence," she said approvingly. "You are far better prepared than you used to be when we negotiated the Partition Treaty."

"You do me too much honor," Jarrod said as he made room for the breakfast that the women were serving.

"Mostly fruit, I'm afraid," Olivderval said, smiling again. "I have to watch my weight and so everybody who comes within my gates has to suffer."

Jarrod smiled for the benefit of the servants and waited until they had withdrawn again before answering. "We've known each other a very long time, Oligarch," he said. She smiled, but covered it quickly. What she had smiled at was his assumption that fifteen years was a long time. "I don't think it any advantage for the two of us to fence. When it comes down to it, we both have the same aims. Let me be blunt. The Magical Kingdoms want a definite sign that Isphardel is committed to fight this war, alone if need be."

Olivderval surged out of her cushions. She stood before him, a solid presence wrapped in floating layers of silk. Her face had begun to sweat and fine rivulets made lines in the powder that she had donned for the interview. "No, we are not," she said with some heat. "You don't understand our country. We've never had to think in terms of fighting. We are an association of free people, well moderately free, and you just can't go around coercing people into armed service."

"There is, I hope, a but in all of this," Jarrod interrupted.

"You really ought to try the fruit," Olivderval countered. "It might sweeten your disposition."

"Divine Oligarch," Jarrod said with a grin, "I don't think you can accuse the Magical Kingdoms of coercion." He cocked his head to one side and wiped the moisture from the bottom of the sweating cup. "I seem to remember that you were the one asking for help."

Olivderval took her time settling back into her cushions, pulling and tweaking where she felt adjustment was needed. "What do you need in the way of reassurance before you can convince the Councils of Paladine and Arundel to intervene in our cause?" she asked.

"Oh, not trade concessions," he said, allaying her fears and enjoying it at the same time. He smiled at her and moved his silver cup back and forth between them. "Truth would be nice, but I recognize that that would be difficult for someone in your position."

He dropped the playful stance abruptly. "I would like to help you," he said, "and know that you have my vote in Council, but I need something more than this to convince the Queens to commit."

Olivderval tucked her legs up. There was nothing in the least coquettish about the move. "No support thus far?" she asked.

"Not a pikeman, not a cavalry officer," he said with regret.

"You've made some moves, though. I have my own intelligence. Suppose you speak about those. At best you'll give advance warning about something your Ambassador will tell me on the morrow, at worst, you'll confirm what my spies have already told me."

"Tough talk from a country that cannot defend its own frontiers," Jarrod said.

"Tough is as tough needs to be, Eminence. We're about to fight for our lives here. The shrines along temple street are filled with worshipers, business is off, the independent banks are refusing loans and we, the Oligarchs, are at our wits' end. What more do you want?"

Jarrod ate several pieces of fruit to keep her waiting and then complimented her on the selection. Once he had wiped his fingers on the napkin provided, he smiled at Olivderval again. "My wife's factor," he said deliberately, "has heard of new sea maneuvers and the possibility of a new weapon."

"Your wife's factor is a very clever man whose days are numbered," she replied calmly.

"Are you going to deny his information?" Jarrod asked.

She looked over at him for a while without replying. Then she smiled. It was a poor excuse for a smile. "If we are to be allies, it is pointless to have secrets from each other," she said with a massive shrug. "I have spent a considerable amount of money developing an advanced version of the Umbrian cannon. If we can develop it successfully, we thought we might attack the southern coast of the Empire. This," she reared up from the cushions, "is strictly between ourselves."

"I shall do my best to keep it that way," Jarrod assured her. "I should have enough to convince Paladine, which is closest to the Umbrian incursion, to send troops onto the Alien Plain. The rest will follow."

"You could have said that before, you know," she said, grudgingly.

"And if I had, you would never have told me about the cannons and your plan to deploy them on ships."

"But I never," she began, and then broke off to laugh. "You snake," she said. "You realize that I'll never trust you again?"

"Oh, yes you will," he said with a smile as he unfolded himself from the cushions. "And, as an earnest, Naxania is calling up the Farod." He smiled broadly over at her. "I grant you that there are a number of domestic advantages in the move, but it might give the Emperor pause and it's a very positive thing to report to your Council."

"The problem with war," Olivderval said as she heaved her way out of her pile of cushions, "is that you and I can no longer spar together, which is a pity, because I enjoyed the encounter. Soon we will be allies in fact as well as name and we shall only be able to tell each other the truth. Shame, isn't it?" She rang the hand bell again, but this time for the young ladies to escort Jarrod out. He pressed his hands together in the ritual of departure. As she came out of her reciprocal bow, Olivderval said, "It may not come to that, you know."

Jarrod shook his head sadly as he turned. "You know it will, dear Oligarch, you know it will."

Olivderval fanned herself as she watched him leave. Magicians are unnecessarily tall, she thought. Then, he's harder than he used to be. She weighed what he had said. He had committed to nothing, but she trusted him. That, she told herself, was a lousy way to do business.

XI

✣ ✣ ✣

After the initial flurry of activity that followed in the wake of the Umbrian declaration of war, the summer wore on in an atmosphere of anticlimax. The Farod had been summoned and put through its paces beyond the Upper Causeway. The area behind the wall had been covered with tents with a wide berth given to both the Place of Power and the Great Maze. The tents and the men were gone now, leaving a dusty and grassless expanse. Puffs of dust rose from beneath Nastrus' hooves as Jarrod rode toward the gates through the massive wall. They stood open and unguarded, but he wondered how long that would last.

'You continue to be uneasy about these Umbrians,' Nastrus commented.

'I don't trust the Emperor,' Jarrod replied. 'Things are just too quiet and his troops are too close to Paladine for my taste.'

'Any human who is capable of encouraging others to kill unicorns cannot be considered trustworthy,' Nastrus said acidly.

'How have your offspring taken the news?'

'Disbelief, anger, disgust, take your pick. It took me a while to *convince them that not all humans are so inclined. It helped that your foal was there. They know him and they like him. Malloran, too, supported me, but then he has a vision of humans and unicorns living together on this world. I'm not sure where he gets this streak of idealism from, but it proved persuasive.'*

'Indeed? I should like to talk to him about it.'

'Yes, I'm sure you would,' Nastrus said with a return to his normal, somewhat caustic sense of humor. *'You are somewhat alike. Do you want to go now?'*

'Now?'

'Why not? Hold on.'

Jarrod emerged from Interim feeling both cold and hungry. He looked around and saw that they were in the forecourt of the castle on the mountain. He wished that Nastrus wouldn't do these translations so suddenly. His resistance to Interim had improved steadily, but still . . . He swung himself wearily down from the saddle, uncinched the girth and went into the undercroft to see if he could find something to eat.

When he reemerged, munching on a carrot, he saw the unicorn that Nastrus called Malloran standing at the bottom of the steps that led up to the Hall. He walked over broadcasting greetings. He felt a probing somewhere in the back of his head. *'. . . Mage Jarrod,'* he heard. Obviously the tail end of a thought.

'Do you hear me clearly?' he asked.

'I have no trouble seeing your thoughts.' A wisp of humor drifted in. *'Although if you are like the younger human who calls himself Joscelyn, I may not always understand them.'*

'Takes after Nastrus,' Jarrod thought a trifle morosely and belatedly tried to cloak the idea.

'Too late,' Malloran said clearly in his head. Goodwill and good humor came with the thought. Beneath them Jarrod sensed steadiness and an amount of pride. *'You have an ease with our kind,'* Malloran continued, *'that your young kinsman has yet to achieve. By the way, Nastrus is my grandsire.'*

'But I thought . . .'

'As he wished you to do. He still considers himself our dominant male.'

Jarrod let that pass. 'He tells me that you have a vision for the future of our two kinds.'

Again an intimation of humor. 'Not so much a vision of the future as a vision from the past.'

'I'm afraid I don't understand,' Jarrod said.

'But you are familiar with the Memory.'

'Yes, the combined recollections of a family.'

'The farther back one goes, however, the harder it is to decipher. All things, it seems, fade in time.'

Jarrod smiled. 'I know full well. I am trying to write a history of Strand and my research has shown me that documents from earlier times are spotty, sometimes unreliable. You have to use both logic and intuition to put together a picture from the pieces that survive.' He sensed both agreement and sympathy. 'But what is it that you have been exploring?' he asked.

'There was a time before we knew of the Guardian, when we did not live on the Island at the Center. There were few of us then and He who Controls the Lines of Force had rescued those ancestors from another world. The Memory is clouded about that time. There is confusion and fear, an overwhelming sense of sadness and loss. Many of my kind were gone and the survivors did not want to remember. There are suggestions, however, glimpses of that former home. There were some who dwelt upon happier times. There are humans in those memories.'

'And were those humans the cause of the losses?' Jarrod asked, half-afraid to hear the answer.

'In part, but sadder yet was that unicorn fought unicorn. I have not been able to decipher why. One thing that is clear, however, stands out in the happier memories. There was a time when human and unicorn lived side by side in harmony, when communication like this was common.' A note of diffidence crept into the stream of images that Jarrod was receiving. 'It is my dream that those conditions might come again on this world.'

'It is a noble dream, friend Malloran, and I for one would do everything in my power to bring it about.' He stopped as a thought struck him.

'It is possible,' Malloran replied to the as yet unformulated question, *'but the Memory has no information on that point.'*

'Yet it is possible that, if the Guardian saved your kind from destruction and took them to the Island at the Center, he might have plucked our kind from the brink of disaster and set them down here?'

'Who can know what the Guardian does or thinks? He is older than the Memory and his power knows no limit. His ways are inscrutable.' The thought had an almost ritualistic cadence.

'But you think we can recreate that other world, the one you saw before the conflict?'

'There is some support among our kin,' Malloran returned, *'but we cannot do it alone.'*

'Granted. I must think on this.' He paused again. *'In the meanwhile,'* he resumed, *'do you know where Joscelyn is?'*

'He and his companion went through the cleft to fish. I do not think they will return much before sundown.'

'Please tell him that I inquired after him and that his mother sends her love.'

'I shall tell him. He seems, by the way, to be more tranquil here than he was before.'

'I am glad to hear it.'

'There is something more you wish to ask,' Malloran stated flatly.

'Alas, yes. We may have another war to fight. If we do not win, your dream will never come to pass. Will your kind help us?'

'I do not speak for the unicorns,' Malloran said ruefully as he turned away.

The Emperor Varodias sat at his ease in one of his withdrawing rooms sipping chai, his feet resting on a padded stool. The Mother Supreme sat opposite him. She was wearing a simple, loose gown that hid her plump figure. A scarf covered her hair.

A far cry from Arnulpha, Varodias thought approvingly. The former Mother Supreme had been intelligent and ambitious, as this one was, but she had been aggressive and overly intent on the glory of the Church. Estrala, the Mother be praised, was a woman one could work with. She was somewhat fanatical on the subject of the Discipline, but that, under the circumstances, was all to the good.

"We are pleased with the reports that we have had," he said, signaling a servingman to pour her more chai, "of the Church's preaching in the matter of our brutalization by elements from Isphardel and from the Discipline."

"It is our duty so to preach," she replied. Her use of the Formal Mode was as assured as his and reminded him that she came from an Electoral family. Just which one he could not remember and that irked him. There was an important connection there.

Estrala pushed herself back into the armchair provided. Her feet swung free of the floor. Her eyes summed the Emperor up. They were grey, penetrating and, from Varodias' point of view, insufficiently deferential. She gripped the arms of the chair and leaned forward. "You find me overly intense," she said. "I can tell that. Indeed, I can tell a great deal from the way you hold your body, the fluttering of your hands, the way your lips tense or relax." Her own face was smooth. "I tell you this so that you will not think that I have any special powers." She paused to look at him speculatively and then she smiled. It was a clear and luminous smile. It lit her face and seemed to affect the space around her. There was a sense of understanding, and even of joy, in that smile. Varodias was not unaffected. It made him very nervous.

"I am the Elector of Ondor's youngest sister," she said as if explaining the obvious. "He was very stupid and he deserved to die. Oh"—she held up a hand briefly—"I don't for a moment think he was guilty of the crime for which you condemned him, he didn't have the brains to mastermind a conspiracy against you, but, as head of the family, he should have anticipated your move." Her head had dropped slightly during the recital. One corner of her mouth twitched upward and she raised her head. There was a challenging gleam in her eyes. "I don't have an Electorate to lose so I can declare, full body, for the Empire"—she took a deliberate breath—"and for the man who rules it." She reached for her cup and took a sip of chai.

Varodias watched her, eyes narrowed. Ah yes, the Ondor connection. He remembered now that he had felt, at the time of her election, that her knowing at firsthand the extent of Imperial power would make her more malleable. He was rapidly revising that opinion. Here she was, sipping chai and looking innocent, but beneath that pink-and-white exterior lurked a sexual predator and, unless his instincts were awry, she was setting her cap for him. It was intriguing, but this was not the time.

"We are happy to hear of your devotion to our person," he said with a chilly smile. "It is always best when the Church and the Crown are in accord. Now, when we are challenged from without and threatened from within, it is even more desirable."

"Great good can come of it, though," Estrala said. If she recognized the rebuff, she gave no sign of it. "New souls will be brought under the sway of the Mother's magnanimity, the heathen shall be converted and Her enemies will be smitten."

"If by Her enemies you mean the Discipline, that may prove difficult. One cannot draw them into battle." It took no effort at all to sound condescending.

"But one can punish those temporal kingdoms that support them," she replied quickly. "Their rulers are members of the accursed Discipline, equally blasphemous, equally doomed." Her voice took on a cathedral ring. "Your Imperial hand will stretch forth and crush them, your rule extend to the far reaches of Strand and the Mother's blessing and Her power shall ride upon your sword." She stopped, mouth open, eyes bright, panting softly.

Varodias pursed his lips. It was possible that the woman might be a little mad, but her fervor made her seem more attractive. He would have to tread carefully with this one, but the fanaticism that appeared to run through her, whatever its underlying cause, would serve him well. She could be an inspiring figure when the spirit was upon her. He would have her address the troops when the time came to move into Songuard. The manservant refilled his cup and Varodias rolled the hot, slightly bitter liquid around his mouth. Emperor of Strand. It had a nice ring to it.

XII

❧ ❧ ❧

The one place on Strand where there was no feeling of complacency, no illusion that everything was as it had been, was Isphardel. In Morlin, Zingara and Jointon, in Belengar, Martesberg and Faringford men and women drilled in increasingly complicated maneuvers. Two small merchantmen, outfitted now as fighting vessels, had been sailed and towed up the Illuskhardin River to the broad body of water that the Isphardis called by the river's name and the Umbrians referred to as Lake Grad. Thick jungle protected the east bank of the Lower Illuskhardin, but the stretch from the northern tip of the lake to the Saradonda Mountains was vulnerable to Umbrian assault. A string of primitive mott and bailey forts had been hastily constructed to guard that frontier and were now manned by a mixed force of mercenaries from the Magical Kingdoms. Smithies were working around the clock turning out weapons and armor.

There was another group of former blacksmiths who were working in feverish secrecy on Tamara Island, set halfway out to sea in the mouth of Belengar Bay. They cast and hammered, chipped and smoothed by the perpetual light of furnaces. They had been sequestered for months, turning out cylindrical iron tubes and metal balls. The tubes were fashioned into cannons and mounted on wooden gun carriages. The finished products were transferred to waiting ships, hidden from the mainland by the island's bulk. The ships then set sail to make the necessary adjustments to their superstructures and to train their crews in the use of gunpowder. In the early days, the recoil of the fired cannons wreaked havoc, but practice, wariness and the instinct to keep their limbs intact brought a measure of order and competence.

While the mood in Stonta, Fortress Talisman and Celador was one of eerie calm and lingering dissatisfaction, the mood in Belengar was jittery. The grain trade was in shambles and the bankers were nervous. Merchants, faced with change, were irritable. Theaters, raree shows and prostitution thrived. The capital was consumed by a wave of manic gaiety on the one hand and an upsurge of religious feeling on the other. Alone among the places of worship, the soaring Church of the Mother on the outskirts of the Old Quarter attracted fewer people than of yore. The Exotic Bird Market also suffered. The purchase of an expensive pet constituted a commitment to the future and the future looked all too uncertain.

On an early autumn night, while a copper nightmoon was rising, twelve ships slipped anchor and headed out into the Inner Sea. When they were out of sight of land, a lantern appeared on the poop deck of the lead vessel, which promptly came about and began to tack east across the wind the way they had practiced so often during the past month. It was not that the captains and crews were not well-seasoned seamen, they were not used to working together with so many other vessels. Things went smoothly that night, however, and they sailed in line, with the nightmoon gibbous off the starboard bow.

They stayed out of sight of land for four days, which in and of itself was unusual. Merchantmen rarely strayed out of sight of land. Surprise was their object now and they were headed for the mouth of the Bardon River, two hundred leagues along the Umbrian coast. Come morning, once the decks had been scrubbed with blocks of pumice, sluiced down and dried, five of the ships broke from the formation. Once clear of the line, portions of the bulwarks were removed and the guns were run out. Each ship had four, two on each side. Cannonballs, kegs of powder, ramrods and swabs appeared from below. Slow matches lay curled in their special fireproof boxes. The topgallants and topsails were reefed to reduce way and the cannons were loaded. Three rounds per gun were fired in a final practice. The powder and the shot were both too expensive to waste. The trick was to fire the cannons as the ship's side was rising on the swell in order to throw the cannonballs high in the air. There was no other way to elevate the barrel far enough and all their targets would be on land.

Well before dawn on the following day, boats were lowered from the seven ships that were not equipped with the cannons. Soldiers swarmed down the netting draped over their sides and the little flotilla headed toward the river mouth. Rowlocks were muffled and silence was maintained. There was a manor house on the bluffs overlooking the sea and, while they expected no resistance, they did not want the alarm given. The manor was not their objective. The party was headed for another estate upriver.

The land was silent as the boats were rowed upstream. Small fishing craft were moored by the banks, smaller versions of the ones pulled up on the beaches by the river mouth. Groves of trees made blacker patches in the dark and, from time to time, the smell of woodsmoke drifted down. The stars had begun to fade by the time they neared the docks that would be their way to Cromlin Castle. The waving heads of the cane crop, miles of them, had already indicated that they were inside the boundaries of the demesne.

They tied up and disembarked at the deserted docks and

crept past warehouses and the two-storied processing plant. They were empty now, last year's produce gone, waiting upon the harvest that was a month away to resume their busy life. The only life that would come to them this year, though, was the leap and crackle of fire. Not yet a while. That could wait upon the retreat. Meantime, up the broad, unrutted road they marched as the misty forms of outbuildings and workers' cottages emerged in the predawn paleness. Birds were roused and singing their greeting of the new day. Humans would be up and about soon. The new soldiers in their unfamiliar uniforms quickened their pace.

There were no guards at the castle gates. The old doors had been closed but not barred and within minutes they were all in the courtyard. The only signs of activity came from the kitchens. The group split up, officers taking their men, as planned, to the various entryways. Then, upon a signal from the leader, the rampage began. Men and women died without knowing what was going on. There was no resistance worth the name. When the Isphardis regathered in the courtyard some had blood on them, but none of it was their own. Some faces were white, some stomachs queasy, but discipline was maintained. Horses were let out of the stables and shooed out of the castle. The same men who had killed women in their beds balked at destroying horses. The countinghouse was emptied of its coffers and then the castle was put to the torch.

An abortive attempt was made to fire the cane fields, but the stalks were still too green to catch. The peasants' cottages, however, caught rapidly and blazed as thatch and dried-out timber burst into flame. Those men and women who, thinking the fire at the castle was a natural occurrence, had not fled were easily dispatched. Then, the grim work done, the Isphardis returned to their boats and set off back downstream, leaving docks, warehouses and plant bright beacons signaling destruction. A pall of smoke obscured the risen sun.

The trip downriver was faster by far than the ascent had

been. The current aided arms made tired from rowing up and from the swinging of swords. While there was no longer a need for caution, words were few. The mission had been a success. They had done what they had been commanded to do, but there was no feeling of joy among them. For most it was as well that the fires were at their backs and that the river was hastening them away. As they swept around the final curve and met the incoming swells from the sea, the manor house up on the cliff to their left was smoldering, the timbered top floors gone, the stone of the ground floor blackened. Their comrades had obviously been equally successful. Isphardel's first counterstrike against the Empire had gone off without a hitch. There would be grog in the messes come noon. There would be time to forget before they reached the next target farther down the coast. It was only a name now. Quern. Within the sennight it would become a place.

Malum sat tight-lipped, face drained of color. The hands resting on the desk in front of him were bunched into fists, the knuckles white. The man who stood before him in the room that he used as a workplace was travel-stained, his stance lopsided from weariness. It had taken five days of almost nonstop riding to reach Angorn. One horse had died under him and two more had gone lame.

"You will say that again, slowly." Malum's voice was as tight as his fists.

"My lord, a thousand men attacked from the sea. Before they landed, the main house was bombarded by the ships. Great iron balls crashed through the walls and brought down the roof. A fire started in the kitchens and spread to the stables and granaries. By the time the soldiers came ashore, all was in chaos. We never stood a chance. Once they had disposed of us they marched inland and burned the manors of Perdom and Chalfont. They trampled down the crops and slaughtered most of the livestock. They took some carcasses back to the ships with them, along with some live hogs and fowl, casks of wine. I do not know how many of our people died . . ."

"And how came you to survive, Mathrion?" Malum asked suspiciously.

"I had been away collecting taxes in the Shire, my lord," the man said quickly, fearfully. "I rode in the following day and by then there was no sign of the raiders or their ships."

"So you never saw the murdering swine."

"No, Lord, but there were a few who escaped, most left for dead. They said the men wore uniforms with linked circles emblazoned on their tabards."

"Isphardis," Malum hissed. He rose from his chair, leaning on the still-clenched fists. "Isphardis, may the Mother blind and wither them." He straightened up, his own eyes staring out as if sightless. "Gone," he said softly, "all gone. All mother's hard work, all my stewardship, all destroyed by those bastards." He fell silent and did not move.

Mathrion waited until the silence frightened him. "My lord," he murmured, "I used part of the tax money to pay for horses to get here. I made the best speed I knew how."

"What? Oh yes; yes, you did well." He seemed to see the man as if for the first time, taking in his bedraggled condition. "Go and find my bodyservant Brandwin. He will get you food, some clothes and a place to sleep." He waved a vague dismissal. Mathrion bowed and turned to leave. He had expected the young master to be upset, but not to the point that he forgot to ask about the rest of the tax money. He made his exit before it came to mind.

Half an hour later Malum stood before the Emperor. Varodias was still dressed in his hawking clothes, with the stout leather patches at wrists and shoulders. His demeanor made it plain that he was not pleased to have been interrupted.

"We were told that this matter would not wait," he said coldly.

"I regret that that is true, Your Imperial Majesty," Malum

replied. He had his emotions firmly in control, though there was still a knot of anger in his chest. "A sennight ago the Isphardis attacked the region around Quern. I am told that about a thousand troops participated. They razed three manors, mine included, slaughtered the inhabitants—men, women and children—destroyed the crops and the livestock. They came by sea, they were well organized, they wore uniforms. This was no marauding band of pirates. They sported the insignia of Isphardel."

Varodias' mouth tightened in anger. "Again? Those heathen dogs have violated our territory again? Killed our people?" The voice was high, almost out of control.

Again? Malum thought. When was the first time? How did the Emperor know and he did not? If it had taken a sennight for the news from Quern to reach him and he had heard no whisper of the other attack, either the two events were close in time or his network of informers, both in the countryside and here at Angorn, were totally inadequate. He decided to gamble. There really was no other option. Not with Varodias.

"Indeed, Sire, and so close together, relatively speaking."

Varodias stopped pacing and looked over his shoulder at his Secretary. "You did not see fit to inform us of the first attack?" he asked, almost conversationally.

"I was aware, Sire, that your sources had informed you at the same time that I received the news," he lied smoothly. "I assumed that you would have summoned me if you wished to consult me." He took a breath. "The really troubling thing is the use of cannons by the enemy."

"The use of cannons? Impossible!" Varodias thundered.

Malum heaved a silent sigh of relief. The gamble had paid off. "Oh," he said, as lightly as he was able with the blood still throbbing in his ears, "they may not have used them on the first attack, but they certainly did when they reduced Quern to rubble."

"Are you sure?" Varodias was standing, hands on hips, staring at him.

"There can be no doubt, Liege Lord. My reports say that large, iron balls battered down my ancestral home. They came from the ships riding offshore."

"Impossible," Varodias exclaimed. "It would take too much coal, and where would they get the coal?"

"We are talking about Isphardis, Sire. They buy, they sell, they take in barter.

"Nevertheless, if they have the secret of the cannon, we are speaking of treason within our ranks." He paused and his face darkened. "Treason within our own household. How else could they have acquired the secret of the cannon?"

"I cannot say, Sire," Malum said unctuously. "I have not taken the liberty of spying upon Your Imperial Majesty's personal servants. I take it, however, that there have been no reports of cannons stolen?"

"None."

"Then it is likely that the design rather than the instruments were stolen. It may well have happened some time ago. These machines cannot have been easily duplicated, especially in a country with no scientific expertise." He gave the Emperor's back a speculative look. "Tell me, Your Majesty, was the secret of the cannon shared with any other Elector-Scientist? To spread the load of research?" Malum had already formulated a list of Electors he would like to implicate in this scandal, ones that had shown no love for him.

Varodias considered. "I discussed certain problems with the Elector of Waldermeer, but they were purely technical. That man is a scientist first and an Elector only by accident of birth." The Emperor's tone was dismissive. "The man is no traitor."

"Nevertheless, Sire, as unworldly as he is, he could have discussed the construction of cannons with someone who appeared to him to be interested only in the theoretical aspects.

He would not have intended to betray Your Majesty, but the
end result would have been the same. I think, perhaps, he
should come to Angorn for questioning."

"Agreed," Varodias said shortly.

"Is there anyone else, Sire, of whom you are unsure? Someone in the program perhaps?" He felt calm now, in control of
things. The knot behind his breastbone had dissolved.

"None that I can think of—for now."

"Very well, but, should something occur to you, no matter
how small, we should investigate it. There may be a ring that is
selling Umbrian secrets to the enemy. If the cannon, why not
the rotifer? This is something that we should pursue with
vigor."

"Traitors," Varodias said, spitting the word out. "Traitors in
our midst. We must root them out, Quern, we must make an
example of them." There was a mad glint in his eye, a sort of
detached heat fueled by something deep within.

Normally speaking, Malum would have retreated from that
look. He had seen it before and it boded no good. Now, however, he had nothing to lose. His estates had been burned to the
ground, proof positive that he was no traitor and while the Emperor was in this disassociated mood, he was suggestible. He
had lost so much, why should he not gain some advantage from
the situation?

"If Your Majesty permits, I shall institute an inquiry into
this matter. It would be best if I could summon suspects under
your seal. Since we are dealing both with matters of state and
scientific expertise, that may require bringing a number of Electors to Angorn under guard. May I have permission to use Imperial troops if need be?" It was a bold thrust for someone of his
rank.

"You may. If we cannot extirpate the enemy within, what
hope have we against those who threaten us from without?
Traitors must be rooted out. They must die for their treason.
Examples must be made." The Emperor's voice had risen stead-

ily and now he was glaring at Malum as if he could make his point more forcefully with his eyes than with his tongue.

"Your Imperial Majesty's command is mine to obey," Malum said, worried that he had gone too far, and bowed. "I will have a writ prepared for your seal and signature and I promise you that I shall not rest until this traitor is rooted out."

Varodias seemed to relax a little. The rigidity went out of his shoulders and the madness ebbed from his eyes. "You have suffered in our cause," he said with a trace of returning warmth. "Your lands have been devastated. We must do something about that." His head bobbed, perhaps confirmingly, but it looked as if an inexperienced puppeteer was pulling the strings.

"Your Majesty is too generous," Malum said, warily, with another bow.

"Aye, we must dispatch troops south to try to ensure that this sort of thing does not happen again," the Emperor said with reassuring brusqueness.

"Where would you station them, Sire?" Malum ventured. "They come from the sea. They come and go as they please. We cannot even guess where they will strike next."

"Quite right," Varodias replied shortly. "The only two places we know they will not appear are Quern and Cromlin. Nevertheless, if we do not send troops, the south will feel abandoned and that breeds disaffection. See to it."

"Of course, Sire." Malum was surprised. Such an order had never come from someone of his rank. He would have to convey the order with self-deprecating firmness and hope that the Emperor had not changed his mind if the order was challenged.

"May I ask, Sire," he said, emboldened, "how you plan to answer this dastardly attack?"

"Oh, they will suffer," Varodias said, walking over to the one comfortable chair in the room and seating himself. "This cannot go unpunished. The Isphardis have taken this to an entirely new level and now they must pay for it." He looked at Malum, a weighing look that made the recipient feel uncomfortable. "We shall take counsel with our military leaders and then we shall take action. These depredations must be answered. In the meantime, anyone caught trading with the Isphardis will be hanged. Do we make ourselves clear?"

"Entirely, Sire," Malum began, but his words were silenced by a rap on the door. The Chamberlain entered.

"Imperial Majesty," the man said with a deep bow. "Forgive the interruption, but the Court awaits you in the Lesser Throne Room."

Varodias' face darkened momentarily and then he nodded. "Send my gentleman of the wardrobe to me." He turned his attention back to Malum. "Good my Secretary, do you attend us in the anteroom and we shall proceed together."

Malum bowed and backed out swiftly. The Emperor had said nothing about restitution for the damage he had suffered, but to enter a full Court gathering with the Emperor was a signal mark of favor.

He followed Varodias down the corridors to the Lesser Throne Room, a chamber larger than most Great Halls in Electoral palaces. The room was more than half-full with courtiers and their wives. The senior officers of the Household were ranged on either side of the throne. The fanfare of trumpets silenced the crowd and into that silence Varodias paced, with Malum ten steps behind him. He took a place to the left of the throne with the lesser officials. Varodias strode up onto the dais, turned and sat. He surveyed the gaily appareled throng.

"My lords, ladies, gentlemen of the Household," he began. The voice was deeper than usual. "We have had bad news. Our southern coast has been attacked by the itinerant dogs of Isphardel. Manors have been sacked. Our subjects have been killed and subjected to rapine. Fields have been set alight, herds slaughtered." He paused to let the facts sink in. "The offense," his voice became more clipped and rose in register, "is intolerable." He turned his head and looked at Malum. "Master Secretary, would you come before us?"

Malum advanced. This was not to his liking. He had always operated in the shadows and now he was being brought forward in front of the Court.

"My Lord of Quern," Varodias said, easily, gently. "Are we correct in saying that your ancestral lands were attacked by the enemy?"

He bowed. "Indeed, Your Imperial Majesty. There have been reports of one thousand men coming ashore." He knew better than to mention the cannons.

"Are we right in saying that there was no resistance. That your estates were overrun with scarcely an arrow being loosed?" The Emperor's tone stayed light and inquisitive, but Malum froze, scenting a trap, but not quite sure in which direction it was laid.

"My men were taken by surprise, Your Imperial Majesty. They were overwhelmed before they had a chance." There was a rustle from the courtiers behind him. They sensed that something was in the wind.

"An example of lax guardianship from afar," Varodias said over Malum's head, aiming his remark at the crowd. There was a murmur of assent. "In fact, my Lord of Quern," Varodias continued, rising, alarmingly, from the throne, breaking all precedent, "would you not say that your guardianship of our coast has been entirely inadequate? That you have failed to protect the borders of our realm?"

Malum's brain raced. What was the man talking about? The southern shore had never been considered a "border of the realm" in that sense. Surely everybody knew that. It didn't matter, he suddenly realized. He was being manipulated. All those soft words in the inner sanctum were a disguise. He was going to be punished for being the bearer of bad tidings. He was going to be humiliated publicly and there was nothing he could do but stand there meekly, with the Court laughing at his discomfiture. Bile coated the back of his throat.

The Emperor walked down the steps from the throne,

slowly, so as to heighten the drama. He stopped on the last step so that he could maintain the advantage of height.

"My Lord of Quern," he said, the voice clear and high. "We find that you have been derelict in your duty toward us. Perhaps if you spent more time on your estates, if you had a greater care for the welfare of this realm, this affront to our Empire would not have happened."

Malum stared up at his Emperor, mesmerized. He was close enough to see that Varodias' eyes were bloodshot and that his mouth was working. He felt a thrill of visceral fear.

Varodias drew in a breath and then spat directly at Malum's shoes. A white glob splattered against the silver buckle on the right black shoe and began to sag downward. Malum stood there transfixed. His eyelids seemed glued open and he did not think that his limbs would answer him. His brain was slow to accept the message. The Emperor had spat upon him. Dimly he heard Varodias' voice saying,

"You may leave us now. You have displeased us."

He had no clear memory of how he left the chamber. His world was in ruins. He had been betrayed. The man whom he had served all of these years had publicly accused him of something that he couldn't possibly have done anything about. It was so senseless. It was so unfair. And then the Emperor had spat at him. His father had spat at him . . .

XIII

❧ ❧ ❧

N axania of Paladine was pacing back and forth in front
of the throne. She was talking to herself, but for public consumption. "Stupidity," she said, "sheer blind stupidity.
What are those benighted Oligarchs thinking of? Have they no
sense? No, of course they have no sense; no sense of tradition,
no notion of how to rule, no common sense. A vast emptiness
to be filled by trade and greed and profit. They cannot see
beyond their purses."

She turned and recognized the assembled nobles as if she
had been unaware of their presence. Her face cleared. "Come
forward, sirs, come forward." She opened her hands in welcome. "We hope you have not been too long awaiting." She
raised her left hand and massaged her temples with her thumb
and middle finger. "The burdens of the Crown are constant
and, on occasion, they consume our attention." The voice
sounded apologetic even in the cadences of the Formal Mode,
the mouth was crooked into a smile, but the eyes, black in this
light, had no apology in them at all.

Jarrod stood at the back of the crowd as usual, not because

he was shy or because his rank did not merit a place in the front row, but because he was so much taller than anyone else. She was up to something, no doubt about that. Bunglebirds from his informants had kept him abreast of developments in Isphardel and he'd expected the Royal Council to be summoned, but this was a much more public gathering. He scanned the crowd. All the usual faces except for Osmir Dan. Had the favorite fallen from grace? He was jerked back from speculation by the cold and practical tone in Naxania's voice.

". . . has, of course, retaliated to these attacks upon his southern shores, but, somewhat surprisingly, his attempts to cross the Upper Illuskhardin have been repulsed. In Songuard, the clans have been attacking Imperial troops. It is only a matter of time, however, before the Imperial armies gain the upper hand." She was standing before the throne, raised a few steps above the rest. She looked thoroughly regal in a white gown stiffened by an elaborate embroidery of pearls. She wore a ruff around her throat, short in the front and flaring high behind her head. It suited her, Jarrod thought, but it had been out of fashion for at least five years. Curious.

"The Isphardi Ambassador has come before us," she continued, "to invoke the military assistance clause in the Treaty of Partition. We seek your advice." She sat herself gracefully on the throne. From somewhere she produced a small fan and flicked it open. "Perhaps the Mage can tell us what the mood in Celador is like." She smiled at Jarrod over the heads of the others.

He was practiced enough not to appear surprised and responded on cue. "I understand, Majesty, that there has been a meeting of the Queen's Council at which the events in the east were discussed. I believe the consensus was that the Empire's incursions into Isphardi territory on the Alien Plain preceded the attacks on the coast of Umbria and that the Umbrians are the aggressors in this war. If Paladine enters the war, Arundel will follow. I think the reasoning was that, since our border is so much closer to the Empire than theirs, we should make the first move." He made the obligatory bow.

"Our Cousin of Arundel is ever mindful of our estate," Naxania said somewhat acidly. "What think you, my lords. Should we take up the cause of Isphardel?"

"If Your Majesty permits?" The words came from Sir Patrus Braise, one of her commanders.

"Say on, sirrah." She waved the fan.

The cavalryman cleared his throat. "The Imperial Army is well equipped, has been kept active quelling domestic disturbances and outnumbers us. Despite the valor of our men, I doubt if we could prevail at this time."

"We agree," Naxania said, favoring him with a smile. "It would be foolish to be unprepared. That is why we intend to resummon the Farod and impose a hearth tax to pay for arms, provisions and training." She paused. "I have also recalled the Lord Darius of Gwyndryth to take charge of our forces once more." The fan snapped back together. "Now, let the discussion begin."

You sly creature, you, Jarrod thought. So that's why the water clock of fashion has been set to run upward and why Osmir Dan has been banished. Well, I can't fault your choice, but it's going to play merry havoc with Marianna.

The man whose motives were discussed sat in a padded chair in one of his withdrawing rooms. Opposite, sipping sherris, sat the Mother Supreme. Other than the omnipresent servants, who might as well have been invisible, the only other occupants of the room were two hunting kites on stands by the window.

"It is not customary," Varodias said, "for priestesses to accompany armies in the field."

"Yes," Estrala replied, "it is a shame that so many men have been returned to the bosom of the Mother without the consolations of the Church."

"The battlefield is no place for a woman."

"But Your Imperial Majesty cannot deny that women habitually accompany the army." She caught the look on his face and smiled gently. "We of the Church are not so unworldly that we are ignorant of prostitutes and camp followers."

"Be that as it may," Varodias felt flustered, "the battlefield is no place for priestesses to be. The conditions are hard and the men are rough."

"I would hope that there is sufficient respect for the Church, even among your soldiers, to keep a priestess from being violated. We pass among the common people every day and come to no harm, and they lack the discipline that your troops are supposed to have."

"We see no reason to put temptation in their path." He tried to sound righteous.

"Temptation is everywhere, Sire," she said, taking a sip of her wine. She looked up blandly. "Why, if you tried to have your way with me in this very room, the servants would make no move to stop you." The eyes were wide and innocent. Varodias' mouth worked but no words came. "But you would not because you respect my office and my holy calling," she concluded.

Was there a wisp of regret in her voice? he wondered. "The situation is hardly analogous," he said as severely as he could. "We are afraid, dear Mother Supreme, that you have failed to persuade us." He stopped and thought for a moment. "We take your point about dying without the consolations of the Church, however, and we see no reason why your priestesses should not accompany the Wisewomen. The tents where they tend the wounded should be perfectly safe." He sat back, pleased with himself.

"Your Imperial Majesty is entirely too gracious," Estrala said, inclining her head and omitting to mention that priestesses already did that.

"We shall make a note to our Secretary about it," he added.

"Ah, and how is my Lord of Quern?" she asked. "One sees so little of him these days."

"His estates were put to the torch by the accursed Isphardis, so we have given him some time to be private, but we cannot let him maunder forever."

"That is very thoughtful of you, Your Majesty," Estrala said. "I hope he appreciates it." She had heard that Quern had been disgraced, but nothing ever seemed to be certain in Angorn. She smiled at the Emperor and prepared to be charming.

Malum, for his part, sat in his rooms in another wing of the palace and brooded. He was not in the least bit pleased at the Emperor's failure to summon him, though he had no wish to be made the object of the sovereign's public wrath again. Brandwin had brought him reports of two other occasions on which Varodias had lost his temper with senior members of the Household. Since none of his privileges had been rescinded, he had decided that he had not been singled out for disgrace. He was still not happy with the way things were.

The Emperor was spending entirely too much time with the Mother Supreme for Malum's liking. He didn't trust the woman. Besides, he knew what the Church's attitude to bastardy was. No blame for the mother, for she had fulfilled her sacred duty by having a child. What blame there was attached itself to that child, especially if it was a male child. What would she think if she knew about his parentage? He snorted quietly to himself. The Mother Supreme and the Emperor were the last people in the world he could tell his secret to.

He shook his head. Dwelling on that and on the recent past was pointless. He needed something that would get him back in the Emperor's good graces. For a start he could arrange for the Elector of Waldermeer to be brought to Angorn. It would be pleasant to summon some of the others as well, but, for the time being, that could wait. It would be best to tread softly. When the time came, though, those who had laughed at him would suffer. Yes indeed they would.

Across the Alien Plain, where the wind blew clean and bracing, bending the tops of the unending grasses, the problems and pettiness of Court life had no place. Indeed, there was so little of man under the vast bowl of the sky that humankind itself seemed insignificant, and yet it was here that some part of the future of Strand might develop. That at least was the hope of the small group of humans who stood on the battlements of the castle and looked south toward the inhabited part of the world beyond the horizon.

Jarrod and Marianna stood beside Joscelyn and a young Magister from the Collegium called Allathwyn. Jarrod couldn't bring his first name to mind and that irritated him. Time was, he thought, when I remembered everything. He glanced down at his wife. She looked so small, surrounded by Magicians. When they had arrived that morning, she had had a long, tearful, reunion with Joscelyn. Jarrod had left them alone together and Marianna had not said what had passed between them, but Jarrod was gratified to see that Joscelyn had put on a clean gown and that his beard had been trimmed.

On the plain below a score of unicorns grazed or raced across the savanna in joyful abandon. Marianna put her arm through Jarrod's. "I haven't seen so many unicorns at one time since the Island at the Center," she said with a sigh. "It's such a beautiful sight."

"And almost all of them are descended from Amarine."

"It's amazing to think that it all started with three little colts." She shook her head. "And it seems like only yesterday, but Nastrus has grey in his whiskers and grown offspring of his own."

A solid-looking unicorn materialized in the grassy forecourt below. "Ah, and that, if I'm not mistaken, is Malloran," Jarrod said.

Marianna looked up at her son, saw his rapt face and smiled. "Undoubtedly," she concurred. "I have a feeling that's what I look like when I'm around Amarine. Let's go down and meet him."

As they emerged from the castle, Marianna faltered and Jarrod grabbed her shoulders to steady her. He was already in touch with Malloran and knew that the unicorn had reached out to her mind.

"Are you all right?" he asked.

"Oh yes. I just wasn't prepared for it."

"Can you hear him well?" Jarrod knew the answer from what he could read in Malloran's mind. It was bizarre to know what his wife was feeling through a third party.

"Not as clearly as I would like. I have to concentrate and, even then, some of the images are blurred."

'It is an honor to meet with my great-grandam's great friend,' Malloran said. And Jarrod knew that the remark was addressed to Marianna.

'How is she?' The question was faint but clear.

'She does not gallop much anymore and she no longer responds to the rut, but she is well enough and much venerated.' There was great fondness around the thought. 'But you did not come here to discuss my family.'

'No,' Jarrod agreed, 'we came to hear more of your plan for humans and unicorns.'

'And to see if you can help us against the Umbrians,' Joscelyn broke in.

'We are not at war with the Empire,' Jarrod cautioned.

'Well we bloody well ought to be,' Joscelyn declared hotly.

'The fact that this particular herd of humans has put a bounty' (the idea of bounty was a hard one for the unicorn to formulate) *'on my kind puts my whole idea in jeopardy,'* Malloran interposed swiftly.

'Can you explain . . .'

'The basic concept is very simple. I want to see unicorns and humans living together in harmony. Given the current situation, however, I think that it would be best if there was a certain distance between the two species.'

'How would you begin to put this plan into effect?' Jarrod asked.

'I would return to the Island at the Center and try to persuade others to come back down here with me.' He moved his neck gracefully toward the plain below. *'The conditions are ideal for unicorns, but I should need certain assurances from humankind before I could do that.'* He turned his attention back to Marianna. *'You could come with me if you like and see Amarine.'*

Marianna's response was tinged with regret. *'I wish I could, but I have young children to look after.'* The tone turned rueful. *'Also, I am not as young as I was.'*

'What kind of assurances?' Jarrod asked.

'An area that is ours alone and guarantees of our safety.'

'We'll have to defeat the Umbrians before we can do that,' Joscelyn said. *'You'd help us, wouldn't you?'* It was a question that Jarrod had already asked.

Jarrod was aware that Malloran had clamped down a tight control on his feelings. *'That would be up to the unicorns,'* Malloran said evenly.

This is a formidable young unicorn, Jarrod thought.

'I thank you for that,' Malloran said in a corner of his mind.

Jarrod allowed humor to surface and then said seriously, *'You will at least consider it?'*

'I shall consider it,' he replied gravely, *'but you and I have been over this ground before.'*

Jarrod bowed his head in acknowledgment. There was, he knew, no point in pursuing matters further. *'We thank you. You know that we support your idea and that we shall do anything in our power to bring it into being. We too, alas, cannot speak for all Strandkind.'*

The group broke up. Marianna took her son off for a walk and Jarrod chatted with Allathwyn to try to get to know him better.

"Are we looking for allies if it comes to war?" the younger Magician asked as they strolled across the grassy peninsula on which the castle was built. His accent confirmed what his name had indicated, that he was from Arundel's Southern Marches.

"Even if they agreed, I don't know what they could do. We're certainly not going to ride them into battle. By the way, could you understand anything of what was going on?"

"Not a thing," Allathwyn confessed with a grin. "It was passing strange. You all just stood there with blank faces. I knew you were talking to each other, if that's the right word, but I couldn't hear a thing."

"As far as I can gather, and I suppose that Marianna and I are the resident experts, not everyone can communicate with unicorns and even those that can, cannot contact every one. It may come with practice, but you'll need a unicorn to cooperate. I'll mention it to Malloran before we leave."

"I should be grateful, Excellence."

"And speaking of leaving, I wonder where that reprobate Nastrus is?" Jarrod was aware as he spoke the words how flat and inadequate mere speech was. If this earnest young man was a unicorn, he would have known exactly how Jarrod felt about his friend. It made him think of the advantages of having unicorns on Strand and reminded him how different the two species were.

XIV

☙ ☙ ☙

There weren't many settlements out on the Alien Plain north of Paladine. The government had done nothing to encourage them. There were some, though, carved out of the vast savanna by ambitious younger sons or desperate peasants. The government had done nothing to discourage them either. They represented a physical presence in the wilderness, proof positive that the Crown's sway extended into the new lands. Some of the early settlers came slinking back to Stronta, defeated by the ever-present wind and the lack of timber, but most seemed to stay, or else died out there with no one to bring the word back. Folks rode out beyond the Upper Causeway as they always had, but they only went so far and they were back for supper.

One of the pioneers who did not fit men's notions was Gareth Bord. He was an energetic man in his thirties who had made a fortune in the linen trade. Five years before his wife and child had died in a boating mishap. He had since remarried, but his second wife was displeased with the family home. There were too many reminders of his previous life. So he bought a large tract of land from the Crown, situated at the eastern end of what some people were calling New Paladine. He built a substantial farm, drilled wells and erected windmills to irrigate his crops, moved in a herd of prize kina, hired men to work the fields and began a whole new life. He became a familiar figure in the markets of Stronta.

He had sent a party out to track down some strays from the herd. When they caught up with them, they found that an Umbrian patrol had already come across them, had killed and eaten one and were preparing to drive the rest back to their base. Heated words had been exchanged, anger had flared, swords were drawn and two of Bord's men were wounded. The kina were herded away by the Umbrians. Gareth Bord was a big man, tall and broad-shouldered, considered handsome by most women. He made an impact when he walked into a room and he was formidable when roused. A sennight after the encounter with the Umbrians, he arrived at the palace demanding justice and restitution. That was the beginning of what became known as the Bord Incident.

Two squadrons of cavalry were sent off into what was perceived as the wild. It was supposed at Court that they would find nothing, that the Umbrians would have withdrawn. That was not the case. The Paladinian force came upon a small Imperial contingent about ten leagues east of the supposed boundary line and routed them. Who attacked whom depended on the teller of the tale. What is certain is that the waist-high grasses caught and burned out of control for sennights, leaving a broad swath of the Plain black and denuded. Naxania promptly sent in more cavalry and called the Farod back to active duty.

Darius of Gwyndryth's appearance at Stronta in the middle of all this activity was not greeted with rejoicing in all quarters. The Queen was warm and welcoming and he sat at her right hand at Hall. Those who saw the two together from close range commented on a certain reserve on the part of the old warrior. The younger courtiers put it down to his old-fashioned ways.

The older ones, who knew their history, read other things into his behavior. Those who had backed away from the Dan faction began to have second thoughts. Darius himself was blissfully unaware of all of that.

He had thought long and hard when Naxania's request had reached him. His first feelings had been ones of vindication. "For the good of the realm and the love we bear you . . ." her letter had gone in part. The phrase, "the love we bear you," was, of course, standard diplomatic language, but the fact remained that she needed him. The memory of their long affair had been polished during his self-exile and had regained much of its luster, but seeing her again would be painful, he knew that. More to the point, was he still capable of commanding an army? He had left with the flags of his reputation flying high. Why take the risk? Ah, but she said she needed him and who knew the Umbrians better than he. He and Lissen were the only foreigners who had ever fought in the Imperial Army. He wondered what had happened to Lissen. Settled down and gone to seed probably. He stopped his pacing and looked at his naked, wavy reflection in the polished metal of the mirror. Hunting had kept him lean—if you ignored the roundness of the belly. He still had his hair and his teeth. He nodded at himself and called for his steward to help him dress. A sennight later he was on his way to Stronta.

He found Naxania virtually unchanged physically. The figure was a little fuller, but that was no bad thing and the hair was as black and glossy as ever. He was relieved, however, that the sight of her no longer prompted the visceral pull of desire. She did him honor in public and was warm and pleasant in private, but made no overt move to renew their relationship and he was grateful for that. He had a job to do.

The first part of that job was establishing a relationship with Sir Patrus Braise, Commander of the Queen's Horse. He found Braise to be a rather dour man in his early thirties who had seen service at the tail end of the Outland wars. Conversation revealed him to be a sound theoretician, but with no experience of actual command in the field. He was polite and helpful and if he harbored resentment, he hid it well. They sat their horses side by side as the cavalry went through their paces outside the walls. Darius made approving comments on the condition of the mounts and the turnout of the soldiers. Indeed, they made pretty figures on the parade ground. How they would respond to rough conditions and how well they could fight remained to be seen.

Once the exercise was over, he made his way back to the apartment at the palace through the streets of Stronta. People, remembering that he was the man who had put down the rebellion against the Queen and spared the kingdom civil war, cheered him. It pleased him that they should still think well of him and he waved back. He was in a good mood as he let himself into the antechamber. He sat down on the bench by the wall and held his boot out to Semmurel, whom he had brought along as his personal bodyservant.

"Once you get me out of this uniform, I want a bath," Darius said. "Parade grounds are dusty places, especially with several hundred horses trampling around. No, on second thought, first some cold ale and then a bath."

"The cold ale is in the great chamber, Holdmaster, but I think the bath will have to wait," Semmurel replied with the license permitted to longtime retainers. He tackled the other boot.

"And why, may I ask?" Darius was prepared to humor him, up to a point.

"Because you have a guest. I put him in the great chamber and brought him ale."

"What's his name?"

"He would not say, Holdmaster. He said he was an old friend of yours and he seemed a harmless enough old man."

"Get my slippers," Darius ordered, standing up. He opened the door to the withdrawing room and strode in. He stopped and a smile grew across his face.

"By the gods, what a sight for sore eyes." He opened his arms and Otorin of Lissen got up and came over. The two men hugged briefly.

"You better get some more ale, Semmurel," Darius said, shuffling into his slippers. "My Lord Lissen and I have some catching up to do."

"What brings you to Stronta?" he asked after they had sat down.

"Arabella sent me when she knew you were coming here."

Darius' eyebrows went up. "News travels very fast. I've only been here a few days."

"Naxania, as is proper, requested her permission for you to serve in the Paladinian forces."

"Yes, of course. I should have done so myself. I must be getting old."

"You've never been too scrupulous about getting the sovereign's permission as I recall. When I was serving as your 'squire' in Umbria, you fought first and got permission afterward." Both men smiled.

"So, she's brought you out of retirement, has she?" He regarded his old friend fondly. "Well, we'll soon have that extra weight off you, though there's nothing we can do about the hair." They fell silent as Semmurel returned with a second mug and the extra ale, served and retreated.

"Oh no, not this time," Otorin resumed. "I'm too old for fighting. I've a wife and children at home. No, all you'll get out of me is information."

"Ah, so you've been keeping your hand in."

Otorin shook his head. "Not really. I've talked to my successor. The old network is still pretty much intact, though a few of my sources have died—of old age and illness I'm glad to say. Some of my better informants were Isphardis who traded with the Empire. That's stopped, of course, but I doubt if the picture has changed much. Which d'you want first, political or military?"

"Oh, military by all means."

Otorin took a long pull at his ale before starting. "Our best guess at his forces is ten thousand cavalry and twice that number of infantry. The Electors are being pressured to equip more men. He has been stretched thin by having to keep troops in three areas. His son is in command of a force that is trying to move down the valleys of Songuard. They are encountering unexpectedly stiff opposition from the clans. Prince Coram is in nominal command, but the real general is our old friend Estivus of Oxenburg. He also commands the cavalry units that are occupying the Isphardi part of the Plain."

"I'm sorry to hear that," Darius said. "He's a capable officer."

"Luckily for you," Otorin said with a chuckle, "his reinforcements have been diverted to other fronts. His headquarters are at Fort Bandor, by the way. The Umbrians also have troops along the east side of the Illuskhardin somewhere between the Saradondas and Lake Grad. They tried going down the western valley, but were forced to pull back. On top of all that, Varodias has had to send cavalry to guard the south against Isphardi raids. Thankless task. They hit, they return to their ships, they sail out of sight and they hit again. No way to predict where they'll land and they resupply themselves from the holds they sack."

"Why bother to try?"

"Politics. The Emperor cannot afford to let the southern Electors think that he has abandoned them if he expects to get their support. And he needs their support. So far Varodias has very little to show for his efforts, except the territory north of the Upper Causeway, both Songean and Isphardi, but that is empty land. It won't last, of course. The Umbrians have superior numbers and, with one important exception, superior weaponry."

"And that exception?"

"Remember the cannon that Varodias was so proud of?"

"I do," Darius said with a touch of distaste.

"Nothing you need worry about in my opinion. They are virtually immobile and they are only effective against a stationary target. Besides, the Umbrians are so besotted with their steam technology that they rely on it for far too much. When it comes to firing cannons, they can't build up sufficient thrust to do very much damage. The Isphardis, on the other hand, have come up with a black powder that does the job. The irony is that the Umbrians have much the same thing, which they use in their arquebuses. The cannons were one of Varodias' monopolies and he hasn't done any meaningful scientific work in years."

"Have they improved on the arquebus?"

"No. It's still awkward to load and needs to be rested on something to be accurate. Bows are still faster and more effective. If they do make improvements, that could change, but I don't think you need worry about them in this campaign. They'll be using the battlewagons they captured from the Outlanders, unless I miss my guess. Varodias' team has done work on them, produced a kind of armored steam chariot. They didn't crack the problem of the armament, though."

"The gods be thanked for that at least," Darius said drily.

"Got a campaign strategy mapped out yet?"

"Have to put an army together first. Then we have to chase the Umbrians out of the occupied territories. That'll be the easy part. Holding the border against them will be the problem."

"I agree. My advice would be to strike quickly. With all that relatively flat ground and all that grass, it'll have to be a cavalry operation. That gives you some extra time to train infantry. What kind of support are you going to get from the Discipline? That might make the difference."

"I have heard nothing. You've been at Celador, no doubt. The Archmage make any kind of committment?"

"Nothing substantial. I'd have a word with that son-in-law of yours if I were you. Now, you ready for the political side?"

Darius shook his head. "I'd rather hear what you've been up to since Sparsedale. Then you can tell me what the situation in this country is. That's more important for the moment than what's happening in the Empire."

The reminiscences lasted until the evening meal, when Darius had to attend the Queen once more, and resumed afterward. As a result, Darius' head was feeling a trifle empty the next morning. He was not best pleased when Semmurel announced another visitor.

"Send 'em away," he growled. "Make it sound polite."

"I am your Lordship's liege man, but, in this instance, I dare not obey you."

Darius groaned. "Show Her Majesty in."

Semmurel smiled slyly. "Not the Queen, my lord. Far more dangerous." He turned and opened the antechamber door. "The Lady Marianna, Duchess of Abercorn," he announced.

Darius was on his feet in a trice, arms held wide.

"Father." She came into his embrace and was lifted briefly from the floor. All traces of lingering resentment seemed to be leached away in the hug.

"How well you look," he said, beaming and holding her at arm's length to look at her.

"As do you. Oh, it is good to see you."

"Semmurel, chai and some sweetcakes. On the double." He handed her to a cushioned chair. "How are the children?" he asked.

"Thriving. The servants at Oxeter dote on them and spoil them dreadfully. It has been a long time since there were children there."

"Both you and they are much missed at Gwyndryth."

"And they miss their grandfather. They send their love."

"And are you happy there?"

"I have my duties as Duchess," she said diplomatically, "the more so since Jarrod must spend most of his time here. That is one of the reasons I did not bring them with me on this trip. I think it is important for Jarrod's vassals to feel that the family will be rooted in Oxeter."

"Vassals," Darius said musingly. "I keep on forgetting quite how large the Ducal holdings are." He smiled at her mischievously. "I have tenants and you have vassals. I must make sure to find out how many men-at-arms he has to supply in times of war."

"Five hundred knights, fully accoutered, one thousand foot with pike or bow in helmet and breastplate, together with victuals and fodder for four sennights," she replied promptly. "They are presently camped half a league south of the city."

Darius whistled in appreciation. "That many. I must say, that husband of yours has acted with admirable speed. None of the other magnates has provided troops thus far."

She smiled back at him. "That husband of mine has done absolutely nothing. This daughter of yours sent out the summonses and, with the help of his Seneschal, reviewed the troops and checked on the provisions."

"I am proud to call you daughter," he said, and she basked in his approval. He checked himself. "You rode to Stronta at the head of this small army, didn't you?"

"I did," she said proudly.

"Yes, I thought so." He wagged a finger at her. "Now see here, young lady, the last time that there was fighting hereabouts, you defied all orders and went into battle. Damned near got killed for your pains. I'm having none of that this time. I'm in charge this time and you'll not cozen your way around me."

Marianna laughed and signaled the hovering Semmurel to pour her some chai. "I was young then, Papa. I had no husband, I had no children, I had no estates to manage. Rest assured, I have no intention of doing more than waving all you brave men on your way." She looked at him and said more seriously. "Besides, if the Queen really means to fight the Emperor, if all this marching and mustering is more than just a flexing of martial muscle, then I can do more good making sure that there are sufficient crops to keep an army in the field. The Empire is a formidable opponent and the Emperor is a stubborn man. This could be a long and ruinous war."

He reached over and patted her hand. "You and I both know that war is wasteful, but the young men see it differently. They lust for adventure and glory, they think that wounds will produce a comely scar and they never seem to think that death will come to them."

"The more fools they, but even older men," she gave him a sidelong glance, "men who should know better, respond to the call, even as old war-horses, long out to pasture, will prick up their ears at the sound of a bugle."

"I don't do it for pride," he said, "or in an attempt to recapture my youth. I know what to do and how to do it. If I do my job properly, fewer young men will die."

"I know, Father, but that doesn't stop me wishing that you wouldn't. I love you and I don't want to lose you. Promise me that you will be careful. You have this overweening sense of duty, which I respect and admire, but you've done more than your share already. Let the others take the risks."

"Don't worry," he said with what he hoped was a reassuring smile. "I value life too much to throw it away. Well now, you haven't come all this way just to see your father. You'll be off to see Jarrod to let him know that his men are here. I expect he'll want to ride out and see them. Tell him, if you would, that I'd appreciate it if he came by to see me. Shall we say a couple of hours before Hall if he's dining at the palace?"

Jarrod was prompt and Darius was back from another meeting with Patrus Braise, this one on the best way to integrate the Abercorn troops with the Royal forces. The greetings were cordial and Darius complimented his son-in-law on his response to the royal call for soldiers.

"All Marianna's doing," Jarrod replied truthfully. "She made it her business to visit all the castles and estates and she's very thorough when it comes to knowing what obligations are owed."

Darius was pleased by the answer. Most men would have claimed the credit. "Well, the Duchy has certainly done its duty by the Crown. Now I need to know what, as Mage of Paladine, you intend to do to help us in the upcoming campaign."

"The High Council of Magic took a wait-and-see attitude."

"That was before a state of war existed between Paladine and the Empire and, even if the Discipline as a whole held back, surely the Discipline in Paladine could be expected to participate?"

Jarrod produced a tight, little smile. "So Her Majesty has said. Several times; at some length."

"She has a point, does she not?"

"It's not as simple as that. The Discipline has never engaged in conflict against the people of Strand. We fought against the Outlanders, but that was different. What if there was a dispute between Paladine and Talisman, or Arundel, should the Discipline then take sides?"

"That's not the point and you know it," Darius said bluntly. "We're talking about the Empire. The Empire doesn't believe in Magic and it's declared war on the Discipline. How can the Discipline not fight?"

Jarrod sighed and then said softly. "Could you please see that there are no servants in either of the other rooms."

Darius pursed his lips and then rose quietly, went to the door of the bedchamber, opened it and peered inside. He recrossed the withdrawing room and opened the antechamber door. "Semmurel," he said. "Go down to the stables and tell the chief ostler to be sure that my horse is groomed and ready first thing in the morning." He waited until the outer door closed and then resumed his seat.

"Thank you," Jarrod said. "I am sorry to be so suspicious, but there are too many ears at this Court and Naxania is probably nervous enough with fifteen hundred men, supposedly loyal to me, camped outside the capital." He shrugged apologetically. "In the matter of the Discipline's intervention," he continued, "I am entirely with you. Our lack of action does not sit well with the people. Greylock, however, has become exceedingly cautious in his old age and, unless forced by circumstances, I cannot go against his wishes."

"What kind of circumstances would make you defy him?" Darius asked.

"They would have to be fairly drastic, I'm afraid. A direct threat to the country. As things stand, that would mean that you would have to be defeated." He opened his hands, fingers splaying. "Even then, if the Archmage declined to move, I could only call for volunteers from the Outpost. I could not compel them. I myself would engage, whether Greylock permitted it or not, but I do not flatter myself that I could affect the outcome of a war single-handedly."

"You've done it before," Darius reminded him.

"Not alone. I had the unicorns and Ragnor."

"What about the unicorns? I hear that there are more of them about these days. Marianna tells me that Joscelyn was involved with them."

"Did she tell you the whole story?" Jarrod asked warily.

"She did, and you'll get no criticism from me. He's back in favor and that's important." He paused. "By the bye, when I talked with Marianna, she seemed set on staying here. Kerris of Aylwyth is a damned good Seneschal, couldn't ask for better, but Joscelyn will inherit. He's been with you people for most of his life and it's time that he learned how to manage his inheritance. Any chance of his spending some time at Gwyndryth?"

Jarrod caught his lower lip between his teeth and stared off into space for a couple of beats. He focused on Darius again. "Difficult question for me to answer. He's still a political liability. Varodias is unpopular at the moment, so Joscelyn's offense is being overlooked, but there could come a time when it would be politically expedient to hand him over to the Umbrians. From that point of view it would be better if he were out of sight.

"As to Gwyndryth, I'm not too sure at the moment. He's a very strong Talent. He could be one of the great Magicians or he could be a dangerous menace, both to himself and others. When this business is over, I want him back at the Collegium. It is vital that he learn his craft and that he learn control. I've had a number of conversations with him during the course of this business with the Weatherwards and I think he trusts me a little more than he used to. I am still his stepfather, however, and he is headstrong. I'm the last person to give him orders in any other capacity than that of Mage. He's still young and I don't think he knows what he wants to do with his life. The last time we spoke, he wanted to be a Weatherward. I see your point and I understand your concern, but the decision to be a practicing Magician or a Holdmaster must be his. I shall recommend that he spend his holidays at Gwyndryth and, if you have not already done so, you should make it clear that he is more than welcome. More than that I cannot do."

"I'll be grateful for anything you can do. At his age I was betrothed, but I suppose that's too much to ask of a Magician."

Jarrod laughed. "Not necessarily, but if you're hinting that I should talk to the boy about sex and marriage, you've got the wrong man. Joscelyn doesn't want to admit that his mother and I have slept together. He'd much rather believe that Daria and her brother were produced by a spell."

"That's right, leave it all up to grandpa," Darius grumbled good-naturedly. "Perhaps you'll have better luck with the Archmage."

"Oh, I don't think Greylock's interested in sex," Jarrod said teasingly, and the meeting ended on a good note.

XV

❧ ❧ ❧

While Jarrod was thinking about Joscelyn and unicorns, Estivus of Oxenburg was sitting in his room atop Fort Bandor's towers. He had an unobstructed view out over the Causeway to the distant horizon. Grey clouds bearing rain scudded overhead, rain that would be wasted on the empty landscape ahead, rain that would have done so much good had it fallen on Umbria instead; might even have averted this grandiose folly that the Emperor had embarked upon. He had men out there in that waste, men he would rejoin on the morrow: too few of them for the task at hand. This had been a safe posting for the Prince before the clans and the Paladinians had become actively involved. As such it had been irksome for Estivus, whose idea of service to the Empire did not include being nursemaid for the heir to the Empire.

All that had changed. Prince Coram had been properly bloodied in a contest for which he could not have been prepared. Fighting in the last war had been clean, direct, a clear and purposeful crusade against an abominable foe. Now the enemy looked more or less like neighbors. They dressed differently, spoke differently, but were recognizable as fellow beings. Nor did they fight like Outlanders; they certainly did not fight in the traditions of the Imperial Cavalry. They did not stand their ground and fight honorably. They set ambushes, swept down from the hills, killed and ran. It was a war of nerves and attrition, of constant wariness and fear. There were no tactics in Songuard, just constant improvisation and, ironically, the Prince, with his lack of formal military training, was probably a better man for the job than he himself was.

He shoved his legs out in front of him and leaned back in the chair. In the months they had spent together, he had come to know Coram quite well. The man was a series of contradictions. As the Emperor's youngest, and most neglected, son, he had grown up without the burden of other people's expectations. He had not been the center of sycophancy and, as a result, did not give himself airs, though he had a firm view of his overall importance. He regarded his father as divinely appointed and himself as having some kind of special dispensation from the Great Mother. It was a feeling that he had seemed to transmit to his men and it appeared to have generated an intense loyalty. He was bluff, hearty, open, cruel on occasion, caring and highly sentimental on others. All in all, Estivus thought, he might make a good Emperor.

He pulled his legs back under him and stood up. To be successful, Coram needed more men. So did he. Varodias had taken two full companies from his command to combat the Isphardi incursions in the south at the same time that he had ordered the drive southward from Fort Bandor. That left him with precious few men to face the Paladinians. Their troops were green, everybody knew that, but his intelligence had informed him that the Lord Observer, as he used to be known, had been brought in to command them. He began to pace. Darius of Gwyndryth was as much of a hero to the Umbrians as he was to the Magical Kingdoms. He had reorganized the Imperial Cavalry and turned the tide of battle against the Outlanders, saving Angorn in the process. Estivus had served under him and had learned much of what he knew from the man. The fact that they were now on opposite sides and would, sometime in the near future, do battle epitomized for him all that was distasteful in the current state of affairs.

No matter, he told himself as he wheeled around and started to recross the floor, I am sworn to the Emperor and, under that oath, I must do my best to destroy a man I admire and respect. Darius had the upper hand in terms of raw numbers and the best that Estivus had been able to do thus far was to give ground slowly and create the impression that he had troops in reserve, that Darius' victories had been against scouting groups only. He had fallen back to the western end of the nameless lake that ran from the Umbrian border to roughly the middle of the Isphardi territory. He had expected an immediate attack, but Darius had pitched camp about two leagues west and seemed content to stage exercises. The one rotifer that had overflown his lines reported small groups riding around square wooden boxes.

Estivus had smiled to himself on reading the report. Others might think the old Lord Observer mad, but he knew what was afoot. He had gone through just such exercises when he was younger. They were meant to counteract the Outland battlewagons and, indeed, had proved successful. Darius must think that he would have to face them again and was preparing his troops to counter them. They were coming, Darius was right about that, but these days they depended on coal to make them go, and that had yet to be delivered. In the meantime, there were two courses of action open to him. He could attack now, while Darius was occupied with the training, or he could wait and devise a strategy to deal with the Paladinian thrust when it came. His instinct was to attack, but the numbers were against him. He had sent a bunglebird to Angorn a sennight ago requesting reinforcements, but he had no means of knowing when, or if, they would arrive. What he needed was a contingency plan that used his knowledge of Darius' methods. He continued to pace.

"We are not content, Quern." The Imperial voice was high and irritable. The lack of an honorific was notable coming from a monarch who set great store by the niceties.

Malum was nervous. This was the first time that he had appeared before the Imperial presence since . . . his mind flinched away from the memory. The circumstances were not reassuring. He stood alone before the throne, but the Court was marshaled behind him. Alone in a pool of space before the three-step dais, but with the officers of the Household ranged on either side of the throne. It was possible, of course, that this appearance might signal his return to favor, made as public as his rejection had been. Indeed, he had told himself that this was so, but the Emperor's opening words were not promising. He felt small and dowdy in his habitual black in front of all these peacocks. No matter what happens, I shall act with dignity, he vowed to himself.

"I am Your Imperial Majesty's loyal and humble servant," he said and bowed from the waist—but not too far. He was pleased with both his voice and his control.

"You are my servant, certes, and the Mother knows you appear humble enough." Varodias paused and the Court laughed dutifully. Malum's stomach twinged. "However," the voice soared on the word, "for our Secretary to issue a summons in our name to an esteemed Elector might be construed as a sign of overweening pride."

Varodias rose from the throne and slowly peeled off his left glove. He maneuvered slowly, in his high-heeled, high-soled boots and descended. Malum retreated three feet to maintain the proper distance and the Court behind him shuffled back as well.

"We understand your zeal in our behalf," Varodias continued, "indeed we commend it." He paused and smiled at the transfixed Malum. The eyes were quite clear.

Fear blossomed in Malum. Tingling filaments spread through his body and he began to sweat. There was no trace of madness in the Emperor. Anything he said now, he meant to say. What was worse was that he was playing a game and thoroughly enjoying himself. The Emperor started to pace to his right. He twirled the doffed glove in his right hand. He turned and started back toward Malum.

"And if," the glove flicked out, barely missing Malum's nose, "we were to discover that the summons was closed with the Imperial seal, we would be very," the voice underlined the word and then repeated the inflection, "very, displeased."

Varodias stopped in front of Malum, glove twirling idly, moving ever so slowly toward Malum's face. Malum could not move, he wanted to, to take a step back to give the Emperor his proper space, to avoid the glove, but his muscles weren't working. He was still sweating, but his mouth was dry. Incongruous, he thought as his mind darted away from the moment.

"What say you, Master Secretary?" The glove drooped, inches from Malum's face.

He swallowed and summoned a will to speak. "It is true, Sire," he would have used a more flattering honorific, but he didn't trust his tongue, "that I advised the Elector that Your Imperial Majesty wished to confer with him on a matter of mutual scientific interest." His voice responded well and his spirits and his nerve strengthened. If Varodias had already condemned him, there was nothing he could do to save himself. Dignity, he reminded himself.

"I admit that I may have misinterpreted a remark made by Your Imperial Majesty in a private conversation." A most inappropriate and unlikely feeling of daring pushed back the web of fear. Let the assembled throng know that he, Malum of Quern, unacknowledged son of the Emperor, had private talks with that same Emperor. "I did order an Imperial Messenger to take that invitation to the Elector. There was never any question of the use of the Imperial seal. I would have had to go to the Lord Chancellor for that, and I am sure that his Lordship will attest that no such request came before him." He caught the look in the Emperor's eye and stopped. The glove started a lazy swing. The braggadocio went out of him.

"My Liege Lord," Malum began. His voice was higher in his ears than it usually was. Dignity, he said to himself. He need not have bothered.

"We are not content, Quern," Varodias iterated.

As Malum bowed his acquiescence, his left cheek came into brief contact with the glove.

"You may retire, my lord," Varodias said as if nothing had happened. He turned on his heel and mounted the dais. Facing out toward his Court again, both hands were gloved again. "If there was sufficient innate decorum in our Court, there would, by now, be a lane by which the Lord Malum might leave our presence." The voice held disdain and the Court reacted immediately. Malum backed down the gantlet, which seemed to narrow as he approached the doors. Dignity, he reiterated and hoped that he was still on the right line for the doors.

His head was traveling in circles when he found himself out in the corridor. A footman came up to him. "I'm quite all right, thank you," he said testily.

"No, my lord, though I am delighted that Your Lordship is in good health," he added quickly. "His Imperial Majesty has instructed me to tell you to wait presently upon his pleasure. He wishes to see you when the Assembly is over."

A chill ran through him and left him momentarily paralyzed. To return . . . alone, his brain said. This had been a charade then, a puppet show before the Court. He was aware, suddenly, that he had a broad grin plastered across his face. "I thank you," he began, and then broke off and laughed. "I don't even know your name."

"My name doesn't matter, my lord," the young man said, and made an attempt at a bow.

Malum's curiosity was piqued. "I am indebted to you, Squire Anonymous. I approve of your reticence. If ever you should need help, and I can be of service, you may call on me." He paused for a beat. "If you do not wish to give your name, may one ask the name of the lord whom you serve?"

The youngster, proud in his livery up until that moment, wished that he was not wearing it. "The Elector Waldermeer," he admitted.

"You serve him well," Malum said, understanding the young man's need to be reassured. He turned on his heel and walked down the corridor.

The first hundred yards was covered by a coarse-threaded red carpet with a curving pattern of dark blue woven around the edges. It had been put down for this particular occasion. Beyond the fringe were the usual stone flags. He wanted to stay out of sight, but within reach, while he tried to understand what was going on. The boy had pumped up his optimism, but the fact was that there was no way to understand what went on in the Emperor's mind. This whole, terrifying, interlude might be whim, might be an elaborate screen for some plot concocted by Varodias. What, he wondered as he walked up and down, had the members of the Court, not his natural allies, seen when the Emperor's glove was whirling in front of his face? If they thought he had been slapped repeatedly, his career was as good as finished.

He took a turn so as not to be out of earshot of the heralds. There was something going on here that he did not understand. That in itself irritated him. He had used his position to create a network of spies throughout the Empire. He, more than anyone else, more than the Emperor, should have seen this coming. If it was not a failure of his network, then it must mean that Varodias was playing a lone hand, for reasons that Malum could not know. Was this the work of the Mother Supreme? Did she suspect his role in the death of her predecessor? What was the significance of using a page in the Elector of Waldermeer's train? It would be two hours before he was given a chance to find out.

Varodias was sitting at the head of a long, deeply polished, plank table. The throne and the dais were gone. The dark blue and white, almost architectural, decorations stood out in a way that they had not before. Malum approached with trepidation. He had been serving the Emperor for a number of years, had been admitted to his presence more than all but a handful of people, men who had been in his service most of their lives, but he still brought awe with him. He made his bow again.

"You played your part well, if a trifle melodramatically," Varodias said.

What part? Malum asked himself. "To serve Your Imperial Majesty is to be constantly challenged." That's what he said, and he sounded convincing when he said it. What he thought was unfocused and uniformly hostile.

"In times of peace, no one thinks that we would have a spymaster. Now we are at war, everyone expects us to have one. I thought it would be best if you were seen to be out of favor."

"I could have wished that Your Imperial Majesty had been a little less thorough." Malum risked a little joke.

Varodias did not smile. "We should not have had to strike you had you acted less stiff-neckedly. There were very few that saw it." He pursed his lips. "There were far more who heard your words. They're bound to be misreported, but they may win you some sympathy and some confidences." He smiled one of his rote smiles. "All in all, a profitable outcome." He had started to look toward the window, but looked back quickly. "Provided, of course, that you have been keeping up with your work?"

Malum did not blink. You've overplayed your hand, he

thought. You've done it once too often. You've let me see the strategy. "I had very little else to do, Sire."

Varodias looked at him suspiciously and then pushed himself back into his chair. "What is your assessment of the way that the war is going?"

"It is early days, yet, of course, and in early days it is always the established army that is at a disadvantage."

"How so?" Varodias questioned.

Malum felt the familiar tightening in the stomach. Knowing the strategy didn't help. "The enemy is disorganized," he said slowly. "They have no trained forces and so they will not meet the established army on the field of battle. That is where trained armies fight the best." He risked a look at the Emperor and continued with a little more confidence. "You end up with what is happening in Songuard."

The Emperor grunted.

"Your intelligence failed to predict the Isphardi raids and their possession of the cannon . . ."

Malum bowed his head. "I had a highly placed source. She did not serve me well. She is dead. The Isphardis have obviously been preparing for a long time, which accounts for their early success. It cannot last. They lack the resources and the resolve."

"And what of the Magical Kingdoms?"

"Naxania goes through the motions of preparedness and has used the circumstances to levy new taxes. The people are not content. The Farod has been called back to duty, which pleases neither lords nor peasants. She has sent a token force onto the Alien Plain under the old Lord Observer, which does not please her senior officers. Arabella, on the other hand, does nothing."

"We trust that your information is more reliable than it has been of late," Varodias said drily. "In the meantime, you may attend us at tomorrow's levee."

Malum bowed deeply and took his leave. Having regained the safety of the anteroom, he took a deep breath. If he was to attend tomorrow's ceremony, it was a palpable sign that he had the Emperor's confidence once again, but for how long? His own confidence had been badly shaken and he would have to tread softly for a while. Fortunately, he had recruited a new agent who should, if the man were to be believed, give him access to the plans of the Magical Kingdoms. Now, if he had a source close to the Mother Supreme . . .

XVI

❧ ❧ ❧

J arrod emerged from the night's trance and straightened his back. It ached; it never used to do that. He checked the beaker to his right in the weakening light of the interlocking pentacles. It was empty. Nothing wrong there. He felt strong, sure, buoyed up by the potions he had taken and the purification he had undergone. Then why did the small of his back hurt? Old age, he told himself, brought on prematurely by all the spell casting he had done, or perhaps all the statues he had posed for after the War. The windows of his workroom, formerly Greylock's workroom, reflected the werelights from the lines that limned the pentacles, but he could tell that it was black outside. There was no urge yet to Make the Day. He got up and stretched. His back felt better. He picked up the empty beaker and strode across the glowing lines, feeling the tingle from each as he passed over it. Once outside, he extinguished them with a blink of his mind and then lit the candles by the same method. He went over to the chair, retrieved his clothes and put them on.

He crossed to the fireplace and picked the last of the three flagons from the trivet that stood in the ashes. It was still warm and he drank the final potion. He could feel it course down his throat and comfort his belly. He wouldn't feel the main effects for another twenty minutes. He went over to a small, brass-bound chest on a shelf in the middle of the bookcases that ran the length of one wall. He opened it and took out a heavy gold ring with a large, dull stone. There had been a time, before he was a Mage, when he had worn it all the time. It hadn't been on his finger for years now. A dereliction on his part. He could only hope that those who dwelt in the Place of Power would be grateful for the rest afforded them and not angered by his neglect. It was another unforeseen outcome of the peace. He slipped it on the middle finger of his right hand and looked down on it fondly. Greylock had entrusted him with it when he had been scarcely more than a boy. Its fire had been extinguished at one point and it had taken the Guardian to restore it. Yet one more thing he owed to that bodiless enigma.

Once the Making of the Day was achieved, Jarrod collected his Staff. It had been created and empowered by Greylock and Naxania, one of the few important pieces of Magic Jarrod had ever seen her perform. It looked like a giant bow, taller than he was, covered with bright runes, quiescent now, but, to Jarrod's eye, gaudy nonetheless. It, too, had languished in the cupboard since the end of the war. He doubted that he would need it now, but it always paid to be prepared. He contemplated changing into a more elaborate gown, but decided against it. Instead he placed the diadem of the Mages of Paladine on his head and pressed it down firmly into his curly hair. It was a plain circlet of diamonds, of little value, but of great age. Thus accoutered, he went down to the stables in the dark and roused Nastrus.

'Why so grand at this disgusting hour?' the unicorn inquired grumpily, submitting to being saddled with distinctly ill humor.

'We're going to visit the Place of Power.'

'*And I suppose this couldn't wait until a body has eaten?*'

'*The fewer people who are aware of it the better,*' Jarrod replied.

The nightmoon was setting as they rode north, the breeze behind them pleasantly cool. Jarrod spent the time rehearsing the words that Greylock had taught him. They were in no tongue that he knew and made no sense that he could fathom. Since Greylock had laid such stress on the sound and intonation, he suspected that it was the resonances created rather than the meaning that summoned the Dwellers and the energies that they imparted. It reminded him that it was time that he began to train a successor. If they were entering violent times again, it was not too early to begin. The circle of megaliths loomed up in the darkness and they rode round to the Causeway side, where Jarrod dismounted.

'*You can come in with me if you like,*' he thought to Nastrus. '*You've been in there before.*'

'*I remember. Not one of my favorite spots, though the grass in there is always green. I think I'll stay here for a while.*'

Jarrod hefted his Staff and walked past the first and lowest of the blocks. The sky was just beginning to lighten, but the mottling on the stone was not yet apparent. Jarrod's memory supplied the rusty color. As he cleared the altarlike rock, the stone in his ring began to glow softly and tiny prickles of sensation washed across his skin. He walked on and skirted the second monolith, this one white and gleaming and of a height with the crosspieces of the menhirs that formed the circle, and came to a halt in front of the third and tallest stele. This one was of a dead and unreflecting black and reared up at least a hundred feet. Jarrod shivered. It had nothing to do with the temperature. It was atop this column that Greylock had been imprisoned, his flesh bound to the stone. This place was not meant for man. There were forces here that could not be controlled or understood.

The potions and the purification sustained him, but he was

nervous. Greylock had had a far greater familiarity with the ancient spirits that governed this area that the Guardian had called a Force Point, but it hadn't protected him. This maundering wasn't helping, he told himself firmly. He gripped his Staff and began to chant the syllables, deepening his voice and letting the sounds roll out. The light in the Ring of the Keepers quickened and the hair on the nape of his neck tingled. He found his arms rising and then his whole body was moving smoothly upward. He floated up to and over the flat top of the towering black slab before settling gently on its surface.

He took a deep breath and began the second round of the chant. He felt the wind at his back, but the fabric of his robe didn't move. The ring grew warm on his hand and the Staff was surrounded by pale green fire. There was a sense of imminence around him, of a presence or presences waiting. He continued with the chant and as he did so the very air seemed to thicken. Cold points of fire rippled over him, as if he had plunged into a mountain tarn. The sensation persisted, but the initial pain diminished as he came to the end of his guttural song.

He was aware of a questioning. It was not inside his head as it was with the unicorns, but rather all around him, soaking into him. His arms came down slowly and the Staff grounded itself on the surface. The green light still flickered along the rune-carved length.

"I am Jarrod Courtak, designated as Keeper of the Place of Power. You know me and have accepted me," he said aloud. The feeling of inquiry did not lessen. "Our country is at war again, a war not of our making. I would know what I must do. I seek your advice." Nothing happened. He waited, wondering if he should repeat his request.

"If you will not advise me," he said finally, "can you show me what is happening so that I may reach my own conclusion?" In an instant the pressure was gone and Jarrod was suddenly aware that the sun had risen, coloring distant clouds with rose and gold. Then the sky went black.

The ring still glowed, but the fire around the Staff had gone out. Jarrod was alert, every sense questing for danger. The potions were working in his body and they would enable him to handle power safely, but he hesitated. No spell suggested itself. His eye was caught by a lighter patch in the sky and as he watched, it brightened. He found himself looking down at a coastline with tiny ships bobbing offshore. It was disorienting looking up into the sky and down upon the land at the same time. As he watched, pinpricks of fire blossomed. The coast of Umbria, he thought. So, the Dwellers were prepared to assist him. That was a relief.

The scene in the sky shifted as did the viewpoint. He was now looking at a group of men and women, richly dressed, sitting around a table. He recognized Olivderval. A meeting of the Oligarchs then. A man he did not know was standing before a map using a pointer to indicate something, troop deployments possibly, or places the Umbrians were expected to attack. He saw mouths move, but there was no sound. Scarcely enlightening. Clouds came in and covered the opening in the heavens and when they had cleared again Jarrod felt himself to be above the valley of the Illuskhardin. He recognized the Central Range to the left and the Saradondas to the right. Scenes came and went, clans gathering and attacking soldiers, ronoronti being driven off, clansmen darting down out of the foothills striking at the armored Umbrians, inflicting little damage and disappearing again, rockslides being triggered to block the invaders' path. He saw Umbrians heading back north but others continuing to press on toward Isphardel. It all looked very messy and inconclusive.

The focus shifted even as he was coming to those conclusions. The view now was of the end of a broad body of water that was not known to him. What was obvious from the aerial view given him was that the ground around the end of the lake was marshy. There were troops about, horsemen for the most part, and they avoided the westernmost end of the lake. The viewpoint widened to include mechanical vehicles making their way toward the Umbrian camp. The grass had been flattened by the cavalry that had preceded them and they were making good time. The view swung to take in a larger force. Small groups appeared to be attacking stationary boxes. Confusing and uninformative, he thought. He felt somewhat cheated.

As if in response, the viewpoint descended and individuals became recognizable. It could have been in response to his unspoken wish, or even that the Dwellers were sharpening their art after years of quiescence. Whatever the reason, he suddenly saw a man who was undoubtedly Darius coaching horsemen in the tactics of attacking square wooden constructs. He still couldn't hear the words, but the gestures made the meaning plain enough. He had the feeling that the two forces he had seen were not too far apart, but he could not be sure and, as he speculated, the scene in the sky changed back to a picture of the Umbrians. It was close this time, in a tent, and, a major difference, he could hear what was being said.

"Guile, gentlemen, that is the secret of victory here." The speaker was Estivus of Oxenburg and he was addressing his cadre of officers. "We are outnumbered, you all know that, and the Lord Observer," he used Darius' old, civilian title deliberately, "commands the opposition. He is a formidable opponent, but he is old and old men tend to try to repeat their triumphs, using the same methods. Knowing that, despite our inferior numbers, we can lead him to destruction. The battlewagons will be here in two days and he will not be able to resist them. They will be his downfall."

The panel in the sky winked out. There was nothing there but the dark, no stars, no fading wash of moonlight from the setting nightmoon, nothing. "More!" Jarrod's voice came out as a demanding croak. "You must show me more." The nothingness was an almost positive denial. He could feel no presence, no Dwellers, no one. "You cannot leave me like this," he said, part complaint, part beseechment. He was speaking to a void. There was no one, nothing there. He bowed his head slowly. No point berating powers who had no human feelings. They had done what he had requested. He was Keeper, not Controller. He told himself these things as he stood atop the monolith and watched the stars bleed back into the sky. The wind ruffled his sleeve points and lifted the hem of his gown gently. Those Who Dwelt had done everything that they were prepared to do for him this time. He resigned himself to it. He was frustrated and unsatisfied.

The smell of the grass was omnipresent, sweet and somewhat cloying, intensified by having been trampled down. Darius inhaled deeply as he turned over on his pallet, made out of grass, of course. A cavalryman's dream, this terrain. Flat, good grazing for the horses, scant chance of being taken by surprise by the enemy; a place where textbook maneuvers could be carried out. Estivus was the best of foes, clever, thorough, scrupulous and challenging. He smiled to himself in the darkness. He had always had a soft spot for the Margrave, knew he had the makings of a superior cavalry commander. It was a pleasure to match wits with him. Some of the probes and feints he had mounted had been novel and effective, had sharpened his own wits, had put a zest back into service that he had not expected to find again. He liked to think that his counters had kept the youngster from sleep on a night or two.

"Permission to enter, sir?" The voice from without the tent flap was short-breathed and nervous.

"Come."

"I'm sorry to disturb you, General," the young officer said after he had ducked through the tent flap, "but our scouts report unusual activity by the enemy. They are on the move, moving toward our position and deploying on both wings."

Darius rolled off the pallet and reached for his trousers. "Quite all right, Ensign Darbo, how close are they?"

"About a league, sir."

"A surprise attack at dawn? Oxenburg knows we have scouts out. Doesn't smell right."

"Permission to enter, sir?"

"Come." Darius was fully dressed by the time the new man entered. "Report," he said, dousing his face from a hand basin.

"The main body of the enemy has halted a scant mile away, sir. Estimated number, four hundred."

"That's almost their entire force," Darius said as he tossed the towel aside. "How long to firstlight?"

"Hour, hour and a half, sir, according to the water clock."

"Roust the men, but do it quietly. Have the cooks dish up a cold breakfast. Silence to be maintained. I don't want them to know we've been roused. Do it."

An hour later the Paladinian cavalry, close to eight hundred strong, was mounted and ready. They were deployed in three long lines, but their orders were that the first two lines would charge straight ahead as soon as there was visibility and that the third line would divide right and left to flank and contain the enemy. Small groups had already been dispatched to the wings to see if the foe had deployed men out there. No reports to that effect had come back.

Darius sat his horse, with his three top officers around him. They were behind the lines of mounted men, but not by much. The disadvantage of flat terrain was that there was no way of overlooking an engagement.

"I do not like this, gentlemen," Darius said quietly. "It is out of keeping. Oxenburg is up to something. Fight hard, but proceed with caution." They saluted and wheeled away. There was nothing more to be said, just the hardest part of battle to endure—the waiting.

The sky paled slowly behind the Umbrians. Helmets and plumes were etched against the faint luminescence. The Paladinians were still invisible, which was what Darius had counted on. He walked his horse around his troops and ended up ahead and slightly to the front of the first line. He intended to attack first, but the men had been warned not to be decoyed. If the enemy turned and fled at their approach, they were to break off the attack. He did not know what trick Oxenburg might have up his sleeve, but he was not about to ride into it. He had been a soldier too long to be easily cozened.

Before the sun breasted the horizon, before it could shine into his men's eyes, putting them at a disadvantage, he raised his sword and dropped it. His men spurred forward, lances coming down, screams of defiance coming from their throats. The enemy reciprocated. Darius saw them surge forward as his men swept past him. The two lines came together, lances snapped, men were pried from their saddles, battle was joined. Darius circled round behind the fighting. His men were pushing the Umbrians back. To be expected given the numbers. He clapped his heels into the grey's flank to get to the other side of the melee. A flank attack from a force hidden in the high grass? He reined in, stood up in the stirrups and scanned the terrain. No counterattack to be seen.

His men were driving forward now and he turned the stallion's head to follow. They trotted past men dead and dying, fallen horses and some, riderless, who were galloping around aimlessly. The pace in front of him quickened. The enemy had been broken and were in retreat. He recognized the change in the horses' gait, the whirling of swords aloft, a certain lack of tension in the air. It made him nervous. The young men ahead of him could sense nothing odd. There was blood in their nostrils and victory rode on their swords. This was what they had been training for. Darius used his spurs and sent the stallion plunging through the ranks of pursuing cavalrymen.

As he reached the front of the pack, he became aware that the Umbrians were not in headlong flight, not routed. They were fighting a rearguard action, turning and confronting their enemies, killing occasionally, dying bravely more often than not. Only one explanation, Darius thought as he wielded his sword, cutting down an Umbrian. Varodias must have become bored with the skirmishing and, safe in Angorn, ordered an all-out assault. The man was capable of it. Poor Estivus, he was a loyal subject, but he also cared for his men.

He was in the front line now and he reined the stallion back a little. The sun was a half globe on the horizon and he lifted his arm to shield it out. Something caught his eye behind the fleeing Umbrians. A squat shape, black against the rising sun. So familiar. That was what young Estivus was up to. Certainty and relief bloomed in him. Now he knew. Battlewagons. Two more, no three, six of them at least. He lifted himself in the stirrups. "Battlewagons!" he screamed. "Battlewagons!" He pointed the sword at them, swerving the stallion to slow his men and alert them to the danger. As he did so, the Umbrians peeled aside, as he knew they would. "Battlewagon drill!" he yelled. "Battlewagon drill!"

The Paladinians, hectored by Darius for sennights about battlewagons, obediently split into small groups and broke formation to get behind the machines so that they could attack their vulnerable point. Unfortunately, the ground here, bordering as it did on the end of the nameless lake, was boggy. Horses slowed and fought for footing. The swift dash to the side, so often practiced, slipped and slid to a delicate walk. The battlewagons stayed immobile, waiting, but the Umbrians, joined now by unsuspected reinforcements that had been waiting for this precise moment, wheeled back and charged down on the preoccupied and mired Paladinians. Darius' troops, intent on the battlewagons, were slow to adjust. They gave a good account of themselves, but it was futile. About three hundred and fifty escaped the trap. Darius of Gwyndryth was not among them. When his body was identified, there was a lance point in his side and multiple sword cuts. Someone had finished him off by cutting his throat.

Estivus of Oxenburg did him homage. He was washed and dressed in clean clothes, his armor was polished and placed beside him. His hands were placed around the hilt of his sword and laid upon his chest. He was borne back to the Paladinian lines, under flag of truce, laid most meetly upon a litter. Estivus himself accompanied the body and delivered a moving speech in which he recalled his early acquaintance with the general and the reverence in which he had been held in Umbria. He swore, upon his honor, that there would be no strife on that field until Darius had been buried. The men who bore the body back to Stronta, and thence to Gwyndryth, said that tears had stood in the Umbrian's eyes.

The body lay in state at Stronta. Queen Naxania, along with the Duke and Duchess of Abercorn and many notables, kept vigil. The common people lining up in the palace courtyard waited many hours to pay their last respects. On the third day, the Holdmaster set out on his last journey back to the Gwyndryth that he had always loved. Villagers along the route turned out and stood silently at the roadside, watching as the cortege passed. After it was out of sight, they spoke among themselves of the beautiful Lady Marianna, pale and drawn, and of her husband the Mage, who rode a unicorn.

The burial at Gwyndryth was, according to Darius' wishes, to have been a simple affair, but that was not to be. That was assured by the arrival of Queen Arabella and the Prince Consort. They were accompanied by the great landowners of the realm, thus assuring that the hospitality of the ancient hold and that of neighboring estates was put to the severest of tests. There was too much for everybody to do for there to be much time for grief, even though the Holdmaster had been greatly loved by his people. There were so many great lords and ladies to gawk at and speculate about, to say nothing of the surprise reappearance of Joscelyn, the young master. But there were greater wonders still to come.

On the day of the burial, shortly after the sun had risen, a great number of unicorns appeared in the hayfields outside the mossy walls of the hold. Chief among them was Amarine, dam or grandam to the rest. The signs of age were subtle, but they were there. The gait was somewhat stiffer than of yore, and the hollows above the eyes were deeper. The lower lip drooped. The guard hairs on the back of the forelegs, beneath the throat and behind the ears, were longer and stiffer, giving her a slightly shaggy look. The Lady Marianna came out to meet her and, for the first time that anyone had seen, she wept. The Mage, too, came out to welcome Amarine's daughter Pellia and young Joscelyn was reunited with Astarus. Together they accompanied the coffin to the family graveyard where, in the presence of royalty, nobility and creatures out of legend, Darius of Gwyndryth was laid to rest beside his long-dead wife.

The monument that he had had erected when his wife died was grey and lichened after all these years. The traditional figure of grief, crouched, the outlines of limbs angular beneath mourning sheath, looked down in anguish at the chalky scar in the ground at her feet. The majority of the carving on her pedestal had dimmed. The new figures, BLVCCI, freshly carved, stood out. Other than the effectiveness of the statue, nothing marked this joint grave out as the resting place of two extraordinary people.

Darius of Gwyndryth had had an eventful and satisfying life. He had extended his estates and they were more prosperous when he died than when he inherited them. He had left behind him a stable succession. These two constituted the chiefest measure of a man. In addition, he had been the first Arundelian Ambassador/military observer to be allowed into the Umbrian capital. He had exceeded his orders and revitalized the Umbrian cavalry. He had even led a portion of them in battle. He had rescued Queen Naxania from the threat of revolt and, once in his life, he had ridden a unicorn. He had enjoyed a full and productive life, but, in death, he achieved more.

Most of the decisions were arrived at in Celador, following his funeral. After consultation with her Council, Arabella issued a call to arms and was heartened by the outpouring of support it engendered. Prince Saxton was appointed head of the combined forces of Arundel and Paladine, a move not greeted with universal enthusiasm by the Paladinian army. The Thane of Talisman, on a diplomatic visit, pledged Cloudsteed Wings and Warcat Battalions in support. He did not say how many. The Discipline, in a hastily called meeting of the High Council, designated Jarrod of Paladine as "Chief Representative of the Discipline in the effort to dissuade the Empire of Umbria from the folly of its recent ways." The method by which suasion would be brought was not mentioned.

War is like a living thing, though it is an unpredictable organ. It grows and it changes in accordance with rules that few can fathom. Oftimes its nature is affected by an event that has little to do with military science. The battle by the nameless lake was such an event. In the grand scheme of things, it was not decisive, nor pivotal. A relatively small number of men were involved. A clever ruse, bluffing the enemy and drawing him in anyhow, had succeeded and an internationally known General had been killed.

Yet the effects of the engagement rippled out. On the Umbrian side, while Estivus was saddened by the loss of a noble man, his troops were jubilant. They had defeated the best general that the Magical Kingdoms had, and when they were outnumbered. The thought of plunder in Paladine occurred to most of them.

XVII

⚜ ⚜ ⚜

E xcuse me, Excellence." The Duty Boy hovered just inside the door.

Jarrod looked up from the desk, irritated at being disturbed. The writing of this chapter of his history was flowing
smoothly, a rare enough occurrence, and he didn't want the
mood interrupted.

"Is this really important," he said crisply. "I gave instructions that I was not to be disturbed."

The boy looked uncomfortable and frightened. "There's a
unicorn downstairs, sir," he said with the suspicion of a wobble
to his lower lip. "It won't go away."

Am I that forbidding? Jarrod thought, with a touch of surprise and a twinge of contrition. "Nastrus?" he inquired in a
softer voice.

"No, sir. I know him, he's the old one. This one's younger."

"Very well, then, I'll come down." He smiled at the boy in
what he meant to be a reassuring way. "You did well," he
added.

When Jarrod got to the foot of the tower, Malloran was waiting for him.

'*I am here to take you to the castle,*' he said in Jarrod's head.

'*Any particular reason?*'

'*We are having a meeting about our place on this world and our obligations to your kind. You have been selected as a representative from your species.*' Malloran clearly felt awkward.

'*This all sounds very formal,*' Jarrod returned, trying to bring some lightness to the thought.

'*It is important to us and, we think, to your herds as well,*' Malloran replied with gravity.

Jarrod probed briefly and withdrew satisfied. He made an automatic obeisance and then tried to describe his reasons. It didn't seem to work.

'*Let me walk you to the stables,*' Jarrod said, recognizing the inevitable. '*I can ask you some questions as we go.*'

'*Such as?*' Malloran inquired as he turned and allowed Jarrod to direct him.

'*How long will I be gone? There might be arrangements to be made. Should I take provisions? If so, are you prepared to carry them? Who else is being summoned? Will that do for a start?*'

'*You are a very practical creature,*' Malloran replied with a hint of amusement.

'*I've been around unicorns for too long. I've learned that you generally don't think of our comforts.*'

'*To answer your questions, I do not know how long this ———— will last.*' The image was one of a consultation–group-participation–discussion–decision-making assembly that had no exact equivalent in Paladinian nor in Common. '*You had better bring provisions for several days and, yes, I am prepared to carry them. As to the others, Amarine has gone to fetch your mate. They in turn will direct your Archmage and the Queen of Arundel. You, I rely on to inform the Queen here. A brother unicorn awaits in your stables to transport her.*'

'You seem to have thought of everything,' Jarrod replied. *'How long do we have?'*

'The sooner the better, isn't that one of your sayings?'

'I don't think you have met our Queen Naxania, have you?' Jarrod asked.

'There is what you call humor, that is not really humor, around that sending. I look forward to this encounter.'

This time the smile reached Jarrod's face.

There were hundreds of unicorns dotted around the base of the foothills when Jarrod arrived. Even looking down at them from a fair height, he detected a current of communication running through them. He was aware of an odd contrast. On the surface, the unicorns were grazing peacefully, or rolling in the grass, or sparring with each other, but, below the bucolic surface, there was a lively debate going on. The passing of thoughts was too swift for him, but, from the feelings that they gave off, there was, at the very least, a difference of opinion down there. He turned back and saw Amarine. He bowed to her.

They could not communicate, but he felt that she was pleased to see him and, if Amarine was here, his wife was probably here as well. The unicorn turned and he followed her. Hunger was gnawing at him. As they approached the castle, Marianna came bustling down the steps. She was wearing a simple kirtle of linsey-woolsey with her hair caught up in a large, patterned kerchief.

"About time you turned up," she said as she embraced him. "I can't tell you how dirty this place was when I arrived."

Jarrod smiled to himself, glad that he didn't have the same kind of total communication with her that he had with some of the unicorns. She had obviously assumed the role of chatelaine of the castle.

"Come along inside and get something to eat. Naxania's in there, but she's still unconscious."

"Who else is here?" he asked as he climbed the stairs to the hall. He stopped on the threshold, amazed. The windows had been cleaned, the floor swept. A table and chairs had appeared in the middle of the long room and a fire had been laid in the great fireplace.

"Arabella and Greylock are resting. We're all sleeping on straw pallets. It's the best I could do under the circumstances. We don't have much in the way of crockery or eating utensils, so we'll just have to pretend."

"I'm sure that it will all be just fine," Jarrod said as reassuringly as he could. "You entertained Naxania at Oxeter so she knows what you can do. In the meantime, I really need to eat something."

"Go and sit down. Enjoy the first of one of many vegetable stews."

The following morning, humans and unicorns gathered at the foot of the mountain range. The humans sat together on a grassy slope about twenty feet above the Plain. Marianna, by virtue of her link to Amarine, stood a few paces in front of them ready to serve as translator. Slightly below them, in full view of the assembled herd were Amarine, Pellia, Nastrus and Malloran. Jarrod gathered, via Nastrus and Malloran, that not all of the assembled unicorns were descended from them, but a considerable number were. Amarine turned to Marianna.

"My friend Amarine," Marianna translated, "says that the unicorns have been debating the place of Strand in their future." She paused to listen. "There are many very young unicorns who are here for the first time and they are enamored of the grasslands and the space that now exists for them to run and rut. They have no direct knowledge of Strandkind, but, now that they have discovered Strand, they wish to stay here."

"Please tell her that we are delighted that they should feel that way and that we welcome their presence," Greylock said, taking charge. "The Alien Plain is vast and there is certainly room for both humans and unicorns."

Marianna turned to him and spoke in her own behalf.

"That's the trouble, Archmage. The young ones down on the Plain don't know us, but some of the older unicorns do, and they have some grave doubts about Strandkind. They do not entirely trust us."

"And they are quite right when it comes to the average Strandsman," Jarrod said for the benefit of the human contingent and thought out for those unicorns he could reach. "We are not typical of Strand." He circled an arm out to include his companions. "Most people on Strand have never heard of you, or, if they have, think of you as something out of legend. Any mingling would have to be done gradually."

'Why don't you suggest that a portion of the Alien Plain be ceded to the unicorns,' Nastrus asked in the back of his head.

'Because I don't own the land,' Jarrod replied. 'The queens do. If I made the suggestion, I could lose my head.'

"What are they trying to say?" Naxania asked on cue.

Jarrod knew the answer, but he allowed his wife to reply. "They would like assurances that they will be left alone to enjoy a portion of this world that we have no use for and guarantees that, if they settle here, they will be safe if they mingle with us."

"We thank the Holdmistress of Gwyndryth," Arabella of Arundel said in the Formal Mode, "for her admirable intercession. However, if this is to be a negotiation over territory, we must tell you that we shall need an extraordinarily good reason to present to our Royal Council."

"They do not understand the concept of negotiation," Jarrod interposed.

"We had thought that the Lady Marianna was speaking for the unicorns," Arabella said, motioning toward Jarrod's wife, who was still standing, but no longer seemed possessed.

"She speaks for Amarine who is the senior unicorn, as it were, but she has no proper contact with the others. I cannot hear Amarine, but I have close contact with several of the others and it is they who are speaking at the moment," Jarrod replied.

Arabella nodded. "We cannot speak for our Cousin of Paladine, and the other rulers of Strand are not present, but, for ourselves, we will not cede land belonging to the Crown in perpetuity. We bear a responsibility to those who will come after us. We have already said that we have no objection to the unicorns having the sole use of a portion of our land south of the mountains, but that is only while I occupy the throne. Upon my death, or should I abdicate, the matter would be subject to the approval of my successor. If that is not agreeable to the unicorns, then we are at an impasse." She looked at Naxania for support.

Naxania was thinking, eyes narrowed, hands loose in her lap. She lifted her head. "We are not knowledgeable as to the capabilities of unicorns," she said.

'She is using the Formal Mode, as the other Queen has been doing,' Jarrod relayed. 'That means she is speaking officially.'

"It does not seem to us that there is anything substantive they could do for Paladine, or for the Crown. If there is some service they can provide us, something that we cannot do for ourselves, we would be prepared to cede territory in perpetuity. Short of that, we would take the position of our Cousin of Arundel."

Clever, Jarrod thought. She's hedging her bets. If the unicorns have some powers that would be useful to her, she wants them to come to her first. Then an idea came to him.

"We are all members of the Discipline here," he said. "We know that the Discipline fought mightily against the Outlanders, that it was indeed the Discipline that eventually defeated them. The High Council of Magic ceded their claim to territory on the Alien Plain during negotiations on the Treaty of Partition. However, the right of ownership by conquest still exists and these mountains were nowhere shown on the maps. The Discipline can claim these mountains by right of conquest and, one can assume, a fair amount of land around them.

"Not only that," he added, warming to his theme, "the castle behind us was built by Magic, with the assistance, I may say, of unicorns. It has been inhabited by a Magician, my stepson Joscelyn, continuously for a number of years, so we have not only conquered, we have also occupied." He paused and looked at his companions. The Archmage was smiling, Arabella was pensive and Naxania was clearly not beguiled.

"And your conclusion, my Lord of Abercorn?" she asked pointedly, using his Paladinian title to remind him that he was her vassal.

"I think, Majesty," Jarrod replied coolly, "that the Archmage should formally claim sovereignty of the mountain range and its surrounding territory for the Discipline. The Treaty of Partition never set northward boundaries, since it was unknown territory. The precise boundaries were to have been negotiated later."

"I think that the Mage of Paladine has proved his point," Greylock cut in quickly, before Naxania opened her mouth, "and I hereby proclaim the mountain range that forms the northern border of the Alien Plain, together with a portion of the lands surrounding it, to be . . ." he faltered. He looked around. "The word sovereign doesn't really apply to us, does it?"

"To be the legal property of . . . ?" Jarrod suggested.

"To be the inalienable property of the Discipline of Strand to have and hold from now and henceforth." The voice came from behind Jarrod, but he recognized it. Joscelyn. He didn't turn around, but he saw the look of pride on his wife's face.

"Excellent," Greylock said. "So says the Archmage of Strand before members of the High Council of Magic and the rulers of Arundel and Paladine."

"It is a shame, Archmage," Naxania said acidly in the Common Mode, "that you don't have a flag to plant."

"With the permission of Your Majesties," Jarrod said, using the cadences of the Formal Mode so as not to give offense, "I have one more suggestion to make." He smiled at them both and rose to his feet. "We all came here by unicorn. We are the only people in the world who know what is out here. Varodias of Umbria has no knowledge of this area, nor have the Isphardis and the Songeans. What harm would it do if the majority of the unicorns we see below us moved onto their territory? You royal ladies are surely not going to talk about these proceedings, and you would have no way of knowing what happens in territories other than your own." His tone of voice was deliberately ironic.

He smiled at them, pleased with himself. "We should, of course, have some unicorns hereabouts because we shall need to contact them, but, should there ever be a challenge to the royal authority on this matter, Your Majesties, should you decide to go along with this suggestion, could always claim that you denied the unicorns the use of your lands and were unaware of where they went thereafter."

Arabella smiled back at him. It wasn't her usual, crowd-winning smile, it was much smaller and conveyed reluctant approval. "We would recommend to our Council the recognition of the Discipline's authority over the mountain range that seems to circumscribe the Alien Plain. Surrounding lands, where they impinge on the Arundelian hegemony, will require further negotiation."

As tough as her "cousin," Jarrod thought. He turned his head toward Naxania.

"We would not object to the Discipline's possession of the mountains," she said. She stopped briefly to consider. "Indeed, we cannot. Resident occupancy for more than five years, under our Common Law, constitutes ownership." She smiled at Jarrod. It was not a friendly smile. "We are sure that the Duke of Abercorn was aware of that when he came up with this idea. If the unicorns choose, with the Archmage's permission, to dwell in the mountains, you will hear no objection from us. If, however, they venture upon what we consider Paladinian land, we shall be much exercised."

'What, exactly does she mean by that?' Malloran asked.

'Ah,' Jarrod said, 'That was royal parlance for, I will turn my head aside and ignore what is really going on, but, if I was ever challenged, I would be blameless.'

'I confess that there is much I have to learn about Strandpeople,' Malloran admitted, echoed by the other unicorns who shared in the thought process.

"Perhaps," Jarrod said out loud, "we should terminate this meeting with the understanding that the unicorns can stay on Strand for the time being, ranging freely within sight of the mountains. We ask of them that they think of ways in which they can help Strand," he paused momentarily. "And its rulers."

"The Mage of Paladine makes eminent sense. We concur," Arabella said.

"Indeed," Naxania said. She drawled the word and there was no friendliness in the way she said it.

'Amarine says that she agrees,' Malloran said inside Jarrod's head.

"Archmage?" he asked, "Any last comment?"

He did not expect Greylock to respond but, "I am delighted to welcome the unicorns to the Discipline's portion of Strand," he said with a broad smile. He stood up and walked forward until he was clearly in front of the group. Then he lifted up his arms and spread them wide to encompass the unicorns and the plain. "I welcome you on behalf of the Discipline," he said in as loud a voice as his years would allow.

Naxania stood abruptly and drew her cloak about her. She made an infinitesimal bow in the direction of the Archmage and set off uphill. A unicorn appeared at Arabella's side to take her back to the castle. One picked his way toward Greylock.

"Very good," the Archmage said to Jarrod, and patted him on the shoulder. "I'm not sure you realize precisely what you've done."

"You forget, Archmage, that I have been writing a history, so, yes, I realize what I have just done, and I wish I could say that it was a carefully thought-out program. Unfortunately, it all seemed to fall into place in an instant."

"A lot of the best things do," Greylock said with a smile. "And it's every bit as satisfying as if you'd sat down and plotted it all out, isn't it?"

Jarrod moved and hunched his shoulders uncertainly, the whole managing to suggest a yes.

"Well," Greylock said reassuringly, "the repercussions of what you said today will still be being felt generations from now."

"I wish you hadn't said that, Archmage," Jarrod said as he followed his mentor uphill.

XVIII

꙼ ꙼ ꙼

The Discipline may have been distant from the conflict, but, as its leaders were debating, men and matériel, fodder, food and weapons came ashore at the Isphardi ports. Stores and bulky items like ballistae and the stones they would loft were reloaded on barges and towed up the Izingari and the Lower Illuskhardin. Tent cities blossomed and were struck as the men of the Magical Kingdoms marched north. They made a brave sight in their unblemished armor, flags waving in the following wind as they set out. After two days, the armor was no longer worn, in deference to the realities of the Isphardi climate. Unbeknownst to the men who marched, the Weatherwards stationed on Tamara Island in the mouth of Belengar Bay were laboring mightily to slow and control the storms that swept in off the sea at this time of year. As a result of their efforts, the rains held off for a sennight, easing their journey toward the front, but that did nothing to reduce the heat.

Ahead of the advancing army, a band of Weatherwards who had landed at Morlin were riding north on a relay of posthorses. They crossed the Porodel River at Martesberg, where their unusual height was noted by a man who was in the pay of Malum of Quern, but they had disappeared again long before the bunglebird reached Angorn. The spy, a none-too-successful trader in hard woods, assumed that they were headed for the Umbrian lines. They were, however, aiming for the southern reaches of the Gorodontion Mountains. Their mission was to use the weather to make life miserable for the Emperor's men. They looked forward to the task.

The Magical Kingdoms may have been slow to commit and slower still to organize, but once the enterprise was launched, the results were awesome to behold. Mangonels and ballistae were outlined against the sky as they made their way along the road that ran on top of the Upper Causeway. On the plain below thousands of men marched and rode eastward, wagons creaked their way behind them. Crowds would gather every morning to watch them pass. Women held their children up to see the heroes going off to war. Bands marched at the head of the columns to lift the spirits and keep the men in step, horses pranced and the sunlight gleamed on helmets and on lance points. Great lords, their destriers magnificently caparisoned, their surcoats emblazoned with the emblems of their houses, rode at the head of their contingents. It was all very festive.

One great lord who did not ride with his men was Jarrod Courtak. He had other things to do. Command of the Abercorn forces fell to Jarrod's chief vassal, the Earl of Thorpe. He was a seasoned warrior, having seen service in the Outland War, and was well respected. Jarrod did not know him well, but the man's reputation was good. Jarrod's main contribution had been the expenditure of considerable amounts of money to equip the men. The footmen's body armor was made of good stout leather, reinforced with metal plates, as were their caps. They were well shod, their pikes were newly made and the iron on them was of good quality. The wagons that followed them contained bowstaves, strings and arrows, spare armor, shoes and weapons as well as good plain food. There was nothing fancy about the Abercorn troops, but the men were well content.

Their Duke did not spend much time in the northern area of engagement. Neither side could keep secrets from the other. Umbrian rotifers flew above the Kingdoms' advancing forces and cloudsteeds circled about the positions that the Umbrians had taken up behind the Jodderon. He had visited the Magicians who had ensconced themselves on the Upper Causeway beyond the reach of the crossbowmen, who used the top of the massive barricade that the Margrave had built across the roadway as a vantage point. There they practiced the spells of illusion that they would employ when the time came.

Jarrod's main preoccupation was Songuard. There were Weatherwards on the western slopes of the Gorodontion Mountains, they had been there time out of mind, but their job was to control the weather over the eastern half of Paladine and that could not be disrupted. There were no longer any Weatherwards in the Saradondas and, since the Umbrians now controlled every approach to those mountains, no hope of getting any there by conventional means. Jarrod therefore enlisted the aid of the unicorns to transport the three young Weatherwards who had escaped with their help from the Empire back to the mountains. The Weatherwards had had one experience of travel through Interim and had survived it, and they were keen to exact revenge on their former captors.

Consequently, Jarrod and the three young men, aboard Nastrus, Malloran and two other unicorns, appeared shortly after dawn at the southernmost station. The first thing they did after recovering from the journey was to go out in search of one of the Songean clans. Easier thought upon than achieved, for the Songeans were masters of the mountains and, unless encumbered by their herds of ronoronti, would not be found if they did not want to be. In the event, it was the Songeans who found the Magicians. Jarrod came awake under the prompting of Nastrus.

'*What is it?*' he asked.

'*There are human beings around and watching us.*'

Jarrod peered out into the darkness. There was a sickle moon, the sign in Paladine of the approaching harvest, just past the zenith and made vague by thin, high clouds. Not much useful light from that. He moved cautiously to the pile of dry wood that had been gathered earlier and fed the embers of the fire. He could have created his own illumination, but the Songeans were, by and large, not well disposed to Magicians, and Jarrod deemed it best not to rouse the superstitious in their nature. He shook the nearest Weatherward gently and placed his finger on his lips as the young man came awake. He motioned for the lad to do the same to the other two.

'*Any clues as to who they are or how many?*' he asked Nastrus.

'*Meat eaters, but local ones.*' The thought came sheathed in disdain. '*As far as I can judge, there are about twenty of them.*'

'*If this turns nasty, save yourselves. You can always come back for us later.*'

Nastrus snorted. Jarrod ignored him and rose slowly to his full height. The branches were beginning to catch and he was certain that the Songeans could see him in the flickering light. He raised his arms, hands open.

"We come in peace," he said. It was one of the few Songean phrases he knew.

'*Pity you can't converse with them the way you do with us,*' Nastrus commented. '*It would save a lot of misunderstanding.*'

'*Not now, Nastrus.*' Jarrod's eyes were probing the dark beyond the firelight. A figure emerged and then another. He did not risk looking behind him, but he was sure there were other clansmen there.

"Which one of you speaks Songean?" he said in Common to the Weatherwards.

"I speak some. Not very well." The voice came from below.

"Stand up nice and slow then. The rest of you stay where

you are. Say something diplomatic and ask, very politely, who they are."

A guttural exchange with rolling r's took place. "What did they say?" Jarrod asked.

"They ask who we are and what we are doing here and whether the unicorns are our prisoners."

"Tell them that the unicorns are our honored friends and that I am a friend of Sandroz of the Central Range."

Another exchange took place. "They do not know this Sandroz," the Weatherward reported, "but they say that if the unicorns are our friends, we are welcome among them."

"Thank the gods for that." Jarrod lowered his arms. "On your feet, you two. Make no sudden moves."

'I don't know what you would do without us,' Nastrus remarked with evident satisfaction.

The Songeans emerged from the shadows and surrounded the party. The other three unicorns drifted into the light, aligning themselves behind the Magicians, and the clansmen pressed their palms together and bowed low. Jarrod could feel the thoughts emanating from the unicorns. *'Vain creatures,'* he thought out with what humor he could muster. *'Please don't do anything to jeopardize this meeting.'* The thought was not well-received.

One of the Songeans stepped forward. Jarrod presumed that he was either the clan chief or the leader of this particular band. He spoke and the Weatherward translated. "They wish to know what we are doing in their mountains."

"Tell them that we are here to fight the Umbrians and ensure the safety of their herds and their womenfolk. That the Umbrians are our implacable foes."

"I don't know the word for implacable," the youngster complained.

"Then improvise," Jarrod said tersely. "And offer them the warmth of our fire. Be diplomatic."

The guttural exchange resumed, accompanied by hand gestures from the Weatherward indicating the fire. The Songeans advanced cautiously and then sank to their haunches in a loose semicircle. Jarrod hastened to add wood to the fire.

"Ask them," he said over his shoulder as he stooped to rearrange branches, "if there are any Umbrians in the vicinity."

"There is a party down in the valley that they have been following for a ten-day," came the translation. "They captured part of the clanherd and drove off the rest."

"Ask them if they would aid us if we destroyed these herd-despoilers?" Jarrod asked, remembering the Songean word at the last moment.

"Clanleader Yorrorula would welcome our help, but, he says, deeds are the fleece, words are but the promise of a calf."

"So be it," Jarrod said, bowing to the man who had been speaking for the clan. "If they will show us where these despicable ronoronti thieves are, we will undertake to restore the honor of the clan."

"Can we really do that?" Aristach whispered urgently.

"If we don't, this mission is dead," Jarrod said quietly, but with conviction.

By noon that same day, the party found itself belly down on a rock outcropping overlooking the valley. Below was a group of forty Umbrian horsemen camped by the side of a stream. They were taking their midday ease. Their mounts were hobbled and there was a large cookpot suspended over a fire. The men had taken off their helmets and breastplates, though most seemed to have sheathed swords at their belts. Waterskins or wineskins were being handed round and most of them had wet hair, indicating a dousing in the stream. They were relaxed. No sentries were posted.

Jarrod wriggled backward and beckoned for the Magicians to follow him. They came together in a group. "Two ways of doing this," he said tersely. "Spell of invisibility and knives. We could probably dispose of twenty before they knew what was happening and leave the rest to the Songeans." He looked at the faces crowding in on him. "Slicing throats not to your liking, gentlemen? A shame; you'll have to get over that. War's a messy business. The best reason against that approach, however, is that we leave the Songeans to complete the business. Creating an avalanche is chancy, might leave too many of them alive. Fire is best, I think."

He looked from one to the other without a smile, hoping that the intensity of his mood was having an effect. He knew where he was going, and it wasn't pleasant. "Remember how to create a circular force field?" He looked at the white faces surrounding him again. "Good. Remember how to bring it in toward the center? Third year work at the Collegium if I remember correctly. Very well then. Here's what we'll do, and remember, make sure that the horses stay outside the force field. The Songeans will be able to make good use of them and it will increase our stature among them."

"I'm not prepared for this, Magister," Gordiam said. "This isn't weather Magic, I don't know if I can do this." There was a whining note to his delivery.

"You are Magicians first, Weatherwards second," Jarrod said harshly. "I don't know what the Collegium has been teaching recently and I don't care. We have a job to do. It entails Magic. You are all graduates of the Collegium. As Mage of Paladine I am your superior in the Discipline and I demand not only performance, but obedience. I have assigned three of you to perform a lower grade spell. All you will be doing is confining them. I shall be the one destroying them. If that disturbs your infantile stomachs, leave." His voice modulated slightly. "If you do, of course, your prospects of advancement will be nil. The choice is entirely up to you." He looked at each of them in turn. His face was practicedly bland. He terrified them.

Ten minutes later the four Magicians were seated cross-legged with their backs to a large boulder. Each one held the image of the Umbrians below, stream flowing, fire crackling be-

neath the cauldron, horses grazing around them. At a nod from
Jarrod the younger Magicians began to weave a net of air
around the men in the valley. Once they knew it to be solid,
they moved it in on the group. The Umbrians on the edge of the
gathering leapt to their feet as they felt the touch of the spectral
enclosure. They flailed and their arms and fists met resistance.
The barrier did not give much, though it did not hurt them. It
pressed forward inexorably, propelled by the combined will of
the Weatherwards and the Umbrians were tumbled backward
by the invisible net.

Jarrod sat a little apart. He had gone within himself, centering his energies, seeking the balm of power that admits of no
right or wrong. He had a job to do, a duty to perform. It was
distasteful, but this was war. He had known war before, as
these youngsters had not. He had been responsible for . . . His
mind flinched briefly from the admission . . . a great many
deaths. But they were not Strandsmen, part of him prompted.
Enemy, he told himself. Necessary, he said.

He settled himself briefly, pushed his shoulders back a little
and called for a view of the valley. He saw through the eyes of
one of the Weatherwards. The Umbrians were being steadily
concentrated. He conjured fire and applied it to the picture in
his mind. He blanked his vision. He could not, however, mask
his ears. He heard the screams of the Umbrians. He knew, then,
that this moment would haunt him for life. This was of his devising. It was war, he reminded himself, an act of war. It was
necessary. He did not convince himself. He came out of his
semitrance, unfolded himself from his sitting position and left
without a word.

He was avoided for days. Oh, not ostensibly. The Weatherwards were appropriately deferential, but he couldn't get them
to talk. Even the Songeans, who could be expected to relish the
victory, were reticent to begin with. That dissolved rapidly,
however. Once the awe that the feat engendered had been di-

minished by a certain distance, the Magicians were inducted into the clan. The Magicians and, especially, the unicorns were taken up into the hills and feted.

It was a three-day performance of dancing, feasting and drinking. The Weatherwards, unaccustomed to the effects of fermented ronoronti milk, suffered. One by one they appeared before Jarrod for reassurances. Jarrod heard them all and dispensed what advice and comfort he could. He felt that his counsel was hollow, but it seemed to strengthen the young men. The only one who was not contrite was Aristach and Jarrod decided to take him along if the conflict widened. His single-minded need for revenge against the Umbrians could be useful. Even as he thought it, Jarrod doubted his decision, decided to send him home in the meanwhile, but knew, in his heart, that, if he had to use Jubal Aristach against the Umbrians, he would. When the feast was over, he dispatched two of the Weatherwards to the south with a guard of young clansmen.

Trading on the esteem the clan chief held him in, he proposed ways in which the clans could slow and harass the Umbrians without Magical intervention. The two Weatherwards had departed with a full warriors' send-off. Jarrod and Jubal Aristach disappeared without warning. The Songeans had no way of knowing that the Mage went south, while the other, somewhat sullen young Magician, had been sent back to the Outpost.

As for Jarrod, he was next seen strolling, or rather not strolling, into the tent of the general commanding the allied troops in North Isphardel. The Commander, at this stage of the game, was one Magrius, self-styled Holdmaster of Dwallyth. He was free-lance, hired by the Isphardis and in nowise allied to the Arundelian monarchy. He had, however, been successful in the war against the Empire and was a popular hero in Isphardel. He was relaxing on a couch when Jarrod's tall shadow cut across his light.

"How did you get past my guards?" was his first question.

Jarrod was impressed by his self-confidence. "They did not see me," he said simply.

"That so?" He pushed himself up into a sitting position. His lips curled at the corners. "I could use you in my front line."

"I have already done you more service than you could countenance," Jarrod replied drily, "and I am here to do you even greater service."

"Speak on, Magician, I'm always grateful for information. If it proves true, there'll be a reward for you."

"Oh, I don't think a reward is necessary," Jarrod said, pushing back the cowl on his cloak. There was no reaction. "Do you know who I am?" he asked.

"From your height, you're a Magician, what else do I need to know?"

Nothing, Jarrod thought, though he was disappointed not to be recognized. "In that case," he said, "you should know that there are spies in your camp and that your plans are known to the enemy."

Magrius straightened up slowly. "There are spies in my camp? Can you prove that?" He sounded belligerent.

"Your battle plan," Jarrod said offhandedly, "is to mount an all-out attack along the bank of the Illuskhardin, curl around behind the Umbrian forces and attack the rest from the rear. Not so?" He did not wait for an answer. "I know because I watched as a Songean chief extracted the information from an Umbrian captive." He produced a sour smile. "I am inclined to believe him."

"And you undoubtedly have a suggestion," Magrius said, finally sitting back, tone sarcastic.

Jarrod pursed his lips, offended by the man's attitude. "They have adjusted to take advantage of your strategy," he said slowly. "If you attacked in force up the center, instead of along the riverbank, you could win a decisive victory."

"I see," Magrius said in an almost jocular tone. "And I'm supposed to believe you because you turn up in my tent unexpectedly and are very tall?"

"Not exactly," Jarrod said, smiling for the first time. "I have men up in the mountains who are prepared to bring lightning down on the enemy before you attack to soften them up. If that doesn't happen, you'll know I was lying." The smile broadened. "I have also arranged for the Songeans to launch an attack from the rear as soon as they see both lines entangled."

The Arundelian looked at Jarrod speculatively. "It sounds very inviting, Magician, and I do not doubt your personal probity, but you are asking me to risk a great deal on your say-so."

Jarrod smiled again. "Well done," he said. "Were I in your place, I would have my doubts. The Umbrians killed my father-in-law, that's true. He was a good man and I respected him. I never got to know him well enough to love him though. I regret it now, but his death hasn't warped my judgment. I've been in the mountains trying to rally the Songean clans. I think I've made some headway, but one never knows with them. Can I guarantee that they'll attack? No. My inner self says they will, for what that's worth. Besides, you don't have to make a move until the lightning strikes begin. Best of all, no one saw me arrive and no one will see me leave. My reputation is already established, I don't need the credit for this action. From here on in, this is your battle. Make of it what you will." He pulled his cloak around him, turned and headed for the tent flap.

XIX

⚜ ⚜ ⚜

M alum of Quern sat with the Emperor. Under other circumstances, it would have been accounted a rare privilege, but Malum was aware that in his case it was motivated by the Emperor's wish to keep a public distance from him. On top of that, Varodias was in a bad mood and, for once, had every right to be. News of the defeat of the Imperial forces in northern Isphardel had reached Angorn that morning. There had been an extremely stormy Council meeting to which Malum had not been invited. Though there was no way that he could be linked with the defeat, he was nervous. He was always nervous around Varodias these days.

"We assume that you have heard the news." The voice was tightly controlled.

"Alas yes, Majesty."

"How could this have happened, Master Secretary?" The control slipped slightly. "An Imperial Army bested by despicable Isphardis and green troops from the Kingdoms more fitted for plowing fields than warfare. It makes no sense. We have been betrayed; there can be no other explanation. If there is treason, we count on you to sniff it out."

"I hold no brief for the Elector of Nimegan," Malum said cautiously, "but he has always been loyal to the throne. He has never been implicated in any kind of sedition. His wife and his youngest son, of whom he is very fond, are here at Angorn. I am not competent to judge his military skills, but I do not think he would knowingly betray you."

"What then?" The question was delivered sharply, with a touch of anger.

"My intelligence from the battlefield indicates that there was a bombardment of lightning bolts just before the fight was joined. It shocked and blinded the troops and by the time they had recovered, the enemy was upon them. To me that bespeaks the subtle hand of the Discipline. The troops sent against us are but chaff, and we the flail, but the Discipline fights by other rules."

Malum saw that the Emperor's color had darkened. Mention of the Discipline could be counted on to divert Varodias. Now, if he could come up with a way to turn that to his advantage, to strengthen the regard in which the Emperor held him.

Varodias' fists were clenched. "And what can we do against these unbelievers, these merchants of darkness?" he demanded, eyes bright and wide. "How can honest men counter their unnatural ways?"

Then the answer came to Malum. His pulse quickened. "When we were dealing with the Weatherwards," he said, knowing that he might be provoking unpleasant memories, "I developed a machine that immobilized them, as your Imperial Majesty may remember. It was lost in the landslide, but it can be duplicated."

Varodias sat forward in his padded chair. "We did not know that you were so scientifically inclined." Varodias was wildly ironic.

"We needed something portable and I had help from some

more qualified than I," Malum said modestly, relieved that the Emperor had forgotten the previous failure.

"That was the only one?" The Emperor's complexion had returned to its normal pallor.

"Yes, Sire, but I can duplicate it."

Varodias sat back with the beginnings of a smile. "Then do so. We shall train men to use them and send them to the battle-front. We shall grant you a patent and you shall be provided with whatever materials you require. You will be reimbursed by the exchequer—only if they work, of course," he added. "Will they take long to assemble, think you?"

"I shall proceed with the matter immediately, Sire," Malum said, rising and bowing.

"Good; very good," Varodias said, nodding and rubbing his gloved hands together. "You shall report directly to us on your progress."

Malum bowed again and backed to the door. There was a decided spring in his walk as he made his way back to his rooms. How quickly things can change, he thought with satis-faction. With this one stroke he was about to become a very rich man. More importantly, he had impressed his father. The scientific aptitude that he had inherited had proved to be the key. It was, he felt, entirely fitting. Life was looking up.

Jarrod Courtak's life, by contrast, was spent looking down; down at the valley where the Umbrian forces under Prince Coram were trying to make their way south, down at the treacherous paths that led across the mountains from one clan holding to the next. He was accompanied by the unicorns and a returned Jubal Aristach. There were days of trekking and chilly nights spent sleeping in the open. Despite the clans' traditional dislike of Magicians, he was well received, mainly, he was sure, because of the presence of the unicorns, whom the Songeans regarded as divine incarnations. What surprised him most, however, was that he always seemed to be expected.

The life led by the clans was a hard one and, by Kingdom standards, primitive, yet their system of communications was remarkably effective. He knew of the recapture of Fort Bandor within days of its occurrence. The clansmen of the Central Range, so the story went, had stormed the castle with the help of a few foreigners who rode cloudsteeds. Whatever the truth of it, it made Jarrod's work of chivvying the clans into attacking the Umbrians a great deal easier. The Chiefs of the Saradondas were not about to allow the clans of the Central Range to gain all the glory. While spears, knives and light bows were no match for Umbrian arms or Umbrian armor, the Emperor's men were outnumbered and kept on the defensive. They did not dare, moreover, to venture into the hills to hunt. While the Prince continued doggedly to press onward, the steam had gone out of the drive.

"I think we've done all we can here," Jarrod said to the young Weatherward one morning. Jubal's face lit up. "No, we're not going home quite yet, I'm afraid. I think we should pay Fort Bandor a visit first. Cheer up," he said, slapping the lad on the shoulder. "It will mean sleeping in a bed for a couple of nights."

After bidding the clan elders farewell and thanking them for their hospitality, Jarrod let the unicorns, with the exception of Nastrus and the three-year-old that Aristach was riding, know that they could leave. If their arrival had delighted the clanspeople, their sudden disappearance into thin air stunned them. Before they could recover, the two Magicians and their mounts vanished too.

They came out of Interim at the edge of the woods behind Fort Bandor.

'This place has changed since last we were here,' Nastrus commented. And indeed it had.

The formidable walls still loomed high, cutting off the view to the north, but whereas before they had stood clear, they were now fringed by wooden buildings, most of them deserted by the look of things.

Jarrod turned to his companion. "I think we shall have to go around and in by the front gates. And if there is any talking to do, leave it to me."

"Wouldn't a spell of invisibility be a good idea?" Aristach inquired nervously.

"If the fort is in friendly hands, our sudden materialization might provoke an attack, but I think a small disguise would be in order."

Jarrod concentrated, visualizing the two men and the unicorns. He fixed the image in his mind and then started to make alterations, much like a painter might do upon a canvas. The horns disappeared from the unicorns and Nastrus became a roan. Then he tackled the harder job of making himself and Aristach smaller. He opened his eyes and rode around the Weatherward. The transformation looked convincing.

Aristach watched him and then looked down at himself. "How did you do that?" he asked.

"Practice. And, no matter what happens, don't try any spells unless I tell you to. We shall be moving and maintaining the illusion is a lot harder than setting it up."

You might have used your magic to do something about your appearance,' Nastrus said. *'You could both do with a good grooming.'*

'And I don't need any distractions from you either,' Jarrod replied. *'Lead on to the front gates.'*

When they rounded the front corner tower they saw guards outside the entranceway, indicating that the gates were open. The sight of the sentries, however, made Jarrod's stomach tighten. They were Umbrian. So much for the reliability of the clans' intelligence system. "Grab hold of your unicorn's mane and prepare to go into Interim," he muttered to Aristach. Nastrus, however continued ahead. He ambled up to the guards, paused while they were looked over and waved along, and then went in through the gates.

'Are you mad?' Jarrod thought out at him. 'In the name of the gods get us out of here!'

The unicorn ignored him and continued to pace forward. Jarrod glanced up at the battlements and saw more Umbrian soldiers looking down on them. 'Do you want to get us all killed? What kind of game are you playing?' Nastrus' mind, however, was opaque. Jarrod prepared to go within himself for whatever power he could summon, but his attention was distracted by a Songean boy of about fourteen or fifteen who came running up and bowed. Jarrod realized that he had let go of the illusion and began to raise a force field around them.

'No need for that,' Nastrus said smugly. 'The boy was smart enough to recognize a unicorn when he saw one in spite of all of your shennanigans. The bow was for us, not you.'

Jarrod sat straight, expecting an arrow between the shoulder blades. He glanced at Aristach and saw the look of incomprehension and fear in his eyes. "Hold on," he said. "There's something funny going on."

At that moment, a lean man with a straight back, bowlegs and a touch of grey around the temples came out of a doorway and approached. He was wearing civilian clothes, but there was no mistaking the military bearing.

"Welcome to Fort Bandor, Magician," he said as he approached. "To whom do I have the honor of speaking?" He spoke in Common and his accent was unmistakably Talismani.

A cloudsteedsman, Jarrod thought with relief. So the Songeans had been right. "I am Jarrod Courtak of Paladine," he said, "and my companion is Jubal Aristach."

"The Jarrod Courtak?" the man inquired pleasantly.

"The same, I'm afraid. And you are?"

"Forgive me, Eminence, I'm Wing Commander Alost Sarad."

"What exactly is going on around here?" Jarrod asked, looking back up at the battlements.

"Oh, don't worry. Those are my men. They are wearing captured Umbrian uniforms in case a rotifer decides to fly over."

"Most effective, I assure you," Jarrod returned, throwing a leg over Nastrus' back and sliding off. He motioned to Aristach to dismount.

'You might have told me,' he thought out reproachfully to Nastrus.

'I know very little about human coverings, but I sensed no aggression.' The unicorn was offhand.

"Do you think you could arrange for my friends to get water, food and a good grooming? We have been living in the mountains for some sennights," Jarrod said.

"By all means," Sarad replied. "Do you think they will follow the boy?" Jarrod nodded and the Wing Commander spoke briefly and gutturally to the Songean. He turned his attention back to the two Magicians. "If you don't mind my saying so, my lord, you both look as if you could do with a bath and a change of clothes."

The Magicians followed him and Jarrod's head was filled with Nastrus' amusement. An hour later, bathed, shaved and wrapped somewhat ignominiously in sheets since their robes were not yet dry and there were no clothes on the post that would fit them, they joined the Wing Commander and his officers for the midday meal. If the cloudsteedsmen saw anything funny in the getup of their guests, they were either too well schooled or too much in awe of Magicians to express it.

"Sarad," Jarrod said to break the ice, "are you by any chance related to . . ."

The Wing Commander cut in, smiling, having obviously fielded this question any number of times before. "Borr Sarad is my father."

"He is an old friend of mine from the days of the Commission on the Outland," Jarrod said. His forehead wrinkled. "I seem to remember his telling me that his sons were farmers."

"My older brothers are. Father always liked to think of himself as a man of the soil." There was a slightly distant feel to the words. "I honestly think he believed it—and it certainly endeared him to the voters." The tone had sharpened. "I was trotted out for occasional elections, both as a boy and when I was in a Cloudsteed Wing." A smile, a slightly sour smile, appeared on his face. "Now that he has retired, his wish has come true and he complains that he is bored and that the grandchildren are always underfoot."

No love lost there, Jarrod thought sadly. "No doubt he will be proud of this exploit of yours, and probably a bit envious," he said.

The smile, what there was of it, vanished. "He doesn't know about it," Sarad said. "No one does, except the Umbrians. They loosed bunglebirds before we subdued them. They're such tricky creatures in flight once they're well loosed that we couldn't bring them down. We launched cloudsteeds after them, but to no avail. That's why we keep on alert. There's no knowing when the Umbrians will counterattack."

"Well no one challenged us behind the fort," Jarrod said.

"When you appeared behind the castle, you weren't disguised and the clansmen in the woods arrived with your description before you rode through the gates," Sarad corrected.

"It seems that I underestimated you, Wing Commander. I shall make sure upon my return that your father is aware, among others of course, of the excellent job that you and your men have done."

"The praise can wait. What we really need are reinforcements."

"I shall see to that on my return to Stronta," Jarrod said. "In the meantime, I need someone to keep an eye on the Umbrians who are trying to link up with their brethren in Isphardel."

"Oh, the ones commanded by the Emperor's son? I think we can do that, so long as it is only surveillance you want."

"The Emperor's son commands them?" Jarrod said.

"According to the garrison members we captured."

"Interesting. All the more reason to keep an eye on him."

"It will be a pleasure, Eminence."

"And if you could contrive to make it seem that you came from the south . . ."

"I don't think you'd have an argument from anybody here about that," Sarad said with a genuine smile.

"The clans have slowed them down considerably and have cut off their supplies, but, let's face it, they will never be able to face them in a pitched battle."

"Be honest, Eminence," one of the officers said, "this is nothing but a side show. The big tournaments are in Isphardel and with Prince Saxton on the Plain."

"Saxton?"

"Yes, hadn't you heard? He's replaced old Gwyndryth and is facing off against the Umbrians across the Jodderon River."

Jarrod smiled good-naturedly. "I have been out of touch for too long, it seems," he said pleasantly, as befitted an officers' mess. "It would be best, I think, if my friend Jubal Aristach and I were back in Stronta, damp robes or no." He looked around. "If any of you have messages for loved ones at home, we would be more than happy to see them delivered." He raised his hands as a hubbub broke out and waved for silence. "Come now, gentlemen," he said. "You know you're going to have to write them out and please have the name and address printed clearly on the outside of each letter. We shall be leaving in about an hour."

"That was a very nice gesture," Jubal said as they were walking out of the Hall.

"You've never been in a war before, have you?" Jarrod replied. "No, of course you haven't. I grew up in war, and I hoped never to see it again, but there you are. These men are far from families, and wives, and sweethearts. It is a simple thing to do, but it is enormously important to them." He looked at the young man, with his uncreased face and his look of expectation and was saddened. "Not too long ago," he said, "I taught you how to kill. This is a lesson in how to give hope." He lengthened his stride and walked away.

XX

istories are deceptive. That was something that
Strand had yet to discover. The first history was
being written by Jarrod Courtak, who had been working at his
version for a number of years but had yet to publish a volume.
His research depended heavily on the Archmagial Archives in
Celador and thus saw things from the Discipline's perspective.
This was no bad thing since the Discipline was fairly even-
handed given the spread of its influence. What got recorded,
however, tended to be the doings of Mages, Archmages, Kings
and Queens. There was scant record of the quotidian.

Thus, the decision of Prince Saxton to attack the Empire's
position across the Jodderon has been variously ascribed to his
wisdom or whim, orders from his wife, from Queen Naxania or
the Archmage Greylock. What in fact propelled him forward
was a diminishing supply of food. Varodias and his advisers
had expected wholesale desertions among the Farodmen as the
harvest approached. This time, however, crops had been pre-
bought and the men on the banks of the Jodderon were quite
happy to let the women and the boys back home bring in the

harvest. If they made a mess of it, it didn't matter, the money had already been paid. The problem for Prince Saxton, Sir Patras Braise and the rest of the commanders was that those same women and boys who might have supplied the army were in the fields and the stocks in grain barns were depleted.

The catapults had been winched laboriously down the face of the Causeway and reassembled behind the Allied lines. Practice shots had been lobbed at the battlewagon, but, since they were mobile, little damage was done. A line of arquebuses, propped on forked staves, kept the Allies from attempting a river crossing. The high morale of the troops, men less used to the monotonies of army life than their more professional Umbrian counterparts, had begun to ebb. Faced with these mounting problems, Prince Saxton decided to take the initiative. Having done so, he paid a visit to the Magicians atop the Causeway.

When the sun came up the following morning under lowering skies, the watchers on the Umbrian controlled portion of the Upper Causeway trained their spyglasses on an amazing sight. All along the west bank of the river stood rank upon rank of soldiers stretching back as far as the eye could see. An officer was dispatched to alert the general.

"We estimate a force of at least a hundred thousand men, sir," he reported. "I don't know where they came from. None of the rotifers mentioned massive reinforcements moving this way in the past few days. On the face of it, it's impossible, but they are there."

"If it is impossible," Estivus said, "then sorcery must be involved. I think it's time to try out Secretary Quern's secret weapon." He turned and issued orders.

Half an hour later a hideous, high whine split the air and was carried north by the prevailing winds. The Magicians carefully positioned among the troops instantly clapped their hands to their ears, their bodies writhing in pain. The link between them collapsed upon the instant and two thirds of the allied host winked out of existence. There were still troops massed along the riverbank, but not in the overwhelming numbers that the dawn had revealed. Trumpets blared and flights of arrows darkened the sky. Catapults heaved stones weighing up to forty pounds into the opposing lines. A second trumpet call rang out competing with the infernal noise the Umbrians were making and the Allied infantry surged into the water. The stakes impeded them and the first fusillade from the arquebuses took their toll, but they took too long to reload and the archers picked them off.

As the first contingents of infantry struggled ashore, the left wing of the Umbrian cavalry swept down on them. Men fell and the river began to run red, but the soldiers of the Kingdoms kept coming. The lines became jumbled and horsemen were pulled from their saddles. Pikes and knives came into their own in close quarters and the Umbrians were pushed back slowly but surely. The battlewagons had a head of steam up and the crossbowmen using them as a platform had their weapons cocked, but the situation ahead was too muddled for them to be sure of hitting the enemy.

Out on the northern wing a classic cavalry battle was shaping up. The river was wider and shallower there and Prince Saxton's men had less trouble crossing. Oxenburg shifted two squadrons farther out and used his main force to counter the frontal assault. He meant to give ground slowly, destroying as many of the enemy as he could, until he had lured the Allied cavalry far enough away from the river for the reserve squadrons to execute a flanking maneuver and take them from behind.

Unfortunately for the Margrave, the element of surprise was not going to come from his reserves. They were waiting shielded by a screen of young trees in a bend in the river. Three blasts on a bugle was to be their sign to sweep down on the enemy and catch them between two Umbrian contingents. One minute they were virtually alone on the plain and the next they were surrounded by a herd of unicorns that appeared from no-where. There were two Magicians among them, one, it was later reported, with red hair, but if they thought that these were an-other Magical illusion, they were soon disabused. The unicorns charged down on them, used horns and hooves on their mounts, unseating many as the horses reared and bucked try-ing to escape the torment of the slashing hooves and pricking horns. The horses bolted, carrying the remaining riders ig-nominiously away. Their work done, the unicorns vanished as suddenly as they had appeared.

The superior discipline of the Umbrian troops saved them from disaster. When the reserve wing failed to materialize, Es-tivus of Oxenburg rallied his men and withdrew in good order. At the end of the day, the Allies had lost more men, but they had secured the east bank of the Jodderon. Not wanting to out-pace his infantry, Saxton broke off the pursuit of the Umbrians and returned to his men with part of the Umbrian baggage train. It was accounted a great victory though none in the Allied camp knew that it was owed to the unicorns.

Prince Saxton was too busy reorganizing his troops and visiting the Wisewomen's tents to check on the wounded to miss his family overmuch. When he did think of them it was in terms of safety and tranquillity. Tranquillity, however, was not what his wife was experiencing. She had just had a highly disturbing au-dience with the Mage of Arundel. She had used the skill she had developed over the years that she had been on the throne, the ability to listen and appear sympathetic without committing herself. Now, in the privacy of her withdrawing room, she went over the interview again.

Arabella had been mildly surprised when Sumner pre-sented himself in full regalia for a private audience. She put it down to the insecurity bred by his relatively humble birth and concentrated on putting him at his ease. First she bade him take a seat and then had chai and shortcake served.

"To what do we owe this visit, my Lord Mage?" she said pleasantly when the niceties had been completed.

"A matter of grave import, Your Majesty," Sumner replied. "Have you seen the Archmage of late?"

"He dined with us two nights ago."

"And how did you find him?"

Arabella smiled. "A little distracted and somewhat tired, but otherwise good company."

"Did he discuss the war, Your Majesty?"

"It was a social occasion, my Lord Mage."

"If I may be frank, Your Majesty, Greylock avoids the subject on all occasions. Nor, for that matter, will he discuss matters pertaining to the Discipline." He shrugged. "As you yourself know, with so many of us off east aiding the armies, there are many places to be filled, a great deal of administrative detail to be finalized, and yet our Archmage stays in his tower and does nothing." He shook his head. "I fear that Greylock is no longer capable of performing the duties of Archmage. His previous, notable, contributions during the late war have taken their toll.

"He is a good and worthy old man," Sumner said sententiously, "but I fear that he is no longer capable of discharging the office of Archmage—especially not in a time of war. I say this with deep regret, but Greylock has become a liability and at a most-sensitive time."

"We are not clear what it is, exactly, that you are suggesting, my Lord Mage. Are you asking that the High Council of Magic appoint an acting Archmage?"

Sumner waited, seeming to consider. "No, I think we need to do more than that. If we appointed an acting Archmage, that person's authority would be constantly undermined by Greylock, whether he intended it or not. I think, alas, that he needs to be deposed and replaced."

Arabella's eyebrows rose in question. "Have you discussed this with the Archmage?"

"It would do no good, ma'am. He has been sounded out discreetly by the Dean and several Magisters from the Collegium. He sees nothing amiss."

"Then surely we must inform him and a special Council meeting must be convened to deliberate the matter."

"In ordinary times that would be most commendable, but we are fighting a war and the Discipline's contribution has already been grievously hampered. I fear that we cannot afford the time for formal deliberations."

She gave him her most beguiling smile. "Are you proposing to nominate us, Eminence?"

"Your Majesty would make a superb candidate," Sumner replied diplomatically, "but you have a Kingdom to rule and, with your husband away at the wars, all the weight devolves upon your shoulders."

"Shoulders, may we remind you," she responded with a touch of asperity, "that have borne that weight since we were a small girl and you were still a student at the Collegium."

"Just so; just so, Your Majesty." He bowed his head. She might be a great deal younger than he, but she could dominate him effortlessly.

"So," she said, pleasant once more, "who is your candidate?"

"The Collegium's representatives on the Council are united behind me, ma'am."

"And you will, of course, vote for yourself."

"I was hoping for your support, ma'am."

"You make an interesting case, my Lord Mage," Arabella said, making the words sound encouraging. "We must think upon this." She stood, signaling the end of the audience.

Sitting now in the withdrawing room, she had done her thinking and the more she had thought, the less she liked the situation. Sumner was right in characterizing Greylock as ineffective, but an Archmage had never been removed from office. Sumner was an ambitious little upstart, but he could be dangerous. If what he had said was true, he had a working majority of the High Council behind him, especially since Jarrod Courtak, the other likely candidate to be the next Archmage, was out of contact. Still, it wouldn't do to oppose the man openly. No; that could lead to an accident or a too-strong dose of mandragore slipped into Greylock's bedtime posset. No, she would have to be more subtle, or more brutal than that. She smiled to herself. It was not a pretty smile, rather it was the unconscious expression of one who had wielded power for a long time. Sumner had made a mistake in coming to her, but then men tended to be vain and simple creatures. Her mind made up, she rang the hand bell on the table beside her.

Greylock was roused from sleep by two of the Queen's Guard. They gestured him to remain silent as he struggled into wakefulness.

"Your pardon, Eminence," one of them said quietly. "Her Majesty has discovered a plot against your life. It is imperative that you get dressed immediately and come with us. Take the triple tiara of the Archmages and your Staff, those she most especially mentioned. Otherwise take only what you most immediately need."

"Where are we going?" Greylock demanded as he complied.

"Just come with us, my Lord Archmage," the young soldier said urgently. "You will be safe with us. You have our bond on that. The Queen will contact you later."

"Oh, very well," Greylock said grumpily. "I just hope that all this hugger-mugger is justified. Get the Duty Boy to help me pack."

"No Duty Boy tonight, Eminence. We've brought a saddlebag."

It was at that moment that the gravity of the situation sank home. He hoped these men had not murdered the lad, but resistance was obviously futile. He fetched the box that held the triple tiara of the Archmages and retrieved his Staff from the corner of the room. He stuffed smallclothes, shirts and hose into the bag, donned a workaday robe and pronounced himself ready. Surely, he thought, if they meant to kill me, they wouldn't go through this farce of spare shoes and breechclouts. He still wasn't sure, though, as he followed the men down the curling stairs. The courtyard was disconcertingly quiet and their footsteps correspondingly loud. They walked across the city without the aid of torches, keeping to the main thoroughfares. No watch challenged them.

Greylock glanced up. The nightmoon was past its zenith. It must, he thought, be at least the second hour of the day. He hadn't thought to look at the water clock before he left his rooms. Where in the name of the gods were they taking him? His unease deepened as they approached the gates. Lights were on in the guardroom, but no one seemed to be on duty. One of his escorts unlocked the small door set in the larger and gestured him through. This, thought Greylock, does not bode well. These two cutthroats in soldiers' uniforms will take me outside the city and do away with me. Then they will steal the tiara and make off. He straightened his back and began the litany of concentration under his breath.

I am Archmage of Strand, he told himself as the calmness took him over. If these ruffians try to lay a hand on me, I shall destroy them.

"Not much farther, Eminence," the talkative one said in tones of such solicitude that Greylock's certainty wavered. "The cloudsteed's just over there. It's a good, reliable beast and it knows the way to Stronta without your having to do anything."

"Stronta? I'm going to Stronta?" Greylock exclaimed.

"Yes, Archmage. Queen's orders. She says you'll be safe there. All you have to do is stay in the saddle."

"Yes, yes, yes, I've ridden a cloudsteed before," Greylock said testily, relieved that his worst fears were mere night fumes. "Am I going alone, or will you two be coming with me?"

"Darley here will fly with you, sir. Her Majesty wanted it all kept hush-hush."

"You've done very well and I thank you," Greylock said generously. "Tell me your name. I'll not forget you when I return."

"It's Arencort, sir, Fillis Arencort, but you don't need to do anything special. We're just carrying out orders."

"Well, I'm grateful to you both, nevertheless," Greylock said with spirit. They had stopped and the outlines of two cloudsteeds bulked in the scant silver from the moon.

"Let me just get you settled on the steed and then you'll be on your way, Eminence." He paused and then added awkwardly, "And may the gods bring you back safe to Celador."

"They will, son, they will," Greylock said with a confidence he did not entirely feel. "Go now with my blessing." He made a vague sign that he hoped would do and turned to the silent partner. "Come now, friend Darley, let us to steed." Pleased with the sound of it, he added, "The night sky is ours and the future is friendly, but unknown."

It was a phrase that would crop up later in ballads of the era.

XXI

❧ ❧ ❧

On the Alien Plain, just north of the Upper Causeway, two great armies feinted and probed each other for weaknesses. The skies above them were also filled. Umbrian rotifers lumbered around, spewing smoke and steam. Cloud-steeds swooped gracefully. Both sides took pains to consolidate their possessions by digging trenches. In this the Umbrians had the edge because they used their battlewagons to disrupt the allies' attempts to complete theirs. The sharpened stakes that held horsemen at bay were useless against the armored steam chariots. Darius' method for disabling the the battlewagon had been to attack them when they were at rest or moving very slowly. While Varodias and his team of scientists had never been able to duplicate the Outlanders' peculiar weaponry, they had managed to increase the speed of the vehicles. In this particular operation they simply disrupted the digging and crushed the pointed stakes to splinters. The Allies, for their part, forced the Umbrians to spread their encampment out to minimize the damage done by the rocks hurled by the mangonels. After a time, though, suitable rocks were in short supply.

Ironically, the lack of local ammunition had been caused by the Discipline when it removed the remnants of the Giants' Causeway.

It was a dragging and dispiriting time for all concerned, but most especially for those young bloods who had ridden bravely out expecting glory and feats of individual valor. Darius' lasting legacy had been the reformation of the cavalry on both sides. The day of the headlong charge and the individual challenge was gone, replaced by disciplined units carrying out precise maneuvers in a coordinated fashion. It took a great deal of practice, and practice was boring.

The stalemate was hardest on Estivus of Oxenburg, compounded by too many messages from one source and too few from another. The Emperor was impatient. He reminded the Margrave that he had been provided with the finest in Umbrian technology and he expected to see results. Estivus knew that it would be not only fruitless, but dangerous, to point out that these weapons were of limited use given the actual conditions, or that he had already captured the Songean and Isphardi portions of the Alien Plain and was successfully defending them across an extended front. He became adept at sending back soothing and optimistic replies.

As worrying was the fact that he had had no word from Fort Bandor for a long time. After the first sennightly report had failed to appear, he had waited for three days and then sent a messenger. The messenger had not returned. He had sent a group of six scouts. None had returned. It was unlikely that the Songeans had taken over the place, but, even if they had, someone would have escaped, or one of the men he had sent would have turned back when he saw what had happened. He had sent a rotifer to fly over the fort and the pilot had reported that the flag was flying from the battlements and that Umbrian soldiers manned the walls. They had waved at him. There had been no signs that a fight had taken place and certainly no signs of a siege. It was all most puzzling.

His train of thought was broken by the appearance of his orderly at the tent flap. He saluted smartly. "Yes, Patsern, what is it?"

Patsern was a grizzled veteran of the Outland Wars. He had been wounded a number of times and limped when he walked. It did not affect his ability in the saddle, however, and he had reenlisted when the call came. He did not hesitate to give his commander the benefit of his advice, but only in private.

"Beggin' the General's pardon, but the Captains are outside."

"Is it that time already?" Estivus stood up. "Show them in." He waited until his senior officers had filed in. "Take a seat, gentlemen." He waited again until they were settled. "As you know, His Imperial Majesty is anxious for us to attack the enemy. Things are not going as well on the southern front as he would like and the people are hungry for news of a victory. It is up to us to provide that victory. I have held off so that we can incorporate the new recruits and to give your men a chance to hone their skills. The time has come to put those skills to the test. We have nothing to fear from the Magicians. I intend to put crossbowmen on the right wing and to the rear to counter the unicorns should they put in an appearance. With those two elements neutralized, we should be able to have ourselves a nice, normal battle." The officers chuckled. "Now, here's what I propose . . ."

To a man, the others in the tent leaned forward.

Jarrod was to find the Archmage in residence in his rooms on his return to the Outpost. They had, of course, been Greylock's rooms before they had been his, but if the Archmage was paying a visit to his former home, Jarrod would have expected him to stay at the palace as befitted his state. Having seen Nastrus stabled, he went directly up the tower stairs. He stopped on the landing and signed to the Duty Boy to announce him. Greylock looked up as he came in.

"Ah there you are," he said, the voice quavering slightly. "I wondered when you would show up. D'you want some wine or some ale? I'm afraid I don't have the head for them these days."

"Water and something to eat would be good," Jarrod said to the Duty Boy. He turned back to the Archmage. "I hope you don't mind if I have something to eat, sir. I've just come through Interim and it always makes one ravenous."

" 'Course not. Come over here and tell me what you've been up to. All I know is that Agar Thorden is muttering darkly about your being away all the time."

"Poor Agar; I'd feel sorrier for him if he didn't enjoy the responsibility."

"True enough," Greylock admitted. "I assume that you have been with the military. How are things going?"

Jarrod waited while the Duty Boy put a plate of bread and meat down for him and filled a goblet with water. Then he brought the Archmage up to date between bites of food. "So you see," he concluded, "while things seem to be going fairly well for the armed forces, they are going rather poorly for us."

Greylock sighed and rubbed his eyes. "There's always something, isn't there. I had hoped to be able to end my days in peace and quiet, but that's obviously not going to happen." He looked across appraisingly. "D'you know why I'm here?"

"No, sir. I was rather wondering."

"Had to leave Celador in the dead of night. The Queen's orders."

"Arabella banished you?" Jarrod said incredulously.

"No. She may well have saved my life. Our good friend Sumner was moving to replace me and Arabella thought that he might resort to assassination. So, I was bundled out of bed in the middle of the night and put on a cloudsteed."

Jarrod swore under his breath. He looked at the old man, perched on the edge of the chair he had always sat in when Jarrod had been summoned before him as a boy. He seemed so much smaller now. "What are we going to do?"

"There's nothing that we can do from here. I've sent a message back saying that there was a major problem at the front and that I have gone to see for myself." He smiled, revealing yellowing teeth. "As it turns out, the Umbrians are using some kind of machine that puts us out of commission, so I have not lied."

"I hadn't heard that they were using it in battle. It'll be the same one that they used against the Weatherwards. We should have expected that."

"There doesn't seem much that we can do about it." Greylock said, sounding resigned.

"The first thing we can do is take a fast carriage ride along the Causeway and visit our colleagues. Did you bring your Staff with you?"

"I did, but I don't think . . ."

Jarrod cut in before the Archmage could complete the sentence. "Just seeing you there will put heart into the men and between us we'll cook up something impressive."

"If you say so." Greylock sounded doubtful and Jarrod felt a twinge of regret. This was the man he had revered and feared and now he was diminished to the point of going meekly along. He rose. "I'd better see Agar before he finds out that I'm back and comes looking for me." He smiled. "Then I'll have to tell him that we'll be leaving again. I have a nasty feeling that that will be as hard as confronting the Umbrians."

Greylock chuckled. "Rather you than me, lad. Off you go then."

It took three days before the journey down the Causeway got started. One of those days was spent with the Queen and her advisers. His news of Bandor and the doings in Songuard and on the southern battle ground was more recent than anything they had heard thus far. One side effect of the meeting was that what had been planned as a quiet trip to the battlefield became something far grander. He had not mentioned the goings on at

Celador, for that was Greylock's right, but Naxania insisted that the Archmage should be properly attended as befitted his high office. Instead of the two of them in a single carriage, the party consisted of six mounted soldiers, the carriage for the two Mages, a coach for four attendant Magicians, including Jubal Aristach, a larger, rougher version for servants, a cook wagon and a baggage wain.

The journey seemed to take forever and yet it ended sooner than Jarrod expected. They came upon the Magicians' encampment on this side of the Jodderon and the army could be seen spread along the easterly bank, backs to the river. The Magicians were curious as the little cortege approached, coming out of their tents. Curiosity turned to joy when they saw the Archmage descend. They clustered around him, bowing in greeting. They repaired to the largest of the tents while the baggage was unloaded.

"How do you come to be here?" Jarrod inquired when the civilities were over. "I thought the last battle gained far more ground." There was a silence until a heavyset man in a blue robe that could have done with a washing spoke up.

"Three days ago the Umbrians attacked in full force before dawn. We had just finished Making the Day when we heard their accursed machines coming to life. We were far enough away, the gods be thanked, that they did not affect us badly. The battlewagons led the assault just as the light began to come. Our men were slow to react. The machines just plowed into our lines, catching many in their tents, rolling over them. Then the sky machines came over, dropping great rocks on the picket lines. A lot of horses were hurt or killed outright. We retreated then. The battlewagons don't come close enough to do us harm, but those flying machines can come whirling down the wall as fast as a man can run. We are powerless against them. They didn't bother to use the noise machine," he added bitterly. "They know we cannot hurt them."

Jarrod had been searching for the man's name while he

spoke and then it came to him. Roark Cafftar, an Arundelian who taught at the Collegium and specialized in sympathetic Magic.

"The Archmage and I think that we can," he said, avoiding the Archmage's eye. "That is why we have come." He saw tense faces relax and eyes brighten. "I'm sorry, I shouldn't have interrupted. What happened next?"

"They forced our men back for the greater part of the day and then we seemed to be having some success on the far wing. It was too far off for us to see. Besides, there was dust swirling everywhere and steam rising from hot horses, but the enemy looked to be curling back on that flank and a couple of squadrons of their cavalry were pulled out from the center and sent galloping off that way. Our main force took heart and the movement backward ceased. The lines were locked together, swaying first one way and then another. It was like watching a massive snake undulate, except for the noise, that is. Anyway, to make things short, around the eighteenth hour trumpets began to bray and the two sides disengaged."

"Aye," a second man, whom Jarrod did not recognize, said. "Here we are, more or less where we started. All that time, all that effort, all those lives, gone for naught."

"No," Greylock objected, "not for nothing. The Umbrians have been held in check. They have been taught that they are not invincible and shown that the Magical Kingdoms have the will and the stomach for this fight. Those men did not die in vain."

There was silence. The Archmage had spoken. If there were thoughts or questions, they went unvoiced. To have the head of the Discipline in their midst inspired deference, and in some, awe. Greylock got arthritically to his feet.

"They should have my quarters prepared by now," he said. "I shall go and refresh myself. The road up here is smooth, but being cooped up in a carriage is hard on old bones." He smiled at them all. "I am glad to see you all and I commend you for your steadfastness. It has not been easy for you." He turned to Jarrod. "If Your Eminence would accompany me. We have much to discuss."

"Willingly, Archmage." He nodded to the assembled Magicians. "We shall talk again later." He, too, smiled at them before turning and following the Archmage out.

When they were installed in Greylock's newly erected tent, sipping watered wine, the Archmage voiced the question that had obviously been on his mind since he left the meeting. "What, in the name of the gods, are we going to do? We can parade around in our finest robes, waving our Staffs to hearten our people and the troops, but that's not going to help them on the battlefield or restore their faith in the Discipline for very long. We're going to have to do something."

"If you'll permit a suggestion?"

Greylock waved at him to proceed.

"The first thing we should do is to confer with Prince Saxton. There would be no point in our contriving a grand gesture if his troops aren't in any condition to follow up. And I think our first visit should be incognito. In fact, we should be invisible when we go through his lines. When we find out what he needs most, we can act accordingly."

"You sound very sure of yourself."

Jarrod smiled a little grimly. "I have a feeling that a lot of the damage that machines do to us is in our minds. We have been told since first we walked through the Great Maze that Magic can't work in the presence of machines and so we believe it. Oh," he said to forestall a protest, "I don't mean to suggest that machines have no physical effect on us, but I think those effects can be minimized. Take the meeting we just had, for instance. Our colleagues admitted that the war wagons had no effect on them because they were too far away and, up on the Causeway, they are safe from them. They are terrified of the rotifers, however. This new weapon paralyzes them because it is new and because the noise reaches out and assaults them. It is extremely unpleasant to the ear, granted, but just as much to lay folk as to us. Under normal circumstances, noise, however loud, does not cripple us. We can work perfectly well close to some kinds of machinery. A grist mill is a machine, and fullers' hammers when powered by water are machines. Yet a Village Magician thinks nothing of casting a spell while standing next to them . . ." he let the sentence trail off.

"Theory is theory, practice is practice," Greylock said, just as he had when Jarrod was an Apprentice. "But you're right about talking to Saxton. Tonight after dinner, I think. For the moment you can go away and let me get some rest."

Jarrod put his cup down. "I'll see you at dinner."

I shall have to be careful with him, he thought. He must be seen to be involved in whatever we come up with, but I can't tax him too much. I have to keep him alive so that he can return to Celador and deal with that stable cur Sumner. He went in search of his own quarters.

After dinner Jarrod went back to his tent and got out a long dark cloak before rejoining the Archmage. Greylock looked at it speculatively.

"A little warm for that, isn't it?"

"We'll need them, though, and it'll be worth a little discomfort. First off we'll have to get down off this wall and a cloak will help with that. Secondly, it will be dark and with cloaks on we won't need much in the way of an invisibility spell. The alternative is to ride back to the ramp on the other side of the Jodderon, ford the river and . . ."

"All right, all right. I see your point." Greylock went over to a press and got out a light cloak. "Will this do?" He held it up.

"That will be fine," Jarrod said. "Now, I think we should discuss what we are going to say to the Prince."

"Did you spot his tent this afternoon? It would be a shame if we spent the night wandering around the camp looking for it. I mean we can't just stop a soldier and say, 'excuse me, we're invisible, but could you tell us how to get to the general's tent?' "

Jarrod laughed. This was a good sign. Greylock wasn't known for his sense of humor. "Yes, I did. Mind you, it looks simple enough from up here, but it's bound to be a lot more muddled once we're down there."

An hour later they performed a modified spell of invisibility. They left the tent and walked over to the northern side of the Causeway. Jarrod helped the older man onto the mercifully broad parapet and then climbed up beside him.

"Spread your arms and hold the cloak out," he said.

"I was doing this before you were born," the disembodied voice replied. "Let's get on with it."

Jarrod took a deep breath and went within himself, summoning memories of flight when, for a brief time, he had ridden in the body of a raptor. He began his chant and felt progressively lighter as the words came forth. When it was over he was an autumn leaf about to drop, a wing feather spiraling in the soft air. He stepped off the parapet and felt the air fill his cloak. He kept the images firmly in his head as he floated down. The sudden presence of ground beneath his boots took him by surprise and his knees bent in reflex.

"You all right, lad?" came the voice on his left.

"I was about to ask you the same."

"Give me your hand," Greylock said. "Since you know where we're going, you'd better lead." Jarrod groped around until he made contact.

Thus linked, and stepping carefully, they made their way past campfires and around groups of soldiers gaming. The men they saw appeared to be relaxed, but close to each fire there was a stock of pikes leaning into each other or a pile of bows with a line of quivers behind them. These were the lucky ones. There were tents behind the lines where the wounded lay and moaned. Even they could count themselves among the fortunate. Somewhere out of sight there were mounds of recently dug earth. Those who slept beneath them would never wake. They came at length to the great square tent in the middle of the encampment. Two sentries stood on either side of the entrance-way, staring resolutely ahead. The two Magicians walked quietly between them and ducked inside. The sentries, eyes fixed forward, never saw the tent flap move aside and fall back into place.

The inside was richly furnished. There were thick Isphardi carpets on the floor to keep out the damp and cushion weary feet. Hinged chairs with tooled leather seats and small tables inlaid with nacre were dotted around. Wrought-iron stands held lighted oil lamps. A campaign table took up one side, sand shaker, inkwell and pens were neatly laid out with a pile of blank sheets of parchment and some scrolls. The walls were covered by hangings, which was fortunate since it meant that no shadows could be seen from outside. The Magicians might deceive the eye, but they could not shed their shadows. Opposite the table was a large carved chest and a stand holding armor. At the back, in stark contrast to the luxury of the other appointments, was a simple truckle bed. The Prince's quarters were understatedly magnificent. They were also empty.

"If we are to wait," Greylock whispered, "I'm going to sit down." A few seconds later one of the chairs disappeared, not because it had been Magicked from sight, but because Greylock's body and clothes hid it.

In the event, they did not have to wait long. They were alerted by voices approaching and the stamp of feet as the sentries came to attention. The Prince half entered and turned in the entranceway to bid a final good night to his unseen companions. When he turned back, two dark shapes stood in the wavering lamplight. His hand went instantly to his sword hilt.

"No need for that, my son," Greylock said, stepping forward. "You shall get no harm from us." The cry in Saxton's throat died without utterance and his hand fell back to his side.

"I am honored by your presence, Archmage," he said,

recovering nimbly from his shock, and bowed. As he came up he glanced over his shoulder.

"No blame attaches to your guards," Greylock said. "They did not see us enter. No man could have done." He turned slightly and indicated Jarrod. "I think you know the Mage of Paladine."

"Be welcome, Eminence." The Prince's bow was not quite as low as the one with which he had greeted the Archmage. Jarrod returned it gravely. "Come, let us sit," he said briskly, "and do you tell us what brings you to my tent this night." If the man was surprised to see the two Magicians, he controlled himself admirably.

"We have come to assist you in driving the Umbrians back," Greylock said, "but we need to know if your men can do it now or whether you must wait for reinforcements."

Saxton laughed shortly. "The gods only know when or if they would come. I can do with whatever help I can get and the time begins to run short. The winter comes early in the north. But, if you will forgive my saying so, the Discipline has proved, shall we say ineffective? so far. What can you do for us now that you could not do before?"

"The point is well taken, your Royal Highness," Greylock admitted with a rueful smile. "This new machine of the Umbrians has the capacity to disable us and make us incapable of spell casting. The Mage of Paladine, however, has a theory about that"—he put a slight emphasis on the word theory— "and he has convinced me to assist him in redressing the balance. That must be the first task. Should it succeed, we will be able to help you in many ways. In any case, we can summon up the weather and turn it against them, befuddle them, take the heart out of their men."

Saxton's face brightened. "It would make all the difference," he said. "What do you need to know?"

They sat and talked until the third hour of the following day. The Prince insisted that they sleep at the camp, but the

Magicians, knowing that their bodies would have them awake early to Make the Day, declined. So he roused his orderly and bade him fetch horses and provide an escort to guide them back over the river and up the ramp onto the Upper Causeway. It had been a long night, but all three men were content.

XXII

⚜ ⚜ ⚜

They took to their beds after the Making of the Day and though there were tongues awagging on the Upper Causeway, there were none who dared to question openly or disturb their sleep. Once the Mages were up, however, there was no lack of activity. Jarrod summoned a carpenter from the camp below and set him to work fashioning wooden boxes with crooked handles coming from their sides. Greylock had Magicians lowered down the wall on the inland side to hunt for a list of herbs. The rest he set to cleaning up the campsite atop the Causeway and to drawing the double pentacle that they all knew betokened a rite of purification and preparation. They were also bidden to fast and to practice the five points of concentration. Something was afoot, something major, that much was obvious, and it galvanized those members of the Discipline who had spent two unproductive and frustrating months marooned from their fellows.

After the evening meal had been consumed, Greylock rose from the table and addressed them. "My dear colleagues," he said in a voice so soft that those at the far end of the trestle table had to strain forward to hear him, "the time has come for us to take the offensive. Tonight the rune fires of the pentacles shall burn and in them the Mage of Paladine and I shall sit, together with our good brother Roark Cafftar." He pretended not to notice the visible start his words produced in Cafftar and looked round benevolently at the others. "The rest of you will not be left out of this great enterprise. On the morrow we shall destroy the machines that have caused us so much grief. That done, we shall make great Magic together to drive the Umbrians back whence they came." He paused and when he resumed his voice had taken on a greater resonance, as if the voice of his younger days had come back to him. "Together we shall engineer a great victory over these poor, misguided men, these unfortunate tools of an evil Emperor." As he spoke, his hands rose to shoulder height on either side of his body, he seemed taller and broader and it was as if a light shone through the skin of his face.

Jarrod, who knew what his master was going to say, was moved. This was the Greylock he had known, the man whose fierce precision had molded him. Listening now to the words one could not help but be stirred. The Archmage's certainty was infectious and he could see how they made the sinews stiffen and the pride return. If I were a believing man, he thought, I would offer up prayers of thanks to the deities for this.

Greylock's hands descended slowly in a widening arc. "Much will be demanded of you and the greatest task will be the overcoming of your own fears, the setting aside of things you thought immutable. If you do, the Umbrian machines will have no power over you. It will be your power, the age-old power of the Discipline, that will be triumphant." He paused and looked at them. "I know that you can do it, but will you? Will you undertake this trial with me and for me?"

"Aye! Aye!" "Hear him! Hear him!" The cries rang out and Jarrod felt the tears pricking at his eyelids. He sniffed vigorously.

Before the sky began to pale, the three men came out of their trance and looked upon one another with the almost complicitous smile of greeting that comes to those who have shared something out of the ordinary. Sitting there in the middle of the pentacle, bathed in the dubious light of the rune fire that limned the ancient, geometric and sorcerous figures, the three naked men presented very different aspects of the human animal. Greylock, shorter than the others, but broad and stocky, showed loose skin where flesh had been. The ribs of the barrel chest could be counted, even in this light. The rounded paunch above the spindle shanks was an anomaly. Cafftar, on the other hand, had entirely too much flesh and dark hair that grew along his shoulders and in the small of his back. Jarrod Courtak, youngest of them, was lean but muscled, a dappling of curly hair across the chest and the white lines of old scars crisscrossing his back.

They rose together, though no sign was given, crossed the lines and left the pentacles. Greylock turned, made the smallest of gestures and the lights went out. They donned the clothes that had been left out for them. The Archmage and Jarrod struggled into the stiff, embroidered gowns they had brought from Stronta. Cafftar had an easier time with the plain, but clean, Magician's robe. The Mages picked up their Staffs and the three walked down the roadway toward the Umbrian lines. They stopped when they came to the wooden boxes laid out in a row.

"Friend Roark," Greylock said, "these boxes are representations of the devices that the Umbrians have been using against us. I know you to be a master of sympathetic Magic and that is why you are with us. We need you to help us destroy them."

"What Talent I have is at your service, Archmage," the man replied cheerfully, his normally surly nature subsumed by the potions he had ingested through the night. "The problem is we don't know where they are until they turn them on and, if they do, we won't be able to do anything about it."

"Oh, we have a marvelous plan to draw them out," Jarrod said, "and when they start their wailing, you will be protected against them by these." He held out two small pieces of soft cloth. "When the time comes, you will put these in your ears. It will cut down on the noise, but, more importantly, the spells that the Archmage and I have laid upon them will counter the vibrations that the machines emit. Once the Archmage and I have pinpointed the whereabouts of the machines, all that you need do, using your arts of sympathy and similarity, is to meld the images of the real with these simulacra. When we destroy the one, we will destroy the other." He smiled encouragingly.

"It seems simple enough," Cafftar replied, and Jarrod wondered if, perhaps, the potions had not been too strong for him.

"The dawn approaches," Greylock said. "We should prepare."

"Very well. Now remember," Jarrod said to Cafftar, "when you see our spell begin to manifest itself, and you won't be able to miss it, I promise you that, put the cloth in your ears and tamp it down. Muster your strength to block all sounds. The Archmage and I will have a shield up by then, so you will come to no harm. Is that understood?"

"Entirely and, if I understand you aright, when you give the sign I must join the thought of the Umbrian machines to these boxes and together we shall annihilate them." He grinned at the thought.

"Entirely so." Greylock nodded his approval. "My Lord Mage, may we have a word apart?" He drew Jarrod farther down the Causeway. "What is all this about a shield?" he demanded when they were out of earshot. "You never said anything about a shield."

"There will be no shield," Jarrod replied reassuringly. "I simply said it to give him confidence. I don't need any Magic from you at this stage. That will come later. I just need you to ignore the efforts of their machines and stay on your feet." He handed two more pieces of cloth to the Archmage. "These will help protect you, but, since we are closer to the enemy, some noise and some vibration will probably leak through. I need you to fight them off and stay on your feet. I'll be behind you and I'll support you if necessary, but I can't do this without you, you know that."

Greylock sighed and then reached up and patted Jarrod's cheek. "You're a good lad, but you're becoming altogether too big for your britches. You, support me? Have a care, young man. Look to yourself. Be sure you do your portion properly." The voice had started gently and hardened into mock anger. Jarrod was well satisfied.

"Your pardon, Archmage," he said with a smile. "I meant no disrespect."

"Let's get on with it then," Greylock said briskly. He planted his Staff and stood, head up, feet apart. "Will this do?"

"Admirably. Now, if you would put the cloth in your ears and prepare yourself to withstand the effect of the machines. When I have located them, I'll signal you and then we'll go back to Cafftar and finish the job."

He watched Greylock stuff the cotton in his ears as he moved behind him. He followed suit, not because he thought it would do any good, he knew there was no spell on the material, but because he knew that Cafftar would be watching. He bowed his head briefly and the two men began to chant. They were generating different spells, but the two seemed to commingle and generate harmony. The sound and the tension rose as the energy flowed into them and was contained by the potions. An eldritch light began to flicker around each Staff as the runes inscribed upon them came alive. It danced from one Staff to the other. To Jarrod's eye the movement seemed playful, but the power building up inside him was reaching the point of pain. He gripped his Staff, the great, curved bow of it feeling light in his hand, and paced solemnly around his mentor, keeping his face toward him, memorizing every wave in his hair and stitch in his gown. Everything he looked upon was preternaturally clear and, at the same time, he was aware of the growing light behind him and the ceiling of grey clouds above. It was time.

He resumed his place behind the Archmage, but the picture he had formed from the front was sharply etched in his mind. He took that image and projected it out and up onto the clouds and there, looming over the Umbrian camp, huge, stern and menacing, was Greylock, Staff in hand. There, Jarrod thought, that should flush them out. He stopped concentrating on the image and was pleased to see that it did not waver. He probed out toward the camp below and was aware of the growing consternation as men came awake and beheld the portent above them. Men ran to snatch up their arms, orders were shouted and more men tumbled out of tents to see what was amiss.

Soon enough the noise began, soft at first, but winding up rapidly to the familiar high-pitched screech. He gritted his teeth against it and saw Greylock begin to tremble. He placed his free hand on the other man's shoulder to steady him. The foreign machines did not bother him, but that was the Guardian's doing and no virtue of his own. Greylock had nothing to protect him except the idea that Jarrod had tried to instill, but he had to stay upright until this was over or the illusion would disappear and all would be lost. How was Cafftar faring under the onslaught of noise and vibration? No time to look. First find the machines and silence them.

He narrowed his concentration, calling up the energy that was boiling through his blood. There! He had one. And another. A third and fourth. Back a little, away to the left, a fifth. More? No. Five was all. He divorced his sight from his body, rising in mind above the Causeway, always aware of the man beneath his hand, straining to remain conscious, to stay on his feet. Jarrod saw the enemy lines and here and there among them the men who knelt beside their wooden boxes cranking the handles that produced the fiendish howl. He gathered the energy from his body and hurled it down the path of the vibrations. It would not hurt the machines, impervious constructs of wood and metal, but human minds were another thing. His mind's eye saw the bodies crumple and the sound wheezed down to silence.

He shook Greylock's shoulder, turned him and half supported, half dragged him back down the Causeway. The werelight around the Staffs still glowed and the forces summoned by the call to power still prickled and popped against the inside surface of Jarrod's skin. He could see Cafftar ahead of them, kneeling in front of the boxes, hands still over his ears.

"On your feet," he said roughly as they came up to him. "We must work fast before they think to move them. "Are you all right?" This was gentler and addressed to Greylock. The old man swallowed and blinked. Dry lips stretched in an imitation of a smile. He shook his arm free and pulled the cloth out of his ears. "What did you say?" he asked.

"You've just answered me," Jarrod said and took the cotton out of his own ears. He turned his attention back to Cafftar. "Fix these boxes in your mind. I have a picture of the Umbrian ones and I want you to reach out and join your vision to mine until the two are one." He gave the man a sharp look. "Yes you can," he said, as if he were reading the other's thoughts. "It's akin to shape-changing. You've done that before, everybody has."

"I, I'll try, my lord."

Jarrod clapped him on the arm. "Just reach for my mind and when we meld, release every scrap of energy you have in you on those boxes." He turned to Greylock. "Eminence, do you stand guard over us and use your power to block anything the enemy may do to retaliate." Greylock nodded and shifted his Staff so that he could lean on it. His skin was grey and Jarrod knew that, without the protection and the feeling of well-being generated by the potions, the Archmage would have collapsed.

His mouth set in a grim line. He caught Cafftar's eye and the

Magician began to intone what Jarrod recognized as a spell of assimilation, gathering the essence of the boxes, fusing it in his mind with images of the Umbrian machines conjured up by his imagination. Jarrod crystallized his own real vision and his memory of the construct he had seen on the mountainside. He reached out for Cafftar's consciousness, much as he would when contacting a unicorn. Don't fight me! He thought it so hard that he almost said it aloud. And then it was there, blurred at first, but growing ever clearer. Jarrod shifted those boxes and superimposed them on the ones pulsing in his own mind. The outlines of both wavered, oscillated, slid one into the other until the lines were united and only one set of images remained. "Now!" he shouted.

There was a blinding flash, both in Jarrod's mind and on the Causeway at their feet. Afterimages striated behind closed eyes and repeated. He heard Cafftar cry out and sensed that Greylock had staggered back. The picture in his mind had vanished and a dull ache filled the space. He opened his eyes and looked down. There was a fine strew of splinters and sawdust on the pavement. The early morning breeze picked it up and played with it briefly before whirling it away. To the east, the sun shouldered its way over the horizon and the pink underside of the clouds turned golden. The pudgy Magician was on his knees again, holding his head once more. He moaned softly. Jarrod looked over his shoulder. Greylock sagged against his Staff, his head hanging, the breath rasping in and out.

"It is done," Jarrod said, feeling the onset of the euphoria that marks the end of major Magic making. His voice sounded like a rusty hinge.

In the late afternoon a herald rode up onto the Causeway bearing an invitation from Prince Saxton to dine that night. The two Mages were resting after the morning's endeavors, but they came out to greet him.

"We shall be honored," Greylock said, "but I have a favor to ask. We are somewhat weary. The performance of great Magic ages one," he smiled, "though in my case you cannot tell. I would ask that we dine early."

"The Prince has suggested the nineteenth hour and he will send a litter for you."

"Tell His Royal Highness that the Mage of Paladine and I will be delighted to attend him," Greylock replied.

Two hours later, a troop of cavalry in full dress uniform came to escort them to the dinner. They rode down the ramp and back across the river and thence through the camp. Soldiers gathered and cheered them as they passed and the Mages bowed from side to side in acknowledgment.

"This is a great day for the Discipline," Jarrod said. "We must make sure that news of this reaches Celador. It will put Sumner's nose out of joint."

"Was it for that you put my image on the clouds?"

"What better symbol to put fear and trembling into the bones of the enemy than the Archmage in all his splendor?" Jarrod said in mischievous ingenuousness.

"This is all very pleasant," Greylock said of the full-throated troops around them, "but it will go as fast as it has come if the battle is not won."

"The battle is not ours to win but theirs," Jarrod replied. "Besides, we shall have the help of all our colleagues next time."

They dismounted before Saxton's tent and were greeted with due state and then ushered inside to change into their robes. The dinner itself, attended by all the senior commanders, was held in the open air so that as many of the men as possible might see.

"If Oxenburg decided to attack now," Jarrod, seated on Saxton's left hand, remarked, "your men would be leaderless."

"I have doubled the sentries against the eventuality, but I doubt they have the stomach for it." He grinned and it made him look years younger. "That was a very impressive display you put on. Even I, and I knew what was going to happen, was abashed by a giant Mage with flaming Staff hovering in the skies."

"Are your troops ready to fight tomorrow?"

"They will be. Their mood has turned completely. Is there anything special that you require of us or that we can do for you?"

"I would be grateful for the loan of a spyglass," Jarrod said. "It would make it easier to generate illusions on the far side of the field."

"You shall have one before you leave," Saxton promised.

The festivities broke up early. The Captains repaired to Saxton's tent to go over their orders for the morrow and the Magicians returned to the Causeway to instruct their colleagues on what would be expected of them at dawn.

"How are you holding up?" Jarrod asked his mentor as they prepared to dismount.

"Well enough, all things considered," Greylock replied. He smiled wryly. "You wake up in the morning and flex your fingers to get them working, then you stretch slowly and carefully. You say to yourself, 'Ah, it's going to be one of the bad days,' or, if you're lucky, 'Not bad,' and you get out of bed with a sort of quickening of the spirit."

"So you know at the beginning of the day how things will go," Jarrod remarked.

"Well, not quite. The weather has something to do with it. So, I believe, has one's general mood. You know," Greylock continued, warming to his subject, "passions don't die, or fade all that much, contrary to popular belief. They just don't last as long. The one emotion that does grow, I'm sorry to say, is vexation and with it come frustration, irritability and shortness of temper. Magic, of course, can alleviate the symptoms, but it becomes a trap. The more you use it, the older you eventually feel. You know that, but the easement it brings is a powerful temptation. It is easy to become addicted even while you know that such overreliance is self-destructive."

He drew back and reached out a hand to grasp Jarrod's arm. "I'm sorry," he said with a smile. "You asked a simple question and I replied with a homily." He shook his head. "I fear I have become the sort of man who, when asked a mere, polite, 'How are you?' launches into a detailed description when all the other really wanted to hear was a, 'Well, an I thank you.' "

Jarrod smiled back. "You can always use the long version with me."

The following morning, in a darkness close to absolute, the Magicians gathered to Make the Day. The lamps of the heavens were shuttered for Aristach and another Magician had been up all night shepherding storm clouds in from the south. They hung now, unseen, above the Plain. The men seated on the pavement, facing toward the east and reaching for the sleeping sun, had blocked all awareness of their surroundings, but despite their concentration on the daily ritual, there was a feeling of anticipation. This was the day when, thanks to the Archmage, they would emerge from their collective impotence.

As the outlines of the Umbrian camp began to emerge in shades of grey, Jarrod, leaning on the chest-high stone and looking down, could feel the pent-up resentment in the men behind him. He turned and looked through their ranks to Greylock, who stood a little way behind the rest, Staff in hand.

"It is time, my Lord Archmage," he said formally.

"Let us use our powers for the good of the people of the Kingdoms," Greylock responded.

Jarrod nodded to the other. "You know what to do." He turned back to watch what would come. He heard the soft chanting and his skin prickled as he felt the energy begin to build in the men at his back. Without looking round he knew that two had detached themselves and were concentrating on the clouds that moved turgidly above their heads. It worked in Isphardel, he thought, it should work here. He noticed a fog forming around the Allies' front lines and smiled to himself. The first move was under way.

It started as a mist at ground level and thickened and spread. It was as if the clouds had descended to wrap themselves around the waiting troops. The bank of opaque blackness extended up for twenty feet and out across the Plain for as far as the eye could see. Jarrod leaned forward, closed his eyes and pictured the scene. Borrowing from his memory of the interior of the Great Maze, he added ripples of iridescent light to the surface that faced the Umbrians.

Light had seeped onto the Plain, but it was wan and sickly. The sun had not shown itself and there was no trace of a breeze. The air hung heavy and there was the tension that precedes a storm. As if on cue, a peal of thunder broke the silence, followed almost immediately by another. That should wake them up, Jarrod thought, and when they had rubbed the sleep from their eyes they would see what their sentries had already seen, a towering curtain created by Magic. Now for the second move. He turned and signaled to the Magicians who were controlling the clouds.

Blinding light exploded and Jarrod threw up his arm to shield his eyes. It was followed within a breath by a crash of thunder that sounded like the world ripping apart. Lightning forked down again and again, searing its way into the Umbrian encampment. Earth and other things fountained up. Jarrod trained the spyglass on the area and tried to focus his watering eye. A boulder dropped through his circle of sight. It meant that they had woven the dark curtain well. Impenetrable to the Umbrians, it did not exist for the Allies and the ballistae and mangonels were gauging their distances accurately. It pleased him.

The bombardment continued for another twenty minutes with earth, and arms, and sometimes parts of men, flying out from the point of impact, then the clouds resumed their march, grumbling and sparking as they went. Somehow Aristach and his colleague had managed to keep the rain aloft, immured in the thunderheads, and fires flickered where the lightning had struck. There were a number of bodies, or blackened heaps that could be bodies, on the cratered ground, but most of the men had scrambled away to safety. Two of the battlewagons had been battered into canting ruin.

The Umbrians, however, had earned their reputation as determined fighters. They had been surprised and they had been put to flight by an unnatural storm. They had saved themselves, true, but they had not been routed, had not lost their courage. The spyglass revealed that they were regrouping about a mile and a half behind their original position. The faint sound of bugles teased the ear.

Jarrod's sense of satisfaction was tempered by a sadness. The Discipline had fought before, had fought against the Outlanders for centuries. Jarrod himself had committed acts of violence, sometimes to protect himself, as he had had to do on the Island at the Center, sometimes to protect Strand. He had virtually exterminated the Others, would have killed every last one of them had the Guardian not intervened. But the scene below the Upper Causeway was different. The havoc wreaked by the lightning storm was a deliberate act of war by the Discipline, as an organization, against fellow Strandsmen. It had not been designed to contain them, or render them ineffective. Magic meant to kill them. It was as if a certain innocence had been irretrievably lost that day. The previous war had been clear-cut when it came to morality. Now things were far more complicated. He sighed. That other world, the world outside the Discipline, the world of politics and anger, was a harsh mistress. He lifted the spyglass again and swept the area.

He watched as the Allied Army advanced in impeccable order over the ruins of the Imperial camp and something in Jarrod responded to the skirling of the pipes and the sight of an army marching toward victory, a victory that he would have a part in. The movement of the Magicians behind him brought him back to his immediate surroundings. Of course, the troops still needed the Magical curtain to keep the enemy guessing and at bay. He moved with the rest until they stood once more between the two armies. Now he would find out whether his gamble had paid off. He only knew Estivus of Oxenburg from the stories his father-in-law had told, had seen him at Ragnor's funeral, no more than that, but he was betting that the Umbrian would try to neutralize the sorcery before he launched a counterattack against the Allies. He trained his spyglass on the enemy.

It was his ears and not his eyes that gave him the news he sought. The cough and sputter of engines coming to life. The sound did not affect him, but he glanced at the others. There were signs of strain on their faces, but no one had collapsed. Perhaps when the battlewagons passed them. In the meantime, here they came, heading for the Allied lines, hoping to dissolve the Magic with their mechanical presence. He had guessed right. The Umbrians were more afraid of Magic than they were of the armed might of the Kingdoms. The battlewagons rumbled by below. After the sounds that nature had made, the noise from the machines seemed thin, flat and unimpressive.

The battlewagons swept on, gaining speed. Jarrod slitted his eyes and peered through the curtain he had helped to create. The Allied forces had seen what was coming and had fallen back slightly, preparing to deal with the unnatural weapons. He watched as the wagons steamed into fog and were swallowed up by it. Once they were through, the Allied troops, armed with metal spikes, swarmed over them. Some fell, some were crushed under the treads, but they were quickly replaced. Spikes found the vulnerable crack on the housing of the treads and, one by one, the battlewagons ground to a halt. Darius' tactics had been adapted by another generation. That was all that needed to be done. The men inside were trapped, their fate un-

known to their comrades. All that the other Umbrians could see
was that their vaunted machines had disappeared into the darkness that swaddled the enemy. Gone.

The time had come for the Magicians' final contribution to
the battle. Jarrod turned back to the group on the Causeway.
Greylock moved through them and came to stand by Jarrod's
side.

"Gentlemen," he said, "the illusions that we create today
may well be the key to victory. As you know, they will have to
keep just ahead of the attack and that is going to require every
scrap of concentration you can muster. Courtak and I need a
steady, even, flow of power and I am confident that you will
provide it. He smiled at them and when he spoke again it was
with a lift in the voice. "The Emperor of Umbria, in his overweening pride and stiff-neckedness, has seen fit to declare war
on the Discipline, believing that we are impotent against him.
Very well, let us now show Varodias the error of his ways. Let
us demonstrate to these Umbrians what the Discipline can do
when roused."

The Magicians sat down cross-legged on the Causeway
while the two Mages stood by the parapet scanning the battlefield. The Umbrians had established a new line, with squares of
infantry interspersed with crossbowmen and arquebuses. This
will require something special, Jarrod thought. As if in response, the banshee wail of pipers warming up split the air.
Worse than the whine of the Umbrian boxes, he thought, and
yet he felt the network of power beginning to build among the
Magicians on the pavement. He went into himself to prepare.
He had to be both channel and molder. He opened himself and
the power began to flow into him, a bloom of heat racing
through his veins followed by the icy prickle of control as he
absorbed and directed. He could feel a portion of that power
being siphoned away by Greylock.

Something to affright the enemy, to sap their will to fight or
run, to make the blood run cold so that muscles did not re-

spond, that was what was needed. Did he have something like that inside him, he wondered briefly before the first images came to him. As he began to embroider them, other horrors crowded in. Somewhere, behind all that, he was aware that rune fire was blazing around Greylock's Staff. He stiffened the reality around the creatures swarming in his mind. He looked at Greylock.

"Now!"

Greylock's arms shot up. The Staff blazed. A great roar came from the throats of the men massed below and Jarrod clothed them with his imaginings. From the Umbrians' point of view, they burst out of the magical cloud not as mere men, but as ravening beasts out of nightmares. Horned and fanged, tall, snouted and tusked, slavering muzzles with long, caried teeth, furred and scaled, with curving claws, they poured across the battered grass toward the enemy. The shrill and piercing tones of the pipes added to the illusion of otherworldly terror. Jarrod strove to fix the images as the men trotted forward, paused to let the archers get off a flight, and moved on again. Truth to tell he was enjoying himself. This was a once-in-a-lifetime chance to bring forth the creatures of the fireside tales that set the teeth of children to chattering, a chance to tap the darker corners of his imagination.

Down on the Plain to the east, Estivus of Oxenburg rode his charger up and down the lines exhorting his men to hold fast.

"Not real! Not real!" he yelled, waving his sword aloft. "Pictures meant to frighten babes not fighting men. They cannot harm you! Illusions! No more than illusions! Stand, men of Umbria. Stand and fight for your Emperor and the Great Mother will protect you." The ranks held, even as the arrows began to find the range, but they were not convinced.

Jarrod trained his glass on the far wing. The Allied cavalry were holding back, waiting for the outcome of the shock of combat in the center. The Umbrians opposite them, lance butts planted on boot toe, watched and were prepared. We need something to distract them, he thought. Then he had it and he smiled at the contrast his mind had suggested. He set himself to conjuring. His hands came up as he bent in the effort of concentration. The fingers spread and curled as if they held an invisible ball. All at once, out on the Alien Plain, a herd of unicorns appeared. Heads lowered, manes and tails streaming in the wind their speed created, they careened toward the mounted men on the Umbrians' right flank, swinging aside before they came in reach of the lances, whirling, prancing away to turn and charge again.

In the center the infantry battalions of both sides came together and the sending dropped away, leaving man to face man. The clash of metal on metal rang out and sparks flew. The heat of furious bodies began to create a mist of its own and Greylock lowered his arms. As he did so, the net of power dissolved slowly and evenly, leaving the Magicians with a brief sense of emptiness and loss before the euphoria that follows spell casting took them over.

Jarrod picked his spyglass up off the parapet and trained it on the distant ground between the cavalries to see if the battle had been joined there too. To his surprise, his herd of unicorns was still there. Impossible, he thought. The Magic's done. Yet there they were, attacking now in earnest, harrying the enemy flank, darting in and out with horns poised to gore. Not a sending, not creatures of his imagination and memory, but living unicorns come to the aid of the Allies in their time of need. His heart went out to them in unspoken thanks and he handed the glass to Greylock and indicated where he should look.

"This I had not thought to see," the old man said. "What noble creatures that they should risk themselves for us."

"And for the land they hope to gain for themselves," Jarrod added.

Greylock ignored him. "Ah, I see that that boy of yours is with them," he said as he fiddled with the focus. "We made a wise decision there."

Jarrod smiled wryly. "Well, he's certainly showing initiative. More importantly, the unicorns have proved that they can help the Kingdoms. The Queens will surely agree to cede them the land around the mountains."

"Only if we win," Greylock said pragmatically.

The damage inflicted by the work of the Magicians, both physical and mental, had redressed the balance. The lines were intermingled, a pocket of Allies forging forward here, a section farther on pushed back. Men made heedless of danger by the rush of spirit that claims them in the heat of the fight were locked in hand-to-hand combat. Swords and daggers were the weapons now that battle was truly joined. Bow and arquebus were cast aside. This was warfare at its most simple. The instinct to kill and to survive was paramount. Prince Saxton, sitting his horse behind the lines, received reports from his Captains and doled out his reserves to keep the momentum going while those on the line cursed and thrust, were cut and bled and died. Oxenburg and a corps of knights rode up and down, flinging themselves off their horses and into the battle whenever the enemy threatened to break through.

It became increasingly difficult to see the progress of the fight as the morning wore on and Saxton knew that it was time for his final throw. He had heard that unicorns, miraculously fighting on his side, were keeping the Imperial cavalry off-balance and on the defensive. His horsemen were fresh and doubtless keen to join the fight. He sent a messenger racing north with his instructions. In obedience to his orders, the bulk of the Allied cavalry swung wide and came down upon the flank of the distracted Umbrians. As they galloped in to close, the unicorns vanished. Lances splintered as the two groups met, but the Umbrian horses had suffered enough that day. They were skittish and hard to control and all too ready to abandon the field. A retreat became a rout.

The Allied cavalry gave chase, thundering through the grass. Their opponents seemed in no mood to turn and face them, but the Allies had been tricked before and rather than be led on into some prepared trap, pulled up themselves, turned and fell upon the Umbrian rear. The slaughter lasted but half an hour. The Umbrians, caught between two forces had nowhere to run. They fought with a bravery born of desperation, but they were doomed. When the trumpets rang only six hundred still stood among the piles of bodies. The Margrave of Oxenburg, whose horse had been cut down from under him sometime before, was not among them.

XXIII

❧ ❧ ❧

It is said that the only thing that travels faster than the wind is bad news. That is not true where bunglebirds are concerned. Their lurching, unpredictable flight makes them hard to bring down and their unassailable homing instincts make them reliable messengers. The first couple arrived from Bandor and, thanks to the fact that two of the bunglebird keepers were in Malum's pay, he was at the cote before anyone else was notified. It was not an edifying experience. The stench of ammonia from the droppings was overwhelming. The birds sat on their perches, grooming themselves and shedding feathers. The keeper showed him the small scrolls that had been attached to the birds' legs. That was how Malum learned of the fall of Fort Bandor. That was bad news for the Empire, but more worrying, especially to Malum, was the absence of news about Prince Coram.

A couple of sennights later two more bunglebirds arrived, these sporting the colored leg bands that identified them as coming from the Imperial Army on the Plain. They carried no message, however, and had not been coached to repeat any news. The implication was that the Imperial Army under Estivus of Oxenburg had been destroyed. If Prince Coram had not been at Bandor when it was captured, then he would have been with Oxenburg. It could be that both of them were dead. If it was true of Oxenburg, that would be a pity. Malum liked the man. He was one of the last honest, loyal, hopelessly old-fashioned aristocrats. If the Prince was dead, that was an entirely different netful of hedgehoppers.

It would mean that Malum was the Emperor's only living relative—much good would it do him. Even if he convinced Varodias of his parentage, the Electors would never accept him as heir. With Coram gone and the war going badly, it would only be a matter of time before the Electors tried to remove the Emperor and Varodias was getting old. With the Emperor gone, Malum would have no one to protect him. The Prince had been his insurance of continued influence, but if Coram was dead, he had nothing but his own wits to rely on. He sat in his bedchamber reviewing his options. For now, at least, he would have to do everything he could to support Varodias, not out of any particular filial feeling, but out of his strong sense of self-preservation, and for the good of the Empire, of course.

His head came up sharply as Brandwin entered. He smiled. He had become fond of the lad. He saw that the boy's sleeves were too short and his britches scarcely covered his knees. He had been too preoccupied to notice that the youngster had grown again. They changed so fast at this age. He looked at his bodyservant as if he were a stranger. Curling fair hair, pink cheeks made more obvious by pale skin, a golden fuzz signaling the beginnings of a beard, a strong chin marred by pimples. He had broad shoulders, a small waist and well-muscled legs. He had lost the prettiness of boyhood, but he would be a good-looking young man. Time to think of finding him a suitable wife, the daughter of a prosperous merchant or a middle sister from the minor nobility. He had served well and deserved advancement, but a replacement would have to be found first. Malum would be sorry to see him go.

"What is it?" he asked, though he thought he knew.

"A Gentleman Usher, my lord. The Emperor wants to see you."

"Brush out my short cape then and fetch me the shoes with the silver buckles." Malum heaved himself out of his chair and went over to the basin held by a tripod that stood close against the wall. He splashed water on his face and Brandwin was by his side with a towel. I shall miss him, Malum thought. And I am occupying myself with my servant, he decided with a flash of self-appraisal, so that I don't have to think about this audience.

Varodias sat in a chair slightly elevated above the others in a small, plain room off his bedchamber. There was nothing so obvious as a dais, just a gentle rise in the floor disguised by rushes. Malum bowed before him. Varodias inclined his head slightly in return.

"What have you to tell us?" he asked without the usual courtesies. To Malum's practiced eye the man seemed under strain. He glanced around quickly to make sure no scribe lurked.

"There is trouble within the Discipline, Your Imperial Majesty. The Archmage left Celador in the middle of the night and reappeared at Stronta. The Queen was not expecting him, nor was anyone else. He gave out that he was on his way to the front, but I am reliably informed that there was a move to replace him with the Mage of Arundel. I tend to place credence in that since I know Mage Sumner to be an ambitious man. Indeed, he made a bid for the Archmageship when Ragnor died. On the other hand, one of my agents saw the Archmage and the Mage of Paladine riding out along the Upper Causeway in the direction of the Allied Army." He paused and Varodias waited, his usually nervous hands quite still.

"There are reports," Malum continued, "that reinforcements are being sent to Fort Bandor using cloudsteeds borrowed from Talisman. The Isphardis are buying grain and kina and are about to impose a new tax to support the war. The war itself remains popular both there and in the Kingdoms." If the Emperor was aware of a possible defeat on the Alien Plain, he was disguising it well. That was scarcely reassuring.

Varodias waved a hand to cut him off. "Small stuff," he said dismissively. "What of battle plans? What is going on in Songuard?"

He let his face express frustration. "My knowledge of the situation in Songuard has been curtailed by the capture of Fort Bandor. I have had no success in suborning any of the local chieftains. Clan rivalries seem to have been set aside for the moment in favor of Umbrian baiting. I doubt it will last, those animosities run too deep. As far as military information is concerned, I am less than satisfied," he admitted. "My best access ended with the death of General Gwyndryth."

"Darius of Gwyndryth was your agent?" Varodias exclaimed, taken by surprise.

Malum allowed himself an enigmatic smile. In fact it was Darius' personal servant who was his source.

"Have you heard anything from young Oxenburg, or from his command?"

"There has been a battle," Malum said, taking a gamble and extrapolating from the arrival of the messageless bunglebirds and the fact that he had heard nothing from his own men in the Army of the North, "but I do not know the outcome." And if I knew there had been a disaster, I would not be the first to tell you, he thought. Why put one's head on the block for other men's mistakes?

"We fear the worst," Varodias said glumly, chewing his lower lip. Then he turned his gaze on Malum. "If we hear," the voice was quiet and unemotional, "that the Archmage overcame your machines and that our men were defeated by Magic, not only will your monopoly be void, but you will refund every groat advanced you by the Treasury."

Malum felt cold all of a sudden. The old wolf would be more likely to have him executed and then all his property would be forfeit to the Crown. If that seemed likely, he would break his silence and tell the Emperor that he was his bastard son. He had promised Estragoth that he would never speak of it, but Estragoth was dead and he would have nothing left to lose. He bowed low. "I am ever Your Imperial Majesty's devoted servant," he said. "Your word, Sire, is my will."

"Let it be so," the Emperor said coldly, and the audience was at an end.

Malum left feeling that he was living on borrowed time.

Prince Coram was alive, but far from happy. Food had been running low and a foray into the hills for game had become imperative. He should not have designated himself as one of the five men to sneak out during the dark of the moon, he knew that now, but, at the time, it had seemed right. None of the others had his skill at hunting and the venture had been simple and safe enough. The clansmen did not patrol at night. It had gone well at the start; five men on horseback moving more or less silently past the lackadaisical sentries who were expecting, this night as on all the nights during the past moonphase, an Umbrian camp huddled in upon itself. Once past the Songeans, they had flushed a gathering of seven lowland deer. By the time the sun was rising they had killed three and were set for their return. That was when they found that the lower slopes were swarming with clansmen, far more than they had suspected. They settled in to wait for night, when they could cross back through the lines again. The Songeans seemed to have other plans.

Tribesmen streamed in from all directions and the Umbrians pushed themselves back into the thicket in which they had hidden to avoid discovery. A major gathering of the clans was afoot, that much was obvious. Coram knew that his party should get back to their comrades with the news, and with the food. The news was foremost and they tethered their horses in the brake, abandoned the carcasses and tried to regain their companions on foot. The first foray did not succeed, nor did the second. The morning of the third day saw a wholesale descent by the Songeans on the Umbrian force below. Coram and his party could do no more than witness the massacre.

There was no point in trying to reach the valley floor, the soldiers of Coram's now tiny force knew that, and any attempt to regain the sheltering fastness of Bandor by way of the valley had gone. Escape over the mountains and back into Umbria was the only viable alternative and so they retrieved their mounts and set their horses' heads upward and east, toward a distant freedom, though their hearts were heavy and their spirits disconsolate. Better, they thought, to have been with their comrades and honorably dead than alive and bent on personal preservation. They were aware of what people would say, that they had deserted their comrades in arms. It was not true, but who would vouch for them save Coram. He would be believed. For the sake of their own reputation, they would have to see that he reached Angorn alive. They tried to make the trip across the mountains back to the Empire's side, dangerous as it was, sound like his idea.

As they climbed up into the Saradondas, they found themselves virtually alone in the upward-stretching vastness of rock and scree with occasional patches of tussocked grass and ice-pure streams. The only life they saw were horned sheep, small antelopes, rockrabbits and, overhead, wheeling and waiting, the omnipresent raptors. Prince Coram had a chance to think. Here, in the thin air, beneath the peaks that no sane man could think to own, beneath the unchanging and indifferent wheel of stars, human affairs were a matter of indifference. Could one find water? Was there food? Wood for fire? These were what counted. Somewhere, between foothill and the col between the peaks, Prince Coram arrived at a philosophy that was his own. The privation of the peaks, the relative solitude and the seeming closeness of the stars contributed a mystical quotient that had nothing to do with the Great Mother. He could not know it as he struggled upward in the thin air, but it would have its effect on the history of Strand.

To the south of where Prince Coram was climbing toward the summits of the Saradondas, the armies were preparing themselves for combat. The Umbrians had received reinforcements, but they were green. More useful would have been provisions, but the Emperor had not sent those. The men had lived off the land as best they could, but the land they occupied had been stripped long ago and the mountains behind them yielded neither wheat nor kina. The forces before them had been augmented, all the reports agreed on that, and the news, spotty though it was from the valley behind, was not encouraging. Pacing his tent, the Elector of Gottberg felt trapped. He had not asked for this position; in fact he had carefully assured himself a place on the General Staff at Angorn. When he had been picked to succeed Nimegan, his first move had been to remove his wife and his eldest son from Court. He had hoped and expected that this command would be an easy one. The Isphardis were no fighters and the Magical Kingdoms would have their logistical disadvantages, but nothing had turned out the way he thought it would.

His rear was being menaced by tribesmen. They were a minor nuisance, but no more than that. The unicorns were something else. They did a minimum of damage, but they affected his men disproportionately. A number of his troops, the new recruits especially, were superstitious when it came to the unicorns, thought that they were manifestations of the Mother, bounty or no bounty. They undermined morale. He had issued orders for the proper procedure when confronting unicorns, which included the order to kill them, but, as far as he knew, it had been ignored. He was going to have to attack before discipline shredded entirely.

The first Umbrian thrust was an unqualified success. The Allied forces were taken by surprise and pushed back right along the front. Geographic markings were vague or nonexistent along the border, but, as far as could be calculated, Gottberg was certain that they were back in Isphardi territory. The bunglebird he sent to Angorn said, "have the enemy on the run. Am pushing south." Had he waited a sennight, the message would have been different. The Allies had retreated, true, but they dug in their heels and established a new line. The Weatherwards in the mountains, who had eluded repeated attempts at capture—talk around the camp said they fled on unicorns—kept the Umbrians under drenching rain and threw in lightning bolts for good measure. The Allied counterattack cost the Umbrians dearly. Their crossbows were damp and ineffective, the powder for their guns refused to catch. The raw recruits on the Isphardi side made up in enthusiasm what they lacked in finesse. In short, the Umbrians were driven back beyond their old lines. Gottberg sent no bunglebirds and rain set in over his camp again.

Varodias sat in the throne room. He had dressed with care and been barbered for this session. He was angry, had been angry for some time, the more so because he had had no outlet for his pent-up feelings. The news from the battlefront, when there was news, had been disappointing, but his General Staff was adept at evasions. He had them now though. Prince Saxton's diplomatic courier had arrived, had spoken to no one except himself. They were all aware of his arrival—who could not be; they had all tried to intercept the man, the General Staff, Malum, all of them, but the messenger had insisted that his words were for the Emperor alone, had insisted that he be received in private with no one else present. There had been a hidden scribe, of course, but the messenger was not to know that.

He had also received word from the Elector of Estland that his son was safely within the Empire's borders at Harrenberg. The soldier who had brought the news claimed to have been with him and had waxed enthusiastic about the Prince's performance as a commander and about his daring escape. He had thanked the man and sent him off under guard so that he could not tell his tale to anyone else. Malum might know, but he was loyal and discreet, the rest were counting on Coram's death. He settled himself on the throne, adjusting the cushion. After all these years the gesture was automatic. He glanced at the birds to his right and left. Like him they were born to freedom, like him they were leashed. He went over in his mind, one more distasteful time, the ultimatum that Saxton's messenger had delivered and then he gestured to his Chamberlain to let the Generals in.

Varodias acknowledged their obeisances with the minimum of bows. They were nervous, he could see it in their body postures, and this would make them more nervous still. So be it. They deserved no less.

"You are welcome in our presence," he said with a smile that clearly said otherwise. "My Lord of Everington"—his eyes fixed on the greying veteran whose wounds in the previous war had kept him from the field—"do you speak for the rest, as usual?"

"I believe it comes with the position, Your Imperial Majesty," Everington answered with a touch of humor. It was a quality that Varodias had liked, up until now. It had marked a certain independence of spirit that was rare among those that served him. Almost he regretted what was to come. Almost, but not quite.

"Tell us what is happening with Lord Estivus' Command," he asked gently.

"We have had no new reports since last we spoke, Sire, but I have no doubt that things go well."

"Have you not, sirrah, have you not?" The voice was light, high and jocund. Those familiar with the Emperor and his moods would have noticed that the gloved hands were twining and untwining, but Everington was not a courtier.

"The Margrave's a good soldier and he's been supplied with the latest weapons," the General said with conviction. "He can handle anything that Saxton throws at him. I expect that the only reason we haven't heard from him is that he is on the march and too busy driving the enemy back. We'll hear from him as soon as he has established his new lines."

"Your confidence in the Margrave is admirable, General, though a trifle misplaced," Varodias said silkily. "If the reason for his silence was retreat rather than advance, would you defend him as readily?" What game is he playing? he wondered. Surely he knows about Saxton's courier?

"Oxenburg is one of our finest commanders and his loyalty is beyond question," Everington said, sounding stuffy even in his own ears.

"And what if we told you that he had betrayed us? Had ceded the Alien Plain to the enemy?" Varodias still sounded sweetly reasonable, the question hypothetical, but the hands, the telltale hands, were separated, poised and hovering.

Everington looked around to the other officers, seeking support. He found it. "Not possible, Majesty," he said with conviction. "Estivus of Oxenburg isn't that kind of man. He is entirely loyal to the throne. His whole career speaks to that. There are," he admitted, "those among us who felt he was a little young for such a position, but treason? No, that's unthinkable." If the envoy had suggested that, he thought, the man was lying.

Varodias smiled. The news the messenger had brought was disastrous and he meant others to suffer for it. "Would you stake your reputation on that?" he asked. "Better yet, would you stake your life?"

"Your Imperial Majesty is trying to tell me something," Everington said, head held high. The Emperor was known to be changeable, and whimsical, and lethal. He had hoped to avoid this kind of fatal nonsense when he had accepted the post, but this, he supposed, was the price one paid when serving an elderly madman. He breathed deeply. If he was destined to die, he would do it with dignity and, as far as he was able, he would protect his colleagues.

Varodias leaned forward slightly, propping his elbows on the arms of the throne. "What would you say, General, if I told you that I had received an ultimatum from Prince Saxton? That he is poised on the border of the Empire and bids us sue for peace or he will invade the Motherland?"

There was a twitter of comment from the military men, but it was silenced by a wave from Everington. "If Your Imperial Majesty tells me true, I shall of course believe it," he said, low and strong. He looked up at the throne and the man on it and risked Imperial displeasure and his neck. "Is this true, Sire?" he asked.

Varodias looked down on him. The bubble he had protected himself with since the messenger had bowed his way out, the fragile skin that had allowed him to play with his senior officers was wearing thin. The sense that he and his Empire were invincible had been handed a shock that he was still not entirely willing to acknowledge. But Everington was there before him, solid, earnest and concerned. He wasn't the brightest of men, he could be manipulated and coerced, but he was a soldier through and through and he had always been loyal. The games were over. It was time for truth, however unpalatable.

"We received the messenger from Prince Saxton," he said. "He asked our permission to return a number of wounded to us. The Margrave is among them." He stopped to gather his thoughts. "It seems," he continued after a while, "that there was a battle just east of the River Jodderon. Our entire army, battlewagons, rotifers, everything, was overwhelmed." His head came up. "To their credit, there are very few of the wounded. The man did tell me that Oxenburg fought valiantly." The hands, sheathed in grey gloves, wandered, hesitated and moved again, expressing what the Emperor could not.

"The messenger said," the Emperor's voice was perfectly steady, "that the Prince and his armies were poised on the border of our new territory. The Prince offers us generous terms of surrender. We have a fortnight to reply. If he does not hear from us by then, he will invade the homeland." He looked directly at Everington, pale blue eyes boring in. "What say you to that?"

"Bluff," Everington said without hesitation. "Let him try it and we shall set him on his ear."

Varodias pursed his lips and nodded slowly. "We had expected you to say no less." The way he said it did not make it sound reassuring. He took a deep breath and straightened his back. "We shall expect you to secure our northern border," he said crisply. He sat back in the throne and looked at each officer ranged behind the Chief. Some shifted their feet, some dropped their gaze, some did both. "You have no doubt guessed," he said, "that we are playing for very high stakes. The fate of the Empire is in your hands, gentlemen. Should you fail, your necks will be in my hands." He smiled around malevolently. "That will be all," he said.

XXIV

🜲 🜲 🜲

The High Council of Magic was convened in Stronta. It was unusual, but not without precedent, and since the Archmage and two of the more powerful members were Paladinian, it was understandable. Understandable or not, the timing made Sumner and his supporters from the Collegium intensely nervous. Queen Arabella, with her consort off at the wars and royal duties to perform, had no objections, so there was no gainsaying the move. To make matters worse, news of the Archmage's coup, destroying the Umbrians' secret weapon, projecting a towering image of himself on the sky and sending the Empire's battle-hardened troops into headlong flight, had been the subject of gossip and broadsheets for days.

Sumner had far too much time to review the situation on the carriage ride from Celador to Stronta. His state of mind was not helped by the discomforts of the journey. His ample flesh was no protection against the cruel jolting of the iron-shod wheels and sleeping on a straw pallet, albeit in a silken tent, was not in the least to his liking. In fact physical discomfort and the whirling of his brain combined to deny him sleep. The same calculations edged up into his thoughts time and time again, an endless round of votes and personalities. Three from the Collegium and himself made four.

Arabella should be with him, but she had put him off with fair words that sounded like support, but, when parsed, had all the substance of smoke. Handrom, when Dean of the Collegium, had been his supporter, but he owed his elevation to the position of Chief Warlock to the Archmage. He had not seen the man for a while, had had no chance to sound him out and, since he was coming from Talisman by a separate route, would have no chance to do so until they were all at Stronta. The Archmage could not be deposed now; no one would believe that he was too old and feeble, though how he had roused himself and found the strength to perform such magic Sumner could not fathom. Still, the matter of the succession could well come up, especially if Greylock had been weakened and further aged by the spell casting. I should have done away with the man while he dozed the days away in Celador and seized the triple tiara, he thought. Should have, could have; all too late.

The Little Hall, used these days by the palace staff, had been taken over for the Council meeting. It had been freshly painted and the long table and the benches removed. A smaller table had been fetched in and canopied chairs with badges of rank emblazoned set around it. Tapestries now adorned the walls, sweet-smelling grasses and fresh herbs had been strewn among the clean rushes. New candles had been fitted in the sconces and a separate table set up for the scribes. Queen Arabella and the visiting Magicians had been feted and banquets held in their honor, both at the palace and at the Outpost. When Queen Naxania and her guests rode out for a formal picnic close by the Place of Power, the populace turned out to cheer them.

Naxania presided over the first Council session. She sat at the head of the table with the Archmage at her right hand. The Archmage's chair and canopy were grander than hers. Sumner sat opposite him. Arabella sat at the foot of the table with the

Mage of Paladine to her right and the Chief Warlock to her left. The Dean and the two Magisters from the Collegium sat in between.

"We bid you welcome," Naxania said, using the Formal Mode for her opening remarks, "and tell you that it is Paladine's pride and privilege to have you all here. Time was when meetings of this Council were held in Celador, Fortress Talisman and Stronta in revolving session. That tradition lapsed, but perhaps we can start it anew." She smiled and looked at each of them as a monarch will. "We are here not because our Archmage is a Paladinian, but because Stronta is closest to the battlefield. The Discipline has scored a most-notable victory, which all men do acknowledge, but there is more to do and it is for that that we are here conjoined."

The beating of Sumner's heart calmed somewhat as he listened to the Queen's words. Perhaps Greylock was unaware of his plans. He had, after all, left the same night that he had spoken to Arabella. It could be a coincidence. Surely his decision to intervene personally in the war had been made some time before and he had chosen to leave surreptitiously because he feared that he might otherwise be prevented. The sunlight coming in through the windows lifted his spirits. If Arabella had been unforthcoming when they spoke, it could be simply that she was privy to the Archmage's plan and wanted him to go unhindered. Sumner sat back in his chair feeling peaceable for the first time in sennights. He had been fretting needlessly. He found himself smiling and then realized that Greylock was speaking.

". . . machines still affect us, but not to the extent that we had thought. It is the perception of the harm that stifles us. The Northern Army has advanced to the borders of the Empire. We need not fear to cross that line. We have proved that we can overcome or circumvent their machines and that the Great Mother is but a goddess like unto the gods and spirits that our people worship. We have beaten the Umbrians, their general is under guard in the tents of the Wisewomen, but if we do not follow up, it will all go for naught.

"The problem is that the Empire is vast. To subdue it all, so far from home, may well be impossible," Greylock continued, his voice deep and sure. To Sumner's well-trained eye he did not seem to have suffered from his Magic making. He looked old, hair white, eyes pouched, skin wrinkled and, when he spoke one could tell that some teeth were missing, but he had looked like that before. "Varodias' strength is in his centralized command, but that is also his weakness. We do not have to conquer Umbria. We have to convince Varodias that he cannot win and to do that we have to subdue Angorn." The Archmage leaned forward. "Any suggestions?"

"Angorn sits upon a level plain and is not particularly susceptible to any earth tremors that we could induce." The voice was light, dry and detached and came from Amyas Simbrel, Magister of Projected Magic. "It is also well out of range of weather spells, but it would seem to me that the key to success is our ability to frighten the Emperor and his Court into submission." He was warming to his theme and his bony hands began to rub together in a gesture that was familiar to his students and his colleagues.

"To gain maximum credence and hence maximum effect, the plagues or disasters we plan to visit on them should be declared in advance. A murrain on their kina, rodents running amok through the streets, the spirits of their dead seeming to walk at night."

Simbrel was thin and bald and on the short side for a Magician. His eyes were pale and seemed overlarge in his face, but when an idea had seized him those same eyes compelled and he appeared to grow larger. As he spoke, his elbows pressed down on the arms of the chair and he came up in his seat, galvanized by his imaginings, oblivious to his surroundings and the fact that he was a very junior member of this august assembly. "Yes, yes," he said. "We threaten them. 'If you do not do such and such, then we shall do thus and so.' " The body was tense and he darted glances from side to side.

"It might be, 'If you do not pull your troops out of Isphardel, or Songuard, or wherever, we will make your wells run dry, or all your women sterile.' " He looked around, eyes bright, a slightly manic smile on his face. "We could add illusion. The walls could drip with blood . . ." He stopped, realizing what he was saying. The smile turned apologetic. "Well, I'm sure you get the gist of it."

"The precept is admirable, if not exactly original." The speaker was Handrom, sounding every bit the former Dean of the Collegium. "The problem is propinquity. If we had an accurate model of Angorn here, we could, if we combined our energies and drew additional force from the Place of Power, wreak all kinds of havoc, but, as far as I know, no such model exists. So, for ghosts to walk, or blood to drip, Magicians would have to be in the city, or very close to it. Angorn is a long way from the border and Umbrians are even shorter than our own Untalented. We would not go unnoticed in that land. No, victory will have to come by force of arms. I wish it were not so, but I can see no other way."

"There is, I think, another way," Jarrod said, "but there are other matters that we must decide upon and then, perhaps, we can come back to this."

"The Mage of Paladine speaks true," Naxania said, though her tone suggested that she was not pleased to have the timing of events taken over by another. "At this time we would pass control of these proceedings to our Cousin of Arundel."

"Our thanks," Arabella said, equally formal. "What has to be said next does not come easily to us." She had not looked at Sumner, but suddenly his sense of well-being was gone. There was a hole beneath his breastbone where lizards scurried. He held himself very still. "Some sennights ago," the Queen began, "the Mage of Arundel came to us seeking audience. He told us that the Archmage was no longer capable of fulfilling the obligations of his high office and should be set aside. He said further that he, the Mage of Arundel, should be put immediately in his place.

"We did not agree with him then and since that time the Archmage has proved convincingly that he is more than capable of leading us. We are in the midst of a war, a war in which the Discipline has been directly challenged. We cannot afford disaffection within our ranks." She paused and took a breath. "In times gone by this Council has acted as a court of justice. We invoke that tradition now and ask that it be voted on."

"I do not think that is necessary," Sumner said. His voice was quite steady. "I freely admit that I went to the Queen and suggested that the Archmage step aside for the good of the Discipline, be made to step aside if he refused. We are, as you pointed out, at war with the Empire and for months the Archmage had failed to take an active part. It is also true that I suggested that I might fill the office, but not by force. In a time of war the office could not stand vacant. The Queen had a country to rule and would not have the time to devote to the Discipline and to war. I was the next most senior member of the Council at hand and volunteered to fill the post until such time as we all could meet and vote upon the matter. I had but the best interests of the Discipline in mind." He looked around and saw skepticism.

"I rejoice," he said. "Who among us does not, to see the Archmage restored to his former potency. I rejoice in the victory he has given us, but we had no hint of that when I spoke to the Queen as I did. I sought not opportunity for myself, but a redress against what I, and many others, saw as sloth and indecision at the top, a lack of leadership in an hour of utmost peril. Those times are past and I see no need for further action by this Council."

"We think the matter should go to a vote," Naxania said. "All in favor of adjudicating this matter?" She looked down the table and saw four hands raised. "All opposed?" Sumner, the

Dean and the two Magisters. "A tie. I cast my vote in favor. The High Council will hear the case against the Mage of Arundel. Proceed, Cousin."

Arabella turned to the table with the scribes. "Will one of you ask the young man waiting outside to come in?" she asked.

A witness? Sumner thought. They have this all arranged. They are conspiring against me. His eyes were on the door and widened slightly as a young Magician in the brown gown of an Apprentice was shown in.

"Come and stand by me," Arabella said. "There is no need to be nervous. You are among friends here."

"Yes, Your Majesty," the youth said, but he looked far from comfortable. He looked down the table to where Sumner sat and swallowed.

"Members of the Council, this is Apprentice Magician Ostim Bray, who has been studying with the Mage of Arundel as part of his course at the Collegium."

"Ostim Bray," Naxania said, "do you swear that what you will tell us is the whole truth so far as you do know it?"

"I do, ma'am." The pitch of his voice was uncertain, as if it were newly broken.

Arabella smiled at him to put him at his ease. "About six sennights ago there was a meeting in the Mage of Arundel's chambers at Celador, at which some of those here today were present. Is that not so?"

"It is."

"Can you point them out?"

He indicated Sumner, Dean Beriman and the two Magisters.

"You served them wine and overheard some of their conversation?" He nodded. "Tell us what you heard."

"They were talking about the Archmage. They said he had no more Magic left in him. His Eminence said that he should be deposed, that a better, younger man should be Archmage in his place. That the times and the war demanded it."

"Did he say anything else?"

"Yes, Majesty. He said a convenient death would solve the problem." There was a sharp intake of breath from someone at the table.

"What said the others?"

"They started to discuss it, but His Eminence held up his hand and told me I could go, that they would serve themselves. He called me for more wine about an hour later, but they did not speak while I was in the chamber."

"It was hypothesis," Magister Vascoign broke in agitatedly. He was the third of the party from the Collegium and had been silent until now. "A discussion, a game such as scholars play." Sumner shot him a venomous look and he subsided.

"A dangerous game," the Chief Warlock said. "If this were a lay court, the charge would be treason."

"What says the Mage?" Naxania asked, reestablishing order.

"The boy lies, or, to be more charitable, misheard and let his imagination go to work." Sumner sounded confident, but his face was white.

"That can be ascertained," Jarrod said. "By your leave, Majesty?" he asked Arabella. She nodded and Jarrod rose and walked down to where the Apprentice stood. "This is an old truthsaying spell," he said over his shoulder to the others. "I came across it in the Archives." He faced the boy. "Now I want you to relax and concentrate on my voice. No harm will come to you. We are just going to prove that you were telling the truth. Now, look into my eyes and listen to my voice."

He spread his fingers and placed them lightly on either side of the young man's temples. "Look deep into my eyes and listen to my voice. You will hear nothing but my voice. You will relax, be calm and confident and listen to my voice, only my voice; calm and relaxed and listening to my voice . . ." He let the sing-song die away and held the other's gaze.

"You are in the Mage's chamber serving wine, the others are there and they are discussing the Archmage. What are they saying?"

The Apprentice's mouth worked a little and from it came Sumner's voice. "He should never have been elected in the first place. He was a spent force when Ragnor named him and Ragnor was too senile to know what he was doing. Now he sits there useless, dreaming the days away. He should have the grace to die."

"A little too much mandragore in his bedtime posset might help him on his way." The new voice was Simbrel's and he squeaked when he heard it.

"Or he might trip on the hem of his robe and tumble down the stairs." The words were followed by a harsh bark of laughter. It was Sumner again.

"If the Queen could be induced to vote with us, and I do not see why she should not," the Dean's voice said out of the young body, "we would not have to wait for the full Council."

"That will do, Ostim," Jarrod said gently. "You have done well. When I tell you, you will wake and you will feel calm and refreshed. You are coming back to the present now and now you will wake." The boy blinked rapidly and closed his mouth. Jarrod walked back down the table and took his seat.

Arabella turned to the Apprentice and said, "We thank you, Ostim Bray. You may return to the Outpost now. You have done the Discipline great service." They waited until he had left the room.

As the door closed, Sumner got to his feet. "I have had enough of this farce. Who are you to judge me? That man . . ." He froze in mid-sentence, hand stretching to point at Greylock.

Handrom did not seem to have moved, but the rest of them felt the power emanating from him. "I think we have heard quite enough," he said. "I think we should leave it to the Archmage to pronounce sentence on these men."

Greylock lowered his head for a moment and then rose. He did not have his Staff, he did not wear the Archmage's tiara and he wore a simple robe, embroidered at the hem and sleeves, but bearing no runes. He, too, was short for a Magician and age had shrunk him somewhat, but, standing at the head of the table, he seemed tall. A glamour was upon him and he was not simply Greylock, but the incarnation of all the Archmages who had preceded him. He raised his right hand slowly, palm outward and as it rose so did the other three accused.

"You have defiled your oath of service," he said to them and his voice was terrible. "You are not fit to instruct the young, nor to hold office within the Discipline. I would not, however, waste your Talents. Henceforth you will serve at the pleasure of the Archmage and you will not have the freedom to disobey. Go now to the Outpost and wait for my orders."

When they had filed out, he walked around the table to where Sumner stood, still locked in place. He laid his hand on the Mage's forehead. "It grieves me to do this, my brother," he said and, indeed, there was regret in his voice, "but you have brought this upon yourself through greed and ambition." He closed his eyes and took a deep breath.

"By the powers that came to me from Errathuel and all the long line of the Archmages, in the name of the Discipline whose servant I am, I take from you all knowledge of the power that you have borne 'til now." The force emanating from Greylock was palpable to those sitting at the table, but now the Hall began to thrum. "From henceforth," came the voice, terrible and disembodied once more, "you shall be bereft of Talent. You shall be as other men, no more, and in token of mercy you shall bear no memory of the time when you were Talented. Go forth now and make for yourself whatever life you can with the gifts given to you by your parents when you were born."

He took his hand from Sumner's forehead and the thrumming stopped. He turned, walked slowly and wearily to his chair and sat down. He watched as Sumner, blank-eyed and seeming not to know where he was, pushed back his chair. He made his way to the door with jerky steps. He did not turn his head or glance at anyone.

Greylock sighed. The glamour had left him and he was an

old man once more. "I have performed much difficult Magic in my life," he said, "but this was the hardest."

The High Council reconvened on the following day. They had meant to continue their deliberations, but they found they had no heart for it. The Discipline was a closely knit organization, its members set apart from the general populace both by their Talent and by their height. They had been trained together, worked together, supported one another all their lives. Yet they were as diverse as other men and women. The blood of Errathuel showed itself at all levels of society and the passions, weaknesses and prejudices of mankind manifested themselves in Magicians and lay folk alike. The Archmage, the Chief Warlock and Jarrod Courtak dined in their own quarters at the Outpost that night. The Queens, condemned by their station to public display, dined in state in the Great Hall, but, despite their practice and their skill, the Court, expert in gauging the royal mood, knew that something was wrong.

In part to dispel the lingering gloom, but mainly because he was a practical and unsentimental man, Greylock began the next session briskly. "We have much to do." He gestured at the empty space that divided those at the top of the table from those at the far end. "The chairs occupied by our former colleagues have been removed, but their places must be filled. I spoke last night to Sommas Handrom and to Jarrod Courtak and some names came up. However, I think that the ladies should have first right of proposal. Have either of you had the chance to give the matter thought?"

Naxania smiled wanly. "I found it a trifle difficult to sleep last night," she said in the Common Mode. "I have been away from the Collegium for far too long to know who would be suitable to lead. I have some opinions about the higher offices, but I would prefer to wait on those."

"I too have spent far more time on the kingdom than on the

Discipline," Arabella admitted, "but from what I have seen of the staff of the Collegium, I have been favorably impressed by Myrthal Frandy." She was referring to a popular teacher of incantation. "She is well regarded by her colleagues and might make a good Dean. Besides," she added drily, "it is about time that a woman held the post."

"Neither the Mage of Paladine nor I are sufficiently knowledgeable in that area to make suggestions," Greylock said. "Handrom, however, as former Dean, is best placed to decide and we will defer to his judgment." The two women nodded their agreement.

"I agree about Frandy," he said. "She has strong opinions and does not hesitate to speak her mind, but remains well liked." He smiled briefly. "A rare quality. As for the other two posts, I should prefer to visit the Collegium first and talk with some of the Magisters."

Naxania looked around for dissent and found none. "So be it. Now, the Mageship of Arundel is vacant, unless, Archmage, you choose to assume it as your predecessor did."

"No, no," Greylock replied, shaking his head. "There was, alas, some truth to the accusations Sumner made. I am old. I would not have been able to direct the attack against the Umbrians if Jarrod had not shielded me. No, I propose that Sommas take the post. He will be able to keep an eye on the Collegium and guide it through the transition."

"A good choice," Arabella agreed. "Who then will be Chief Warlock?"

"We thought that Agar Thorden deserved the office. He has run the Outpost for a long time. Tokamo has been his right hand until recently and could run the Outpost in his stead."

"Then you will stay as Mage of Paladine," Naxania said to Jarrod. She made it a simple statement, but the others knew that it irked her to have one of her major vassals in that position.

"My land and my family are here, Majesty," he replied gravely. "I would like to be at hand while my children grow up."

"Before we go any farther," Greylock interposed, "I wish to make a solemn statement in Council." He looked over his shoulder to where the two scribes sat. "Are you ready, gentlemen? Very well then. I, Greylock, Archmage of Strand, being of sound mind, do designate Jarrod Courtak, Mage of Paladine, as my heir and successor, subject, at the time of my death, to the approval of this Council." He beamed around, noting the surprise on Jarrod's face and Handrom's unreadable countenance.

"I do not do this capriciously," he added, "nor because I have had a hand in his rearing and in his training, but because he has proved himself worthy. Let me remind you," the voice slipped into a somewhat sententious mode, "that Courtak found the unicorns and learned how to communicate with them. When Strand was in great danger, he undertook the unimaginably perilous trip to the Island at the Center in search of a solution. Having returned safely, he sacrificed the life of his good friend, the unicorn Beldun, albeit at the unicorn's request, to obtain the unicorn's horn. With that horn, he and my predecessor, Ragnor, destroyed the Outlanders and freed Strand from their oppression. Since then he has served the Discipline effectively as a diplomat and negotiator and has administered our activities in Paladine well. When the time comes, he will have more than earned the Archmageship." Greylock smiled. "Of course," he said on a lighter note, "I don't expect that to happen for some time."

The rest smiled dutifully with him. Jarrod wanted to protest that he had had a great deal of help with all these exploits, but he had learned when to keep his mouth shut.

"Now that that is done," Greylock continued, "let us move on to the Umbrians. Jarrod, I think you said yesterday that there was a way of getting close to Angorn without being observed."

"Yes, yes I did," Jarrod said slowly. He was still trying to figure out what had precipitated Greylock's decision to name him as successor at this particular time. The man had made no mention of it the night before. "I was thinking of the unicorns. I would have to go with Nastrus first to pick a spot where we could come out of Interim safely and then we would have to . . ."

"One moment, friend Courtak," Arabella said quickly. "You say 'we'; whom do you mean by 'we'?"

Jarrod's eyebrows went up and his fingers spread slightly. "This is hardly a task to be left to ordinary Magicians. I had rather assumed that we five would go."

Handrom laughed sardonically. "You're a very good Magician, Jarrod, but you are woefully naive when it comes to politics. The royal ladies could not possibly undertake this venture."

"Oh indeed, Chief Warlock, forgive me, my Lord Mage of Arundel, and why is that?" Naxania was smiling, but there was an edge on her voice.

"Queen Arabella's husband is away at war and, should anything happen to her, her children are too young to rule in her stead. As for yourself, Majesty, you have no heirs. What would happen to Paladine if you failed to return?"

"You see, Cousin," Arabella said, wickedly reasonable, "we cannot go if we have children and we cannot go if we do not."

"Your Majesty is pleased to make sport of me," Handrom replied, "but for you to leave the country and put yourself in peril, you would have to consult with your Council of State. In the first place they would not permit it and, in the second place, our plan becomes known. You have men who send you intelligence from foreign parts and so, we can be sure, does Varodias."

Naxania rose swiftly from her chair and crossed to the scribes' table. "You will give me the notes that you have taken since the Archmage made his statement on the succession." She held out her hand. "Thank you. You may leave your things and go." She smiled unpleasantly. "Since the two of you are the only ones outside the Council who know aught of this matter, should the slightest inkling of it emerge outside these walls, we shall know who is responsible. And think on this; anything I might be able to have done to you as your Queen pales in comparison with what the High Council of Magic could visit upon both your bodies and your minds." She walked over to the massive, empty fireplace, tossed the sheets of parchment in and concentrated for an instant. There was a little, whumping noise and the grate was filled with flame. The scribes bowed themselves out as fast as they could.

"Are we decided that we are going to do this?" she asked as she returned to the table. She looked round. "I'll take silence for assent. In that case, I suggest we send a messenger down the Causeway to Angorn under a flag of truce. He can stop on the way and tell Prince Saxton what we intend. We should also inform General Dwallyth. We can send a cloudsteed."

"Do you really think that the Emperor will withdraw his troops?" Jarrod asked.

Naxania laughed, seemingly invigorated. "On the contrary, I think he'll become enraged and redouble his efforts. Varodias is not one to back down when threatened. Part of our message to the Generals should be to keep the troops disciplined and in training and to expect an Umbrian offensive."

"And who shall we send on this mission of ours?" Greylock asked.

"Well," Arabella replied, "I think you, Archmage, should return to Celador. You have been gone a long time and we have a new Mage of Arundel. As for myself," she made a small, self-deprecating gesture, "I do not think that my skills at Thaumaturgy will be particularly useful."

"You are right, Cousin," Naxania said bluntly. "On the other hand, neither Courtak nor Handrom can match my skills at Incantation. It would make sense for me to go."

"But what of your Kingdom? What of your Council?" Handrom asked.

"My dear Handrom," Naxania's voice was full of condescension, "how little you know of monarchs. I shall say nothing to my Council. I shall begin to talk of going on another progress. One of my coaches and a suitable contingent of guards will be seen going south. There is no one to gainsay me. Nor, may I add, is there anyone on this Council who can do so. I intend to go and that is all there is to it." She looked at them, one by one, but no one was foolish enough to challenge her. "Right," she said, "now that that is settled, let us discuss what we are going to do to force Varodias to surrender."

XXV

❧ ❧ ❧

The messenger left with four spare horses. It took him a sennight of hard riding to reach the Allied Army. He stopped briefly to report to Prince Saxton and get fresh horses. Another sennight brought him to Angorn. He was questioned closely by a small, dark man called Quern, but refused to hand over the scroll that he carried. The most he would do and only when it was suggested that he could not come from the Discipline since he obviously wasn't a Magician, was to show the seal with the Archmage's intaglio embedded in it. The following morning he was ushered into the Emperor's presence.

The room was painted to resemble a forest clearing, with a hunting scene on one wall, branches entwining on the ceiling overhead, even mosses and grass and leaves under foot. Varodias was ensconced on an elaborately carved throne and courtiers filled the room. He was offered civil greeting and asked to state his business. He proffered the scroll and said that he did not know what words it contained. The Emperor broke the seal and unrolled it. He slitted his eyes in the way that shortsighted men do and read it. His mouth narrowed and compressed and his cheeks grew red. His eyes, when they lifted from the scroll and focused on the messenger, were hard and bright.

"You may leave us and return to your quarters. We shall summon you when we have composed our reply."

The messenger bowed and backed from the room. The Emperor waited silently, scroll gripped in one gloved hand, fingers of the other drumming incessantly on the arm of the throne. "Out," he said, voice high and clipped. "Out, all of you, except for my Lord of Quern. Do you attend us, my Lord Secretary." When the members of the Court had made their bows and curtsies and taken their leave, Varodias threw the creased scroll at Malum. "Read it!" he screamed. "The Archmage dares to threaten us. That living blasphemy has the gall to send us an ultimatum." The face was blotchy now and the veins in his temples stood out.

Malum scanned the document quickly. Withdraw the forces in Songuard and join in peace talks or Angorn would feel the direct anger of the Discipline. He darted a nervous glance at his master. Varodias was sitting back in the throne, neck cords rigid and breathing heavily. He did not like the look or the sound of it. "Calm yourself, Imperial Majesty," he said as soothingly as he could, knowing that he was risking a further outburst aimed at himself.

Varodias took a deep breath, but his eyes were far from friendly. "Tell us," he said, the voice light and caressing, "could they make good on that claim? Tell us, you who are supposed to be our expert, our chief intelligencer, the man who knows what is going to happen before we do, what, precisely, does the Discipline intend?"

To those who knew the Emperor as Malum had come to know him, this quiet, sarcastic control was far more dangerous than the rages, though the Mother knew they could be lethal. "It is a bluff, my Emperor," he said with as much conviction as he could muster. "A vain attempt to capitalize on a temporary setback inflicted on us. They have neither the troops, the supplies nor the will for a full-scale invasion of the Motherland, so they try this to stampede us into submission. In fact, this," he waved the scroll, "shows desperation. We know that Magic has a limited range. To do this they would have to be in Angorn and how could one of those two-legged pikestaffs come among us?"

"They cannot threaten Angorn from, say, the Saradondas?"

"No, Sire, they cannot. Believe me, I have lived among them and I know that Magicians have to be able to see what they influence or the Magic will not work."

"You are certain?"

Malum inclined his head slowly. "I am."

Varodias sat up again and rubbed his hands together. "Very well then," he said, "we shall throw their challenge in their teeth. We shall send reinforcements to Songuard, raise a new army to confront Prince Saxton and, as for the Discipline, have the messenger beheaded and send his head back to the Archmage." He thought for a moment. "Just to be on the safe side," he added, "we should have the Mother Supreme in Angorn to bring protection to our capital. See to it."

"As your Imperial Majesty commands," Malum said, and began his backward progress out. What was the Archmage up to? he thought as he bowed. There must be something more behind this. This messenger should be put to the torture before he died. With only the head being sent back, no one would know.

The rump of the Council convened again at Stronta and looked over the maps of Umbria. They called in Otorin of Lissen, who had been stationed in Angorn during the Outland wars. He was instructive about what was going on in the Umbrian capital these days, and drew the double keep and the surrounding areas from memory, but was swift to caution that it had been almost twenty years since he had been in Angorn and warn that, as had happened in Celador and Stronta, much must have changed. Jarrod pressed him for details of the Imperial Forest to the south of the capital and Lissen did his best to accommodate. It took a quick trip on Nastrus to confirm that the borders of the forest had not changed.

Once that was established, the debate centered on who would go. Naxania was immovable and Arabella reluctantly agreed to make a very public progress home. Greylock did not need much encouragement to accompany her. Agar Thorden, still uncertain in his recent and totally unexpected elevation, was all too willing to take the Chief Warlock's coach back to Fortress Talisman. That left Handrom, Courtak and Naxania to carry out the program. It was an ideal alliance in theory, each one's strength balanced against the other. Naxania had no equal in Incantation, Handrom had the academic know-how and Jarrod Courtak the intuitive power. It was, in many ways, a marriage forged in the Anvil of the Gods. The only problem was that they all disliked each other.

Malloran and another unicorn appeared in the Place of Power and were introduced to saddles. They made it plain that they did not care for them, but they submitted. They accepted saddlebags with an equal lack of grace though they saw the need for them. Jarrod, meanwhile, had been double-checking maps and Lissen's drawings and going over plans with Nastrus. The unicorn was of little help when it came to details of the mission, but he was an excellent sounding board. Finally there was nothing left to do and, on a night when the moon hung above the horizon as a copper disk, three Magicians and three unicorns arrived at the edge of the Imperial Forest, a scant league south of Angorn.

The three humans ventured forth at daybreak dressed like penitents on their way to the shrine of the Mother in the capital. They cut across the edges of the forest and came out on the main road from the south. It was a simple reconnaissance aimed at familiarizing themselves with the city. If the need arose, they would make themselves invisible, but they preferred to conserve their energies. As luck would have it, they were the first to arrive at the gates, but all that it required to pass was the illusion that they were shorter than they were. Once beyond the gate there was an expanse of cobbles to cross with the looming pressure of the high and ancient walls behind them. Unlike Celador or Stronta, Angorn had not allowed the city to grow. Ahead of them was a broad road that penetrated through a secondary wall of houses, each attached to its neighbor in a disappearing ring. They had expected to be plagued by the presence of machinery, but the common people had little of it.

They spent the day surrounded, overwhelmed on occasion, by noise and crowds and tiny streets with timbered houses leaning out and almost touching. Small people went about their daily tasks, children played in the alleyways and occasional open spaces. The smells of commerce and of cooking assaulted the nostrils. It was all too reminiscent of home and it took the sight of the twin keeps, barricaded behind iron railings and protected by guards, to give them back the sense of mission that they had started out with. There the awareness of machinery was far stronger. The ordinary folk in the streets might be guiltless, but those immured within the palace deserved what they had in store for them. Lacking imperial coins, they ate what they had brought with them and then spent the afternoon seeing as much of the northern part of the city as they could. They scarcely made it back through the gates at dusk. Once within the confines of the forest, they ate poor and slept cold.

The following morning they Made the Day and felt a certain recklessness about it. As far as they knew, the ceremony had never been performed this deep into Umbria. That done, they withdrew into the forest, warded off a clearing against the possible intrusion of a hunting party, and settled down to prepare themselves for a night of activity. They drew pentacles, but did not light them. They prepared potions, but they did not disrobe. They seated themselves in a triangle facing one another and they emerged at dusk feeling strong and united.

The main task this night was Naxania's and it was no easy one. By her Incantation she had to summon up the memory of the departed in those who slept within the walls, catch the images and make them real. Courtak and Handrom had to support her and then make sure that the populace was awake to see what was created. They grouped themselves and then Naxania began to chant, very softly to begin with. There was a hint of a tune, but the rhythm of the words she used was hypnotic, drawing in the other two. She stood between them, hair loose and flowing, long-fingered hands weaving signs into the air before her.

Air, air seemed to be in short supply for Jarrod as he listened to the chant. He had been with Naxania only once before when she had practiced her art and that night of singing had produced the Staff that was back with the unicorns. It was not a night he would go through again and yet, here he was. He summoned power and held it, waiting to feed her when he felt the need. No need now. She was within herself, crooning remembrance and wakening, reaching out to the recent and the long dead. He had a glimpse of cemeteries and wraiths arising at her call. He shut his eyes and concentrated; could feel her song threading through him and Handrom's pool of contained energy. Noise, he thought, noise to waken and affright, to pull from the bedclothes with starting eyes, eyes that would see, would know, would recoil and slam shut against the impossible, and open again. A clap of thunder to rive the heavens answered his thought.

In the palace, Varodias woke and sat bolt upright in his bed. He looked round fearfully and pushed the curtains of the bed aside. Nothing untoward in the room. He had been dreaming, that he knew, but he could not remember the dream. Nothing so bad that it should wake him or surely he would remember.

He swung his legs over the side of the bed. Perhaps no more than a need to relieve himself. Just before he pushed himself forward off the bed he froze. His father stood by the clothespress. A dream, no more. I am still asleep, he told himself, but that did not stop the Empress Zhane from gliding into view. She was young and slim, as he had first known her, but she had died of the dropsy only days ago, was still laid out in state. His hand came up over his mouth as the shades gathered, men that he had condemned to death, some whose faces he had forgotten until now.

In a distant wing of the palace, Malum sat upright in a much more modest bed. Shades were gathering around him too. His mother was the most benign, the others were men whose death he had caused. And then there was Aunulpha, the former Mother Supreme who he had poisoned, fat and malevolent. They seemed substantial, but they would not talk. Their silent presence was accusation enough. He looked down at the foot of the bed and there was Brandwin curled up and sleeping unawares. He kicked out and was relieved when his foot struck solid flesh.

"Do you see them?" he asked as he pushed himself back against the headboard.

"See what, m'lord?" the boy said, the Southern burr he had worked so hard to erase surfacing out of sleep.

"You don't see them? You don't see anyone in this room besides the two of us?"

"No, m'lord, there's no one here. You've just been having a bad dream."

Malum laughed and as he heard it knew that there was an edge of hysteria to it. He had been working too hard, that was it. He risked a glance beyond the bed and the figures were still there. The boy's an innocent, he thought. He can't see them and they can't touch him. "Brandwin, come up here to me," he said. "You're a good boy and you'll be rewarded. "Come up now, and quickly."

"Yes, m'lord," Brandwin said resignedly. It wasn't the first time he'd had this kind of summons.

Daylight brought word from the Emperor. It was well before the levee, but Malum was up and had shaken off the terrors of the night. The Gentleman-of-the-Bedchamber who preceded him had obviously been roused before ready and was sulky and uncommunicative. No he didn't know why the Lord Secretary was being summoned. The Emperor, from what he had seen of him, was healthy. Looked old and tired, but who didn't at this time in the morning? Malum smiled to himself. He made a point of thanking the man as he was ushered into the bedchamber. The Emperor was sitting up against pillows in the huge canopied bed. The bed cap looked jaunty, but the Emperor himself was far from that. He looked his age.

"Did you sleep well?" he asked before Malum had completed his bow.

"Tolerably well I thank you, Your Imperial Majesty," Malum lied.

"Did you see ghosts from your past, or were we the only one?"

"Now that you mention it," Malum said carefully, "I did wake with visions, but they were no more than night phantasms."

"It's in the Discipline's letter, you know," Varodias said. "Your past shall rise against you, that's what it said."

"We must guard against interpreting every bad dream or misoccurrence as a prophecy from the letter come true, Sire. That is what they want us to do. That is why they sent the letter."

"What of their messenger?"

"He was dispatched home yesterday, Sire," Malum replied and knew a tremor of unease.

"Alive?"

"No, Sire. You decreed that we should send back his head and so we did."

"When was he executed?"

"Yesterday morning, but . . ."

"Aha!" It was almost a yelp. "You see. They knew; they knew and these sendings are proof of it."

"By your leave, Majesty," Malum said, "there are other explanations." This uncharacteristic mood must be scotched, he thought. "The sad circumstance of the Empress's death has upset you. It is true that she had been ailing for a long time and death came to her as a release, yet she had been by your side for many years. As the ruler of us all, you must present a brave face. Your grief must be confined within. What more natural then that, when your mind is freed by sleep, thoughts of death and loss should manifest themselves?"

Varodias' face lightened. "We were, in truth, husband and wife for more than thirty years. A long time indeed. It is natural that I should grieve for her." He sounded as if the idea were new to him. The eyes narrowed again and he looked at Malum suspiciously. "But you said that visions of your own dead came to you."

Malum was equal to the occasion. His face showed melancholy. "Ah, Sire, you must understand that the Empress was much loved, almost as much as yourself. For most of us she was the only Empress we have ever known. Her passing has affected the whole nation."

A smile appeared on the Imperial face. "No doubt you are correct. 'Twas but a passing miasma, brought on by sorrow and magnified by the time of night." He nodded to himself. "Aye, that must be it." The smile returned, stronger now. "We thank you for your counsel, Master Secretary. Go you now and break your fast."

Malum was pleased with his performance and almost believed what he had said. The death of the Discipline's go-between and the night's evil dreams were no more than coincidence. His faith was shaken, though, when reports from around the city began to come in. Ghosts were the talk of every marketplace and each man and woman had their own tale to tell. He had the sentries who had been on duty at the gates the previous day questioned, but no one remembered seeing an unusually tall man. He began to feel queasy about the whole episode. The Mother Supreme was in the capital for the Empress's funeral. Perhaps he should consult her.

Jarrod went alone into the city that day. Naxania needed to rest and Handrom was content to let him go. There were more people coming in from the countryside for the morrow's funeral. As Jarrod appeared no taller than those around him, the guards had no reason to notice him. Once inside the walls, he found the atmosphere far more subdued than it had been the previous day. As he overheard snatches of conversation in the streets, he became increasingly contented with their handiwork. He joined the long line that snaked through the palace gates and into the Hall where the body of the Empress lay. The others on the line discussed the coming ceremony. It would start in the morning, weather permitting, in the palace courtyard in front of the Great Hall that connected the keeps. Then there would be a solemn procession to the Cathedral of the Mother, where the Empress would be interred.

Being up and awake so early in the day permitted the three Magicians plenty of time to gather their specimens, dropping them into the cloaks they carried and bringing them back to the clearing on the edge of the forest they had chosen for this operation. As the time for the start of the funeral drew nigh, each made his or her own preparation and then studied Lissen's drawings of the palace and the area between it and the cathedral. The public part of the ceremony was slated to begin at the tenth hour and, given the fact that day had dawned clear and cloudless and the Umbrian passion for precision, would undoubtedly begin on time. The cloaks had been spread out in the shade with two minor geises on them. One prevented their finds from escaping and the other stopped them from preying on each other.

There had been discussion, sometimes acidly polite, on the best time to put their spells in motion. Those in the line to pay their respects to the Empress Zhane had debated the timing of the various rites and where they should be to get the best view of the notables. The Emperor and the Mother Supreme, of course, and most of the Electors and their ladies, but perhaps the most talked about mourner was Prince Coram, specially returned from the war for this sad event. An hour in the forecourt they reckoned before the bier began to wend its solemn way to the basilica. Places at windows and on rooftops along the route had long since gone, but, so went the general wisdom, the best chance to see would be on the avenue. The Magicians had come to the same conclusion.

They had no clocks, but they were used to judging time by the position of the sun. When it was a handbreadth below the zenith, they gathered around the cloaks and studied the insects that crawled around the miniature hills and valleys created by the folds. There were shiny beetles with the antlers of a tiny stag, undulating things with a multiplicity of feet, spiders of every kind, things that hopped and those that would have flown, but for the spell that kept them down. There were slow-moving slugs and insects that skittered on hair-fine, jointed legs, tree lizards and tiny, jeweled snakes, all denizens of the leagues-long forest that was the Imperial hunting preserve, creatures left to breed and multiply undisturbed for centuries.

The three took their time familiarizing themselves with the teem of life they had collected. There were three separate Magics that they meant to do. The hardest fell to Handrom, a spell of summoning. Technically, it wasn't that hard, akin to the finding spells used by Village Magicians, the difference here was the scope. Jarrod's job was to lift them up and send them over the walls and drop them on the area agreed upon. Naxania, meanwhile, would mingle magnified images of the creatures on the cloaks and add them to the mix raining down upon the Umbrians. They looked up one last time toward the sun and, with nods of mutual agreement, began their work.

The forest around them began to rustle as thousands of tiny creatures were drawn up through the leaves. Jarrod started to pull the winds in from the south. The problem was one of finicky control, narrow vector, short duration, continual flow from behind followed by an abrupt drop-off. Tricky stuff, Greylock's sort of Magic, precise and controlled; not his forte at all. Nevertheless, he caught the rising insects in his net of wind, propelled them over the walls and, with the palace, avenue and basilica in his mind's eye, let them go. Naxania was conjuring images which Jarrod was thankful he could not see. The distance and the wind cut off sound, but he could imagine the screams of horror, the beating hands around the terrified faces, the turmoil as those around the route of the cortege struggled to flee. He felt sorry for the Empress. Everything he had heard about her made her out to be a tranquil and domestic soul who suffered from the Emperor's neglect. She had not deserved this, but, after all, war was war.

They finished their work with the guilty knowledge that they had damaged the natural processes of the forest by their actions. They took the cloaks and walked away in different directions, as deep into the woodlands as they could, and shook out the cloaks. It wouldn't reverse the damage, but it would start the healing process. Jarrod, as he pressed through a coppice, found it ironic that he was being so concerned about the life of the forest when there had undoubtedly been human beings trampled to death in the havoc they had caused. This was the second war in which he had been involved in death. They had embarked upon a course and there was no turning back now. If they failed, all the deaths would go for naught, but there must never again be war. Nothing that would provide the excuse and occasion for slaughter. If, indeed, he became Archmage, this he would guard against. This he would prevent. He

flapped the edges of the cloak he held, scattering the tiny creatures that had been so difficult to collect. They, at least, had
survived. Now it was time to go back. There was more to do.

The three slept the rest of the day away. Handrom woke his
colleagues after the nightmoon had risen. He had been up a
while and had prepared potions for the other two against the
work that they would perform this night. It was time to see
what kind of effect their actions had produced on those who
mattered most. The potions were most necessary, for all three
were wearied by what they had already done. Had they not
acted in concert, cushioning the effects for the others, they
would not only be exhausted, but considerably older. As it was,
the strain showed. The lines in the faces were more deeply
graven, they spoke less and moved more slowly. Both Naxania
and Jarrod, younger though they were, would gladly have post-
poned what they contemplated, but neither would admit to
weakness in front of Sommas Handrom, nor indeed to each
other.

This was the hardest yet. They had to journey from their
bodies and yet retain enough solidity to convince those they
visited. That in itself was difficult, but they also had to seek out
the ones they wanted to communicate with and did not know
where in the palace they would be. Naxania was to seek out
Varodias and that was fairly simple. Otorin of Lissen had identified his bedchamber and she had spent time with the Emperor
and could feel his special emanations. The same was true of
Jarrod and Malum of Quern, his chosen target. They had spent
years together on the Commission for the Outland. Prince
Coram, Naxania's second objective was a different matter. He
was not well-known to either of them and they had no idea
where in the palace he slept. It was not strictly necessary that he
be visited, but Naxania wanted it. Her rank as reigning monarch should have its effect on both father and son. Jarrod agreed
with her reasoning, but worried that she would not have the

strength. She had not practiced in years and had already performed a great deal of Magic.

He set the thoughts aside as the chants rose up. They were
cross-legged in front of a tiny fire. A nightmoon barely on the
wane floated over the treetops and the world around them was
preternaturally still. Handrom threw a double handful of simples on the glowing branches. That was something that Jarrod
had not come across before, but, as he inhaled he felt a kind of
separateness from himself, a floating, disassociated feeling even
as he was concentrating on his own spell of displacement.
Something of Handrom's own devising, he thought; not taught
at the Collegium, but quite effective for all that. He was above
the fire and on his way to Angorn.

Naxania found herself directly translated. One instant she
was sitting by the fire, potion churning through her, making
her blood run light and the next she was in Varodias' bedchamber. She looked round with an appraising eye. The furnishings
and hangings were no better than her own. There was a tall
mechanical clock in the corner which made her shudder and,
somewhere in the bowels of the building, she could sense the
sickening rise and thud of far larger machines. I am not really
here, she told herself; they cannot affect me. Ah, but she must
be able to affect Varodias, lying there in his ridiculous cap,
mouth agape and snoring. No servant sleeping in the room she
noted gratefully. She glided to the door and touched the lock
with an ethereal finger. If alerted, the guards could not get in.
Now to wake him. She checked to see that she seemed solid
and then reached out for his mind.

Varodias came awake with a start. He blinked his eyes and
was aware of dim light from the windows. Why were the curtains of his bed not drawn? They had been when he was put to
bed. Then he caught sight of Naxania. His fingers clamped
down on the edge of the covers.

"In the name of the Mother, begone!" he said with as much force as he could.

Naxania laughed. She had dressed her image well in a formal gown. Her hair was pinned up and one of the lesser crowns of Paladine was secured atop. "We are not a shade to be banished," she said, remembering the Emperor's preoccupation with the Formal Mode. "And do not try to reach for the bell pull. It will not work while we are here."

"What kind of sorcery is this?" Varodias asked as he hoisted himself up against the pillows. "Was the defilement of my wife's funeral not enough for you?"

Naxania was impressed in spite of herself. Varodias was old, taken by surprise and alone with someone who could not possibly be there, but he was not quailing.

"We regret that your wife's funeral was disrupted," she said, "but you were warned and you took no heed. We need to talk, sovereign to sovereign, and settle this war that does no good for your people or for mine."

Varodias reached for the bell pull and tugged. Nothing happened. Varodias affected not to notice, but adjusted himself in the bed and smoothed out the edges of the sheet and coverlet.

"We applaud you, Cousin, that was bravely done, but, alas, ineffective. We need to forge a peace here. Your forces are stretched thin and, despite your vaunted mechanical contraptions of war, have fared badly. We have not begun to commit our strength and neither has Arabella. The Warcat Battalions wait in Talisman. No matter what the sycophants that surround you have told you, you cannot win. We could bleed each other to death, but you will never win; never be Emperor of Strand; would go down in history as the destroyer of the Empire. We have fought side by side against the Outlanders. Would you allow all that, the deserved glory and the pride, to be ground down to dust?"

"Why should we believe a shade, a night sending, a bad dream?" Varodias asked with a veneer of belligerence.

"We warned you in advance and you would not heed us," Naxania repeated. "Your father and your wife appeared to you in our behalf and you would not heed us. Did not today's plague convince you? Do we have to visit more on your benighted people before you see sense? These were but warnings. Up until now, more or less, you have fought against our armies. Now you confront the Discipline." She paused and when she resumed her voice was a purr. "A twitch of our finger and your brain would be paralyzed. You would live, cruel as that might be, but you would not be able to speak or move. You would stay like that until it pleased us to release you. You really have no choice."

"Say you so? Say you so?" The Emperor's voice was light and desperate, there was fear in it, but no surrender. "We have ruled this realm since before you were born. Death is something we have faced a goodly number of times. Even if you were not a shade, you cannot affright us with that."

"Oh, but you did not listen to me," Naxania said gently. "You would not die. You would lie here, incapable of communication, while those around you plotted and willed your death. The Empire would unravel in civil war and we would need do nothing. A peace would be made by those who wished to supplant you and you could not gainsay them because you would be paralyzed. You will desire death and there will be those who will try to kill you, some out of ambition, some for what they will sincerely feel is the good of the state and some for love of you, to put you from your misery. They will all fail because your death is in our hands."

"You would not," Varodias said, chalk white against his pillows.

"Oh indeed we would," Naxania said pitilessly. "You are, to use an Umbrian phrase, the mainspring of this war. You declared it, you have pursued it and you can end it."

"What do we have to do?"

"Call your Council into session in the morning and announce a cessation of hostilities. Imperial messengers will be sent to your General on the Isphardi front directing him to stay in place. We shall do the same and we shall direct Prince Saxton to withhold his hand. A peace conference will be convened at Fort Bandor."

"This is but a dream," Varodias said dismissively. "A persistent and disturbing dream, but a dream nevertheless. The Queen of Paladine in our bedroom? Who would believe that?"

"Out of bed," Naxania said. "Now!" The Emperor's eyes bulged, but he obeyed. He went into his cabinet, followed by, coerced by, the image of Naxania. "Write that you will cease hostilities and agree to peace talks at Bandor," she said.

She reached back to Handrom at their base, pouring questions and entreaties at him, telling him what had been agreed. She had no idea if she was getting through, if this kind of transaction was possible. All she knew was that she had Varodias on the run and that the opportunity would never come again. She had to convince Varodias that she was real, despite the fact that, in any usual sense of the word, she was not. He would need something tangible. She stood behind him as he sat at his desk and heard the quill scratch across the parchment. Even as she did so, the air around her darkened until she could no longer see the cabinet. No, not yet, she thought. I cannot go back yet. Then she found that she held a sheet of parchment in her hand. She scanned it rapidly, and smiled as the darkness cleared.

"Here is our promise," Varodias said, holding up a draft without looking back.

"And here is ours," Naxania said, leaning forward and depositing the parchment on the desk. The thunderstruck look on the Emperor's face pleased her enormously.

Jarrod came to himself in a small room taken up by a generous bed and a clothespress. One wall was occupied with a large fireplace, unlit at this time of year, though kindling was laid beneath a trivet. Malum of Quern was sprawled out in the bed and a young man slept huddled against the footboard. He had not expected to find anyone else in the room though he should have allowed for this. A servant sleeping in the room was common enough. He drew on the power within him and wove a sleep spell around the boy. Then he woke Malum.

"Give you good evening, my Lord of Quern," he said civilly as he watched the Umbrian focus, doubt, reject and push himself warily into a corner of the bed. "Have no fear, I shall not harm you."

"Who are you? You look like the Mage of Paladine, but you can't be here," Malum said. "How did you get past the guards?" His eyes were darting around trying to remember where his weapons were. Jarrod interpreted the looks.

"Don't even bother," he said. "I've told you that I intend you no harm and, believe me, there is nothing you could do to hurt me. I have simply come to talk with you, to talk about the good of Strand and the possible salvation of your country."

"Are you real?" Malum demanded.

Jarrod smiled. "When I saw you on that mountainside, I said to myself, that is a brave man. The Emperor is well served." He saw Malum's glance flick down to the body of his servant. "I have not harmed him, I have only ensured that he will sleep through this."

"You harm him and I will make you pay," Malum said.

"You have my word. Now, let us get to cases. This war cannot continue. It will be the ruination of this country. It will, of course, go hard with the Allies too, or would if that were all that was entailed. But you have the Discipline to deal with and I think that we have proved that we can smite you with exquisite precision while sitting safe in Stronta, or Celador." He smiled at Malum's start. "That's right, little man, I sit in my study and talk to you and I can see every shadow in this room and, if I so desired, I could reach out my hand and break your neck."

"I, I do not believe you," Malum said, and thrust his jaw out as if inviting an attempt.

"You are as brave and stupid as your master," Jarrod said, reaching for the power that would make a physical effect. It was slow to come, but perhaps Handrom was occupied with Naxania's needs.

"What's the matter?" Malum challenged. "Can't the phantom make good on his threats?"

Jarrod smiled what he hoped was a superior smile and reached within for something solid. It was there, not much of it, but enough to make his wrist and hand quite weighty. This better do it, he thought, there isn't any more. "I'm here, isn't that enough for you?" he asked. "Do you really need a demonstration?"

Malum surprised him. He swung aside the bedclothes and got out of the bed. He came around it and stood within two feet of Jarrod. "I think," he said, "that you are a figment of my imagination, brought on by the events of the past couple of days. At best, you are a dream sending from the Discipline, but even if you are, I don't see why I should listen to you." He peered up at Jarrod. "There you sit, somewhere in Stronta or Celador, convinced that by appearing to me in the middle of the night, you can bend me to your will." He squared his shoulders and took a stance with legs apart. "Well, you can't. So do your worst. Come on now," he was taunting, "hit me." He tapped his chin and grinned.

"If you insist," Jarrod said and landed a solid punch on Malum's jaw that sent him sprawling across the bed. "I'm sorry, this is not the way I expected these talks to begin." He waited for the Umbrian to sit up. "Does it hurt a lot?" he asked.

"Yes it does," Malum said ungraciously, rubbing his jaw. "All right, what do you want?"

"I want peace and a treaty to back it up."

"Why come to me? You've got the wrong man. I'm just the Secretary to the Council. I don't have any power."

"Too modest by far, little man," Jarrod said sarcastically. "I know." He paused to smile. "You made a bad mistake when you stopped paying Semmurel after General Gwyndryth died. He resented it. We know all about you."

Malum produced a snort that might have been construed as laughter. "If you know so much," he said, "you know that I have very little influence with the Emperor. No one has. He makes up his own mind."

"In this case I think he will listen to you. He has had his own visitation this night. I think he will be looking for an excuse to conclude a peace and it is up to you to provide it."

"And if I do not?" Malum's pride was evident, tinged by fear though it was, and, because it was, Jarrod found it easy to penetrate his mind as he would with a unicorn.

"If you do not," he said slowly, knowing that he would find it almost impossible to carry out the sentence, "your servant would die slowly and most painfully as an object lesson."

"You cannot do that. It is not fair," Malum said agitatedly. "He has done nothing wrong. It was not even his intention to serve me. He was sent here by his father and his term is almost up."

"Nevertheless," Jarrod said inexorably, "if you do not agree, he will suffer first. Did you not know, before you promoted this war, that it is the innocents who suffer? Or were you too far removed from the fighting to think of that?" The voice grew hard. "Other people's boys, other young men, no older than he is, cut down. Did you not think of it because it did not come close to you? Well then, you can learn. The Emperor will be thinking peace upon the morrow. Support the notion or the boy is mine." He smiled, as easy a smile as Malum had ever produced, and as comfortless. "If you and your Emperor cannot see your way to peace," he said, "there is one further sending that we will visit upon you." The smile came again, bright and vicious. "I think I shall let you imagine what it might be."

The smile continued, but Jarrod allowed his body to fade. It seemed to Malum that the smile continued after everything else was gone. He sat back up on the bed and stroked his jaw. The pain was real, there could be no doubt about that. He looked at the foot of the bed where Brandwin slept. A stupid child, he thought, no, not a child, eighteen or close to it, a man. Who would have thought that such a one could be involved in the fate of nations? Who would have thought that he, prepared to sacrifice anyone on the altar of his ambition, would have been hobbled by the son of a vassal? No, he would not be held hostage by some homebred child simply because he had served him well. He was fond of the boy, of course he was. He was supposed to be. He shook him. "Wake up!" he said. "Rouse yourself, you lazy good-for-nothing. I want chai!"

While Jarrod was contending with Malum, Naxania had moved on. She floated down the corridors until she came upon double doors with guards outside. She moved between them, knowing they could not see her, and pushed her way through the closed doors. In the popular mind that was an easy thing to do. Spirits simply floated through and that was that. Reality was different. Well-made doors provided little in the way of access and getting through a solid door took up a lot of energy. She was grateful, therefore, when the man on the bed turned out to be large, blond and with the tanned face and forearms that marked one who had spent considerable time in the sun. She did not have that much time left after her session with the Emperor, so she eschewed subtlety.

"Prince Coram, wake up," she said firmly. She was answered by a swallowed snore as the man rolled over. Her lips narrowed and she aimed a stream of cold air at his ear. He snorted and woke up.

"Coram, listen to me," she said, and was rewarded by a widening of the eyes and a clutching at the sheet.

"Mother?" he said. "What do you want?"

"I am Naxania of Paladine," she said. "I am not your mother."

"Are you sure?" he asked.

"Yes, of course I'm sure," she replied, annoyed. "Do I look like your mother? She was blond."

"Things get changed in dreams," he said. "Don't try to confuse me."

"This is not a dream and I am Naxania of Paladine," she said firmly. "I have just come from talking to your father. He has promised me that the Empire will stop fighting and come to the negotiating table. I need your word that you will support his decision."

"You're pretty," Coram said. "Why don't you come over here and sit by me?" He patted the bed beside him.

"This is serious, Coram," Naxania said, "and I don't have too much time. You know what the situation is. Will you support your father in a drive for peace?"

"You're too beautiful for all that speech," Coram said with a broad smile. "You can be whoever you want. You want to be Naxania of Paladine, that's fine by me. Just get out of all that fancy dress and come to bed."

Naxania began to muster her arguments, but she felt the flow of power that had sustained her ebbing. She had no idea how much time had passed, but her session with Varodias had been lengthy. She looked at Coram and he patted the pillow beside him. She would make no progress here. He was a good-looking man, she admitted and, in other circumstances . . . Her time was almost gone. She smiled at the figure on the bed. "We shall meet again, my lord," she said as she faded.

"Strangest day," Coram said as he turned on his side and pulled the covers up.

XXVI

⚜ ⚜ ⚜

Malum was not in a good mood. Sleep had been impossible and whatever spell the accursed Courtak had put on his servant was still working. He had had to make up the fire and brew his own chai. He had dressed himself. If the Mage had told the truth, Varodias had also received a visitation. He had assured the Emperor that the Discipline could not reach Angorn and twice during the same day he had been proved spectacularly wrong. He was not looking forward to his next interview and it would probably come sooner than later. That judgment was confirmed by a knocking at the door.

He surprised the Gentleman-of-the-Bedchamber by answering it himself and followed him down the corridor. The man looked uncomfortable in his mourning garb. Malum smiled sardonically. He had worn the same kind of clothes for years. He was ushered into the bedchamber, stopped well short of the ornate, canopied bed and bowed. A crooked forefinger drew him forward.

"Give you good morning, Secretary." The voice was a croak

and the Emperor cleared his throat. "Do you know why we have sent for you?"

The Emperor was propped up against the bolsters with a tray beside him, sipping from a cup. His face was sallow and the pouches beneath his eyes were dark.

"Any opportunity to see Your Imperial Majesty is a privilege," Malum tried.

Varodias waved his right hand. "You can spare us the flattery," he said sourly and put his cup back down on the tray. "The other night you saw ghosts. Did you see anything last night?"

"I did, Sire. The Mage of Paladine appeared."

"Despite your 'certainty,' it seems that the Discipline can come and go in Angorn as they please. If what you told us is right, and we are by no means convinced that it is, the Mage and Queen of Paladine, and the Mother knows how many more Magicians, are hiding somewhere in the palace." There was an edge on his voice, but it seemed to Malum that the man was somehow listless. Perhaps the lack of sleep . . .

"I heard no rumors of Magicians before the funeral, Sire, and the Mage told me that he was in Stronta."

"If you go into my cabinet, you will find a piece of parchment left by Queen Naxania," Varodias said sharply.

Malum rubbed his chin reflexively. "The Mage faded slowly from view. If he had wanted to escape unobserved he need only have put me to sleep. He did it to my servant and the fellow was still asleep when I came to see Your Imperial Majesty."

"Nevertheless, we have given orders for the palace to be searched. The woman has a document we signed agreeing to a cessation of hostilities. We would as lief have it back."

"The Mage, too, spoke of making peace," Malum said, remembering the threat that had accompanied it.

"What think you?"

"He had some strong arguments," Malum replied cautiously.

"As did the Queen." Varodias' mouth was grim. "It is your task, Master Secretary, to issue the summons to Council. Do so. The thirteenth hour."

Malum began to back out. "See that you attend," Varodias added.

He walked back to his quarters, his mind a mix of relief and suspicion. Whatever had happened in the thin reaches of the night must have affected the old man deeply. Varodias had acted completely out of character. That was worrying.

In the event, the Emperor proved craftier than Quern had expected. He had convinced the Council of the wisdom of a cease-fire. Convinced was too strong a word. He told them what he had decided and they agreed. Malum drew up a proclamation that was greeted with jubilation in towns and hamlets across the Empire and a delegation was sent to Fort Bandor to begin the negotiating process. The mothers, wives and sweethearts who had expected their men to come home, were disappointed, however. Not only did the boys not come home, but new men were drafted and marched away. Varodias took advantage of the respite to reinforce and resupply his troops.

The negotiations dragged on, and not all the cause could be laid at Varodias' door. The Isphardis were feeling their oats. For the first time ever, they had fielded an army of their own men. During the Outland Wars they had paid for other nations to do their fighting for them. Now they had proved that they could defend themselves. They had not only withstood the mightiest army in the world, they had created a navy and had developed a weapon superior to anything comparable on the Umbrian side. They might never again be in such a strong bargaining position and there was no shrewder group of bargainers than the Oligarchs of Isphardel.

Their requests were not outrageous. They advocated a re-alignment of borders that gave Isphardel sovereignty over the lower half of Songuard in return for the disputed land on the Alien Plain. Geographically, it made great sense. To the southern Songean chiefs it made no sense at all. Varodias' representative took on the role of champion of Songuardian independence. It was all very polite and the Allied side took pains to come to some kind of united front, but the Umbrian side was not deceived. Malum was spending long hours to ensure that the Emperor had the most accurate information possible. The betterment of his relationship with Varodias increased steadily with each accurate forecast. He was feeling pleased with himself when Brandwin announced that he was bidden to the Imperial presence. He went feeling confident.

The Emperor was still flushed with the exertions of hunting when Malum was ushered in. He was walking about in the withdrawing room off the main Imperial suite with a page unbuckling him and two noble attendants hovering.

"Ah, there you are Quern," he said jocularly, obviously energized by the hunt. "Shame you could not have been with us today, bagged two boars; killed one of them myself." It was as close to the vernacular as he ever got.

Malum smiled. "A good hunt is relaxing, my Liege," he said, voice warm and encouraging.

"It also reminds us of our duties," Varodias said, holding out his arms to have the leather pads stripped off. "Where you are concerned, we do not doubt your loyalty, but we do have doubts about your efficiency." He turned, hands over his head, to let the pages complete their work.

Malum produced his usual smile and tried to work himself around without violating protocol. He saw that the eyes were bloodshot. A bad sign. "Majesty," he said as lightly as he knew how, "I do not pretend to attain to the standard set by Your Imperial Majesty, but I do my very best to carry out your intentions."

The Emperor was looking at him from under half-shaded lids. "You would of course say that," he remarked. He put his

head to one side, almost coquettishly. "When it comes to back-
ing what we want, it is surprising how few people these days
are in favor of what we think best for the Imperium." He looked
up at Malum with a simple conviction in his eyes. "Just because
things haven't gone quickly, doesn't warrant dissension, does
it?" The tone was almost plaintive.

Malum, after long practice, knew when to keep silent. The
Emperor shrugged. His shoulders came up and his hands made
small circles of indecision. "She said we could not win, but we
are not so sure about that. Another few months and we shall be
invincible." He leaned forward, intent on convincing. "We shall
drive them back. They will pay, they will all pay . . ." The eyes
were starting and the hands darted about as if looking for something to fasten to.

"Sire," he ventured, hand reaching out.

Varodias ignored him. "We can do it," he said. "We shall do
it. They think they have us, but they do not know us well." He
looked for Malum and seemed to have difficulty focusing. "You
shall see, Master Secretary, you shall see," he said, grasping the
arms of a chair and sinking into it. He stopped talking and a
gloved hand came out, shaking, as if to wave off anything bad
or to acknowledge a crowd.

Varodias drew himself up in his seat and took deep breaths.
The eyes that fixed on Malum were quizzical. The lips were
pinched in. With what looked like a considerable effort, he
pushed his lips out into a smile. "Master Secretary," he said
with a gracious touch to the voice that Malum was not used to,
"we cannot quite recall what it was that we were discussing."
He made himself sit back and he made himself smile. It was a
slightly lopsided smile. "Do you fill us in."

First rule of Imperial service, do whatever he asks you to
do, Malum thought. He didn't like his master's color, but that
was up to the Emperor's Wisewoman—a woman Malum didn't
entirely trust because she had proved incorruptible.

"I am sure Your Imperial Majesty has the right of it," he said as cheerfully as he could. "Your Majesty's espousal of the Son-gean clan leaders was a master stroke." The artificial smile came out before he could stop it. "The Isphardis will have to give way." He spoke with a positiveness that he really didn't feel. Perhaps if he ignored the part about belligerence, the Emperor would let it slide.

The page, his work done, left and the two attendants with-drew to the doorway. The Emperor watched them and then turned his attention back to Malum. "Giving way does not in-terest us," he said quietly. "The Queen of Paladine and the Dis-cipline sought to humiliate us, but they underestimated us, misjudged us. They thought they could frighten us into sub-mission. Compliance was but a tactic, a ruse, a chance to gain time, and that we have done." The voice was gathering strength and the eyes were glittering. "We are strong again. It is time that we took action." His eyes flicked over toward the attendants. "You may leave us," he said.

When the doors were closed he rose from the chair and began to pace, his high-heeled shoes clacking on the floor. "We shall smash them, drive them back, annihilate them."

When the Emperor turned and came back toward Malum, he saw that Varodias' color had risen. "I take it that Your Maj-esty is contemplating a renewal of hostilities?" he ventured.

The other nodded. "We should hit them on both fronts when they least expect it, destroy their armies. Then let the Dis-cipline do its worst." He stopped his pacing. "My Generals, however, have no stomach for a fight. What we need from you is an accurate assessment of the enemy's capabilities. You might also start work on an improved version of your machine."

So the army opposes the plan, Malum thought. He had taken pains to cultivate Estivus of Oxenburg since his return from the wars, but he had had no intimation that a resumption of hostilities was being discussed. Oxenburg was his only source of information within the upper echelons of the army, but the man knew how to keep his own counsel. "I shall send men out into the field forthwith to reconnoiter the enemy's strength, Sire," he said.

"Send them out? Send them out?" The voice rose alarmingly. "We do not need you to send men out. We need information. What use is a spymaster without information? How is it that you are not informed as to the disposition of the enemy's troops, the state of their preparedness? Are you, too, conspiring against us?"

Varodias' face was flushed and his eyes glittered. There was spittle in one corner of his mouth. He's working himself up into one of his rages, Malum thought fearfully.

"I can give Your Majesty a fairly accurate picture of troop dispositions," he said as soothingly as he was able. "I merely meant that I wanted to give the most accurate and up-to-date information possible for such a great undertaking." He produced a weak smile, but Varodias did not seem mollified.

"Fools!" he shouted. "We are surrounded by imbeciles, men with no sense of the Empire's glory, with no loyalty to the will of their sovereign Liege!" He lifted a fist to shake it in Malum's face and faltered. The eyes opened wide and then he dropped to the floor.

Malum stood there shaking, staring in horror at the crumpled form of the Emperor, then he turned and ran for the door. "The Wisewoman," he called. "Fetch the Wisewoman!" He tugged the door open. "Quickly," he said to one of the attendants, "get the Wisewoman here. The Emperor is ill. You," he said to the other, "you come and help me."

The two rushed back to the stricken Emperor. They knelt beside him and straightened him out. The eyes were wide open and starting from the sockets. The face was grey and the tongue protruded. Malum struggled with the fastening of the collar. Let him not be dead, he said to himself. Great Mother, don't let him die. He got the collar open and touched the cheek. It was warm. He felt for the pulse in the throat, but his fingers were shaking too much for him to be able to find it.

"Out of the way. Let me see him." The contralto voice, firm and authoritative, came from above him and Malum moved aside. He stood up as the stout and elderly Wisewoman got down on her knees. Let him live, he thought again as he watched her check over the unmoving body. He found that his hands were clasped.

"He's gone," she said, pushing herself back. "I told him that he needed to be bled regularly, but would he listen to me? Oh no. Always thought he knew best."

"Is he dead?" the attendant asked.

"Of course he's dead. Look at the face. Apoplexy. At least he went fast and without pain."

Malum turned and made his way out of the room. There were others coming now, attracted by the noise. They shouted questions at him, but he ignored them, pushing past them wordlessly. The Emperor was dead. His father was gone without ever knowing the truth. He had kept his secret and his silence too long. The knowledge was useless now. His protector, his father, his Emperor was gone forever. There was a dull ache in his chest and his throat was tight. He compressed his lips and brought a trembling hand up to cover them. Tears welled in his eyes.

A part of him was surprised. He had known that Varodias must die one day. The man was old and, besides, he had made Malum's life a misery on occasions. Why then this surge of emotion? It was all so sudden. No signs of ill health or loss of vigor. Why the man had killed a boar that very morning. No, he admitted to himself, it wasn't just the shock. Something deeper had been unlocked, something he had not known was there. True, he had experienced much the same unexpected rush of feeling when his mother had died, but never before and certainly never since. He had had it in him all this time and had not been aware of it, hadn't recognized his ability to care. It was possible that his father had carried that seed too, but now it was too late.

He had been blundering down the passageways with no destination in mind, but when he looked up to orient himself, he found himself in the corridor that led to Prince Coram's apartments. He straightened his shoulders. Fortune was favoring him, the first person to bring the news to the new Emperor was always well rewarded. Who more fitting to bear the news than the Prince's elder brother? He took a deep breath to calm himself, pulled a kerchief from his sleeve and blew his nose. Then he presented himself at the door. He was ushered in with gratifying speed and was announced.

The Prince came out of the bedchamber, belting a robe about him. His hair was tousled, his face was flushed and he did not look pleased.

"My Lord of Quern," he said with a strained politeness, "what brings you to us?"

Malum advanced until he stood in front of Coram. He looked up into the young and rumpled face and then he went down on one knee.

"Sire," he said and bowed his head.

Coram stood there looking puzzled and looking down on the bowed head. "Is this some kind of a joke, Quern?" he asked.

"Alas, no, Sire. Our father is dead." The word had slipped out. He hadn't meant to say that at all.

"Are you trying to tell me that the Emperor is dead?" Coram asked slowly.

"Yes, Sire. The Emperor is dead, long live the Emperor."

"You said 'our' father," Coram remarked picking up on the inconsistency in order to avoid thinking about the larger import of Malum's words. "You have no right to use the Imperial we." He was distracted, irritated, and he let it show.

Something snapped in Malum then. He had held his secret well, too well. He had served the Empire and his father successfully and had been publicly insulted for his pains. He had stayed in the background and done the dirty work that protected the throne. Varodias had been cruel to him, had used him ruthlessly, but for a reason. This half brother of his, a man he had nurtured, protected by inducing Estivus of Oxenburg to keep him out of trouble, all for the good of the Empire, was lecturing him as if he were the younger one, was treating him as a mere messenger. That he would not bear. A fleeting image of his father came back. Varodias lying on the floor with his tongue sticking out in a final insult. He looked up and then stood. Coram was the taller, so he still had to look up.

"Indeed, Your Imperial Majesty," he dwelt on the title, "I did. I said 'our' father because that is what the late Emperor Varodias was. He settled the estate of Quern on my mother when she found that she was with child and she withdrew from Court for the good of the realm." Not strictly true, but Coram would never know the difference. "The Emperor was well aware of the circumstances of my birth," he said, adding another lie, "but I have never mentioned it. I have been content to serve the Empire."

Coram's eyes narrowed. Until now, he thought. The little man was dangerous. There was obviously ambition behind the self-effacing exterior. If what he was saying was true, and he did not want to believe that, both parents were now dead and Quern had no means of proving his assertion, he was a danger nevertheless. He must be put in his place.

"You forget yourself, my lord," he said curtly. "We assume that you are overcome, as we are, by the Emperor's death."

Anger bubbled up anew in Malum. How dare you condescend to me, he thought. "You are mistaken, my Liege Lord," he said coldly. "I shall grieve for him, and I say 'shall' because the fact of his death, even though I was with him when he died, is still not entirely real to me. I may even grieve more deeply than you, but the fact remains that you and I are brothers." He spaced the last few words out.

So, Coram thought, he raced from my father's body before

the corpse was cold to try to ingratiate himself with me. Well, he has miscalculated. Before he could say anything, a courtier burst into the room and flung himself forward.

"Great Lord," the man panted, "the Emperor, your father, is dead and I am come to render homage to you."

Another one, Coram thought with disgust.

Malum looked down at the prostrate courtier. He was feeling preternaturally calm now that his story was finally out in the open. He had been drunk before, not often, but the feeling had been much the same. A certain separation from what was going on, in control, he had never lost control, but with the freedom to speak his mind.

"Homage?" he heard himself say. "Homage? If you expect to serve your new Emperor well, you'll have to do better than that. You'll have to pretend that everything he says is either weighty or witty. You'll have to laugh at things that aren't in the least funny. You may even find yourself doing things that your conscience deplores. You do it," he said, wagging a finger at the bewildered courtier, "out of loyalty. You do it out of a sense of duty. You do it because . . ."

"That will do, my Lord of Quern," Coram thundered, cutting Malum off. His face was suffused with a deep flush that brought Varodias to mind and Malum stopped as if the breath had been pulled from his lungs. "Guards," Coram said, motioning in Malum's direction with his head. The Secretary had obviously taken leave of his senses and had to be dealt with. This, he thought, is the first decision of my reign. The room was terribly quiet.

"My Lord of Quern," he said briskly, but in a normal tone of voice, "you have rendered considerable service both to our father and to the Empire. We thank you for that. We are aware of the toll that it has taken and we are aware of the recent, regrettable devastation of your lands." He smiled. It wasn't a pleasant smile. "It seems to us that you should return to your estates and devote your time to restoring them. Given your love of our realm, we know that you would be tempted to return to Angorn and to us and would thereby do a disservice to yourself and to your heirs. Therefore, for your own best good, we enjoin you from returning to Court unless we, personally, summon you."

"But Sire," Malum began, suddenly sobered.

Coram nodded to the two guards, who came up on either side of the Secretary.

"We bid you adieu, my lord," he said and turned to go back to the bedchamber.

Malum looked at the retreating back in disbelief. If this was a test of some kind, it was an extremely ill-conceived one. He had not spent the last years submitting to Varodias' whims to be brushed off by this ignorant young man who, but for the accident of birth, would not be able to make his way in the world. Besides, he was owed. He had been faithful to both father and brother.

"You can't walk away from me like that," he said loudly. The courtier, who had spent all this time in bewildered obeisance, scuttled to safety at the side of the room. Coram stopped.

All the years, all the slights and insults, subtle and not so subtle, coalesced in Malum's mind. They were somehow given form by that back. To be rejected now was more than he could bear. "You can't do that." The voice was suddenly watery. That fearsome, judgmental back was turning and Coram's blunt profile was swinging into view. The man was tall, blond and athletic.

"You can't dismiss me like a common courtier," he said as envy and a sense of injustice bolstered him. "I've served the Empire too long and too well for that. And what thanks have I gotten for it, I ask you that?" The voice had risen again and Malum was leaning forward in his intensity. "I asked nothing better than to serve the Empire, and how am I served? You dismiss me as if I meant nothing. Nothing!" The last word was shouted.

"Guards!" The word was clipped and contained the habit of

command. They grasped Malum by the upper arms. "Take him away and see that he's clapped in irons."

"You can't do this!" Malum yelled as he was being dragged out. "You can't rule the Empire without me. You need me! I kept you safe. I gave you Oxenburg."

The doors closed behind his heels, over the marks that their passage had produced. Coram stood and stared at the secured doorway. A pity, really, he thought as he turned and resumed his progress back to the woman waiting for him in the bedchamber, the little man might have been useful, but he was clearly unbalanced. He wasn't well connected, so his disappearance would cause no ripples. Perhaps, if he felt in a good mood during the coronation, he would commute the sentence to internal exile on his estates. That should teach him who could rule.

He looked at the young woman sprawled under the sheets. He had left her side a Prince. He would return an Emperor. He checked his hand. He would have to get dressed. There would be rites to be performed. He glanced down again. He would have to get rid of her. His face went quite blank for a moment, and then he leaned down to shake her awake. He had just confined Quern to irons in the dungeon. He was about to enter the biggest set of irons there were. The difference was, and he smiled to himself at the thought, that he could have Quern executed. The smile broadened. He threw off his robe and, standing naked, yelled for his servants to come and dress him.

XXVII

⚜ ⚜ ⚜

The death of Varodias shocked the nation and brought it together in a way that had not happened since the defeat of the Outlanders. The Empress Zhane had not been known outside Angorn and the Emperor had not been greatly loved by his people, but their deaths, occurring within a year of each other, brought on a feeling of melancholy and a conviction that an era had ended. Churches all around the Empire were swathed in black and attendance at services increased. It increased still further when the rains began to fall. This was widely attributed to the intercession by the departed Emperor with the Great Mother, a notion encouraged by the priestesses.

As Angorn prepared quietly for the funeral, Varodias' body lay in state in the Cathedral of the Mother. People stood patiently in long lines to file past the catafalque and pay their last respects. Coram, meanwhile, had moved swiftly to consolidate his position. He demanded and received an oath of fealty from the Imperial Council and the army General Staff. He sent the Margrave of Oxenburg galloping to the frontier to obtain the same from the Army of the North. By the time the Electors had gathered, their assent was a mere formality.

The funeral itself went off with solemn pomp. Arabella of Arundel, Naxania of Paladine and Boran Marts, the Thane of Talisman, attended for the Magical Kingdoms, despite the fact that a state of war still existed. The Mother Supreme made it clear that the Archmage would not be welcome. Her predecessor might have gone to Ragnor's funeral, but she would not permit the head of the Discipline in her cathedral. She was not to know it, but that dictum was the high-water mark of her influence. Just as she was not bound by Arnulpha's decisions, Coram was not his father and had far less regard for the Church of the Mother than Varodias.

Once the old Emperor had been laid to rest, the mood of the country became steadily more optimistic. Pictures of the new Emperor, a man whom very few had seen, proliferated. His popularity grew when men started to return from the front. While he kept the regular troops in place, the conscripts and the Electoral levies were demobilized. Just in time, some noted, to plant a late wheat crop. The embargo on general trade was dropped and Isphardi merchants began to be seen again in the manufacturing towns. The Oligarchs reciprocated by reinstituting the grain trade. Food shortages in the Empire gradually waned.

The atmosphere at Court also changed. Whereas under Varodias, the capital had been considered a dangerous place, especially for the Electoral families, there was now a young, and unmarried, Emperor on the throne. The daughters of the best families began to take up residence as well as those women whose chief asset was their beauty. The Court was still officially in mourning, but there was a feeling of rebirth and controlled festivity. While the veteran courtiers weighed the chances of the newcomers, there were those who had noticed the way that their Emperor and the Queen of Paladine had enjoyed each other's company.

At Bandor the negotiations resumed and here, too, the atmosphere had changed. There was less bickering and less intransigence. The most dramatic difference, however, was provided by the arrival of Joscelyn of Gwyndryth and the unicorn Malloran. Jarrod Courtak, the Discipline's chief negotiator, came down to the main courtyard to greet them. He embraced his stepson and sent out a warm welcome to Malloran.

"Come on up to my room," he said to the young Magician. "We're short of space here so you'll probably have to share my quarters." He smiled. "It's best if we do our talking there. One has to be a little careful. Almost everybody seems to be in someone's pay." He summoned a groom to take care of Malloran and then took Joscelyn upstairs.

"Now," he said after the boy had eaten, "what brings you here?"

"The unicorns know about the negotiations and Malloran insisted that they be represented. I expect that Nastrus put him up to it."

"Surely they have all the space and freedom they need."

"Has the Discipline's annexation of the mountains come up?" Joscelyn replied.

"No, but the Queens agreed."

"But not Talisman, Isphardel or the Empire. Besides, the unicorns aren't too certain how reliable the Queens are. Then there's the little matter of the bounty."

Jarrod sighed. "This is going to complicate things."

"I don't see why it should. We have the legal right, you said so yourself."

"That's because you've never negotiated," Jarrod said with a shake of his head. "If you want something, you have to give something."

"Well, you can't deny that the unicorns came to our aid against the Umbrians. Anyway, isn't it better to have it out in the open now rather than have it lurking about as a possible cause for a future war?"

"You have a point there, but the Oligarch Olivderval is going to make hay with this."

Joscelyn grinned. "Let me talk to her. If I can't convince her that there's a whole new era, I'll charm her."

Jarrod snorted. "She'd eat you for breakfast. But perhaps you should sit in on our meeting. It might be instructive." He cast a critical eye over the boy. "If you want to charm her, though, we'd better have the barber up."

New era indeed, he thought. The boy had grown up. He was going to be a force to be reckoned with. He reminded him of himself when younger. The red hair apart, they looked a lot alike. He had his mother's eyes, of course, and her coloring, but the build and the mouth and the nose were his, or rather his double's. His own hair had grey in it, more since the adventures at Angorn, and he was getting past the age when he enjoyed sword practice. Perhaps, if these negotiations came out right, Joscelyn would never have to learn the skill. That was certainly a goal worth achieving.

While the negotiators at Bandor continued their work, there were further changes at Angorn. Coram moved with deliberation in the reordering of his Council. His father had seen to it that he did not have his own group of advisers, so he was forced to rely on the old guard while he learned his way. His chief counselor, however, was Estivus of Oxenburg. Estivus became the head of the Imperial forces but was equally influential on the civilian side.

It was partially Coram's boredom with the constraints of mourning and partly his newfound sense of diplomatic timing that caused the Emperor to declare a premature end to the memorial grief and to invite the leaders of Strand to Angorn to finalize the peace treaty and then attend his coronation. The Mother Supreme objected and was turned politely aside. She persisted, demanded an audience with the Emperor, who strongly suggested that a tour of the Mother Churches would be good for her health. She departed breathing imprecations and prophesying dire consequences.

For three sennights the capital saw such a sprucing as it had never known. Repairs were made, paint applied, offal swept from the streets, drains and gutters unblocked. Parks that had not seen flowers in a generation bloomed anew and men who had no wish for employment were pressed into service. The results were gratifying. The old, grey, grim northern capital sparkled beneath a midsummer sun and into the new magnificence came to the great of the world, to the approbation of the populace and the profit of cutpurses, tavern keepers and whoremasters. Whenever the great traveled, the lesser followed in their wake.

The bounty on unicorns had been canceled months ago in accordance with a portion of the developing peace treaty. It was unilaterally abandoned by Umbria. Thus it was that Arabella of Arundel and Naxania of Paladine, having sent servants and baggage trains ahead, rode into the city by the South Gate. In fact both had arrived on the borders of the Imperial Forest and taken the time to restore themselves and don clothes to suit the occasion. They had no trumpeters to announce them, no guard of honor, nor state coach, but that simple entrance riding on a brace of glossy unicorns, with silver hoofs, gold-flecked manes and tails and the nacreous whorl of pointed horns, gathered a cheering crowd that flocked into the streets to greet them. The Thane of Talisman's arrival on a cloudsteed was tame by comparison.

Oh, there were other wonders. The Oligarchs of Isphardel in their silks and their extravagant litters, the Archmage and the Mage of Paladine, accompanied by a younger Magician, all on unicorns. These however arrived directly in the Great Court of the palace and were seen directly by few. That was not the case with the Duchess of Abercorn, who suddenly appeared in a public square on what the instantly knowledgeable declared to be an elderly unicorn. She appeared to be ailing but the crowd was too intimidated by the unicorn to approach closely. She recovered somewhat too soon for those gathered, but was amiably directed to the palace. Truth to tell, unicorns were old news by then. Far more attention was paid that same day to the arrival of a dozen Songean chieftains in their skins and brightly dyed cloaks.

Marianna would have been furious had she known, but she was too busy directing the unpacking of the trunks she had sent on before her. Her husband watched her bemusedly.

"You have come equipped for a year's stay," he said. "There will be no place left for us to sleep, let alone entertain, as I am sure you will want to do." His tone was teasing.

Hers was not. It was brisk and practical. "If you leave me alone, I shall get all this stowed. And it's not all mine by the way. I stopped at the Outpost and got some of the better gowns that Ragnor left you." She flapped a hand at him, waving him to silence as she went to deal with another servant carrying an armful of gowns.

"Let me guess," he said. "This is all for the glorification of Abercorn." He stood with his right arm raised and his left hand on his chest, in formal pose. "No, wait. Better than that. As one of Naxania's major vassals, the better we look, the better we make her look."

Marianna smiled at him over her shoulder. "You're becoming remarkably intelligent in your old age. Now what I need you to do is to use your influence to get suitable lodgings for my dressmaker and the maidservant who dresses my hair."

"And have you brought our clothes from the Island at the Center, the ones we got married in?" He was beginning to sound angry.

She turned and smiled at him. "No, of course not," she said. "First of all, you couldn't fit into them." Seeing the look on his face she held up a hand to forestall him. "Neither could I," she added to pacify him. "No, I have them on display in the Great Hall at Oxeter, alongside the plate."

"But isn't that . . . ?" he began.

"Oh, don't worry about that," she said dismissively, "I had the jewels copied a long time ago."

He smiled back at her. There was nothing else to do.

In another section of the palace, Queen Naxania was receiving a private invitation to the Emperor's quarters after the evening's banquet. Her flesh was more than willing, but her experience prompted her to plead tiredness, but with a regret that left the door wide open. In other corners of the palace debates were going on, informally to be sure, about the positions of each country on the peace treaty. The monarchs and governors might make the final disposition, but they needed to be well briefed. Various parties used the occasion to advance their cause. The Oligarch Olivderval was enormously popular with the Umbrian lords. She had always found Zingaran dancing girls remarkably effective with foreign men and she saw no reason to change.

Balls and festivities abounded and Coram and Naxania found themselves frequently at the same functions. It was common knowledge that they were intimate a good sennight before it became a fact.

In that atmosphere, the settlement of the Umbrian War, as it had somehow become known, seemed almost an imposition, but the rulers of Strand were not light people. They took their duties seriously, but, even among the Oligarchs, there was a feeling that things could and should be settled. Not entirely so, of course, despite the stories and songs that have circulated ever since. There were sticking places centering on the Isphardi demands and the Discipline's claims. Jarrod had been right about that. He also labored mightily to forge a consensus.

The coronation of Coram had not been set to coincide with

an agreement among the warring parties, but on the ninemonth date of Varodias' interment. That date, however, served as a spur. To declare a universal peace on the eve of the coronation was such an obvious idea that it became a positive aim. To achieve that aim a number of problems were banished into a maze of diplomatic language, but everybody at the time felt that a great deal had been accomplished. The peace accord was duly signed in front of an invited audience in the Great Court that fronted the twin keeps. The woodcuts that commemorated the occasion showed a dazzling array of notables and most of them managed to include a unicorn, though none were present at the ceremony.

The unicorns were in the Cathederal of the Mother the following day for the solemn rite as were all the other great ones of Strand. First though, there was the procession. The Queens of Arundel and Paladine rode in individual gilded coaches. Each wore a tiara and both were magnificently gowned. They were followed by the Thane of Talisman astride his cloudsteed, the Oligarchs of Isphardel followed in two large, open coaches pulled by four matching, plume-bedecked greys and they in turn were succeeded by the Electors of Umbria, all on horseback. Then came the Mage of Paladine and his wife in another open coach. The wife, the crowd noticed, was wearing a gown that rivaled those of the Queens and far more jewelry. The Mage, impossibly tall even when sitting down, was dressed in a richly embroidered blue robe. Then came the unicorns, half a dozen of them, glistening in the sunshine. By the time the golden State Coach rolled by bearing the soon-to-be Coram III, the crowd had screamed itself nearly hoarse. He was dressed in his purple coronation robes and waved to the crowd as he passed. Hoarse or not, the people responded with renewed vigor.

Jarrod and Marianna had already taken their places in the cathedral. Jarrod, looking round, decided that whatever else one might think about Maternism, it had certainly produced some extraordinarily beautiful buildings. He had been impressed by the church in Belengar, but the cathedral was more splendid still. Slim pillars soared up to lose themselves in the fan tracery that covered the ceiling. The interior was vast, open and airy. The statue of the Mother that towered above the altar was clearly visible from almost any angle. But, impressive as the statue was, the true glory of the cathedral was its windows.

There were two ranks of them, one above the other, divided by a carved course of stone. In them were richly colored scenes depicting the Parables of the Great Mother. Seen up close, the detail was amazing. Seen in their totality, they made the cathedral seem like an enormous jewel box, more glass than stone. They threw lozenges of rich color over the congregation, the altar and the matching marble thrones on either side of it.

Jarrod surveyed the seated throng. It was an extraordinary assembly of the powerful, with former adversaries chatting quietly and peaceably. He wished he had brought writing materials to make notes, for this was, in every sense of the word, an historic occasion. The thought was interrupted as the orchestra in the gallery began to play a sonorous introit and the chorus launched into an anthem. Down the aisle, causing every head to turn, came the Mother Supreme, in gold robes, followed by four priestesses. She installed herself on the throne to the left and they ranged themselves behind her. The music continued, swelled to a crescendo and died away.

The brief silence was shattered by a fanfare of trumpets and everyone rose to their feet. The choir burst forth into another paean and Coram entered and processed slowly down the aisle. From his shoulders flowed a long purple mantle, edged in gold and lined with ermine, carried by four squires of the body in white satin. His blond hair was unbound. He mounted the steps of the other throne and turned, waiting for the squires to arrange the train before he sat. Then the service began with a hymn in which the Umbrian portion of the congregation joined. The Mother Supreme gave a homily on the might of the

Great Mother and the duties of mankind to Her that, to Jarrod's
way of thinking, both smacked of lecturing and went on too
long.

The homily gave way to another hymn, during which the
Mother Supreme and her priestesses sanctified a vial of holy oil.
When the hymn was ended, Coram came down from his throne
and knelt before the altar. The Mother Supreme anointed his
forehead and pronounced a blessing over him. He rose, bowed
to her and returned to his seat. The squires fussed around after
him, resettling the train, as one of the priestesses read a passage
from The Book Of The Mother. The well-practiced voice rang
out.

". . . And behold, the old order passeth and a new order is
made. Old men shall die and young men will marry. Old
women become barren and young women become fertile. It is
the way of the Mother. The old order passeth, but there will
ever be a new."

True, Jarrod thought, looking around as the Senior Elector
paced up the aisle bearing the crown of Umbria on a dark red
cushion. He supposed that he was a part of that old order,
though he didn't feel in the least old, and that Joscelyn was the
new. He glanced across to where the unicorns stood in their
specially constructed enclosure. The friends of his youth were
there; Amarine, Nastrus and Pellia. They, too, were part of tradition, the subject of minstrels' songs, a part, indeed, of his history, if he ever got it finished. He, in his turn, was part of the
Memory, part of the unicorns' history. Strange, at forty, to feel
that one was a part of history and yet both he and Marianna
were. No getting away from that. He was still too young for
that, surely. Then he smiled, oblivious of the people around
him. If he was irritated by this premature fossilization, Marianna would be outraged by the thought.

The Elector, resplendent in a black cutaway coat with gold
frogging, a lot of gold frogging, a scarlet waistcoat and trousers,
paused before the Imperial throne. He handed the cushioned

crown to the Chief Squire, who turned and showed it to Coram. The Elector reclaimed the crown and, holding it high over his head, mounted the stairs. At the top step he lowered it and placed it in Coram's waiting hands. His errand completed, he bowed and made his way back down the steps. The choir interposed a melodic lament for the old Emperor. Then there was silence.

The trumpets began a fanfare. It started low and simple with only two trumpeters and gained momentum. Other trumpets joined in and the rhythm picked up. Into this musical acceleration that drew the audience with it, Coram rose and slowly raised the crown until, at the moment that his arms were fully extended over his head, the music cut off abruptly. He held the pose for a very long moment and then began to lower the crown. To the watchers, the bulk of the old-fashioned crown seemed to float down, unassisted, until it settled, firmly, on Coram's head.

A roar went up, spontaneously engendered, bursting out from Umbrian and guest alike. The sound from the nave and the side aisles lapped the altar and the two marble thrones. Atop one Coram grinned, overwhelmed by the waves of approbation, while, on the other side of the altar, the Mother Supreme's mouth was set in a straight line. She had been thwarted in her attempt to have the Emperor crowned by her and knew that this new Emperor was no friend of hers. Times had changed. This one, she thought, is going to be much harder to influence than his father.

The sound died away and Estivus of Oxenburg limped out into the light of the central chandelier. He bore the ancient iron sword, relic of the first Emperor, dubbed Sword of Honor, given to the sovereign as a sign that it was his duty to defend the realm. He climbed the stairs handily enough and placed the sword in Coram's outstretched hands. As the new monarch raised it, magesterially slow, the orchestra and choir produced an antiphonal chant of, "Long Live the Emperor."

Down from the throne came Coram, squires ducking around swiftly to cope with the train, looking every inch an Emperor. The jewels that studded the dark-looking metal of the crown winked in the candlelight. The corn-colored hair gleamed. He looked exalted. Behold, Jarrod thought as he passed, the new order incarnate. He looked down at Marianna, whose eyes were shining. If she can have this reaction after her father's death, he thought, this is an even more remarkable woman.

The coronation feast was lavish, and long, and wild, but the party from the Magical Kingdoms abandoned it shortly after the second hour to join the unicorns in their stable. There were guards at the archway leading into the cobbled area, but Naxania and Arabella had but to push back the hoods of their cloaks and the soldiers stood aside. The Queens produced their this-is-for-my-subjects smiles and they were through. The unicorns were loosely boxed along one entire wing of the stables. The emanations that Jarrod picked up from them were ruminative and content. Still, the humans had decided that the presence of unicorns and Magicians in the Umbrian capital might give an excuse for a provocation. It was deemed best that they should leave.

The royal ladies, who would stay behind, as would Marianna, were resigned to the long trip home by coach and were gracious, if somewhat marginal, since they could not communicate. Marianna was tearful in her parting from Amarine. She was afraid in her heart, and she could not disguise it from Amarine, that this might be the last time.

'It was us,' she said to the matriarch of the unicorns. '*Do you realize that? It started with the two of us. If we hadn't been able to communicate, none of this would have happened. We'd still be fighting Outlanders."*

The reply came swathed in humor, with a slight aftertone of reproof. '*I do think that there are others involved.*'

'Oh, I know that,' Marianna answered and a smile appeared on her face. 'I was just thinking, that's all.' She shook her head. 'It's all happened so fast. In my mind it was ten, fifteen years ago at most, when we met in the Anvil of the Gods. But I also have a son who is taller than I am . . .'

'And you worry about him. Don't. There's nothing you can do when they strike out on their own. He will either become dominant in the herd, or he will not. It doesn't concern us. Once one group is gone, we concentrate on the rest.'

Marianna made some awkward gestures, even though she knew that Amarine already understood what she felt.

'You pick the best sire for them that you can find,' Amarine responded, 'though the vain creatures inevitably think that they chose you. You teach them as much as you can and then, at a certain point, you let them go. That is the natural way.'

'You're right of course, but it's harder for us. We don't have as many as you do and they are dependent for so much longer.'

'I would not have your patience,' the unicorn admitted. 'Do you know where your foal is going?'

'Back to the mountains for a while and then he must go back to the Collegium to hone his skills.'

'He will make you proud, as my descendants have made me proud. They have already done much, but they will surely do more. And now, my dear friend, it is time for us to go.'

The unicorns were drifting to the center of the stable court. Jarrod mounted Nastrus and Joscelyn climbed up onto Malloran's back. Marianna rubbed Amarine's muzzle fondly. 'You will come back and see me,' she said.

'I brought my foals here because I felt confined on the Island at the Center and now there is a place for us here, a place where the grass is good and we can run free. I shall be content to die on this world.'

Marianna nodded and moved away to say good-bye to her son. Then, one by one, the unicorns winked out of existence, leaving the three women standing alone in the stable yard beneath the nightmoon.

"We have lived in extraordinary times," Naxania said, turning and picking up the skirt of her gown.

"May the gods grant that the next few years are quiet and ordinary," Arabella commented as she followed.

On the far side of Strand, Jarrod, quicker to recover than Joscelyn, gazed out across the Alien Plain. Below him, shimmering softly in the nightmoonlight, were the shapes of unicorns. His mind went back to the time, so many years ago, when the Princess Naxania had been entranced and produced a cryptic verse about unicorns. Who could have known that it would lead to this, that the discovery of a female unicorn and three small colts would result in the permanent presence of unicorns on Strand? He retraced his steps to tend to his stepson. He would return to Stronta in the morning. His work here was done. He looked up at the castle that he had built with Magic and the help of unicorns. That, too, had been a portent of things to come, but this place belonged to Joscelyn now. To Joscelyn and the unicorns.